CREATED BY

JERRY POURNELLE

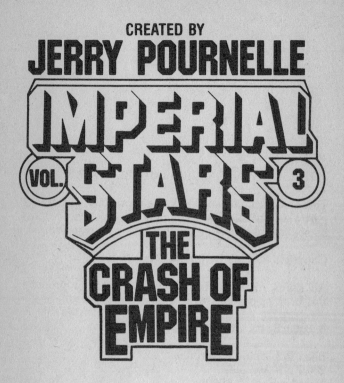

IMPERIAL STARS

VOL. 3

THE CRASH OF EMPIRE

Associate Editor

JOHN F. CARR

BAEN BOOKS

THE CRASH OF EMPIRE: IMPERIAL STARS III

A Baen Books Original

Baen Publishing Enterprises
260 Fifth Avenue
New York, N.Y. 10001

First printing, June 1989

ISBN: 0-671-69826-5

Cover art by David Egge

Printed in the United States of America

Distributed by
SIMON & SCHUSTER
1230 Avenue of the Americas
New York, N.Y. 10020

IT JUST KEPT ON FIGHTING

The contact was immediate and shocking. One of the rebel ships lumbered into the path of the interceptors, spraying fire from what seemed to be as many points as a man has pores. The Service ships promptly riddled it and it should have drifted away—but it didn't. It kept on fighting. It rammed an interceptor with a crunch that must have killed every man before the first bulwark, but aft of the bulwark the ship kept fighting.

It took a torpedo portside and its plumbing drifted through space in a tangle. Still the starboard side kept squirting fire. Isolated weapon blisters fought on while they were obviously cut off from the rest of the ship. It was a pounded tangle of wreckage, and it had destroyed two interceptors, crippled two more, and kept fighting.

Finally, it drifted away, under feeble jets of power. Two more of the fantastic rebel fleet wandered into action, but the wing commander's horrified eyes were on the first pile of scrap. It was going *somewhere*—

The ship neared the thin-skinned, unarmored, gleaming hospital vessel, rammed it amidships, square in one of the red crosses, and blew itself up . . . .

ACKNOWLEDGMENTS

PEBBLE AMONG THE STARS by Gregory Benford first appeared as "Seascape" in the *Faster Than Light* anthology in 1977. Published by permission of the author. Copyright © 1988 by Abbenford Associates.

THE CLAW AND THE CLOCK by Christopher Anvil was first published in the February 1971 *Analog*. Copyright © 1971 by Condé Nast Publications.

THE ONLY THING WE LEARN by Cyril Kornbluth appeared first in the July 1949 *Startling Stories*. Copyright © 1949 by Better Publications, Inc.

REMEMBERING VIETNAM by H. J. Kaplan was published in the December 1987 issue of *Commentary*. Copyright © 1987 by H. J. Kaplan.

BLESSED ARE THE MEEK by G. C. Edmondson appears here by special arrangement with the author. It was first published in the September 1955 issue of *Astounding*. Copyright © 1955 by Street & Smith Publications.

LIMITING FACTOR by Theodore Cogswell made its first appearance in the April 1954 issue of *Galaxy*. Copyright © 1954 by Universal Publishing.

TRIAGE by William Walling first appeared in the November 1976 *Analog*. It is published by permission of the author. Copyright © 1976 by Condé Nast Publications.

HYPERDEMOCRACY by John W. Campbell, Jr. was first published in the August 1958 issue of *Astounding*. Copyright © 1958 by Street & Smith Publications.

CONTENTS

THE CRASH OF EMPIRES

Jerry Pournelle

The fall of an empire may be agonizingly long or mercifully short. Winston Churchill could protest that he had not become the King's First Minister in order to preside over liquidation of the British Empire, but in fact that is what he did; for better or worse, in less than a generation the British experiment in world order was history. During the same period the French Empire ceased to exist. Italy and Germany had already lost whatever imperial pretensions they may have had.

Of course the age of empire is hardly over: the Union of Soviet Socialist Republics is imperial in all but name. Perhaps it, too, will fall.

Paul Kennedy argues in *The Rise and Fall of the Great Powers* that great powers fall because of the economic strain of their military burdens. The United States in particular faces the dilemma of hoarding resources for investment, or spending to keep present military power in order to meet immediate threats.

The dilemma is real, but there is another problem. The United States may not really have any choice, because any resources not spent on military power will not be saved and invested for the future, but immediately consumed. We all know this, and assume that it's "just politics." We also assume that politics is and will remain predominant.

Meanwhile, the United States is transforming itself into an odd form of oligarchy. The nation is, after all, ruled by a small elite elected in effect for life: 98% of all members of Congress were reelected in 1986, and there is no reason to suppose that figure will ever be different. As one observer put it, the two houses of Congress have become in effect the House of Lords twice over, with the only real national contest being for the Presidency.

Of course the President controls the military.

We are brought up on the view that economics and politics control human affairs. Perhaps so; but it is well to remember what is primary. John Keegan, one-time military historian at Sandhurst, says in his *Mask of Command*:

"Marx was able to argue for the primacy of ownership of the means of production as a determinant of social relationships largely because, at the time when he wrote, finance and investment overshadowed all other forces in society, and the military class—exhausted by the Napoleonic wars and dispirited by the defeat of its interests in Russia in 1825 and France in 1830—was at an unnaturally low ebb of self-confidence. Yet military power, represented in its crudest form by the robber-baron principle, can, of course, at any time it chooses, make fools of the financier and investor, as the history of investment in unstable areas of the world makes unarguably evident. It can equally make fools of 'historical' laws. Marx, in his heart, recognized both truths, feared more than any other the temperament—and the military class is ultimately self-choosing by temperament rather than by material interest—that will seize arms simply for the pleasure that blood-letting gives, and constantly urged the politically conscious to learn the habits and discipline of the military class as the merest means of defending and furthering the revolution."

It is self-evident that the *nomenklatura*, the real rulers of modern Russia, have forgotten Marx's warnings. So have the politicians and economists in the United States.

Herewith stories of empire in the future: their rise, and their crash.

Editor's Introduction To:

PEBBLE AMONG THE STARS

Gregory Benford

Republics tend toward centralism. The United States was conceived as a nation of states, but democratic pressures have driven us toward uniformity. This has far-reaching results. The Civil Rights Acts ended one kind of regional diversity. *Roe vs. Wade*, the abortion rights Supreme Court decision, ended another. *Escobedo* and *Miranda* changed the criminal law for every state. Congress is about to undo some of that with the new Drug Law, but the states aren't being consulted. The National Defense Education Act effectively federalized the education system.

The same trends dominate within states. Local school boards are made powerless while state bureaucracy multiplies.

Some will see all these trends as simple justice. Others see a centralized government riding roughshod over local differences. A few will even see the tyranny of the majority that Tocqueville warned us about.

Majority decisions are usually compromises. Uniformity imposed by a majority has the advantage that most of the population—by definition—accepts the national decision. Problems arise when a powerful minority truly believes the majority decision is immoral. In such cases compromises are impossible: how can you compromise between a group that believes abortion is murder, and a group that says that anything less than full free choice is slavery for women? Even so, the pressure for uniformity is overwhelming.

3

Empires have traditionally preserved diversities. So long as the subject states pay their taxes and hold allegiance to the Emperor, they may have whatever local customs and laws that they like.

Of course some local customs are more important than others. So are some of the subject states . . .

PEBBLE AMONG THE STARS

Gregory Benford

Dawn comes redly on a water world.

Shibura sat comfortably in lotus position, watching the thin pink line spread across the horizon. Slowly the Titanic Ocean lost its oily darkness and rippled with the morning wind. Waves hissed on the beach nearby.

The pink line collected into a red ellipse, then into a slowly rising yellow ball. The gathering wetness of the morning fog slowly seeped away. Shibura passed through this transition complete, of a piece, attention wholly focused. Then a small creature, something like a mouse with bat wings and a furry yellow topknot, coasted in through layers of fog and landed on his shoulder. Smiling, he made a finger perch for the animal, noting that its wings were translucent and covered with fine pearly moisture. Shibura and the air squirrel studied each other for a moment. There came the furious beat of wings from above and the faint high cries of pursuit. The squirrel fidgeted; Shibura fished a crumb from his pocket and threw it into the air. The animal leaped, caught it with a snap and coasted away on an updraft. Shibura smiled.

Waterchimes sounded and a small, nut-brown man emerged from his home further down the beach. He began doing exercises on the white beach: hip thrusts; smooth flowing of limbs first one way, then the other; easy leaps into the air. The man's house was a vaulted, delicate structure of curved lattices. The reddish grease-wood gave it the appearance of weight and mass, belied

by the rakish tilt of the columns and cantilevered beams
that would have been impossible in normal Earth gravity. Everywhere there were curves; no angles, no sharp-
ness or sudden contrast to jar the eye.

Shibura enjoyed the man and his house, just as he
appreciated the other homes hugging the tide line of
the Titanic. But they were people of the world, and
given to such things. He was a Priestfellow and lived in
a rude hut of rough canewood. His floor was fine ground
sand.

His food—Shibura reached to the side and found a
bowl of red liquid—simple and adequate. His neighbor
was a dealer in metals who shipped deposits from the
Off Islands for use in the holy factories. The small man
had achieved a station in spiritual life adequate to his
personality, and now reaped the rewards. So it would
come to Shibura. He had but to wait until the Starcrossers
made audience on Seascape again. Then—if the audience was successful and reached cusp—he would fulfill
his role and pass through the holy lens.

The lesson was clear: if the Starcrossers were pleased,
if the Paralixlinnes proved functional, then Shibura (indeed, all of Seascape) would have proved holy in the
light of the stars, complete again for another generation
or more. After that audience would come the material
things, if Shibura wished them.

Within himself he was sure he would not desire such
trappings. He relished the life of austerity and the
denial of the body. Not, of course, for its own sake: that
was counter to the integrated spirit. But he knew that
for himself simplicity was integrity and serenity. Even
the coming of the Starcrossers would not deflect him
from this.

Down the coast Shibura could see people leaving
their homes and walking on the beach, some swimming
and others doing morning meditation. Through the thin-
ning fog he could make out the main road, still void of
traffic. A lone figure moved down it in the quilted
morning shadows: a priestservant, to judge by his robes.
Shibura wondered what the man's mission could be. He
believed he was the only Priestfellow nearby, but he

could imagine no task before him which required a summons so early. Perhaps the man was bound out of town, toward the interior farmland.

Well, no matter. He tried to return to his meditation, but his focus veered. The sun had risen slightly, and its steam brought him even more into the awakening of the morning. He looked up. The great eye of Brutus hung overhead, a half crescent streaked with brown and yellow bands. As he watched, Shibura could see small changes as the great clouds of that turbulent atmosphere swirled and danced. He knew that Brutus was massive and powerful; it sucked the waters away in the second tidetime, stronger than the sun. But now it seemed calm and peaceful, unracked by storms. So unlike Seascape it was, yet Brutus was the parent of this world. Shibura knew this as a truth passed on from the Starcrossers, but it seemed so unlikely. Seascape was a place of quietness and Brutus usually a drove of storms. There were some in the streets who said Brutus influenced the lives of men, but when asked, the Starcrossers said no—men were not born of Seascape, and their rhythms were unkeyed to this world, however much it suited man to live here.

Shibura shook his head; this was disturbing, it took him out of his natural place. All hope of further contemplation vanished when there was a loud jangling of his welcome bells. The priestservant was padding quickly down the short wooded path. His sandals scattered pebbles to the side in his haste. Shibura breathed deeply to compose himself and caught the first sharp tang of the morning tide. The man knocked delicately on the thin door and Shibura called to him to enter. He was an old priestservant who, it was said, remembered well the last audience of the Starcrossers. His robe was tattered and retained the old form of pants and vest beneath his flowing purple outer garments. The man smiled, exposing brown teeth, and ceremoniously handed forward a folded yellow parchment.

Shibura took it and carefully flattened the message against the sand before him. The calligraphy was hurried and inexact. Here and there the ink was smeared.

Shibura noted these facets before reading it; often one could learn more from them than from the literal contents. He prepared himself for an unsettling point.

Slowly, he read. His thumbs bit into the parchment and crinkled it. His breath made a dry rasping sound. After perfunctory salutations and wishes of the day, the message was laconic:

They are coming. Prepare.

The great sphere rode through Jumpspace, unseen and unknown.

Its air was stale. The bridge was dark; hooded consoles made pools of light where men sat calculating, measuring, checking. The Captain stood with hands clenched behind him as the calculation proceeded. There were men sealed within the walls and wired forever into the bowels of the computers; the Captain did not think of these. He simply waited in the great drifting silence between stars, beyond real space and the place of men.

Silvery chimes rang down thin, padded corridors, sounding the approach of Jump. The bridge lay in dull red light. Men moved purposefully about it but everyone knew they were powerless to control what was coming.

Justly so. Converting a ship into tachyons in a nanosecond of realspace time is an inconceivably complex process. Men devised it, but they could never control the Jump without the impersonal faultless coordination of microelectronics.

A few earnest, careful men moved quietly about the bridge as they prepared to flip over into realspace. In the same way that a fundamental symmetry provided that the proton had a twin particle with opposite charge, helicity and spin—the anti-proton—there was an opposite state for each real particle, the tachyon.

The speed of light, c, is an upper limit to all velocities in the universe to which man was born; in the tachyon universe c is a lower limit. To men, a particle with zero kinetic energy sits still; it has no velocity. A tachyon with no energy is a mirror image—it moves with infinite velocity. As its energy increases it slows, relative to us, until at infinite energy it travels with velocity c.

As long as man remained in his half of the universe, he could not exceed c. Thus he learned to leave it.

By converting a particle into its tachyon state, allowing it to move with a nearly infinite velocity and then shifting it back to realspace, one effectively produces faster-than-light travel. In theory the process was obvious. It was Okawa who found the practical answer, some decades after the establishment of Old Nippon's hegemony. The Captain had often wondered why the Jumpdrive did not bear his name. Perhaps Okawa was born of impure strains. Perhaps he was an unfavored one, though passing clever.

A slightly audible count came through the padded rooms of the starship. Silvery chimes echoed, and the Captain closed his eyes at the last moment. A bright arc flashed beyond his eyelids, so he could see the blood vessels as he heard the dark, whispering sound of the void. A pit opened beneath him, he was falling—

Suddenly they wrenched from tachyon space and back into the real universe. There was really no difference between the two; each mirrored the physical laws of the other. There were stars and planets in tachyon space, surely—but no man had ever stopped to explore them. No one knew if a real spaceship transferred into tachyons could be maintained in the presence of dense tachyon matter. The physicists said it was doubtful, and no one cared to test the point.

The ship trembled slightly—or perhaps it was only his own reaction—and the Captain turned to the large screen of the foredeck. There was the F8 star, burning hot and yellow.

"A minute, Cap'n," the Executive Officer said. "Looks like we blew a few on that last one."

"What?"

"The ferrite banks. A lot of them failed."

"The Paralixlinnes, you mean," the Captain said precisely.

"Right. Some are showing flashover effects, too."

The Captain frowned. "I am afraid this might put us over the margin."

"What?"

The Captain grimaced at this insolence. "We may not have enough ferrite memory to make the transition back into Jump. I want a detailed report, if you please."

"Oh." The Executive Officer nodded and turned slightly away, fumbling at his fly. "You think it's that bad?" As he spoke he began urinating into the porous Organiform flooring. "I mean, it could trap us here?"

The Captain stepped away and clasped his hands behind his back. "Well, uh, yes, it might." He knew this public passing of water was acceptable practice on some worlds, the product of crowding and scarcity. He knew it was not supposed to be a sign of contempt. But something in the Executive Officer's manner made him think otherwise. Certainly actions like this were forbidden on his own home world . . .

"What happens if we try it without getting more ferrites?" the Executive Officer said, looking back over his shoulder. His urine spattered on the Organiform and quickly disappeared. Many spots in the ship had such floors and walls; in the long run it was the only way to ensure cleanliness. Dust, liquid, odd bits of paper—all were absorbed and gradually bled into the fuel reserve, to be chewed apart in incandescent fusion torches and converted into thrust.

"The ship's mass will not trigger coherently."

"So?"

A political appointee, the Captain guessed. "We would emerge into tachyon space with each particle traveling at a different velocity."

"Ah, I remember." The man finished and zipped his fly. "Tear ourselves apart. Grind us to atoms."

"Uh, correct."

The Executive Officer had made no attempt to hide himself from view while urinating. The Captain wondered whether the man had any convention of privacy at all. Did he defecate in public? It seemed impossible, but—

"Okay, I'll get that report. Might take a while." The man did not bother to salute.

"See that it doesn't," the Captain said sharply and returned his attention to the phosphor screen. He expanded scale a hundredfold and found the banded gas giant planet. It was enormous, he knew, and radiated strongly in the infrared. At the very center of it, according to theory, hydrogen atoms collided and stuck, fusing together and kindling weak fire. But this vast giant of a world was not their aim. There, not far from the methane-orange limb of the planet, gleamed a blue-white moon: Seascape. He smiled.

Shibura sat, feeling the exquisite rough texture of the floor mat on his ankles and yet at the same time not feeling it at all. There was no sound, and all was sound. He was listening and shimmering in the sweet air of incense, relishing the sticky pull of damp robe on his flesh.

"Thus we proceed to fullness," finished the Firstpriest. "Quit of our tasks. Gathered once more into the lap of sunlight."

Shibura studied the old man's weathered brown face, receptive. The morning had begun with sainted rituals among the crowds of Priestfellows and Priestsisters. As the quiet rhythm of the day wore on, each was assigned a task of convergence, expressed gratitude, rose and departed. The damp of the suntide gradually seeped into the high vaulted room. The cold stone walls became clammy at first and then warmed, adding their own moist breath to the layered smoke of incense. From the rear of the great hall the singing reeds brought a clear, cutting edge of sound that aided the mind to become fixed.

"So we come to the end. All roles are suited but one." The Firstpriest paused and looked into Shibura's eyes. "There is left the place of him who stands on the right hand."

Shibura felt a momentary jolt of surprise. Then he extended his hearing and sensing behind and around him. True; he had not noticed the fact, but the other

Priestfellows were gone. Only he remained. He felt a swell of elation. That implied—

"It passes to you as it once came to me," the Firstpriest said. From beneath the folds of his robes he produced a copper talisman and handed it to Shibura. It was deceptively heavy. Shibura tucked it into his side pouch and straightened the cloth. He knew no reply was necessary.

The ripples of excitement and surprise smoothed and vanished. The Firstpriest began the ritual passes Shibura had heard described but never seen. The old man's hands slipped through the torchlight, now visible, now unseen. Shibura entered into a state of no definition, no thought, no method. To put aside the thousand things and, in stillness, retain yourself. So the motions led and defined him. And inside, the soft tinkling chuckle of joy.

After a time they rose and moved from the great hall. They did not use the usual passage of exit. Instead, they walked slowly through the Organic Portal, as convention required. Shibura had been here only once before, when he was learning the intricate byways of the temple. Their sandals made echoing clicks in the great hall, but when they stepped into the Portal there came a sudden quiet, for they now walked on a firm softness of green. The Portal was a long, perfectly round passage that muffled all sound. It had no noticeable weave or texture, save the uncountable small pores. There were no torches, but the cushioned walls seemed to provide light. It was a hushed and holy place. It was the enduring gift of the Starcrossers.

The two men stopped midway. Near the floor on a small yellow patch was the place of dedication.

Shibura had learned some fragments of the Starcrossers' written language, but he could not decipher all that the patch contained. No one could. He and the Firstpriest squatted together for a long moment and regarded the yellowed print.

ORGANIFORM. *47296A index 327. Absorbent multilayer.*

They passed out of the Portal and through the temple corridor. The Firstpriest began to unfold his memories of the last Starcrosser visit. There were preparations, always extensive and complex. The citizens of the city had to be prepared, and the Priestfellows themselves would have to see to their own personal states of mind as the event approached.

"I received word from the Farseer only this morning. They had been studying the motion of the central band in Brutus, but of course they set aside the usual five time spaces for observation of the Great Bear. That is the ordained place from which the Starcrossers speak."

"But it is not time," Shibura said. "We expected the audience in my third decade."

"I know. I never expected to see another Starcrossing. The last came when I was a boy—almost too young to hold the talisman you now carry. The Firstpriest of that time assured me I would pass through the lens—die— before the Captain came again."

"Why, then?"

"We must remember our place. The Captain is forever Crossing and his path is not so simple that we can understand."

"The men of the Farseer could not be mistaken? They *did* see the lights?"

Shibura knew a few of those patient watchers of the sky. He did not understand the great tube they seemed to worship and saw no true interest in what they did. The stars were but points of light and told nothing. Only the sun and Brutus held any interest for a man of religion, for they alone revealed their structure. The stars were great candles and might possibly say much, but they were too far away. Only through the Crossing did contact with the mightier places come, and then solely in the form of the Captain and his fellows. Nonetheless, only with the Farseer could the dancing of lights be seen and preparations made for the coming of the Captain.

"I have every trust in them. The Farseer was built in the far past, at the command of the Captain. The role of the Farseer is ordained and it is not for a Firstpriest or Priestfellow to question the tenders of the Farseer." The old man's head bobbed in the gesture of instruction. He smiled to show that his words carried no sharp edge and were meant only for reminding. Between the

two men there had come a feeling of closeness. The
Firstpriest's joy that he would again see a Crossing
conveyed itself to Shibura and lightened his step.

After a pause Shibura said, "Was there any message
in the dancing light?"

"The tenders of the Farseer said only that it was
the ritual message. They come. They are now within the
grip of our sun and we must be ready."

Shibura padded ahead and put his weight against
the great door of the temple. They passed out into sunlight. Going down the steps, the bare baked stone face of
the temple at their backs, the murmur of life swelled up
around them. The great square before them was host to
hundreds of people. Knots of friends drifted past amid
the flicking echoes of hundreds of sandals.

The shops which lined the tiled walkways were small
and displayed their wares with abandon, letting robes
spill from their holders; beads and books and spices
competed for the same spot in a display case. The two
men passed through the crowd. Shibura relished the
grainy feel of this uncomplicated existence: talking, laughing, some barterers greeting the price of items with a
feigned sharp bark of disbelief.

The sun lay on the horizon, burning a hole in heaven.
A few men and women clad in religious raiments spoke
of their missions in life, advising of the latest revelation.
Shibura bore them no malice, for they were simple
people who followed their own blind vision.

Five of the women formed a circle and chanted:

I am
Not great or small
But only
Part of All.

Shibura smiled to himself. It was comforting to know
that the purpose of their world was writ large even in
the minds of the most common. These people were, of
course, no less than he. They formed the base of the
great pyramid at whose peak were not priests or merchants or the men of government, but a holy article; the
Paralixlinnes. Shibura had learned much from those
infinitely detailed and faceted cubes. As objects of meditation they were supreme; how fitting that they played

the crowning role even in the vast universe of the Starcrosser.

The Firstpriest made a gesture and they turned down a bumpy avenue of black cobblestone. Rice bins towered over them, their great funnels pointing downward to the rude shop where the grains were sold. The tubs carried indecipherable scrawls in red denoting the strains.

Here the air had its own texture, the sweat of work and reek of spices. Where the two men walked the crowds separated and let them through. Word had passed in the early morning, once the Priestfellows had met in the temple. Now surely everyone in the city knew the time of cusp was approaching. Thus and so: in the damp morning the two men journeyed through the city to the foundry that was the focus of the city itself: the birthplace of the Paralixlinnes.

Shibura glanced upward at friend Brutus, thanking the brown and pink giant for this day. His senses quickened.

The Captain listened intently to the whine of the air circulator. So that was breaking down, too. Nothing in this ship seemed to work anymore.

The last transit through Jumpspace had fractured an entire encasement of Paralixlinnes, even though they were rated to stand up for longer than a year. The ship—indeed, the whole Jump network—was well over into the red zone. With that many encasements gone the ship might well fail at the next Jump. Perhaps the Captain could make it through by enforcing absolute discipline on the next Jump, but he doubted it. Many of the backup men were not well trained; it seemed a corollary of life that political appointees never knew their jobs. But if he ran the calculation through a dozen times perhaps the errors would iron themselves out. A slight mistake in the measurement of the metric tensor, some small deviation in the settings, a flashover in the encasements—any of these, and the ship would blossom into a thousand fiery fragments.

The Captain clenched his hands behind his back and paced the organiform deck. The hooded computer modules were lit, and the sullen murmur of the bridge would be reassuring to one who did not know the facts. The Captain turned and glanced down the bridge. His Executive Officer was talking earnestly to one of the lieutenants. The Captain could be sure that whatever the conversation, it would not concern ship's business. The Executive Officer was a Constructionist, and most of the lieutenants were sharp enough to have fallen directly into line as soon as the ship left its last major port. The Captain knew there were lists aboard of each staff member's political inclination, and he expected the list would soon be used.

The Captain shrugged and turned away. Let the Executive Officer do what he would, this voyage was not finished and the ship was in far more peril than most of the officers realized. Politics could wait. If there was some failure at Seascape this ship might very well never leave realspace again. He turned his attention back to the large screen. They were following a smooth ellipse in toward the gas giant that loomed ahead. At the terminator the Captain could see flashes of gigantic lightning, even at this distance.

This planet was at least nine Jupiter masses; its compressed core burned with a lukewarm fusion reaction. The physics of the thing would make an interesting study. He had never visited this system before, and while reading the description had wondered why an experimental station did not orbit the gas giant for scientific purposes. But then he realized Seascape had a telescope and would see the station. No one wished to perturb the priests of Seascape with an artificial construct in their skies. Such things had proved unsettling on other worlds. So the great gas planet went unstudied and Seascape, according to the computer log, displayed very little social drift. The society there had lasted over ten thousand years, and the Captain was quite aware that he should do nothing to upset it.

He gave an order and the view shifted from the swirling bands to a point of light that orbited the great planet. The view expanded, focused. Seascape shimmered in blue-white. At first it appeared to have nothing but vast oceans, but as the eye accommodated to its light a few details emerged. Lumps of brown were strewn randomly, as though by a careless Creator. At the edge of the horizon lay the only continent. The Captain wondered idly if a drone Ramscoop was by chance making delivery now, but a quick scan of the orbital index indicated nothing around Seascape that would fit the parameters. He made a mental note to complain—for the nth time—about the lack of communication with the drone operation. Worlds like Seascape needed tools, cutting bits, sometimes rare metals and ceramics; if the drone were off schedule or failed in flight there was no way of knowing whether the client world was carrying on manufacture any longer. More than once the Captain had brought his ship out of Jump to find a servant world without necessary materials. Without the few pieces of crucial high technology that the Ramscoop should have brought, the manufacturing process broke down. Without a cause to move them the priests had to search for some other aim, and usually they failed. The world began to come apart at the seams. Not only was the Jumpship's mission worthless, but sometimes fatal damage was done to the client society itself.

The Captain ordered a further magnification and the mottled brown continent became a swollen mark on the planet's limb. There was a belt of jungle, a crinkling gray swath of interior mountains, convoluted snake-rivers and—in the island chains to the north—frigid blue wastes.

An orderly passed by; the Captain accepted a warm mug of amber liquid. He sipped at it gingerly, made a face. He paced the deck again till he came to an area of Organiform and then poured the cup into the floor. In the light gravity the drink made an odd slapping sound as it hit the Organiform and was absorbed.

The Captain glanced back at the screen, where the single continent was spreading over the edge of the planet.

Seascape was tidelocked so that the single continent always faced the banded giant. It was rare for an Earth-like planet to be a moon and even rarer when the geological mix in its crust was hospitable to man. The

Captain wondered what it would be like to live on a
world where the Sun was regularly eclipsed by a gas
giant planet; what color was the halo? There were so
many unique things about any world: winds that deaf-
ened, oceans that laughed, tranquility beside violence.
Even the routine miracles of the xenobiologists could
not wash away the taste and sound and smell of what
was new and alien.

"Cap'n!"

The Captain turned. It was totally unnecessary to
shout on the bridge. The Executive Officer was taking
his time; he stopped and spat expertly into the Organiform
carpet. The Captain went rigid.

"About time we sent them a burst, don't you think?"
the other man said casually.

"It's day at their observatory."

"So what?"

"They cannot read laser flashes in broad daylight,
obviously."

"Use radio. Hell—"

"Their culture was not designed to need or use radio.
They haven't developed it and if we don't introduce it,
perhaps they never will."

The Executive Officer regarded him shrewdly. "That's
probably right."

"I know it is right," the Captain said.

"Yeah, I guess I could look it up if I had the time. I
thought we ought to tell the natives we were coming in
faster than usual."

The Captain regarded him with distant assessment.
"And why is that?"

"We can't afford to spend much time here. Get the
components and leave. There are good political reasons
to be ahead of schedule this time."

"I see," the Captain said evenly. He glanced up at
the screen where the ocean world was rolling toward
them and savored the view one last time. His few
moments of introspection had lifted some of his troubles, but now the weight of working with such men
returned. He breathed deeply of the cycled air and
turned back to the Executive Officer. Men might fly

between the stars, threading across the sky, but they
were still only men.

The message found them as they entered the Kodakan
room.

Shibura padded quietly behind the Firstpriest. They
had reached the door when he felt a slight tap on his
shoulder and turned. A man stood beside him panting
heavily in the thick air. The chanting from within
drowned out his words. Shibura gestured and the man
followed him out into the foyer of the holy foundry.

"We are beginning the game," Shibura said rapidly.
"What is it?"

The man still gasped for breath. "From the Farseer."
Pause. "Starcrossers."

"What?" Shibura felt a sudden unease.

"The Watcher sent me at the run. The Starcrossers
will not circle the sky five times. They come two circles
from now."

"That is not congruent with ritual."

"So the Watcher said. Is there a reply for the
Watcher?"

Shibura paused. He should speak to the Firstpriest
but he could not now interrupt the Kodakan. Yet the
Watcher waited.

"Tell him to omit the Cadence of Hand and Star." He
juggled things in his mind for a moment. "Tell the
Watcher to spread word among the populace. The
Firstpriest and I shall go to the small Farseer to watch
the next circling of the sky. The Firstpriest will want to
see if events are orderly among the Starcrossers."

The man nodded and turned to leave the foundry.
Shibura reflected for a moment on his instructions and
decided he could do no better without further thought.
And he could not miss the Kodakan.

He entered the chamber quietly. He made the canonical hand passes diagonally across his body to induce
emotions of wholeness and peace. The low hum of
introduction was coming to an end. Shibura took his
place in the folded hexagon of men and women and
began his exercises, sitting erect. He aligned his spine

and arms and found his natural balance. He raised his
hands high and brought them down in a slow arc,
breathing out, coming *down* into focus, outward-feeling.
In his arm carrier he found the gameballs and beads.
He began their juggling and watched as they caught the
light in their counter cadences. Sprockets of red and
blue light flashed as they tumbled in the air. The familiar dance calmed Shibura and he felt the beginnings of
congruence in the men around him. Across the hexagon
the Firstpriest juggled also, and a feeling of quietness
settled. The sing-chant rose and then faded slowly in
the soft acoustics of the room. The factory workers
signaled readiness and Shibura began the game.

The first draw came across the hexagon where a
worker of iron fingered his leaves nervously. The man
chose a passage from the Tale and unfolded it as over-
ture. The play fell first to the left, then to the right. It
was a complex opening with subtle undertones of dread.
Play moved on. Gradually, as the players selected their
leaves and read them the problem gained in body and
fullness.

*For the older man came down from the hills on the
day following, and being he of desperate measure, he
sought to bargain on the rasping plain. Such was his
mission of the flesh that he forgot the custom. There are
things of trade and there are things not of trade; the
old man forgot the difference. He sought gain. The
things he loved he had made himself, but he knew not
that to give to himself was necessary to find himself and
others. There came a time . . .*

All entries made, the play passed to Shibura. Shibura
began the second portion of the Kodakan: proposal of
solution. The draw danced among the players and the
air thickened.

It came to this: you are one of two players. You can
choose red or black. The other player is hidden and you
hear only of his decisions. You know no other aspects of
his nature.

If you both pick red, you gain a measure. If both
choices are black, a measure is lost. But if you choose

red and your opponent (fellow, mate, planet-sharer) votes black, he wins *two* measures, and you lose two.

In the end it gains most measure for all if all play together. He who cooperates in spirit, he who senses the Total—it is he who brings full measure to the Kodakan.

Kodakan is infinitely more complex than this simple trading of measures, but within the game there are the same elements.

Today the problem set by the workers carried subtle tension.

The Starcrossers come in audience yet they take from us our most valued.

If the Paralixlinnes be our consummation—

—Apostles of first divinity—

—Why should we give them over to the Starcrossers? We shall suffer loss of Phase.

We shall lose our moorings. Go down into darkness.

But now the play returned to Shibura. He pointed out the automatic ships that came to Seascape. Did these machines without men not bring valued supplies, components for the working of the Paralixlinnes? Bore they not new and subtle devices? Delicate instruments, small lenses to bring insight to the making of the Paralixlinnes?

The gameballs danced and the spirit moved out from Shibura. The workers caught the harmony of the moment. Shibura indicated slight displeasure when divergent moods emerged, rebuked personal gain, and drew closer to the workers. The Firstpriest added tones of his own: praise of the workers; admiration of the delicate iron threads that honeycombed the Paralixlinnes; love of workmanship.

So, Shibura asked then, as one casts food upon the Titanic and through the mystery of the eternal currents there returned the fishes and the deepbeasts; so the Starcrossers gained the Paralixlinnes and Seascape received the Ramships with their cargo of delights.

The mood caught slowly at first and only with the rhythm of repetition did the air clear, the tension submerge. Conflicting images in the game weakened. The players selected new leaves, each bringing to the texture of events some resonance of personal insight.

Shibura caught the uprush of spirit at its peak, chanting joyfully of the completion as the play came to rest:

In pursuit
Of infinity
Lose the way
Thus: serenity.

The Firstpriest imposed the dream-like flicker of gameballs and beads. The muted song was clothed in darkness. Then stillness.

Accept them as the flower does the bee. The fire burning, the iron kettle singing on the hearth, an oiltree brushing the leadened roof, water dripping and chiming in the night.

The hexagon broke and they left, moving in concert.

Shibura stood with his arms folded behind him and listened to the clicking of the implements. The Firstpriest was engaged with the small Farseer, and attendants moved around the long tubular instrument, making adjustments. Shibura looked out the crack of the great dome and down at the sprawling jumble of the town as it settled into dusk. Even at this distance he could see the flicker of ornamental torches and make out the occasional murmur of crowds.

In the main street the canonical pursuit was in progress. Bands of young men in tattered rough garments ran down the avenues, laughing and singing and reenacting the sports of the Fest. There came the muffled braying of domestic animals. The *segretti* were loose; Shibura could see one of the long-limbed animals chasing a group of men under the yellow torchlights.

The *segretti* snapped at a lagging man, but he dodged away at the last moment. The animals were fairly harmless anyway, since most of their teeth had been pulled. Their three legs still carried the sharpened hooves that could inflict wounds, but these were easily avoided by rolling away if the man was quick about it. The *segretti* chase was the most ancient of the Fest ceremonies. It spoke of the earliest days of man on Seascape, when he had not tamed the animals of the inner continent and was prey as often as he was hunter. Shibura had run like that once, taunted the *segretti* and felt the quick darting fear as the animal brushed too close. But that was behind him. He would not know it again.

"It is there," said the Firstpriest. "All seems in order."

Shibura turned away from the view. He murmured a phrase of pleasure and relief, but still he felt a gnawing anxiety. Things were askew; the Starcrossers should not perturb the ancient ceremony this way. He felt restive. Perhaps the Game earlier in the day had not truly brought him to completion.

The Firstpriest was conferring with the attendants of the instrument. Shibura knew its function, just as he knew the role of the machines in the foundry and the mines and the optical shops, all of which came together to make the Paralixlinnes. It was only necessary to know their role, not the details themselves. These were the only rightful machines for life on Seascape. Occasionally, through the long scroll of history, men had tried to extend the principles in the Farseer or devise new ways in the foundry. Sometimes they even succeeded, but the radical nature of what they did caused unease and loss of Phase. History showed that when these men died their inventions passed with them.

One of the attendants stepped around the long tube and her flowing robe caught his eye. She had long delicate fingers and moved with grace across the gray stone floor. Her sandals seemed to make a quiet music of their own.

Ah, Shibura thought. *Ah* it was and *ah* it did.

When the audience was over, the Starcrossers gone and he released from his priestly vows, this was what he would seek. A woman, yes. A woman to have in the yearly fortnight of mating. A woman for companion in the rest of the long year. A warm molecular bed of cellular wisdom, receptive. Shadowed inlets of rest. He would not seek adventure or wealth. No, he would seek a woman.

There came a hollow clanking as the Firstpriest came down from the perch.

"The Starcrossing is as before. Their ship is not changed from the last audience." The Firstpriest smiled at Shibura and took his arm. "Would you like to see?"

Shibura nodded eagerly and mounted the iron stair. He settled into the carved oaken chair, and another woman attendant helped him strap in. She turned a massive crank and heavy oiled gears interlocked. It required several moments to bring the tube around, and beads of sweat popped out on her brow. Shibura watched her with interest until the eyepiece swung down to meet his face.

He pressed his eye against the worn slot. At first the field of view seemed dark, but as his eye adjusted he caught a fleck of light which moved from the left into the center. The dot seemed to grow until suddenly it was a silvery ball moving lazily through the great night. Shibura had heard of this but never seen it: The ship that crossed between stars in the wink of a moment. Not like the Ramship which required more than a man's life to make the journey, and carried only instruments or supplies. This ship knew the dark spaces too well for that.

Tomorrow a smaller craft would detach itself from this sphere and dip down into the air of Seascape. Tomorrow was so soon. He and the Firstpriest and all the others would have to labor through the night to make adequate preparations. The people had to be brought to awareness in large meetings; there was no time for the usual small gatherings.

Shibura felt a gathering tightness in him. It was not well to rush things so.

"Come," the Firstpriest called up. "We must go."

The woman labored and the gears meshed again. Shibura wished he had more time to study the ship, to memorize its every line. Then he hurried down the cold stone steps and went to help.

The morning air shimmered over the Canyon of Audience. A swarm of birds entered it from the south and flew its length in W formation. They fluttered higher as they came toward Shibura, probably rising to avoid the murmur of the gigantic crowd. Shibura stood with the others at the head of the valley, the crescent of Brutus at their backs.

The hills were alive with people. They were encamped in the low hills that framed the valley; most had been waiting since yesterday. Delegations were here from the inner continent, an entire fleet from the Off Islands, pilgrims of every description. These were more people than Shibura had ever seen before. The massive weight of their presence bothered him, and he had difficulty focusing on the moment. He knew he was tired from the long night of performing blessings and meditations before the Paralixlinnes.

"*Seistonn*," the Firstpriest murmured, placing a gentle hand upon Shibura's shoulder.

"I am distracted. I hope the Paralixlinnes prove suitable."

"I am sure the workers have done well."

"Would that I were a foundry worker," Shibura said. "They have only to watch now."

"For others there is process. For us there is the comfort of duty." The Firstpriest smiled. To Shibura the crescent of Brutus seemed to form a halo around the Firstpriest's head. The halo rippled and danced in the rising warm air of morning.

Shibura nodded and turned, hands behind back, to regard the incredible view before them. A Prieststeward said there might be a million people here. It was probably no larger than the audiences of antiquity, since the population of Seascape varied little, but the variety astonished Shibura. This was the most important spiritual event of their lives, and the most impassioned were demonstrating their prowess to pass the time. There were men who could pop metal bands wrapped around their chests; women who babbled at visions; children who whispered to dice and made them perform; a wrinkled gray man who could stop his heart for five minutes; walkers on water; religious acrobats; a man who had been chanting hollowly for three days. All this added to the murmurs that came from the hills, aswarm with life.

Far down the valley, toward the west, they saw it first. An excited babble of sound came toward them as the word spread, and Shibura looked up into the gathering blue sky. A white dot blossomed. He prepared himself. The Priestfellows arrayed themselves in the formal manner and watched the dot swell into a winged form. It fell smoothly in the sky, whispering softly as the evening wind. Abruptly it grew and a low mutter came from it. There was a distant roll of thunder as the ship glided down the valley, turned end for end, and slowed. A jet of orange flame leaped out of the tail with a sudden explosion. Shibura wrinkled his nose at the sulphurous stench. The ship came down with lazy grace in the middle of the prepared field.

The sound of its arrival faded slowly, and there was no answering mutter from the crowd. All lay in silence. The Priestfellows paced forward under the direction of the Firstpriest, who carried the banner and welcoming tokens.

A seam opened in the side of the pearl-white ship. A gangplank slid out and after a moment a human figure appeared. He wore a helmet which after a few moments he removed. Other people appeared beside him, all clothed in a ruddy golden cloth.

Shibura watched the ancient ritual and tried to memorize as much as he could of each moment. In a way it was hard to believe these men had spanned the stars. Their aircraft was beautiful and sleek, but it was only a small shuttle compared to the spherical ship he had seen the night before. These men were taller and moved differently, to be sure. In the universe at large they were like the Manyleggers of the Off Islands who spun gossamer webs, bridging the gap between distant orange flowers. Yet here they seemed only men.

His time came: he stepped forward and was presented to the Captain, a tall man with a lined face full of character. Shibura presented the log of Seascape's history since the last audience. There were records of crop yields and births, accidents and deaths, details of factory and farm. The Captain turned and introduced the Executive Officer in prescribed manner. Shibura looked at this man and saw an unbuttoned pocket in his vest; a snagged bit of cloth near his knee; brown hair parted wrongly near the crown of the head; dirt beneath the fingernails; one thumb hooked into a wide belt. The Executive Officer stood with one knee bent, hips cantilevered.

Shibura greeted him. The man pursed his lips and looked at the Captain. The Captain whispered the opening two words and the man picked it up, completing about half the ceremonial response before bogging down. The Captain shifted uneasily and prompted him again. The Executive Officer stumbled through the rest of the reply.

The ceremony proceeded on a raised, hardpacked field near the ship. They were visible all the way down the vast canyon, but their words could only be heard by those nearby. Nonetheless there was no distant murmur of conversation from the other hundreds of thousands in the canyon. All stared raptly at the Starcrossers. All Starcrossers but the Captain and Executive Officer stood together in a group, smiling but not partaking actively in the formal ceremony. Shibura stood at the right hand of the Firstpriest and noted carefully each movement and word. When the moment came the Captain turned and addressed the people at large. His voice boomed out in the canyon. He knew the words well.

Something caught Shibura's eye and he glanced to the side. The Executive Officer was not standing in place. Instead the man paced impatiently and studied the faces on the nearby hillsides. As Shibura watched he produced a shaped instrument from his belt and began fiddling with it. He raised it to his mouth, and green smoke billowed up into the soft air.

Occasionally, as the Captain continued speaking, the Executive Officer would take the implement from his mouth and begin pacing again. The smoke smelled of something like barley. Shibura knew this action was not correct. The Firstpriest seemed oblivious and did not take his vision from the Captain. As the Captain concluded, the Executive Officer put away the implement and took out a polished metal cylinder. He tipped it up to his mouth and appeared to drink from it. When Shibura next looked back at him he was wiping his mouth with the back of his hand.

When the Captain finished there was a sudden crescendo of windbells in unison and the formal procession began. Shibura led the Priestfellows up the slight rise and over the lip of the canyon. The Firstpriest and the Captain entered the waiting ornamental carriage. The Captain said something to the Executive Officer, and the man turned to look at Shibura. There were masses of people everywhere, but aside from the music there was silence. Shibura bowed to the Executive Officer and gestured at the second carriage. The Priestfellows knew what to do; they arrayed themselves in the remaining carriages. With a lurch the procession began back toward the city.

Though their driver was expert, the carriage creaked and groaned with the strain. It was probably several thousand years old and had completed this task many times before. It seemed to know the ruts of the worn road.

The Executive Officer appeared uninterested in talk. Shibura studied him in the filtered light as they rocked and jounced their way along. The man had a day's growth of beard and gritted his teeth at the sway of the carriage. Something caught his interest on a hillside and he leaned out the window to look at it. He screwed up his eyes against the sun's glare and then beckoned to Shibura with his finger. Shibura leaned forward.

"What're they doing up there?"

Shibura followed his pointed finger. "They are performing religious exercises." Near the road a man was rippling his stomach, hands locked behind spine, balanced on the balls of his feet.

"What whackers. That's what you skinheads do?"

Shibura did not know what to say. True, he had no hair. Every Priestfellow was required to symbolize his renunciation of the flesh, and a shaved head was the most common selection.

"No," he said finally. "We perform other tasks."

That seemed to end the matter. The Executive Officer slumped back in his seat and closed his eyes. There he remained for the rest of the journey.

The noise of arrival wakened him. Shibura climbed down and held the door for the Executive Officer. The two followed the Firstpriest and the Captain through the great doors of the temple. The vaulted hall was cool and refreshing. In the flickering of the torches the crucibles seemed to glow with pearly moisture. The Starcrossers trooped in and began opening the carryslings they had brought. The Firstpriest and the Captain moved to the far end of the great hall and finished the ritual of welcome. Then they began to speak as they watched the examination of the crucibles.

The Executive Officer paced around the great hall with his hands behind his back. Shibura followed him at first, but when he realized the man was going nowhere in particular he returned to the center of the hall in case he was needed for some other purpose. Each Starcrosser was accompanied by a Priestfellow. Several Starcrossers set up a bank of machinery near Shibura.

Near him a Starcrosser knelt before a crucible and waited for the Priestfellow to unfasten the latch. Inside was a Paralixlinne cushioned in velvet reedwork. Shibura avoided looking too closely at the work; he did not wish to become fixed on the Paralixlinnes and be unready if he was summoned. At each crucible the Priestfellow turned away as the examination proceeded. The block of orange within was about a meter on a side, with delicate black ferrite stains embedded along fracture interfaces and slippage lines. Each corner was dimpled with an external connection; a Starcrosser slipped a male interfacer into each and studied the meters he carried with him. The intricate array within the Paralixlinnes seemed to dance in the flickering light with hypnotic regularity.

Shibura tried to allow the slow rhythm in the room to relax him. He felt a welling unease but he could not place the cause. Abruptly he realized that the Executive Officer was nowhere in the great hall. He glanced around but no one else seemed to notice it.

He padded quickly to one of the side antechambers and found nothing. Then he crossed to the side foyer and glanced among the columns there. Against one of them, in near darkness, something stirred.

As his eyes adjusted Shibura recognized one of the

Priestsisters standing rigidly, back pressed against the stonework. Her eyes were wide, her hands clenched.

The Executive Officer had his knee between her legs, his hand caressing her hips.

He was speaking to her and she stared straight ahead, rigid. He moved his knee to widen her legs beneath the folds of her robes, and Shibura came forward.

The Executive Officer caught the faint slap of sandals on stone. He turned and saw Shibura.

Casually he released the woman and stepped back. She stared at him, still frozen. He regarded Shibura for a moment and then turned and walked casually away.

Her eyes showed too much white. She was on the verge of hysteria. Wordlessly he gestured toward the great hall and after a moment she seemed to comprehend what he meant; she nodded and shuffled away. The Executive Officer was gone, but the man had not walked in the direction of the great hall.

Shibura followed him, not quite knowing what to do. Beyond the foyer was a maze of meditation chambers; he spent several moments threading his way through them fruitlessly. He stopped and listened for a telltale sound. Even the talking from the great hall did not penetrate this far into the temple, and there was a pensive silence so still that Shibura could hear the sound of his own breath. Normally one could pick out the sound of sandals approaching, but the Starcrossers wore some form of boot with a padded sole which made no noise.

Shibura moved quickly along the torchlit corridors. He found nothing. In a few moments he reached the Organic Portal and decided to go back. Probably the Executive Officer had returned to the great hall.

Turning, he glanced down the bore of the Portal. The Executive Officer stood with his back to Shibura, his knees slightly bent in a familiar stance. Shibura felt a sudden rising premonition. In the dull glow of the Portal walls he saw a thin yellow-amber stream appear between the man's legs. It spattered soundlessly on the floor.

Shibura rushed forward. The soft padding muffled the sound of his approach. Something welled up from

within him. He smacked the man smartly on the back
with the flat of his hand.

"No. This is a most holy place!"

The Executive Officer took a half step forward to
catch himself. He fumbled at his fly, blinking at Shibura.
Then his jaw tightened.

"What in hell—?" He shoved Shibura away. "You just
take off."

"No. This is the Portal from the Captain. It—"

"You don't know what this is. We don't run off into
the bushes the way you do." He kicked at the floor.
"This stuff absorbs it."

Shibura stared at him, uncomprehending. "And you
stroked the woman, the Priestsister, in an inappropriate
manner."

"Spying, huh?" The Executive Officer had regained
his composure. He shook his fist. "You guys want to tell
us about women? Huh—you're unqualified."

Shibura said slowly, "We have our own—"

"You have *nothing*. Nothing we didn't give you. *We*
fixed you so you wouldn't screw too much, wouldn't
overpopulate. So you got a mating season, like animals.
We did it."

"The mating fortnight is the natural Fest time of all
men—"

"No, skinhead. *I'm* a man. You're a test-tube experiment."

"That is an untruth!"

"Yeah? You're trained for obedience. To kneel down
to Jumpship men—real men."

The Executive Officer's lip curled back. Casually,
openhanded, he cuffed Shibura. The Priest's head snapped
to the side. "See? Made to take it."

Shibura felt something terrible and strange boil up in
him. His pulse quickened. Sweat beaded on his forehead. He could not find focus in this swirling of intense
new feeling.

"We . . . are following the path of certitude . . ." he
began, quoting from the ceremony of dedication.

"Right, that's a good boy. You just run along now,
I've got some more business to attend to here."

Shibura started to turn away and suddenly stopped.

The Executive Officer was unbuckling his pants. With a muffled grunt he started to squat and then looked at Shibura again. "What are you waiting for? Get going."

"No. No!"

The man hitched up his pants and held them together with one hand. He stepped forward, bringing a fist around—

Shibura blocked the arm. He clutched at the man's hands, not knowing what to do, and felt a sharp blow in his ribs. The pain startled him and he pushed, nearly losing his balance. Cloth ripped. He grappled at the other man as they fell together. The floor seemed to rush upward into his eyes. He landed with the Executive Officer's weight on top. His face pressed into the softly resistant foam. He caught the stench of urine and gasped. He wrenched upward and got free of the weight. He rolled away. The Executive Officer was flailing after him, and Shibura came up on his heels, ready to spring.

There was some distracting noise but he ignored it to concentrate on his opponent, who was slowly getting to his knees. The noise came again. It was a voice.

"Hold! Shibura, move back—" It was a Priestfellow.

Shibura froze. He allowed arms to encircle him, half listened to their river of words and exclamations. His thoughts ran furiously, and the Organic Portal seemed bathed in hot red light. The Executive Officer glared at him and raised a hand to strike, but another hand appeared and blunted the blow. The other man's face moved away, saying something, and was gone.

The sounds came as though from a great distance, hollow and slow. He stumbled away from there on the arms of two Priestfellows.

There was a sharp burning in his nose. He wiped at it and his fingers came away smeared scarlet. He tried to speak and found his mouth clotted, as though stuffed with acrid cotton.

Word of the event had reached the great hall. There was a babble of voices. With carryingholds and slings the Priestfellows were removing the Paralixlinnes.

Shibura stood and watched numbly. The two Priestfellows still held his arms. He saw the Captain looking over at him, lines furrowed on his brow.

After a time he blinked and saw the Firstpriest standing before him. The old man regarded him for a long moment and then said softly, "No word will be repeated of this. I have heard of the event. I think it best you do not follow us to the canyon. The Captain wishes to depart soon."

There was another long silence; and then, "I know this is a difficult time for you. Let this moment pass away."

Shibura nodded and said nothing. The two Priestfellows at his side went to help with the loading of the crucibles, and after a pause Shibura moved to the doorway of the great hall. The sudden silence of the room reminded him that he was now alone. All others were making preparations and entering the carriages. At the doorway he watched them go, a long line of ceremonial carts. The Paralixlinnes were sealed in their crucibles, which were in turn sheathed in sleeves of polished darkwood. Each neatly filled a cart.

At a call the procession began to move. The carriages departed first, and then the long line of carts rattled away down the cobblestone streets and into the damp heat of the early afternoon. Dust curled in their wake.

Shibura stood with one hand on the massive burnished temple door as the procession slowly wound away. His mind seethed. The Executive Officer's words had battered Shibura more than the fists. The picture endlessly repeated itself in Shibura's mind: The unbuckling. The abrupt squat. The grunt as he settled himself—

It had been the act of an animal. Not a man.

A man knows the time to fondle a woman. A man senses what is sacred.

Such animals as that Officer now had the Paralixlinnes and would carry them away. The purity of those forms would be profaned by the touch of the Executive Officer. The work of a generation was delivered into the hands of that—

Out of the confusion in Shibura's mind came a thought. Shibura was a young man. The Firstpriest would pass

away and Shibura, he-who-stands-on-the-right-hand,
would become Firstpriest. He would supervise the slow,
serene craftsmanship that made the Paralixlinnes. He
would follow the right path.

But when next the Starcrossers came, the Paralixlinnes
would be safely hidden in distant mountain caves. They
would be revered as they were meant to be.

Shibura clenched his jaws tight and smiled a terrible
smile. The Canyon of Audience would prove a different
host next time.

A landslide starts with the fall of a single pebble.
Thus did the Empire begin to erode.

Editor's Introduction To:

THE CLAW AND THE CLOCK

Christopher Anvil

Empires fall for many reasons. Sometimes they choose the wrong enemy.

In 1914 Woodrow Wilson told the world that the United States was too proud to fight. Some thought that meant we couldn't do it. Hitler made much the same mistake 27 years later.

THE CLAW AND THE CLOCK

Christopher Anvil

Iadrubel Vire glanced over the descriptive documents thoughtfully.

"A promising world. However, considering the extent of the Earthmen's possessions, and the size of their Space Force, one hesitates to start trouble."

Margash Grele bowed deferentially.

"Understood, Excellency. But there is a significant point that we have just discovered. We have always supposed this planet was a part of their Federation. It is not. It is *independent*."

Vire got his two hind ripping claws up onto their rest.

"Hm-m-m . . . How did we come by this information?"

"One of their merchant ships got off-course, and Ad-

miral Arvast Nade answered the distress signal." Grele
gave a bone-popping sound, signifying wry humor.
"Needless to say, the Earthmen were more distressed
after the rescue than before."

Vire sat up.

"So, contrary to my specific instructions, Nade has
given the Earthmen pretext to strike at us?"

"Excellency, restraint of the kill-instinct requires high
moral development when dealing with something as
helpless as these Earthmen. Nade, himself, did not
take part in the orgy, of course, but he was unable to
restrain his men. It was the Earthlings' fault, because
they were not armed. If they had been in full battle
armor, with their tools of war— Well, who wants to
crack his claws on a thing like that? But they presented
themselves as defenseless offerings. The temptation was
too great."

"Were the Earthmen aware of the identity of the
rescue craft?"

Grele looked uneasy.

"Admiral Nade feared some trap, and . . . ah . . .
undertook to forestall treachery by using an Ursoid
recognition signal."

Vire could feel the scales across his back twitch. This
fool, Nade, had created out of nothing the possibility of
war with both Earth *and* Ursa.

Vire said shortly, "Having given the Ursoid recognition signal, the Earthmen naturally would not be prepared. Therefore Nade would naturally be unable to
restrain his men. So, what—"

Grele gave his bone-grinding chuckle, and suddenly
Vire saw it as amusement at the ability of Nade to
disobey Vire's orders, and get away with it.

Vire's right-hand battle-pincer came up off its rest,
his manipulators popped behind his bony chest armor,
three death-dealing stings snicked into position in his
left-hand battle pincer—

Grele hurtled into a corner, all claws menacingly
thrust out, but screaming, "Excellency, I meant no
offense! Forgive my error! I mean only respect!"

"*Then get to the point!* Let's have the *facts!*"

Grele said in a rush, "Admiral Nade saved several

Earthlings, to question them. They saw him as their
protector, and were frank. It seems the Earthmen on
this planet have a method for eliminating warlike traits
from their race, and—"

"From their race *on this planet alone?*"

"Yes. The planet was settled by very stern religion-
ists, who believe in total peace unless attacked. They
eliminate individuals who show irrepressible warlike
traits."

Vire settled back in his seat. "They believe in 'Total
peace, unless attacked.' *Then* what?"

"Apparently, they believe in self-defense. A little
impractical, if proper precautions have not been made."

"Hm-m-m. How did the crewmen know about this?"

"They had made many delivery trips to the planet. It
seems that the Earthmen call this planet, among themselves, 'Storehouse.' The code name is given in the
documents there, and it is formally named 'Faith.' But
to the Earthmen, it is 'Storehouse.' "

"Why?"

"These religious Earthlings have perfected means to
preserve provisions with no loss whatever. Even live
animals are in some way frozen, gassed, irradiated—or
somehow treated—so they are just as good when they
come out as when they went in. This is handy for
shippers who have a surplus due to a temporary glut on
the market, or because it's a bad year for the buyers.
So, within practicable shipping distance, Storehouse
does a thriving business, preserving goods from a time
of surplus to a time of need."

Vire absently grated his ripping claws on their rests.

"Hm-m-m . . . And the basis of this process is not
generally known?"

"No, sir. They have a monopoly. Moreover, they use
their monopoly to enforce codes of conduct on the
shippers. Shippers who employ practices they regard as
immoral, or who deal in goods they disapprove of, have
their storage quotas cut. Shippers they approve of get
reduced rates. And they are incorruptible, since they are
religious fanatics—like our Cult of the Sea, who resist
the last molt, and stick to gills."

"Well, well, this *does* offer possibilities. But, would

the Earthmen be willing to lose this valuable facility, even if it is not a member of their Federation? On the other hand—I wonder if these fanatics have antagonized the Earthmen as the cursed sea cult antagonizes us? That collection of righteous clams."

Grele nodded. "From what Admiral Nade learned, it certainly seems so. The crew of the distressed ship, for instance, had just had their quota cut because they had been caught 'shooting craps'—a form of gambling—while on their own ship waiting to unload."

"Yes, that sounds like it. Nade, I suppose, has his fleet in position?"

"Excellency, he chafes at the restraints."

"No doubt."

Vire balanced the possibilities.

"It is rumored that some who have attacked independent Earth-settled planets have not enjoyed the experience."

"The Earthlings would be bound to spread such rumors. But what can mere religious fanatics do against the guns of our men? The fanatics are skilled operators of a preserving plant; of what use is *that* in combat?"

Vire settled back. Either the Earthmen were truly unprepared, in which case he, Vire, would receive partial credit for a valuable acquisition; or else the Earthmen *were* prepared, and Nade would get such a dent in his shell that his reputation would never recover.

"All right," said Vire cheerfully, "but we must have a pretext—these religious fanatics must have delivered some insult that we want to avenge, and it must fit in with their known character. If possible, it must rouse sympathy, even, for us. Let's see . . ."

Elder Hugh Phillips eyed the message dourly.

"These lobsters have their gall. Look at this."

Deacon Bentley adjusted his penance shirt to make the bristles bite in better, and took the message. He read aloud in a dry methodical voice:

" 'Headquarters, the Imperial Hatchery, Khlaftschiffran' —lot of heathenish gabble there, I'll skip all that. Let's see '. . . Pursuant to the blessings of the' . . . heh . . . 'fertility god Fflahvritschtsvri . . . Pursuant to the bless-

ings of the fertility god, What's-His-Name, the Royal
Brood has exceeded expectations this season, all praise
to So-and-So, et cetera, et cetera, and exceeds the
possibility of the Royal Hatchery to handle. We, therefore, favor you with the condescension of becoming for
the next standard year an Auxiliary Royal Hatchery,
consecrated according to the ritual of Fflahvrit . . . et
cetera . . . and under due direction of the Imperial
Priesthood, and appropriate Brood Masters, you to receive in addition to the honor your best standard payment for the service of maintaining the Royal Brood in
good health, and returning same in time for the next
season, undamaged by the delay, to make up the deficiency predicted by the Brood Masters. The fertility
god, What's-His-Name, directs us through his Priesthood to command your immediate notice of compli-
ance, as none of the precious Brood must be endangered
by delay.' "

Deacon Bentley looked up.

"To make it short, we're supposed to store the royal
lobsters for a year, is that it?"

"Evidently."

"There's no difficulty there." Bentley eyed the message coldly. "As for being consecrated according to the
lobster's fertility god, *there* we part company."

Elder Phillips nodded.

"They *do* offer good pay, however."

"All worldly money is counterfeit. The only reward is
in Heaven."

"Amen. But from their own heathen viewpoint, the
offer is fair. Obviously, we can't accept it. But we must
be fair in return, even to lobsters. We will take care of
the Royal Brood, but as for their Priesthood"—he cleared
his throat—"with due humility, we must decline that
provision. Now, who writes the answer?"

"Brother Fry would be ideal for it."

"He's on a fast. How about Deacon Fenell?"

"No good. He went into a cell on Tuesday. Committed himself for a month."

"He did, eh? Able's boy, Wilder, would have been
good at this. Too bad."

Phillips nodded.

"Unfortunately, not all can conquer their own nature. Some require grosser enemies." He sighed. "Let's see. How do we start the thing off?"

"Let's just say, 'We will put up your brood for so-and-so much per year. We decline the consecration.' That's the gist of the matter. Then we nail some diplomacy on both ends of it, dress it up a little, and there we are."

"I wish Brother Fry were here. This nonsense can eat up time. However, he's *not* here, so let's get at it."

Iadrubel Vire read the message over again intently:

From:
Central Contracting Office
Penitence City
Planet of Faith
To:
Headquarters
The Imperial Hatchery
Khlaftschiffranzitschopendischkla
Dear Sirs:
    We are in receipt of your request of the 22nd instant that we put the excess of the Royal Brood in storage for a period approximating one standard year.
    We agree to do this, in accord with our standard rate schedule "D" appended, suitable for nonpreferred live shipments. Kindly note that these rates apply from date of delivery to the storehouse entrance, to date of reshipment from the same point.
    We regret that we must refuse your other terms, to wit:
    a) Accompaniment of the shipment by priests and broodmasters.
    b) Consecration to the fertility god, referred to in your communication.
    In reference to a), no such accompaniment is necessary or allowed.
    In reference to b), the said god, so-called, is, of course, nonexistent.
    In view of the fact that your race is known to be

heathen, these requests will not be held against you in determining the rate schedule, beyond placing you in the nonpreferred status.

We express our appreciation for this order, and trust that our service will be found satisfactory in every respect.

> Truly yours,
> Hugh Bentley
> Chief Assistant
> Central Contracting Office

Vire sat back, absently scratched his ripping claws on their rest, reached out with a manipulator, and punched a call-button.

A door popped open, and Margash Grele stepped in and bowed.

"Excellency?"

"Read this."

Grele read it, and looked up.

"These people are, as I told you, sir, like our sea cult—only worse."

"They certainly take an independent line for an isolated planet dealing with an interstellar empire—and on a sensitive subject, at that."

"Not so, Excellency. It is independent from *our* viewpoint. If you read between the lines, you can see that, for *them*, they are bent over backwards."

Vire absently squeaked the sharp tips of his right-hand battle claw together.

"Maybe. In any case, I don't think we would be quite justified by this reply in doing anything drastic. However, I think we can improve on this. Tell Nade to get his claws sharpened up, and we'll see what happens with the next message."

Hugh Phillips handed the message to Deacon Bentley.

"There seems to have been something wrong with our answer to these crabs."

"What, did we lose the order? Let's see."

Bentley's eyebrows raised.

"Hm-m-m . . . 'Due to your maligning the religious

precepts of our Race, we must demand a full retraction and immediate apology . . .' When did we do that?"

"There was something about that part where we said they were heathens."

"They *are* heathens."

"I know."

"Truth is Truth."

"That is so. Nevertheless—well, Brother Fry would know how to handle this."

"Unfortunately, he is not here. Well, what to do about this?"

Phillips looked at it.

"What is there to do?"

Bentley's look of perplexity cleared away.

"True. We can't have lobsters giving us religious instruction." He looked wary. "On the other hand, we mustn't fall into the sin of pride, either."

"Here, let's have a pen." Phillips wrote rapidly, frowned, then glanced at Bentley. "How is your sister's son coming along? Her next-to-eldest?"

Bentley shook his head.

"I fear he is not meant for righteousness. He has refused to do his penances."

Phillips shook his head, then looked at what he had written. After a moment, he glanced up.

"If the truth were told, some of us shaved by pretty close, ourselves. I suppose it's to be expected. The first settlers were certainly descended from a rough lot." He cleared his throat. "I am not so sure my eldest is going to make it."

Bentley caught his breath.

"Perhaps you judge too harshly."

"No. As a boy, he did not *play* marbles. He lined them up in ranks, and studied the formations. We would find him with his mother's pie plate and a pencil, holding them to observe how a space fleet in disk might destroy one in column. I have tried to . . ." Phillips cleared his throat. "Here, read this. See if you can improve it. We must be strictly honest, and must not truckle to these heathens. It would be bad for them as well as us."

"Amen, Elder. Let's see, now—"

*   *   *

Iadrubel Vire straightened up in his seat, reread the message, and summoned Margash Grele.

Margash bowed deferentially.

"Excellency?"

"This is incredible. Read this."

Grele read aloud:

" 'Sirs: We acknowledge receipt of yours of the 28th instant, and are constrained, in all truth, to reply that you are heathen: that your so-called fertility god is no god at all; that your priests are at best misled, and at worst representatives of the devil: and that we can on no account tolerate priests of heathen religions on this planet. As these are plain facts, there can be no retraction and no apology, as there is no insult, but only a plain statement of truth. As a gesture of compromise, and to prove good will, we will allow one (1) broodmaster to accompany the shipment, provided he is not a priest of any godless 'religion,' so-called. We will not revise the schedule of charges on this occasion, but warn you plainly that this is our final offer. Truly yours . . .' "

Grele looked up blankly.

Vire said, "There is a tone to this, my dear Grele, that does not appear consistent with pacifism. Not with pacifism as *I* understand the word."

"I certainly see what you mean, sir. Nevertheless, they *are* pacifists. We have carefully checked our information."

"And we are *certain* they are not members of the Federation?"

"Absolutely certain."

"Well, there is *something* here that we do not understand. This message could not be better planned if it were a bait to draw us to the attack."

"It is certainly an insulting message, but one well suited to our purpose."

"That, too, is suspicious. Events rarely fall into line so easily."

"Excellency, they are religious fanatics. There is the explanation."

"Nevertheless, we must draw the net tighter before we attempt to take them. Such utter fearlessness usually implies either a formidable weapon, or a formidable protector. We must be certain the Federation does not have some informal agreement with this planet."

"Excellency, Admiral Nade grows impatient."

Vire's right-hand battle claw quivered. "We will give him the chance to do the job, once we have done ours. We must make certain we do not send our troops straight into the jaws of a trap. There is a strong Space Force fleet so situated that it *might* intervene."

General Larssen, of the Space Force, looked up from copies of the messages. "The only place in this end of space where we can store supplies with *no* spoilage, and they have to wind up in a fight with the lobsters over royal lobster eggs. And we aren't allowed to do anything about it."

"Well, sir," said Larssen's aide, "they *were* pretty insulting about it. And they've had every chance to join the Federation. It's hard to see why the Federation should take on all Crustax for them now."

" 'All Crustax,' nuts. The lobsters would back down if we'd ram a stiff note down their throat. Do we have any reply from the . . . er . . . 'court of last resort' on this?"

"No, sir, they haven't replied yet."

"Much as I dislike them, they don't pussyfoot around, anyway. Let's hope—"

There was a quiet rap, and Larssen looked up.

"Come in!"

The communications officer stepped in, looking serious.

"I wanted to bring you this myself, sir. The Interstellar Patrol declines to intervene, because it feels that the locals can take care of themselves."

Larssen stared. "They're a bunch of pacifists! All *they're* strong at is fighting off temptation!"

"Yes, sir. We made that point. All we got back was, 'Wait and see.' "

"Well, we tried, at least. Now we've got a ringside seat for the slaughter."

Admiral Nade was in his bunk when the top priority message came in. His aide entered the room, approached the bunk, and hesitated. Nade was completely covered up, out of sight.

The aide looked around nervously. The chief was a trifle peevish when roused out of a sound sleep.

The aide put the message on the admiral's cloak of rank on the nightstand near the bunk, retraced his steps to the hatch, opened it wide, then returned to the bunk. Hopeful, he waited, but Nade didn't stir.

The aide spoke hesitantly: "Ah . . . a message, sir." Nothing happened. He tried again.

Nade didn't move.

The aide climbed over the raised lip of the catch tray, took hold of the edge of the bunk, dug several claws into the wood in his nervousness, and cautiously scratched back a little of the fine white sand. The admiral was in there *somewhere*. He scratched a little more urgently. A few smooth pebbles rattled into the tray.

Just then, he bumped something.

Claws shot up. Sand flew in all directions.

The aide fell over the edge of the tray, scrabbled violently, and hurled himself through the doorway.

The admiral bellowed, "WHO DARES—"

The aide rounded corners, and shot down cross-corridors as the admiral grabbed his cloak of rank, then spotted the message.

Nade seized the message, stripped off various seals the message machine had plastered on it, growled: "The fool probably wants *more* delay." Then he tore open the lightproof envelope that guaranteed no one would see it but him, unfolded the message itself, and snarled, " '. . . received your message #4e67t3fs . . . While I agree—' Bah! '. . . extreme caution is advised . . .' That clawless wonder! Let's see, what's this? '. . . Provided due consideration is given to these precautions, you are hereby authorized to carry out the seizure by force of the aforesaid planet, its occupation, its annexation, and whatever ancillary measures may appear necessary or desirable. You are, however, warned on no account to engage forces of the Federation in battle, the operation to be strictly limited to the seizure, et cetera, of the aforesaid planet. If possible, minimum damage is to be done to the planet's storage equipment, as possession of this equipment should prove extremely valuable . . .' Well, he's a hard-shell, after all! Let's see . . . 'Security against surprise by Federation forces will be employed without, however, endangering success of the operation by undue dividing of the attacking force . . .' *That* doesn't hurt anything. Now, the quicker we take them, the better!"

He whipped his cloak of rank around him, tied it with a few quick jerks of his manipulators, strode into the corridor, and headed for the bridge, composing an ultimatum as he went.

Elder Phillips examined the message, and cleared his throat. "We appear to have a war on our hands."

Deacon Bentley made a clucking noise. "Let's see."

Phillips handed him the message. Bentley sat back.

"Ha-hm-m-m. 'Due to your deliberately insulting references to our religion, to your slandering of our gods, and to your refusal to withdraw the insult, we are compelled to extend claws in battle to defend our honor. I hereby authorize the Fleet of Crustax to engage in lawful combat, and have notified Federation authorities as the contiguous independent power in this region that a state of war exists. Signed, Iadrubel Vire, Chief Commander of the Forces.' Well, it appears, Elder, that our message was not quite up to Brother Fry's level. Hm-m-m, there's more to this. Did this all come in at once?"

"It did, Deacon. The first part apparently authorizes the second part."

"Quite a different style, this. 'I, Arvast Nade, Commander Battle Fleet IV, hereby demand your immediate surrender. Failure to comply within one hour, your time, following receipt of this ultimatum, as determined by my communications center, will open your planet to pillage by my troops. Any attempt at resistance will be crushed without mercy, and your population decimated in retaliation. Any damage, or attempted damage, by you to goods or facilities of value on the planet will be avenged by execution of leading citizens selected at my

command. By my fiat as conqueror, your status, retro-
active to the moment of transmission of this ultimatum,
is that of bond-sleg to the conquering race. Any lack of
instantaneous obedience will be dealt with accordingly.
Signed, Arvast Nade, Battle Fleet Commander.' "

Deacon Bentley looked up.

"What do we do with this?"

"I see no alternative to activating War Preventive
Measures, as described in Chapter XXXVIII of the
Lesser Works."

"I was afraid of that. Well . . . so be it."

"We can't have a war here. As soon as we saw a few
of these heathen loose on the planet, we'd all revert to
type. You know what *that* is."

"Well, let's waste no time. You take care of that, and
I'll answer this ultimatum. Common courtesy requires
that we answer it, I suppose."

Arvast Nade got the last of his battle armor on, and
tested the joints.

"There's a squeak somewhere."

"Sir?" said his aide blankly.

"There's a squeak. Listen."

It could be heard plainly:

Squeak, squeak, squeak, squeak, squeak.

The aide got the oil can. "Work your claws one at a
time sir . . . Let's see . . . Again. *There* it is!"

"Ah, good," said Nade, working everything soundlessly. "That's what comes of too long a peace. And this
stuff is supposed to be rustproof!"

There was a polite rap at the door. The aide leaned
outside, and came back with a message. "For you, sir.
It's from the Storehousers."

"Good. Wait till I get a hand out through this . . . uh
. . . the thing is stiff. There, let's have it."

Reaching out with a manipulator through a kind of
opened trapdoor in the armor, and almost knocking
loose a hand-weapon clamped to the inside, Nade took
hold of the message, which was without seals or embel-
lishments, as befitted the mouthings of slegs.

Behind the clear visor, Nade's gaze grew fixed as he
read:

From:
Central Contracting Office
Penitence City
Planet of Faith
To:
Arvast Nade
Commander
Battle Fleet IV
Crustax
Dear Sir:

We regret to inform you that we must decline the conditions mentioned in your message of the 2nd instant. As you may be aware, the planetary government of the planet Faith does not recognize war, and can permit no war to be waged on, or in the vicinity of, this planet. Our decision on this matter is final, and is not open to discussion.

> Truly yours,
> Hugh Bentley
> Chief Assistant
> Central Contracting Office

Nade dazedly handed the message to his aide.

"And just how," he demanded, "are they going to enforce *that?*"

Elder Phillips's hand trembled slightly as he reached out to accept the proffered hand of the robed figure.

"Judge Archer Goodwin," said the dignitary politely. "Elder, I bring you tidings of your eldest son, and I fear you will not find them happy tidings."

Phillips kept his voice level.

"I suspected as much, Judge."

"With due allowance for the fallibility of human judgment, Lance appears unsuited to a life of peace. Study bores him. Conflict and its techniques fascinate him. He is pugnacious, independent. He sees life in terms of conflict. He is himself authoritative, though subject to subordination to a superior authority. He is not dull. The acquisition of useful skills, and even a quite deep knowledge, are well within his grasp, potentially. However, his basic bent is in another direction. On a different planet, we might expect him to shine in some limited but strategically-placed field, using it as a springboard to power and rank. Here, to allow him to pass into the populace would require us, out of fairness, to allow others to do the same. But the proportions of such traits are already so high that our way of living could not endure the shock. You see, he not only possesses these traits, plus a lust to put them in action, but *he sees nothing wrong with this*. Accordingly, he will not attempt to control his natural tendencies. Others of even greater combativeness have entered our population, but have recognized the sin of allowing such tendencies sway, unless the provocation is serious indeed. Then—" Judge Goodwin's face for an instant bent into a chilling smile, which he at once blinked away. He cleared his throat. "I am sorry to have to bring you this news."

Elder Phillips bowed his head. Somehow, somewhere, he had failed in proper discipline, in stern counsel. But, defiant, the boy always— He put down the thoughts with an effort. Others took their place. People would talk. He would never live this down, would never know if a word, or a tone of voice, was a sly reference.

His fists clenched. For an instant, everything vanished in rage. Sin of sins, in a blur of mental pictures, he saw himself seek similarly afflicted parents—the planet teemed with them—rouse them to revolt, saw himself outwit the guards, seize an armory, arm the disaffected, and *put this unholy law to the test of battle!*

So real was the illusion that for an instant he felt the sword in his hand, saw the council spring to their feet as he stepped over the bodies of the guards; his followers, armed to the teeth, were right behind him as he entered—

With a sob, he dropped to his knees.

The judge's hand gripped his shoulder. "Be steadfast. With the aid of the Almighty, you will conquer this. You can do it. Or you would not be here."

Arvast Nade studied the green and blue sphere swimming in the viewscreen.

"Just as I thought. They lack even a patrol ship."

"Sir," said the aide, "another message from the Storehousers."

Nade popped open his hatch, and reached out.

Gaze riveted to the page, he read:

From:
Office of the Chief
War Prevention Department
Level VI
Penitence City
Planet of Faith
To:
Arvast Nade
Commander
Battle Fleet IV
Crustax
Sir:

We hereby deliver final warning to you that this Department will not hesitate to use all measures necessary to bar the development of war on this planet or in its contiguous regions.

You are warned to signify peaceful intent by immediately altering course away from our planet. If this is impossible, signal the reason at once.

Hiram Wingate
Chief
War Prevention Dept.

Nade lowered the message. He took another look at the screen. He looked back at the message, then glanced at his aide.

"You've read this?"

"Certainly, sir. Communications from slegs have no right of privacy."

"How did it seem to you?"

The aide hesitated. "If I did not know they were disarmed pacifists, who destroy every warlike son born to them—well, I would be worried, sir."

"There is certainly a very hard note to this message. There is even a tone of command that can be heard in it. I find it difficult to believe this could have been written by one unfamiliar with and unequipped for war."

Nade hesitated, then activated his armored-suit communicator.

"Alter course ten girids solaxially outward of the planet Storehouse."

Nade's aide looked shocked.

The admiral said, "War is not unlimited heroics, my boy. We lose nothing from this maneuver but an air of omnipotence that has a poor effect on tactics, anyway. Conceivably, there are warships on the far side of that planet. But if these softshells are just putting up a smudge with no claws behind it, we will gobble them up, and I will add an additional two skrads free pillage to what they have already earned. The Storehouse regions being off-limits, of course."

The aide beamed, and clashed his claws in anticipation.

Admiral Nade adjusted the screen to a larger magnification.

Elder Phillips formally shook hands with his son, Lance, who was dressed in battle armor, with sword and pistol, and a repeater slung across his back.

"Sorry, Dad," said the younger Phillips, "I couldn't take this mush-mouthed hypocrisy, that's all. It's a trap, and the fact that you and the rest of your generation let themselves get caught in it is no reason why *I* should."

Tight-lipped, the elder said nothing.

His son's lip curled. Then he shrugged. "Wish me luck, at least, Dad."

"Good luck, son." The elder began to say more, but caught himself.

A harsh voice boomed over the gathering.

"Those who have been found unsuitable for life on this planet, do now separate from those who will remain, and step forward to face each other in armed combat. Those who will do battle on the physical level, assemble by the sign of the sword. Those who will give battle on the level of tactics, assemble by the stacked arms. Those who will give battle on the plane of high strategy, assemble by the open book. You will now be matched one with another until but one champion remains in each group. Those champions will have earned the right to life, but must still prove themselves against an enemy of the race or of the Holy Word. In any case, settlement shall not be here amongst the scenes of your childhood. Let any who now have second thoughts speak out. Though a—"

A shrill voice interrupted. "Overthrow them! We have the guns!"

There was an instantaneous *crack!* One of the armored figures collapsed.

The harsh voice went on, a little lower-pitched:

"Anyone else who wants to defy regulations is free to try. The punishment is instantaneous death. I was about to say that anyone who has second thoughts should speak out, though a courage test will be required to rejoin your family, and you must again submit to judgment later. The purpose of the Law is not to raise a race of cowards, but a race capable of controlling its warlike instincts. Naturally, anyone who backs out of *this*, and fails the courage test, will be summarily killed. Does anyone on mature consideration regret the stand he has taken?"

There was a silence.

The armored figures, their faces through the raised visors expressing surprise, glanced at the outstretched rebel, then at each other.

Elder Phillips's son turned, and his gaze sought out his father. He grinned and raised the naked sword in salute. The elder, startled, raised his hand. Now, what was that about?

"Very well," said the harsh voice. "Take your positions by your respective emblems."

Elder Phillips, watching, saw his son hesitate, and then walk toward the open book. The elder was surprised; after all, some fool might think him cowardly, not realizing the type of courage the test would involve.

The voice said, "After a brief prayer, we will begin . . ."

Arvast Nade glanced at the ranked screens in the master control room.

"There is no hidden force off that planet. It was a bluff." He activated his armored-suit communicator, and spoke briskly: "Turn the Fleet by divisions, and land in the preselected zones."

Hiram Wingate, Chief, War Prevention Department, watched the maneuver on the screen, turned to a slanting console bearing ranks of numbered levers and redly glowing lights, and methodically pulled down levers. The red lights winked off, to be replaced by green. On a second console, a corresponding number of blue lights went out, to be replaced by red.

Near the storage plant, huge camouflaged gates swung wide. An eager voice shouted over the communicator. "Men! Squadron A strikes the first blow! Follow me!"

Arvast Nade, just turning from the screen, jerked back to take another look.

Between his fleet and the planet, a swarm of blurs had materialized.

The things were visibly growing large on the screen, testifying to an incredible velocity.

Abruptly the blurred effect vanished, and he could see what appeared to be medium-sized scout ships, all bearing some kind of angular symbol that apparently served as a unit identification.

Now again they blurred.

Nade activated his suit communicator.

"Secondary batteries open fi—"

The deck jumped underfoot. A siren howled, changed pitch, then faded out. Across the control room, a pressure-monitor needle wound down around its dial, then the plastic cover of the instrument blew off.

The whole ship jumped.

A tinny voice spoke in Nade's ear. "Admiral, we are being attacked by small ships of the Storehousers!"

"Fire back!" shouted Nade.

"They're too fast, sir! Fire control can't keep up with them! *Look out!* HERE COMES—"

Nade raised his battle pincers.

Before him, the whole scene burst into one white-hot incandescence.

*   *   *

General Larssen, watching on the long-range pickup, sat in shock as glare from the viewer lit his face.

"And they don't believe in war! Look at *that!*"

"Sir," said a dazed subordinate, "that *isn't* war."

"It isn't? What do *you* call it?"

"Extermination, sir. Pest control. War assumes some degree of equality between opponents."

Lance Phillips, feeling dazed and drained, but with a small warm sense of achievement, straightened from the battle computer.

"I didn't do too badly?"

"Best of the lot," said the examiner cheerfully. "Your understanding of the geometrical aspects of space strategy is outstanding."

"I had a sense of drag—as if I couldn't get the most out of my forces."

"You didn't. You aren't dealing with pure abstract force, but with human beings. You made no allowance for that."

"But I did well enough to survive?"

"You did."

"What about the others?"

"They had their opportunity. Those who conquered will be saved. Any really outstanding fighters who lost because of bad luck, or superb opposition, will also be saved."

"We get a chance to do battle later?"

"Correct."

"We fight for our own planet?"

"That's right."

"But—how long since the planet was attacked?"

"Yesterday, when this trial began. Prior to that, not for about a hundred years."

"*Yesterday!* What are we doing here? We should—"

The examiner shook his head.

"The attack never amounted to anything. Just a fleet of lobsters wiped out in fifteen minutes."

Lance Phillips looked quite dizzy.

"I thought we didn't believe in war!"

"Of course not," said the examiner. "War, of the usual kind, has a brutalizing effect. As likely as not, the best are sent to slaughter each other, so at least the physical level of the race is lowered. The conquered are plundered of the fruits of their labor, which is wrong, while the conquerors learn to expect progress by pillage instead of by work; they become a burden on everyone around them; *that* leads to a desire to exterminate them. The passions aroused do not end with the conflict, but go on to make more conflict. We *don't* believe in war. Unfortunately, not everyone is equally enlightened. Should we, because we recognize the truth, be at the mercy of every sword-rattler and egomaniac? Of course not. But how are we to avoid it? By simultaneously understanding the evils of war, and being prepared to wage it defensively on the greatest scale."

"But that's a contradiction! You can't distinguish between offensive and defensive weapons! And we have too small a planet to support a large-scale war!"

The examiner looked him over coolly.

"With due respect to your logic, your understanding is puny. Now, we have something here we call 'discipline.' Think carefully before you tell me again to my face that I am a fool, or a liar. I repeat, 'How do we avoid war? By simultaneously understanding the evils of war, and being prepared to wage it defensively on the greatest scale.'"

Lance Phillips felt the objections well up, felt the overpowering certainty, the determination to brush aside nonsense.

Simultaneously, he felt something else.

He opened his mouth. No words came out.

Could this be fear?

Not exactly.

What was it?

Suddenly he recognized it.

Caution.

Warily, he said, "In that case . . . ah . . . *how—*"

Iadrubel Vire scanned the fragmentary reports, and looked at Margash Grele. Grele's normally iridescent integument was a muddy gray.

"This is all?" said Vire.

"Yes, sir."

"No survivors?"

"Not one, so far as we know. It was a slaughter."

Vire sat back dazed. A whole battle fleet wiped out—just like that. This would alter the balance of force all along the frontier.

"What word from the Storehousers?"

"Nothing, sir."

"No demands?"

"Not a word."

"After a victory like this, they could—" He paused, frowning. They were *pacifists, who believed in self-defense*.

That sounded fine, in principle, but—how had they reduced it to practice? After all, they were only one planet. Their productive capacity and manpower did not begin to approach that of Crustax and—

Vire cut off that line of thought. *This* loss, with enough patience and craft, could be overcome. Two or three more like it would be the finish. There was just not enough potential gain to risk further attempts on that one little planet. He had probed the murk with a claw, and drawn back a stub. Best to avoid trouble while that grew back, and just keep away from the place in the future.

"Release the announcement," said Vire slowly, "that Fleet IV, on maneuvers, has been caught in a meteor storm of unparalleled intensity. Communications have been temporarily cut off, and there is concern at headquarters over the fate of the fleet. It will be some time before we will know with certainty what has happened, but it is feared that a serious disaster may have occurred. As this fleet is merely a reserve fleet on maneuvers in the region of the border with the Federation, with which we have friendly relations, this, of course, in no way imperils our defenses, but . . . h'm-m-m . . . we are deeply concerned for the crewmen and their loved ones."

Grele made swift notes, and looked up.

"Excellency, might it not be wise to let this information out by stages? First, the word of the meteor shower—but our experts doubt the accuracy of the report. Next, a substantiating report has come in. Then—"

"No, because in the event of a real meteor shower, we would make no immediate public announcements. We have to be liars in this, but let's keep it to the minimum."

Grele bowed respectfully, and went out.

"Damned gravitor," said Squadron A's 2nd-Flight leader over the communicator, "cut out just as we finished off the lobster fleet. I was signaling for assembly on my ship, and aimed to cut a little swath through crab-land before going home. Instead, we've been streaking off on our own for the last week, and provisions are slim on these little boats, I'll tell you that! *What* outfit did you say you are?"

The strange, roughly minnow-shaped ship, not a great deal bigger than the scout answered promptly:

"Interstellar Patrol. We have a few openings for recruits who can qualify. Plenty of chance for adventure, special training, top-grade weapons, good food, the pay's O.K., no bureaucrats to tangle things up. If you can qualify, it's a good outfit."

"Interstellar Patrol, huh? Never heard of it. I was thinking of the Space Force."

"Well, you *could* come in that way. We get quite a few men from the Space Force. It's a fair outfit, but they have to kowtow to Planetary Development. Their weapons aren't up to ours; but their training isn't so tough, either. They'd be *sure* to let you in, where we're a little more selective. You've got a point, all right. It would be a lot easier—if you want things easy."

"Well, I didn't mean—"

"We could shoot you supplies to last a couple of weeks, and *maybe* a Space Force ship will pick you. If not, we could help—if we're still in the region. Of course, if not—"

The flight leader began to perspire.

"Listen, tell me a little more about this Interstellar Patrol."

Lance Phillips stared at rank on rank of mirrorlike glittering forms stretching off into the distance, and divided into sections by massive pillars that buttressed the ceiling.

"*This* is part of the storage plant?"

"It is. Naturally, foreigners know nothing of this, and our own people have little cause to learn the details. You say a small planet can't afford a large striking force. It can, *if* the force is accumulated slowly, and requires no maintenance whatever. Bear in mind, we make our living by *storing* goods, with no loss. How can there be *no* loss? Obviously, if, from the viewpoint of the observer, *no time passes for the stored object*."

"How could that be unless the object were moving at near the velocity of light?"

"How does an object increase its speed to near the velocity of light?"

"It *accelerates*."

The examiner nodded. "When you see much of this, you have a tendency to speculate. Now, we regularly add to our stock of fighting men and ships, and our ability to control the effects of time enables us to operate, from the observers viewpoint, either very slowly, or very fast. *How* is not in my department, and this knowledge is not handed out to satisfy curiosity. But—it's natural to speculate. The only way we know to slow time, from the observer's viewpoint, is to accelerate, and increase velocity to near the speed of light. A great ancient named Einstein said there is no way, without outside references, to distinguish the *force of gravity* from acceleration. So, I think some wizardry with gravitors is behind this." He looked thoughtfully at Lance Phillips. "The main thing is, you see what you have to know to be one of our apprentice strategists. We accumulate strength slowly, take the toughest, most generally uncivilizable of each generation, provided they have certain redeeming qualities. *These* are our fighting men. We take a few standard types of ships, improve them as time goes on, and when we are attacked, we accelerate our response, to strike with such speed that the enemy cannot react. We obliterate him. He, mortified, blames the defeat on something else. His fleet was caught in a nova, the gravitors got in resonating synchrony, *something* happened, but it didn't have anything to do with *us*. Nevertheless, he leaves us alone."

"Why not use our process to put his whole fleet in stasis, and use it as a warning?"

"*That* would be an insult he would have to respond to, and we are opposed to war. In the second place, we agreed to give you an opportunity to fight for the planet, and then live your life elsewhere. There has to be some outlet somewhere. We can't just keep stacking ships and warriors in here indefinitely."

"After we get out—*then* what happens?"

"It depends on circumstances. However, fighting men are in demand. If, say, a properly keyed signal cut power to the engines, and after some days of drifting, the warrior were offered the opportunity to enlist in some outfit that meets our standards—"

"Yes, that fits." He hesitated, then thrust out his jaw. "I know I'm not supposed to even think about this, but—"

The examiner looked wary: "Go ahead."

"With what we have here, we could rival the whole works—Federation, Crustax Empire—the lot. Well— why not? We could be the terror of all our opponents!"

The examiner shook his head in disgust.

"After what you've experienced, you can still ask *that.* Let's go at it from another direction. Consider what you know about the warlike character of our populace, and what we have to do to restrain it. Now, just ask yourself: What could such a stock as this be descended *from?*"

A great light seemed to dawn on Lance Phillips.

"You see," said the examiner, "we've already *done* that. We had to try something a little tougher."

Editor's Introduction To:

THE ONLY THING WE LEARN

Cyril Kornbluth

"The only thing we learn from history is that we learn nothing from history."
George Bernard Shaw, *The Revolutionist's Handbook*

It probably doesn't matter to those killed in the Korean and Vietnam wars that Western Civilization has enjoyed the second longest period of peace in history; but it is so. Since 1945 there have been minor conflicts but no major wars among the western powers.

The last era of extended peace was under the Roman Empire. It is usually called the Pax Romana; it might with as much justice be known as the Peace of the Legions.

The legionnaires of that time were career soldiers, liable for duty anywhere on the frontiers. They built their camps in the afternoon, and destroyed them the next morning, seldom staying in one place for long. They could look forward to permanent settlement and perhaps their own small plot of farmland when they retired; not before. Their life was hard, but they protected the peace.

Like all soldiers throughout history, the legionnaires would take any benefits the government offered. Successive candidates for Emperor offered; and eventually the legionnaires came to believe that soldiering was more a matter of accumulating rights than discharging duties.

That road led to the fall of Rome, an event that still

dominates much of Western history. Rome still dictates our ideal of what the world should be: a place of quaint diversity, but united by a common language, and sharing a common set of basic rules of decency.

Cyril Kornbluth was a veteran of the Battle of the Bulge, where he received the injuries that ultimately killed him. Kornbluth's reflections on the only thing we learn from history were written shortly after that War.

THE ONLY THING WE LEARN

Cyril Kornbluth

The professor, though he did not know the actor's phrase for it, was counting the house—peering through a spyhole in the door through which he would in a moment appear before the class. He was pleased with what he saw. Tier after tier of young people, ready with notebooks and styli, chattering tentatively, glancing at the door against which his nose was flattened, waiting for the pleasant interlude known as "Archaeo-Literature 203" to begin.

The professor stepped back, smoothed his tunic, crooked four books on his left elbow, and made his entrance. Four swift strides brought him to the lectern and, for the thousandth-odd time, he impassively swept the lecture hall with his gaze. Then he gave a wry little smile. Inside, for the thousandth-odd time, he was nagged by the irritable little thought that the lectern really ought to be a foot or so higher.

The irritation did not show. He was out to win the audience, and he did. A dead silence, the supreme tribute, gratified him. Imperceptibly, the lights of the lecture hall began to dim and the light on the lectern to brighten.

He spoke.

"Young gentlemen of the Empire, I ought to warn you that this and the succeeding lectures will be most subversive."

There was a little rustle of incomprehension from the audience—but by then the lectern light was strong enough to show the twinkling smile about his eyes that belied his stern mouth, and agreeable chuckles sounded in the gathering darkness of the tiered seats. Glow lights grew bright gradually at the students' tables, and they adjusted their notebooks in the narrow ribbons of illumination. He waited for the small commotion to subside.

"Subversive—" He gave them a link to cling to. "Subversive because I shall make every effort to tell both sides of our ancient beginnings with every resource of archaeology and with every clue my diligence has discovered in our epic literature.

"There *were* two sides, you know—difficult though it may be to believe that if we judge by the Old Epic alone—such epics as the noble and tempestuous *Chant of Remd*, the remaining fragments of *Krall's Voyage*, or the gory and rather out-of-date *Battle For the Ten Suns*." He paused while styli scribbled across the notebook pages.

"The Middle Epic is marked, however, by what I might call the rediscovered ethos." From his voice, every student knew that that phrase, surer than death and taxes, would appear on an examination paper. The styli scribbled. "By this I mean an awakening of fellow-feeling with the Home Suns People, which had once been filial loyalty to them when our ancestors were few and pioneers, but which turned into contempt when their numbers grew.

"The Middle Epic writers did not despise the Home Suns People, as did the bards of the Old Epic. Perhaps this was because they did not have to—since their long war against the Home Suns was drawing to a victorious close.

"Of the New Epic I shall have little to say. It was a literary fad, a pose, and a silly one. Written within historic times, the some two score pseudo-epics now moulder in their cylinders, where they belong. Our ripening civilization could not with integrity work in the epic form, and the artistic failures produced so indicate. Our genius turned to the lyric and to the unabashedly romantic novel.

"So much, for the moment, of literature. What contribution, you must wonder, have archaeological studies to make in an investigation of the wars from which our ancestry emerged?

"Archaeology offers—one—a check in historical matters in the epics—confirming or denying. Two—it provides evidence glossed over in the epics—for artistic or patriotic reasons. Three—it provides evidence which has been lost, owing to the fragmentary nature of some of the early epics."

All this he fired at them crisply, enjoying himself. Let them not think him a dreamy litterateur, or, worse, a flat precisionist, but let them be always a little off-balance before him, never knowing what came next, and often wondering, in class and out. The styli paused after heading Three.

"We shall examine first, by our archaeo-literary technique, the second book of the *Chant of Remd*. As the selected youth of the Empire, you know much about it, of course—much that is false, some that is true, and a great deal that is irrelevant. You know that Book One hurls us into the middle of things, aboard ship with Algan and his great captain, Remd, on their way from the triumph over a Home Suns stronghold, the planet Telse. We watch Remd on his diversionary action that splits the Ten Suns Fleet into two halves. But before we see the destruction of those halves by the Horde of Algan, we are told in Book Two of the battle for Telse."

He opened one of his books on the lectern, swept the amphitheater again, and read sonorously.

> "Then battle broke
> And high the blinding blast
> Sight-searing leaped
> While folk in fear below
> Cowered in caverns
> From the wrath of Remd—

"Or, in less sumptuous language, one fission bomb—or a stick of time-on-target bombs—was dropped. An unprepared and disorganized populace did not take the standard measure of dispersing, but huddled foolishly to await Algan's gunfighters and the death they brought.

"One of the things you believe because you have seen them in notes to elementary-school editions of *Remd* is that Telse was the fourth planet of the star, Sol. Archaeology denies it by establishing that the fourth planet—actually called Marse, by the way—was in those days weather-roofed at least, and possibly atmosphere-roofed as well. As potential warriors, you know that one does not waste fissionable material on a roof, and there is no mention of chemical explosives being used to crack the roof. Marse, therefore, was not the locale of *Remd*, Book Two.

"Which planet was? The answer to that has been established by X-radar, differential decay analyses, video-coring, and every other resource of those scientists still quaintly called 'diggers.' We know and can prove that Telse was the *third* planet of Sol. So much for the opening of the attack. Let us jump to Canto Three, the Storming of the Dynastic Palace.

> "Imperial purple wore they
> Fresh from the feast
> Grossly gorged
> They sought to slay—

"And so on. Now, as I warned you, Remd is of the Old Epic, and makes no pretense at fairness. The unorganized huddling of Telse's population was read as cowardice instead of poor Air Raid Preparations. The same is true of the Third Canto. Video-cores show on the site of the palace a hecatomb of dead in once-purple livery, but also shows impartially that they were not particularly gorged and that digestion of their last meals had been well advanced. They didn't give such a bad accounting of themselves, either. I hesitate to guess, but perhaps they accounted for one of our ancestors apiece and were simply outnumbered. The study is not complete.

"That much we know." The professor saw they were tiring of the terse scientist and shifted gears. "If but the veil of time were rent that shrouds the years between us and the Home Suns People, how much more would we learn? Would we despise the Home Suns People as our frontiersman ancestors did, or would we cry: 'This is our spiritual home—this world of rank and order, this world of formal verse and exquisitely patterned arts'?"

If the veil of time were rent—?

We can try to rend it . . .

Wing Commander Arris heard the clear jangle of the radar net alarm as he was dreaming about a fish. Struggling out of his too-deep, too-soft bed, he stepped into a purple singlet, buckled on his Sam Browne belt with its holstered .45 automatic, and tried to read the radar screen. Whatever had set it off was either too small or too distant to register on the five-inch C.R.T.

He rang for his aide, and checked his appearance in a wall mirror while waiting. His space tan was beginning to fade, he saw, and made a mental note to get it renewed at the parlor. He stepped into the corridor as Evan, his aide, trotted up—younger, browner, thinner, but the same officer type that made the Service what it was, Arris thought with satisfaction.

Evan gave him a bone-cracking salute, which he returned. They set off for the elevator that whisked them down to a large, chilly, dark underground room where faces were greenly lit by radar screens and the lights of plotting tables. Somebody yelled "Attention!" and the tecks snapped. He gave them "At ease" and took the brisk salute of the senior teck, who reported to him in flat, machine-gun delivery:

"Object-becoming-visible-on-primary-screen-sir."

He studied the sixty-inch disk for several seconds before he spotted the intercepted particle. It was coming in fast from zenith, growing while he watched.

"Assuming it's now traveling at maximum, how long will it be before it's within striking range?" he asked the teck.

"Seven hours, sir."

"The interceptors at Idlewild alerted?"

"Yessir."

Arris turned on a phone that connected with Inter-

ception. The boy at Interception knew the face that
appeared on its screen, and was already capped with a
crash helmet.

"Go ahead and take him, Efrid," said the wing
commander.

"Yessir!" and a punctilious salute, the boy's pleasure
plain at being known by name and a great deal more at
being on the way to a fight that might be first-class.

Arris cut him off before the boy could detect a smile
that was forming on his face. He turned from the pale
lunar glow of the sixty-incher to enjoy it. Those kids—
when every meteor was an invading dreadnaught, when
every ragged scouting ship from the rebels was an
armada!

He watched Efrid's squadron soar off on the screen
and then he retreated to a darker corner. This was his
post until the meteor or scout or whatever it was got
taken care of. Evan joined him, and they silently studied the smooth, disciplined functioning of the plot room,
Arris with satisfaction and Evan doubtless with the
same. The aide broke silence, asking:

"Do you suppose it's a Frontier ship, sir?" He caught
the wing commander's look and hastily corrected himself: "I mean rebel ship, sir, of course."

"Then you should have said so. Is that what the
junior officers generally call those scoundrels?"

Evan conscientiously cast his mind back over the last
few junior messes and reported unhappily: "I'm afraid
we do, sir. We seem to have got into the habit."

"I shall write a memorandum about it. How do you
account for that very peculiar habit?"

"Well, sir, they do have something like a fleet, and
they did take over the Regulus Cluster, didn't they?"

What had got into this incredible fellow, Arris wondered in amazement. Why, the thing was self-evident!
They had a few ships—accounts differed as to how
many—and they had, doubtless by raw sedition, taken
over some systems temporarily.

He turned from his aide, who sensibly became interested in a screen and left with a murmured excuse to
study it very closely.

The brigands had certainly knocked together some

ramshackle league or other, but— The wing commander wondered briefly if it could last, shut the horrid thought from his head, and set himself to composing mentally a stiff memorandum that would be posted in the junior officer's mess and put an end to this absurd talk.

His eyes wandered to the sixty-incher, where he saw the interceptor squadron climbing nicely toward the particle—which, he noticed, had become three particles. A low crooning distracted him. Was one of the tecks singing at work? It couldn't be!

It wasn't. An unsteady shape wandered up in the darkness, murmuring a song and exhaling alcohol. He recognized the Chief Archivist, Glen.

"This is Service country, mister," he told Glen.

"Hullo, Arris," the round little civilian said, peering at him. "I come down here regularly—regularly against regulations—to wear off my regular irregularities with the wine bottle. That's all right, isn't it?"

He was drunk and argumentative. Arris felt hemmed in. Glen couldn't be talked into leaving without loss of dignity to the wing commander, and he couldn't be chucked out because he was writing a biography of the chamberlain and could, for the time being, have any head in the palace for the asking. Arris sat down unhappily, and Glen plumped down beside him.

The little man asked him:

"Is that a fleet from the Frontier League?" He pointed to the big screen. Arris didn't look at his face, but felt that Glen was grinning maliciously.

"I know of no organization called the Frontier League," Arris said. "If you are referring to the brigands who have recently been operating in Galactic East, you could at least call them by their proper names." Really, he thought—civilians!

"So sorry. But the brigands should have the Regulus Cluster by now, shouldn't they?" he asked, insinuatingly.

This was serious—a grave breach of security. Arris turned to the little man.

"Mister, I have no authority to command you," he said measuredly. "Furthermore, I understand you are enjoying a temporary eminence in the non-Service world which would make it very difficult for me to—ah—tangle with you. I shall therefore refer only to your altruism. How did you find out about the Regulus Cluster?"

"Eloquent!" murmured the little man, smiling happily. "I got it from Rome."

Arris searched his memory. "You mean Squadron Commander Romo broke security? I can't believe it!"

"No, commander. I mean Rome—a place—a time—a civilization. I got it also from Babylon, Assyria, the Mogul Raj—every one of them. You don't understand me, of course."

"I understand that you're trifling with Service security and that you're a fat little, malevolent, worthless drone and scribbler!"

"Oh, commander!" protested the archivist. "I'm not so little!" He wandered away, chuckling.

Arris wished he had the shooting of him, and tried to explore the chain of secrecy for a weak link. He was tired and bored by this harping on the Fron— on the brigands.

His aide tentatively approached him. "Interceptors in striking range, sir," he murmured.

"Thank you," said the wing commander, genuinely grateful to be back in the clean, etched-line world of the Service and out of that blurred, water-color, civilian land where long-dead Syrians apparently retailed classified matter to nasty little drunken warts who had no business with it. Arris confronted the sixty-incher. The particle that had become three particles was now—he counted—eighteen particles. Big ones. Getting bigger.

He did not allow himself emotion, but turned to the plot on the interceptor squadron.

"Set up Lunar relay," he ordered.

"Yessir."

Half the plot room crew bustled silently and efficiently about the delicate job of applied relativistic physics that was "lunar relay." He knew that the palace power plant could take it for a few minutes, and he wanted to *see*. If he could not believe radar pips, he might believe a video screen.

On the great, green circle, the eighteen—now twenty-four—particles neared the thirty-six smaller particles that were interceptors, led by the eager young Efrid.

"Testing Lunar relay, sir," said the chief teck.

The wing commander turned to a twelve-inch screen. Unobtrusively, behind him, tecks jockeyed for position. The picture on the screen was something to see. The chief let mercury fill a thick-walled, ceramic tank. There was a sputtering and contact was made.

"Well done," said Arris. "Perfect seeing."

He saw, upper left, a globe of ships—what ships! Some were Service jobs, with extra turrets plastered on them wherever there was room. Some were orthodox freighters, with the same porcupine-bristle of weapons. Some were obviously home-made crates, hideously ugly—and as heavily armed as the others.

Next to him, Arris heard his aide murmur, "It's all wrong, sir. They haven't got any pick-up boats. They haven't got any hospital ships. What happens when one of them gets shot up?"

"Just what ought to happen, Evan," snapped the wing commander. "They float in space until they desiccate in their suits. Or if they get grappled inboard with a boat hook, they don't get any medical care. As I told you, they're brigands, without decency even to care of their own." He enlarged on the theme. "Their morale must be insignificant compared with our men's. When the Service goes into action, every rating and teck knows he'll be cared for if he's hurt. Why, if we didn't have pick-up boats and hospital ships the men wouldn't—" He almost finished it with "fight," but thought, and lamely ended, "—wouldn't like it."

Evan nodded, wonderingly, and crowded his chief a little as he craned his neck for a look at the screen.

"Get the hell away from here!" said the wing commander in a restrained yell, and Evan got.

The interceptor squadron swam into the field—a sleek, deadly needle of vessels in perfect alignment, with its little cloud of pick-ups trailing, and farther astern a white hospital ship with the ancient red cross.

The contact was immediate and shocking. One of the rebel ships lumbered into the path of the interceptors,

spraying fire from what seemed to be as many points as
a man has pores. The Service ships promptly riddled it
and it should have drifted away—but it didn't. It kept
on fighting. It rammed an interceptor with a crunch
that must have killed every man before the first bulwark, but aft of the bulwark the ship kept fighting.

It took a torpedo portside and its plumbing drifted
through space in a tangle. Still the starboard side kept
squirting fire. Isolated weapon blisters fought on while
they were obviously cut off from the rest of the ship. It
was a pounded tangle of wreckage, and it had destroyed
two interceptors, crippled two more, and kept fighting.

Finally, it drifted away, under feeble jets of power.
Two more of the fantastic rebel fleet wandered into
action, but the wing commander's horrified eyes were
on the first pile of scrap. It was going *somewhere*—

The ship neared the thin-skinned, unarmored, gleaming hospital vessel, rammed it amidships, square in one
of the red crosses, and then blew itself up, apparently
with everything left in its powder magazine, taking the
hospital ship with it.

The sickened wing commander would never have
recognized what he had seen as it was told in a later
version, thus:

> "The crushing course they took
> And nobly knew
> Their death undaunted
> By heroic blast
> The hospital's host
> They dragged to doom
> Hail! Men without mercy
> From the far frontier!"

Lunar relay flickered out as overloaded fuses flashed
into vapor. Arris distractedly paced back to the dark
corner and sank into a chair.

"I'm sorry," said the voice of Glen next to him,
sounding quite sincere. "No doubt it was quite a shock
to you."

"Not to you?" asked Arris bitterly.

"Not to me."

"Then how did they do it?" the wing commander asked the civilian in a low, desperate whisper. "They don't even wear .45's. Intelligence says their enlisted men have hit their officers and got away with it. They *elect* ship captains! Glen, what does it all mean?"

"It means," said the fat little man with a timbre of doom in his voice, "that they've returned. They always have. They always will. You see, commander, there is always somewhere a wealthy, powerful city, or nation, or world. In it are those whose blood is not right for a wealthy, powerful place. They must seek danger and overcome it. So they go out—on the marshes, in the desert, on the tundra, the planets, or the stars. Being strong, they grow stronger by fighting the tundra, the planets, or the stars. They—they change. They sing new songs. They know new heroes. And then, one day, they return to their old home.

"They return to the wealthy, powerful city, or nation or world. They fight its guardians as they fought the tundra, the planets, or the stars—a way that strikes terror to the heart. Then they sack the city, nation, or world and sing great, ringing sagas of their deeds. They always have. Doubtless they always will."

"But what shall we do?"

"We shall cower, I suppose, beneath the bombs they drop on us, and we shall die, some bravely, some not, defending the palace within a very few hours. But you will have your revenge."

"How?" asked the wing commander, with haunted eyes.

The fat little man giggled and whispered in the officer's ear. Arris irritably shrugged it off as a bad joke. He didn't believe it. As he died, drilled through the chest a few hours later by one of Algan's gunfighters, he believed it even less.

The professor's lecture was drawing to a close. There was time for only one more joke to send his students away happy. He was about to spring it when a messenger handed him two slips of paper. He raged inwardly at his ruined exit and poisonously read from them:

"I have been asked to make two announcements. One, a bulletin from General Sleg's force. He reports that the so-called Outland Insurrection is being brought under control and that there is no cause for alarm. Two, the gentlemen who are members of the S.O.T.C. will please report to the armory at 1375 hours—whatever that may mean—for blaster inspection. The class is dismissed."

Petulantly, he swept from the lectern and through the door.

Editor's Introduction To:

REMEMBERING VIETNAM

H. J. Kaplan

Empires grow for many reasons. While it's easy to be cynical about high motives, they can't be ignored. It was not so long ago that most Americans thought it self-evident that most nations of the world would be better off under the tutelage of the United States. We could teach them the secrets of economic development while initiating them into the arts of self government.

The Vietnam War had a pivotal effect on American life. Prior to that war we had entered an unprecedented period of economic growth. There could be no doubt of the future. We were going to the Moon. Communism would be contained by military force; meanwhile, the economic machinery which we now understood—Keynes was on the cover of *Time*'s last issue for 1965, and even Richard Nixon said, "We are all Keynesians now"—would generate ever-increasing wealth, which we would use to eradicate poverty, ignorance, and want, first from the United States, then from the world.

We could do anything, and only a few like Russell Kirk muttered darkly about hubris, nemesis, and catastrophe. *Time* summarized it all in December, 1965: "If the nation has problems, they are the problems of high employment, high growth, and high hopes."

We had similar optimism about foreign affairs. Kennedy had announced that we would bear any burden and fight any foe to advance the cause of freedom. Was the Diem regime in Vietnam corrupt? There could be only one answer to that. Diem had invited us there, but he was not worthy; bring him down, to make room for genuine democracy. We were not merely containing communism, we were building nations.

We poured forth blood and treasure, and sent conscript soldiers to die in places whose names they could not pronounce.

We also made promises we did not keep, as H. J. Kaplan, retired from the U.S. Foreign Service, reminds us.

REMEMBERING VIETNAM

H. J. Kaplan

In Saigon between 1965 and 1966, while I was serving as counselor to the American embassy, I lived for about fourteen months in a street called Phan Dinh Phung, a name that had unaccountably slipped my mind, until I came across it again in *The Palace File*, by Nguyen Tien Hung and Jerrold S. Schecter,* a recently published history of the last years of the war. I had tried now and then, for one reason or another, to recall my Saigon address, but desultorily; not to the point, say, of going to a library and finding a map of the city. Life is short, there is always too much to do. And here it was, emitting a faint mnemonic pulse, on the very first page of a book I had opened unwillingly—because who wants to go back to all that?—and finally read with bated breath, passionately, as if I did not know how it was going to come out.

Of course I knew, in a general way, how it was going to come out, although the concluding chapters of *The Palace File* provide no end of details I had failed to register at the time, or registered and then forgot: about how South Vietnam's gold reserves fell into Hanoi's hands; the heroic last stand of the ARVN (the Republic of Vietnam's ground troops) at Xuan Loc; the

* Harper & Row, 542 pp., $22.95.

hopeless attempts to persuade the U.S. Congress to authorize emergency aid, if only to slow down the pace of events and extricate the most endangered people, the most valuable equipment; the beginning of the South Vietnamese exodus.

Hung and Schecter deal briefly and grimly with these incidents, their concern being not so much to wring our hearts as to clinch the argument they have been making, to the effect that in order to get the South Vietnamese to agree to the Paris Peace Accords of 1973, Henry Kissinger and Richard Nixon made secret promises (later repeated by Gerald Ford) to President Nguyen Van Thieu that were never kept. This is the central thesis of *The Palace File*, which is based on a series of hitherto secret communications between the American President and Thieu:

Both President Nixon and Secretary Kissinger promised Thieu that the Seventh Air Force at Nakorn Phanom would be used to bomb North Vietnamese targets if the Paris Accords were violated. [Seventh Air Force chief] General Vogt's oral history clearly demonstrates that his forces were not only a deterrent, but he expected to mount a full-scale response to North Vietnamese violations. Certainly, the letters from President Nixon to President Thieu were commitments that had not been made public or shared privately with the Congress. . . . [F]or the South Vietnamese, however, they were, in fact, part of the understanding.

On April 23, 1975, while the decimated ARVN 43rd regiment was firing its last munitions east of Xuan Loc, holding its ground and inflicting enormous losses on a vastly superior enemy force, Gerald Ford (who had by then succeeded Nixon as President) raised the white flag. In a speech at Tulane University in New Orleans, he said: "America can regain the sense of pride that existed before Vietnam. But it cannot be achieved by refighting a war that is finished as far as America is concerned." The Vietnamese who heard these words— Hung, for example, who was in Washington, desperately lobbying Congress—were devastated, of course, but not surprised. Nor was there any outcry in the country, so far as I can remember, our people having long since—long before the signing of the "peace" agreement in January 1973—turned its back on Vietnam.

A week later, to be sure, Hanoi's tanks breached the gates of Thieu's palace and a new era—the aftermath—began. For several days, like an unshriven ghost, Saigon came back to lead the evening news. Our troops were long gone, but our embassy staff and other civilians had to be extracted. And then all those unbelievable things happened in Southeast Asia: millions murdered by the Khmer Rouge in Cambodia; hundreds of thousands of Vietnamese "boat people" adrift in the South China Sea, raped and despoiled by pirates. Still, a great power cannot lose itself indefinitely in a situation where "all's to be borne and naught's to be done." So the curtain came down.

Few Americans are aware that in the autumn of 1987—more than twelve years after the war's end—the boat people are still coming out at the rate of 1,200–1,500 a month, an astounding exodus for a people whose sense of self is so deeply rooted in the burial places of their families; or that the ethnic Chinese, including tens of thousands who supported Hanoi in the war, have been expelled from Communist Vietnam or interned; or that Hanoi's army is still bogged down in Cambodia defending a puppet government—*nguy*, the term they once applied so invariably to Saigon; or that the Vietnamese are hungry, even in the bountiful South, hungrier than they have been since the famine that followed the collectivization of the land by the Communists in the North in 1955 and 1956.

The litany goes on, but is anyone listening? Certainly not the "useful idiots" of the Susan Sontag–Mary McCarthy school, that goes without saying—but what about the rest of us? We did the best we could for those people, and the worst; and never learned to distinguish the one from the other. And when the last of our troops left the country in 1973, two years before the fall of Saigon, we had finally reached a consensus: enough was enough.

It still holds, it seems to me, but uneasily. In the

fullness of time we built a monument in Washington to mourn our dead. We have had a trickle of novels, memoirs, and films, welling up from many sources, irrepressibly, about mayhem in the jungle and bewildered young men who could not fathom why they were there; and compensatory fantasies of the Rambo type, of course; and even a few attempts, conscientiously financed by foundations and think tanks, to review the historical record on public television. But these, much like the rare works of political and military analysis published in the past few years, have been strangely received, if at all: praised or damned mechanically, as it were, in feeble response to reflexes that have somehow lost their spring. It is as if the Vietnam that once so roiled our body politic, and gave rise to so much reportorial posturing, pop anthropology, and anguished moralism, had been relegated to oblivion, so that we have trouble remembering what it was all about.

And now we have this *Palace File*, a moving account (and from an unaccustomed angle) of one of the most shattering events of our history. It is a *scandalous* book, in the biblical sense of the word, producing serious new evidence and argument to prove that we as a nation not only failed our Vietnamese allies but shamelessly betrayed them. It has been available for more than a year now, but—"woe unto him through whom the scandal comes!"— to date I have seen only one review.

Granted, there must be others, beyond my ken, but I think it safe to assume that *The Palace File* has failed, as they say in the trade, to take off.

This morning's New York *Times* carries the third or fourth of a series of reports on postwar Vietnam. A number of memoirs and studies of former members or supporters of the Vietcong, now for the most part in exile, have been published by David Chanoff and Doan Van Toai. And most importantly, Ellen J. Hammer has brought out her long-awaited—corrosive and devastating —account of the overthrow and murder of Ngo Dinh Diem and his brother, Nhu.*

* *A Death in November*, Dutton, 373 pp., $22.50.

According to Toai, once a fellow-traveler of the Vietcong and now a research associate at the University of California in Berkeley, there is more ahead; and all this would suggest that the amnesia that followed so hard upon our Vietnamese obsession may be coming to an end. It was never total, and now it remains to be seen whether the larger public, and not just one corner of academia, is ready to go back to "all that." There are always issues more pressing than the past, even the relatively recent past; and this truism is true *a fortiori*—notoriously—for a people as perennially and programmatically unfinished as ours.

Witness the latest episode in the continuing struggle between the White House and Congress over the direction and management of our foreign affairs. When *The Palace File* appeared, the welkin was beginning to ring with revelations and rumors about Reagan's faux pas in Iran and Nicaragua and the possibility, so eagerly embraced by his adversaries, that the law had been violated not only by members of the White House staff but by the President himself, so that for the second time in little more than a decade we seemed to be circling around a constitutional crisis—hardly a propitious moment to be digging up old graves in Southeast Asia.

And yet, as the famous rabbi said, *if not now, when?* If the choice is right the moment is right, by definition. Twelve years have passed since Nguyen Tien Hung left the presidential palace in Saigon with the dossier of top-secret letters from Richard Nixon and Gerald Ford (at least some of them, presumably, drafted by Henry Kissinger) which form the armature of this book. Hung's story needed to be fleshed out, organized, and properly Englished; and Jerrold Schecter, a professional journalist who had covered Southeast Asia for *Time*, published a scholarly study of political Buddhism, and served a term in our own "palace," the office of the National Security Adviser, during the Carter administration, was well prepared for the job. The result of their collaboration is a remarkable piece of work, always moving if not always persuasive: at once the story of the Vietnamese debacle as seen from inside Thieu's office and a graphic account of the paralysis that overcame American power at the moment of truth—a subject not so far from our present preoccupations, after all.

Near or far, we cannot escape it. The paradox of memory is that it deforms, as it were, truly. We end by becoming a mysterious amalgam of what we remember and what we forget. Hence the significance for me of a Saigon street name, and for our country of the circumstances of Saigon's decline and fall—painful though it be to go back to "all that."

So now I am struggling to summon up the memory of the people who lived in my house on Phan Dinh Phung—of the Vietnamese especially, because I know at least vaguely what has become of my round-eyed colleagues: Levine and Falkiewicz (who will have forgiven me, I hope, for calling them Jacobowsky and the Colonel) and various others who shared these requisitioned digs for a while and then went back to the West and about their business; whereas the Vietnamese have long been beyond my ken: Huong the grumpy cook, Mai the chambermaid, Li the Chinese driver, and the hard-faced security types who hung around day and night, guns bulging under their chinos and floppy sport shirts, and above all my bohemian friend, Tran Thi Do (or Thérèse, as we called her, using her Catholic name,* who shopped and interpreted for us and once prepared a memorable melon soup when Henry Cabot Lodge and some military brass came to dinner, to the enduring mortification of Huong. She showed up briefly in Washington, a year or so after my return, when I was about to leave for my new post at NATO in Brussels; and I saw her in Paris during the peace talks in 1968 to which I was seconded from Brussels, and tried to persuade her to stay. Her mother had a little money in France, and her brother was a doctor in Cannes. But she was, she said, consumed with homesickness, *le mal du pays,* and insisted on going back and disappeared from view, like so many others.

All these people had visitors, relatives from their vil-

---

* Real names have been altered, for obvious reasons.

lages, sometimes from enemy-infested areas, and Huong —a militant Buddhist who took an equally dim view of the Saigon government and the Vietcong—spent hours talking to them, so that (when there was time and he was willing to distill for me a little of what they said) I sometimes fleetingly had the feeling that I could touch something out there in the mysterious countryside and surmise, if not quite understand, how these people were experiencing the disorder that was roiling the South at that time.

None of this would seem to have much to do with *The Palace File*, which is the story of the immolation of the republic we helped bring into being after the French left Indochina in 1954—and to which, however imprudently, we pledged "our lives, our fortunes, and our sacred honor." No less. The pledge was made and renewed by five successive American administrations, rarely in such resounding rhetoric but perhaps more importantly in deeds, so that when the South Vietnamese began to falter in the early 60's we induced them to fight on by dispatching a half-million of our own troops to their country, building a vast military infrastructure, and organizing a consortium of Asian and Pacific nations to aid them or at least bolster them morally in their struggle.

These early years, however, are only sketchily evoked in *The Palace File*. The authors focus on the period after 1971, the decline and fall, their purpose being not only to make us feel the "pity and terror" of it but also to assert a thesis, namely, that our behavior during the last years—and specifically our failure as a nation to honor Nixon's promises to Thieu—"constitutes the betrayal of an ally, unrivaled in American history."

The verdict is severe. It is all very well for an old-world country, perfidious Albion, say, to be cynical about its alliances. "England has neither permanent friends nor permanent enemies. It has permanent interests." But this is not for us. We need to think of ourselves as a moral people, perhaps this is the most permanent of our interests. Faced with that terrible sentence from *The Palace File*, we look for attenuating circumstances, and although these are not hard to find they turn out to be the very same arguments that persuaded us to abandon our friends in Vietnam in the first place. The incompetence and fecklessness of our allies made them difficult, if not impossible, to defend; the costs were staggering, incommensurate with any good we might achieve; a growing number of Americans had come to feel, however wrongly, that the war was immoral to begin with, or had lost its moral sanction because of the manner in which it was fought. Etc.

These arguments—and I have cited only a few—were at least arguable. They could be answered but they were mutually reinforcing and finally overwhelming, unless we were willing to go back to the beginning and carry the war to the North, the source of all our troubles. But this was ruled out because it might embroil us with the Chinese. Or so we believed.

A misbegotten affair, and quite hopeless—such was the view of Sargent Shriver, the American ambassador to France in 1968, long before Nixon wrote his letters to Thieu. He suggested that I should leave the Harriman–Vance delegation to the peace talks in Paris (the open ones that were being conducted while Kissinger and North Vietnam's Le Duc Tho were doing the real negotiating in secret) and do something useful, like coming to work for him. The Vietnam game was over, there was nothing for it but to get out.

Shriver was a good man, amiable and intelligent, but I was dismayed by his readiness to walk away from "all that"—as if the government of a great power could simply repudiate the debts of its predecessors. "So we made a mistake. Let's admit it and cut our losses." But what, then, would happen to the South Vietnamese?

On Phan Dinh Phung I knew no one except the Japanese ambassador who lived across the street and was good enough to invite me to dinner when I moved in; and people to nod to, of course, including an old man who sold *pho*, a highly seasoned North Vietnamese soup, from a pushcart. A dead ringer for Ho Chi Minh, according to Falkiewicz, but his *pho* was delicious.

Thousands of people lived and doubtless still live on our street, one of those great broad southern French avenues of Saigon that run interminably east and west, plane-tree-shaded and elegant until one approaches Le Van Duyet, where a Buddhist monk made a torch of himself in 1963 and hastened the downfall of Ngo Dinh Diem; turning meaner and more populous as you proceed westward, bearing north toward the air base at Tan Son Nhut where Thérèse's mother, if memory serves, owned a house, although she lived on Hai Ba Trung. Or south toward the teeming Chinatown of Cholon—the Big Market. The sense of the place comes back slowly, a patchy disjointed sense, because it takes time and leisure to assimilate a great city; and we had almost none of either.

I say we, meaning the embassy people, but I really cannot speak for the mass of Americans. And mass was increasingly the word. Soon after my arrival in Saigon in 1965, and quite apart from the growing plethora of journalists, the city began swarming with motley assortments of Americans, some of whom seemed to have precious little to do: aspiring writers accredited by countercultural publications; hungry photographers without fixed assignments; delegates of various cockamamie committees; pop anthropologists—they brought a 60's atmosphere to the city center, with their guitars and marijuana and Australian bush hats.

Remembering them now it occurs to me that they were a bizarre little fringe benefit, as it were, of our decision to elbow the South Vietnamese aside and take over their war. But was there ever such a decision? If so, it had been deemed too cosmic for my ears when I went through Washington, en route to Honolulu and Saigon; nor had it ever been announced, out of a "decent respect for the opinion of mankind," to "a candid world." Declarations, formalities, national mobilization— these things were long out of style. We had the Tonkin Gulf resolution, to be sure, and we had dropped some bombs on Northern boat docks in August 1964; and then, if memory serves, on enemy concentrations in the South in February 1965, when the "Rolling Thunder" program (of air attacks on the North) was getting under way. The idea was not so much to do serious damage as to warn Hanoi to cease and desist. I remember sitting with Ambassador Maxwell Taylor in the MAC-V (Military Assistance Command–Vietnam) situation room and watching General Westmoreland describe, pointer in hand, how the marines would land on the beaches at Danang.

The South Vietnamese were not consulted on these operations; they were merely informed, usually *ex post facto,* if at all. They were reeling from a combination of troubles: political chaos in Saigon, increasing infiltration from the North, larger-scale Vietcong attacks. Which brings back an even earlier memory of MAC–V, probably my first, when as a new official at the embassy I was paying a courtesy call and General Richard Stilwell came out of his boss Westmoreland's office, shaking his head sadly, and said to a colleague of mine who was steering me toward the exit: "This is it. These little fellows can't hack it." What "it" was I've forgotten; but the words have stayed with me. If the "little fellows" could not *hack it,* a new term for my lexicon, we Americans of course could.

My point is that this was a pivotal moment. I had been accredited to the Republic of Vietnam, a troubled, weak, misgoverned, and possibly doomed nation. But now Saigon's role, in the scenario we were writing in collaboration with Hanoi, seemed to be fading away. Surely, this was not what we wanted; and yet no one seemed to realize that this was the effect of everything we did.

Sometime during those early days, having occasion to go to the Tan Son Nhut air base, I found the tarmac littered with mounds of personal effects, suitcases, bundles, wall hangings, ceramic elephants, children, dogs, and unhappy wives; and perhaps some happy wives. The families of American personnel were being evacuated. Until then my colleagues had been living the lives of embassy people everywhere, more or less: office and field work, social activities, church, schools, sports—the whole peacetime bit, including ordinary human contact with local people. In the Foreign Service this sort of thing is encouraged, as everyone knows, except in notoriously hostile countries. The Saigonese I first met were anything but hostile, however critical or skeptical they might be about us. Coming from my last post in chilly Geneva, I found them voluble and easy enough to talk to, if not always open and easy to understand. The cultural gap was huge, obviously, if you had never served in Asia; but why should that daunt a proper Foreign-Service type? I engaged a lovely young person who appeared every morning in a pale green *ao dai*, to teach me some Vietnamese.

Then suddenly, by March or April, all that was gone, or going. The Vietnamese tended, except in their roles as "counterparts" or office help, mysteriously to disappear. More precisely, as I labor to recall that time, it was we who became preoccupied and lost sight of them. No sooner had the marines landed at Danang and army and air-force units begun to settle in all over the country than we became almost exclusively absorbed with one another; and with the media, which proliferated so that our daily briefings began to resemble mass meetings. I made a great fuss about getting the ARVN to hold daily briefings, but it was hopeless; they were hardly attended and it was rare that any news came out of them.

Certain embassy officers, to be sure, kept trying to maintain some semblance of a normal diplomatic atmosphere. They organized and attended receptions, cocktails, dinners, just as they might have done in Tokyo, London, or Rome; they went to the racetrack on Sundays or picnicked on the Saigon River with diplomatic acquaintances and friends or played tennis or swam at the Cercle Sportif, a dilapidated relic of the French colonial days. Not to speak of the liaisons that sprung up, still, with the elegant Vietnamese women one encountered in such places. But not for long. It soon became impossible for such women to dine out with Americans, for fear of being taken for bar girls. The military flood was rising implacably to engulf the official establishment, so that by the end of the summer of 1965 the correspondents, Americans as well as foreign, sometimes had to be reminded that I was still a civilian, and that my boss was not General Westmoreland but Ambassador Henry Cabot Lodge.

Not that it made much practical difference. Barry Zorthian, the Information Chief, was also a civilian; and yet he had officers, including at least one general, on his staff, and military briefings were held under his auspices.

Of course, the Southerners did not actually disappear, nor did we really cease to see them. During the so-called "American war"—from 1965 to 1970—they suffered far more casualties than we did. But politically, and in the world's eyes, the struggle was now between us and Hanoi.

Nguyen Tien Hung, the co-author of *The Palace File*, was a professor of economics who lived in Washington, D.C., with his American wife and children. That he happened to stop at his mother's house on Phan Dinh Phung when he briefly returned to Saigon in the autumn of 1971 is of no particular consequence, except to me. We were there at different times, but some ghostly trace of us (according to a quite plausible Vietnamese superstition) must continue to hover over the place; so now I can think of him as a sort of neighbor.

The American role in the war was winding down in 1971 and Hung, with the candor of an economist, believed that if the South offered to supply the North with rice and other commodities, Hanoi might be induced to leave the republic in peace; and he hoped during his visit to interest Thieu in this idea. Thieu, on the other hand, was eager to hear Hung's views on the mood of the United States, on which his fate depended, just as the North's implacable ambition depended on the supplies it received from the Soviet Union. But the important thing about this meeting was simply that the two men hit it off, and Hung—although initially suspect as a member of a Diemist family—was invited back.

On his next trip, however, in the spring of 1972, he had to wait for some days before he could see Thieu, who was very busy at the South Vietnamese Joint General Staff (JGS). The Communists, on the night of Hung's arrival, had launched their Easter offensive, sending tanks and motorized artillery for the first time massively across the Demilitarized Zone (DMZ), the demarcation line between North and South established by the Geneva conference of 1954. The South Vietnamese should have been prepared for this but weren't; they were accustomed to operating with the help of Westmoreland's computerized command center, MAC–V, and the JGS was ill-equipped to maneuver and supply their regional and regular forces with the requisite speed. Still, they were learning. Surprised and badly mauled at first, they rallied and drove Hanoi's troops from Quangtri, taking heavy casualties but destroying about half the invading force.

The other half, however, did not withdraw across the DMZ. Despite the vigorous pounding it took from General Truong's artillery and from American aircraft based in Thailand, it remained in the South, rebuilding and augmenting its strength with fresh troops and new Soviet equipment—and signaling ominously that Hanoi was shifting into the conventional mode. The Vietcong had been decimated during the Tet offensive, early in 1968, and all but eliminated as a fighting force thereafter: the peasants and city dwellers of the South had been invited to the General Uprising (foreseen in the Communist scenario as the climactic phase of the class struggle) and failed to come. So the future, Hanoi was saying, belonged to the regular army, and the question of what to do about the North Vietnamese military presence in the South had become—for Saigon, especially —the key issue in the secret negotiations that Henry Kissinger was conducting with Hanoi's Le Duc Tho in Paris—negotiations about which Thieu suspected that he was being told only what Kissinger wanted him to know.

This was a crucial moment. Even in the Vietnamese political context, where prevarication was normal and mistrust a matter of elementary prudence, Nguyen Van Thieu impressed his associates as an inordinately suspicious man—the proverbial paranoiac with ample grounds for his paranoia. In 1963, as a young colonel in command of the Fifth Infantry Division, he had played a curiously ambivalent role in the overthrow of Ngo Dinh

Diem. The affair had left him with a sense of transgression that he never managed to shake off, nor did he ever forgive the officers responsible for murdering Diem and his brother and thus, in his view, turning a political act into a common crime. The cruelest letter in *The Palace File*, therefore, and surely the most shocking, is the one in which Nixon, exasperated by Thieu's refusal to approve a penultimate draft of the Paris Accords, reminds him of the fate that befell Diem in 1963 and suggests that something of the sort might happen again. But it will take a year of secret diplomacy to bring matters to such a point.

Meanwhile I can imagine Thieu in 1972 plying Hung with questions. What are the Americans up to? Why does Nixon allow that man to talk to the Communists behind my back? Le Duc Tho, who treated Kissinger with a mixture of arrogance and condescension, had broken off the talks in March, as if to say: time out, chum, while you get a load of *this*; and then produced an offensive which had cost Hanoi 75,000 casualties and mountains of materiel but might well, if the North Vietnamese troops were permitted to remain in the South, win them the war.

To be sure, Thieu received a heartwarming letter from Nixon at this juncture—the sixth item in the Palace File—announcing the mining of Haiphong harbor, which had berthed some 350 Soviet ships during the preceding year, according to the CIA. This would certainly bring Le Duc Tho back to Paris again, even if he had not intended to come back in any case—but to what end? With what agenda? And why, if not to legitimize the present situation, should the Americans talk to him before he withdrew his troops to the North?

It is difficult, knowing what we now know, not to get ahead of this story. Hung, of course, could not possibly be expected to answer Thieu's questions. Nor could anyone else. This was early 1972, remember, and Nixon was still glowing from his February trip to China and looking forward to visiting Moscow in May. Watergate was an apartment complex on the Potomac, nothing more. In his first letter to Thieu, written on the eve of his departure for Peking, Nixon had graciously defined

the position he would take if the subject of Vietnam
came up: "I want to assure you that I will set forth
clearly and forcefully the position of the United States
and the Republic of Vietnam that the war in Vietnam
must be ended through direct negotiations with Hanoi
or, failing that, by the growing ability of the Republic of
Vietnam to defend itself against Hanoi's aggression."
And a few paragraphs later: "With respect to my visit to
Moscow in May, I wish to make it clear that the United
States has no intention of dealing over the heads of its
friends and allies in any manner where their security
interests might be involved." But wasn't this precisely
what Nixon had already sent Kissinger to Paris to do?

Alas, the fate of the Smaller Kingdom was at stake,
and the lords of the Larger Kingdom seemed increasingly distant and distracted. In raising such questions,
as he did repeatedly throughout that fateful year, Thieu
was doing what came naturally. He was worrying out
loud. Small wonder that he kept Nixon's letters in his
desk drawer and reread them, according to Hung, again
and again.

Withal, there were omens and signs in these letters
that Thieu could not read at all, even with the help of
Hung and other American-educated members of his
staff. On April 6, 1972, Nixon had written to assure him
that the United States viewed Hanoi's Easter offensive
as "a flagrant and outrageous violation of both the Geneva Accords of 1954 and the 1968 understandings"
(i.e., the bombing halt negotiated by the Harriman-
Vance mission in Paris) and to assure him that "the
United States . . . will not hesitate to take whatever
added military steps are necessary. . . ." So far so good—
especially the delphic reference to added steps. They
could only be what Ambassador Bunker and General
Abrams had already hinted at: aeronaval action against
the North.

For Thieu this was a consummation devoutly to be
wished. His feeling was that the war was now entering
a new and decisive phase. The South was increasingly
prosperous and secure, although the departure of more
than a half-million Americans would cause some painful

economic problems for a time. The Vietcong had largely
disappeared, except as a façade for Northern troops.
The PAVN, Hanoi's regular army, was now removing
the camouflage, as it were, unfurling its banners and
preparing to move massively and in its own name.
Thieu's instinct as a military man was to seek to spoil
these preparations. But how? Bombing Northern rail-
heads and roads had never seriously impeded infiltration, even when the PAVN was losing 50 percent of its
men on the way down through the jungle. Something
had to be done to interdict the massive Soviet input at
the other end. Indeed, the failure to take such measures had always puzzled the South Vietnamese and
made them wonder, as they were only too prone to do
anyway, about our ultimate intentions. And so, when a
letter from Nixon arrived on May 9, announcing that
Hanoi's harbors were at last to be mined, it was welcome, to say the least.

But why must there always be a worm in the apple?
"The foregoing actions," said Nixon's letter, "will continue until . . . the implementation of an internationally
supervised cease-fire throughout Indochina and the release of prisoners of war." And when these conditions
were met, "We will stop all acts of force . . . and U.S.
forces will be withdrawn from Vietnam within four
months."

Now Thieu was reconciled by then to the departure
of our ground troops; they had in fact for the most part
already left; and he assumed—at that point everyone
assumed—that our air and naval power would remain
available to intervene in case of need, especially if a
cease-fire negotiated and sponsored by us was broken.
What bothered him in Nixon's letter was that there was
no reference, again, to the presence of the North
Vietnamese in the South.

This, for Thieu, was not only a military threat, since
the PAVN was bigger and better equipped than his
army; it was also a political nightmare. The Southerners
were being asked to stake their lives on the assumption
that an independent South could and would survive.
Would not the presence of the PAVN, combined with
the departure of the Americans, undermine that assump-

tion—and even suggest that Washington and Hanoi had made a deal at the expense of Saigon?

To nurture such suspicions, which had the effect of a chemical weapon on the nerves of the Southerners, had always been an essential part of the *dau tranh*, the military-political struggle—"the scientific application of Leninist principles," a member of the North Vietnamese delegation once told me in Paris, "under circumstances prevailing in our country." To Nguyen Van Thieu, who had fought with the Vietminh against the French and acquired some grasp of Communist tactics, all this seemed too obvious for Nixon to miss—unless, as Thieu thought Nixon's emissary in Paris was doing, Nixon was also looking for an excuse (after the requisite "decent interval") to cut and run.

The odd thing is that in all the wrangling over treaty drafts which now ensued (and went on and on until Thieu was bludgeoned into accepting the Paris Accords in January 1973) a sort of prudery prevented either side from alluding to the obvious fact that the basic problem was not in the text but on the ground. Hanoi, having sacrificed hundreds of thousands of its young men and endured daily bombing for eight long years, was simply not going to remove its troops and give up its designs on the South unless it was forced to do so; and this would require energetic and costly moves by the ARVN and continued American air and naval support, including a sustained effort to interdict the PAVN's lines of supply.

What mattered, then, was the relationship of forces, and what Thieu failed or refused to understand was that the American President, even after his overwhelming electoral triumph of November 1972, was no longer in a position to rethink and refight, even on a much reduced level, a war which the American people expected him to end. The repatriation of our troops had lessened political pressures, to be sure, but it had also in a curious way increased the public's impatience with the situation, its desire to have done with it at last. Initiatives like the Cambodian incursion, or the mining of Haiphong harbor, could be taken only within a perspective of withdrawal; and Nixon would pay a heavy political price for each.

This, of course, was the consequence of the strategies of "flexible response" and "limited war" inherited by Nixon from the Kennedy and Johnson administrations—strategies based on premises (e.g., the political situation in China, the patience of the American people, the Soviet interest in détente) that had proved to be utterly false; and it meant that already in 1972, before Watergate, when Nixon was approaching the apogee of his power, actions that demonstrably "worked" in Southeast Asia were debilitating failures in Washington, since they strengthened the hand of the McGoverns, the Kennedys, and the Abzugs, for whom the victory of Hanoi was inevitable and, in any event, a lesser evil than continued support of the South Vietnamese regime.

For all the hours that Thieu spent poring over Nixon's letter of May 9, one phrase seems to have escaped his notice, or to have been dismissed as inconsequential: the one about prisoners of war. Of course peace would mean an exchange of prisoners, this went without saying. But we know how ardently Nixon dreamed of rescuing our men before the November elections, or at least before his second inauguration. This mixture of motives and feelings is very much in the American vein, as recent events remind us. It never occurred to Thieu, on the other hand, presiding as he did over a country whose casualties were numbered in the hundreds of thousands, that the fate of a few hundred hostages could loom so large in an American President's mind.

Never, that is, until long after the event. Exhaling his bitterness in 1979, in an interview published by the German weekly *Der Spiegel*, Thieu said: "What he [Kissinger] and the U.S. government exactly wanted was to withdraw as fast as possible, to secure the release of U.S. prisoners. They said they wanted an honorable solution, but really they wanted to wash their hands of the whole business and scuttle and run. But . . . they did not want to be accused of abandoning us. That was the difficulty."

An understandable bitterness, but misdirected and unfair—such was the gist of Kissinger's reaction to the

Spiegel interview. And so he privately wrote to Thieu, who now lives in London, in January 1980: "I continue to believe that the balance of forces . . . could have been maintained if Watergate had not destroyed our ability to obtain sufficient aid . . . from the Congress in 1973 and 1974. Had we known in 1972 what was to come in America, we would not have proceeded as we did."

There is something moving in this letter—almost (but not quite) a *mea culpa* from a man little noted for brooding on his own mistakes, although he has repeatedly made the point, as readers of his memoirs will remember, that statesmen are often obliged under the pressure of events to make fateful decisions on the basis of insufficient or uncertain information. But this is not one of the wittily rueful obiter dicta that adorn Kissinger's memoirs; here he is writing to a man who now sees himself consigned to a sort of hell, the ruin of his people, and protesting—sincerely, no doubt—that his intentions were good. The fact remains that both the balance of forces and the American will to provide sufficient aid were profoundly affected, before Watergate, by Kissinger's negotiations (over a period of four years) with Lel Duc Tho.

Thieu, in any event, never replied to Kissinger's letter, although he allowed Hung to include it in *The Palace File*.

Phan Dinh Phung, after whom "my" street in Saigon was named, was a distinguished scholar, the leader of a 19th-century movement against the French. After the surrender of the boy emperor, Ham Nghi, he stubbornly continued the struggle, was betrayed, captured, and punished, according to Phan Boi Chau's *History of the Downfall,* in a particularly barbarous manner: the bones of his parents were dug up and burned. This story still causes the Vietnamese to shudder, I am told, despite the many new forms of barbarism they have experienced in more recent times, presumably because something more precious than Phung's corporeal existence was at stake: his spiritual links to home and homeland, to the generation of the departed and the generations to come, symbolized by the graves of his parents and the household altar where the ancestral spirits were enshrined.

To what extent these beliefs still hold I never was able to learn, my friends in Saigon being of different minds on the subject, and there was little time to talk about such things. But it was because of these graves and altars that the Vietnamese were said to be so deeply attached to the villages they have been fleeing from in such surprising numbers since the war.

For outsiders there is nothing more difficult than to understand and measure the persistence of old ways of thinking in evolving cultures, especially in those that are violently invaded by new ideas—first, because the point of departure, the original mind set, remains so foreign to us, and then because it is not a person whose thinking and behavior we are trying to understand, which would be complicated enough, but an infinitely various people who reflect the old and the new in an infinite variety of modes and combinations, so that we are driven to oversimplify what otherwise we would be unable to grasp at all.

This can lead to gross misjudgments, as when Frances FitzGerald in her immensely successful *Fire in the Lake* (1972) argued that there was a profound harmony, an almost mystical accord, between the praxis of the Vietnamese Communists and the ancient system of values and beliefs—that Communism, in short, was not only the wave of the future in that unhappy country but also, curiously, the wave of the past.

This book created a considerable stir, as I recall, because it was no longer merely saying that our intervention in Southeast Asia was ill-conceived and doomed, which many had said before, but that it would be a good thing if the other side won. But then it did win, and our allegedly wise and prescient adversaries, with their deep roots in Vietnamese tradition, proceeded to wreak such horrors and atrocities on their people, and on the Laotians and Cambodians as well, that the cleansing fire in FitzGerald's lake, the Communist victory in Indochina, must now be seen as it is seen by millions of prisoners and refugees: as one of the worst disasters of our time. (Not that Miss FitzGerald has ever made her apologies to the boat people, as many other former supporters of the Vietnamese Communists have done.)

In Washington, once, I ran into Dang Duc Khoi, who used to serve on the staff of Vice President Nguyen Cao Ky, and asked him to forget Frances FitzGerald's politics and tell me what he thought of her account of the old Vietnamese ethos. Generally, for reasons I *feel* rather than understand, the Vietnamese are loath to talk about their religion, but in this case Khoi was fairly rabid: "It's bullshit, she's got it all wrong." From which I concluded that Khoi was unable to forget Miss FitzGerald's politics, and let it go at that. Most of *Fire in the Lake*, after all, despite the promise of the opening chapter, is political: a rehash of the conventional wisdom of the Saigon press corps on the themes I encountered so often (since the correspondents came to see me every day) that I ended by keeping lists of them under such rubrics as VNNDG, meaning the Vietnamese Are No Damned Good, and VCTFT, meaning the Vietcong Are Ten Feet Tall, etc.—such being the foregone conclusions toward which questions, in that atmosphere, were almost always directed.

The point here is not that the conventional wisdom was wrong, or, for that matter, right, but that it was terribly lacking in background and context. Frances FitzGerald at least began with an attempt—practically unique in the journalism of the war—to understand the Vietnamese on something like their own terms. But knowing little to begin with, unable to speak or read Vietnamese, she was obliged to go to France and sit at the feet of Paul Mus, a renowned sociologist who had spent much of his life in Indochina.

There was no American Paul Mus, for the simple reason that we were not interested in the Vietnamese. We became intensely involved with them, perforce, but briefly; and what we learned about them was superficial and functional, as when our "grunts" learned to say *dee-dee* when they needed to move people in a hurry, or *ba-mee-ba*, when they wanted a beer. There were exceptions, of course, personal or professional, but on the whole we kept an extraordinary distance from these people, it seems to me now, even as we made our presence felt in every corner of the country. Indeed, the distance grew in direct proportion to our numbers.

That Phan Dinh Phung gave his name to our street is of little consequence to our story, unless it served to remind us that there were other possible paths to national liberation available to the Vietnamese, before and after the rise of Ho Chi Minh's Lao Dong, or Communist party. As Western imperialism ebbed, exhausted by Europe's internecine wars, Asia experienced a rebirth of self-assertion, confused and tentative at first, pulled this way and that by ancient popular traditions and modernizing impulses, so that the Vietnamese in their struggle against the French had access to a wide range of ideas and models, from the Japan of the Meiji restoration to the Japan of the postwar constitution, from the China of the Kuomintang to the China of Mao, not to mention phenomena intellectually if not geographically more distant, from Gandhi to Nehru to Lee Kuan Yew of Singapore.

What we now call Vietnam came under French colonial rule in the heyday of empire and had been subject to French cultural and economic influence for centuries. Vietnam's misfortune—and ours—was that the period of its decolonization coincided with the extraordinary vogue of Marxism among the French intelligentsia after World War II; and that the most talented and charismatic of its anti-colonial leaders, Ho Chi Minh, opted for Leninism early in his career and stuck to it as it evolved into Stalinism, brilliantly adapting its conspiratorial methods to local conditions, emulating (in the movement he forged) the energy and discipline of the Bolsheviks, their patience and also, alas, their peculiar unconcern with the consequences of their action on the people for whom, theoretically, it was undertaken. As they were the instruments of history, their conscience was always clear. Their task was neither to agonize about means nor to indulge in utopian blue-printing of the future, but to smash the old state and set up a new one, after which they would "proceed to build socialism," as Lenin said on the evening of the October *Putsch*, with only the foggiest notion of what this entailed.

So the accent of Ho Chi Minh's Lao Dong, or Communist, party was always on how to win, not on what it would do with its victory; and this helps to explain why the state the Communists wound up with in the North after the French gave up and went home remained essentially a war machine, geared and oiled and rigged for further fighting, and not much good for anything else.

But very good for that—especially since the Soviets and the Chinese seemed prepared to fuel the machine forever. It took some hubris to imagine that the soft, slothful, disorganized South could prevail against it or even survive, unless Hanoi could be persuaded to turn its energies elsewhere. But this was unlikely. In his long march to power Ho was known by many other names, and so was the Lao Dong, but the main thrust of their action was always the same: first against their Vietnamese rivals to establish their monopoly of the revolutionary project, so that no nationalist would have anywhere else to go; and only then against the foreigner.

The latter, whether French or American or Chinese, was condemned by the iron law of history; his departure could and should be accelerated by the *dau tranh*, the movement, but it was inevitable in the long run. The great thing was to ensure that it happened under the leadership of the anointed party, so that there could be no question, afterward, about who was in charge. Thus the Bolshevik praxis, carefully studied by Ho during his long exile in China, Moscow, and Western Europe, not only permitted but required him and his comrades to eliminate other nationalist leaders, even if this meant assassinating them or betraying them to the French police.

The name of the game was power, undiluted, unshared— and unlike the interminable and insufferable chatter of the Frenchified intelligentsia, so busy plotting against one another in the South, it was played for keeps. Indeed, the very existence of an independent South was intolerable, and the major affair of the North, once it had secured its base, was to put an end to it. With military supplies assured and the Northern population thoroughly regimented, only tactical concerns dictated prudence for a time. But all this, as my friend Khoi used to say, was *connu et archi-connu,* "clear beyond a shadow of a doubt," except to the contemporary versions of Lenin's "useful idiots" in the West.

He might have added that there were useful idiots in Saigon, too. The South was at once indubitably Vietnamese and indubitably different, and the number and quality of Southerners who said *vive la différence* were such that the Lao Dong was obliged for the moment to concoct an elaborate lie about its intentions, especially after news of how the common folk in the North were faring under Communist rule—stories of famine and bloody repression—began to seep through the bamboo curtain. Hence the creation of the National Liberation Front (NLF) and its military arm, the Vietcong, every unit (as we now know from Hanoi itself) carefully controlled by its core of Lao Dong cadres; and the constantly reiterated promise that the South, until it rallied spontaneously to Communism, would be allowed to go its own way.

Connu et archi-connu! Instructed by experience, the Northerners who had fled to the South—now grown to more than a million—could hardly be expected to fall for this line, but there were others (increasingly as the Diem government disappointed and outraged them) who believed it and others who joined the NLF, or supported it for one reason or another, without believing it or half-believing it or simply hoping that something would happen to make it come true—enough of them to start the war against the South that was as fatal to them in the end as it was to the declared enemies of the Lao Dong.

So much for ancient history—and by way of explaining why the street of Hung's family was called Phan Dinh Phung. Most of the streets of central Saigon were renamed after the French left in honor of the heroes and slogans of the independence movement, ancient and modern, which the Republic of Vietnam claimed to incarnate in defiance of Hanoi. The republic's writ, to be sure, did not run everywhere in the South. During the Buddhist troubles of 1963 it did not always run the full length of Phan Dinh Phung. But now that South Vietnam had got rid of the nefarious and incompetent Diem and his brother—so I was told in Washington and Honolulu when I was briefed for my new assignment—it would pull itself together with our help and offer a haven to the nationalist forces that the Communists had repressed or extinguished in the North: to Catholics and Buddhists, political parties like the Dai Viet and VNQDD, as well as to the Southern sects and ethnic groups, the Cao Dai and Hoa Hao, the Chams and Khmers and Montagnards, that had either survived the age-old drift of the Vietnamese from the Red River delta toward the Mekong, or sprung up during the past hundred years under French imperial rule.

Arriving in Saigon in January 1965, with no inkling of the chaos we had unleashed by sponsoring the overthrow of Diem two years earlier, I thought it a reasonable proposition that, given time and tranquillity, the republic should be able to survive and enhance the world's varietal richness. The South had always been Vietnam's New Found Land or, more recently, its California, offering room and resources for all, and now—the curtain having come down in the North—a promise of freedom. It was a promise as yet more honored in the breach, to be sure, but the republic was barely seven years old and under siege from the day it was born. This much I had gathered from what I had heard and been able to read during the long journey from Geneva to Washington and then to Honolulu and Saigon.

Memory has a way of proliferating; the spirit bloweth where it listeth. The point I was making to begin with was simply that I had forgotten the name of Phan Dinh Phung. And the point of my point, no doubt, was that this was the manner of our involvement in Vietnam. In a few short years, a moment on the scale of history, we went from total obsession to a sort of amnesia. The map of that country was once engraved in our minds, and most of us now can no longer remember whether Hué, the old imperial capital, is north or south of Danang. But of course we cannot leave it at that.

Soon after my arrival, I was shocked to discover that the Communists controlled most of the countryside, in some cases outright, in others functioning as a sort of shadow government alongside the nominal authorities; and they were growing increasingly bold in the cities, where the junta of generals who had overthrown Diem had been pushed aside by Nguyen Khanh, an inept and buffoonish fellow who had been helped to power by an inveterate plotter named Thao.

Under General Khanh the remains of the administration so carefully constructed by Diem and his brother (also murdered in the coup) were dismantled, and any notion that there might be a respectable civilian alternative was rudely put down, so that the Southerners began to suspect with astonishment and terror what was in fact the case: that they were now adrift, and that those who had destroyed Diem's government had done so without the faintest idea of what was to take its place—except, being military men already accustomed to receiving their equipment, munitions, and training from us, that the Americans would provide.

But the Americans, for the moment, had nothing but military assistance to provide. They were willing and at that stage apparently even impatient to wage war, but aside from mouthing platitudes about freedom and justice and winning hearts and minds, and a generous readiness to bear the expense, they had no clue about how to rebuild a South Vietnamese polity. They simply had not thought that far ahead, nor did they think it their business, even now, so that years would pass before a group of the more reasonable army officers—the most capable of whom was Nguyen Van Thieu—would be able to put something viable together.

Two incidents come back to focus the absurd disorder of that time. In the first I am walking down a broad boulevard with Howard Simpson, an embassy officer who (being slated for transfer) is bequeathing to me some of his functions and what little he can of his vast experience, having served several tours of duty in Vietnam, beginning with one in the early 50's. Suddenly down the road comes a column of tanks and armored trucks, with an odd-looking Vietnamese officer standing in the turret of the lead tank, and Simpson stops short at the sight of him.

"Thao, you old bastard," he yells. "What's up?"

The officer, who is wall-eyed, pudgy, and grinning, raises his hand, stops the column, and shouts back: "Howie! How you?"

"Never mind how me! What in hell are you doing?"

"Nothing special, Howie. I am making a coup!"

He pronounced the *p* in coup, presumably to make it clear to a benighted American. And then the column moved on. What happened to the coup I do not recall. Those first weeks in Saigon were hectic, this being the period when the Vietnamese seemed to be coming up with a new government with each new phase of the moon. But far from being considered an amiable lunatic, Thao—who came of a wealthy Southern Catholic family and had a brother high in the apparatus of the Lao Dong in Hanoi—had an extraordinary talent for ingratiating himself with every faction. And throughout all this Thao held important posts in the South Vietnamese government and remained close to certain elements of the American establishment, especially the CIA—until, after Khanh fell, he was identified as an enemy agent by officers of Thieu's military security, tracked down, and killed. Ten years later the new Communist masters of Saigon confirmed that he had been one of theirs and proclaimed him a national hero, although there are South Vietnamese nationalists, I've been told, who still believe that he was playing a double game: a Machiavellian romantic, they say, who had read too much André Malraux.

What the CIA concluded, if anything, I never found out, but there must have been many in the agency, as there were elsewhere in the American establishment in Saigon, who were not surprised at the rapid disintegration of the republic in 1964 and 1965. These were people—the most eminent being Ambassador Frederick Nolting and General Paul Harkins, the predecessors of Lodge and Westmoreland—who had warned that by intervening as we did, with no assurance that anything better would follow the removal of Diem, we were creating a huge vacuum and assuming a responsibility for which we were quite unprepared. And this of course is exactly what happened. In the confusion that resulted, phenomena like Thao and Khanh flourished briefly while the Vietcong all but completed their conquest of the countryside and began (but still prudently) to strengthen their urban networks.

And this brings me to my second epiphany—a sad little joke told by my old friend Bui Diem, who was later to serve as Vietnamese ambassador in Washington. In his memoirs, Bui Diem* confesses that he had supported the overthrow of Diem in the hope and expectation that it would be followed (at our insistence, if necessary) by the creation of a constitutional government to which, he believes, the great majority of the South Vietnamese would have rallied. Instead, he says, the amorphous junta drifted "from incompetence to incompetence" and the stage was set for "a firm hand at the helm" which Khanh, if only because he was willing to act at that moment, was simply assumed to be:

> As a result, Khanh was treated from the start as a strongman who enjoyed America's staunch friendship. Defense Secretary Robert McNamara was even sent to South Vietnam to stump the country with him, as a visible symbol that the United States stood beside the new leader. This kind of performance did not come naturally to McNamara. On one occasion he grasped Khanh's hand and declared, *"Vietnam muon nam!"* Unfortunately, whoever taught McNamara the Vietnamese phrase had neglected to also teach him the proper intonation. So instead of saying "Long Live Vietnam," what he actually said, to the vast amusement of his audience, was "Vietnam, lie down!"

In the face of all this, the failure of the Communists of the North and their Southern allies to win the "hearts

* *In the Jaws of History*, by Bui Diem with David Chanoff, Houghton Mifflin, 343 pp., $18.95.

and minds" of the city folk is surprising, to say the least. Perhaps it was simply a matter of time. But one reason, precisely, for the vast increase in the urban population that occurred in the early 60's was that the Saigon government, while progressively losing its grip on the countryside, was still able to afford some protection in the towns. From their sanctuaries along the borders, in Cambodia, Laos, and North Vietnam, the Communists could move forces in and out of the country to collect rice and recruits and to enlarge the "leopard spots" of "liberated territories" almost at will—so that, even if Saigon had a competent administration, the security problem could never be solved, only palliated, unless we did what Lyndon Johnson and Dean Rusk kept assuring the Communists that we would not do: go into the sanctuaries and "widen the war." Instead we relied on attrition to discourage an adversary who was willing and able to take a hundred casualties for every one of ours—and who in fact would sacrifice many hundreds of thousands of men in the coming decade and still field a force of twenty divisions for the final assault on Saigon.

Quite apart from the appeal of their ideology (always limited in the South) and the very real prestige they had acquired in defeating the French, the Communists of the North and their Southern allies were operating from positions of strength. It was the Soviet–Hanoi alliance that was the superpower in Southeast Asia; and the strength of the Communists on the ground was immeasurably bolstered by the sympathy of people everywhere who saw them as victims of imperialism heroically fighting for self-determination and freedom—and the United States in the role of a neocolonialist bully seeking to prop up a puppet regime. They were increasingly adept at generating and exploiting this perception, so deeply rooted in the guilt and self-doubt of the West, whereas the American leadership never learned to take it seriously or to factor it into its calculations. And yet, as we all know now, it was bound to be extremely important—perhaps decisive—in the end.

In short, everything favored the Communist enterprise, and this would have been a good time for us to heed the counsel of prudence and declare not victory, as Senator Aiken of Vermont was to suggest some years later, but defeat: to leave the squabbling Southern generals to their own devices and take our advisers and Green Berets and AID administrators home to ponder the complexities of "nation-building" in Southeast Asia. Such an outcome would have been an unhappy one for the Southerners, but not so devastating as what was to happen ten years later. And it would have spared us an infinite grief.

Nowadays all this is so dreadfully obvious, *connu et archi-connu,* that one tends to forget how out of the question it was in 1965. Lyndon Johnson would not hear of it. The young press corps in Saigon (including such future antiwar activists as David Halberstam of the New York *Times*) would not hear of it, either—these being the hawkish fellows who had roused John Kennedy against Diem on the grounds that he was incapable of winning a war for which they, at least, were ready to "bear any burden, pay any price." And at home the great majority in Congress would not hear of it—not in any case without setting off a great national debate about "Who lost Indochina?"

So we sent in our troops and helped the generals sort themselves out and by dint of enormous sacrifices over the next five years created, or more exactly recreated, the situation half-jokingly described by Senator Aiken. By the early 70's, when we were withdrawing the last of our ground forces, the republic had a reasonably competent government and a credible army; and it had been largely freed—after the bloody paroxysm of Tet in 1968 and the joint U.S.–South Vietnamese operation in Cambodia in 1970—from the threat of internal subversion. Thus it was possible for the first time to issue weapons to village self-defense forces in areas once controlled by the Vietcong.

The North had not given up, of course, nor would it in the foreseeable future. But it could be contained as long as the South was willing to fight and we were prepared to supply the means required to maintain the military balance, including the occasional intervention of our naval and air forces.

So this was the upshot of what the Vietnamese think of as the "American war"—from 1965 to 1971. The South lived—dependent upon us, to be sure, but hardly more so than the North was dependent on Moscow. We could therefore now do as the good Senator suggested: declare victory, and go home.

Needless to say, this is not what we did—not quite, and therefore not at all. It is a complicated story, and *The Palace File* tells it well. Richard Nixon withdrew our armed forces as efficiently and rapidly as they had been inserted by Lyndon Johnson, and with the same sort of consultation with our allies, i.e., none, and meanwhile sent Henry Kissinger to conduct secret diplomacy with Le Duc Tho, which had the effect (however unintended) of assuring the Northerners that the prize would be theirs if they only persisted, and of suggesting to the Southerners that something sinister was afoot. At the end of the so-called peace process we persuaded, indeed forced, South Vietnam to put its head in a noose, the Paris Peace Accords of January 1973, while solemnly swearing that if the trap were sprung we would be there to cut the rope and chastise the villains.

All this was not only explicitly stated in Nixon's letters to Thieu but reinforced by military planning, e.g., inviting the South Vietnamese corps commanders to our air-force headquarters in Thailand to show them how precisely we were planning to target our attacks if the Communists violated the cease-fire. And then, of course, the trap was sprung, in full view of the world, and lo! we were not there.

In our entire history, Hung and Schecter maintain, there is no precedent for such a betrayal. But they immediately mitigate the condemnation by raising, if not settling, some obvious questions. How valid were the commitments of Nixon and Ford? Why were they never made public? Did Nixon and Kissinger cynically betray our allies in the hope of achieving a "decent interval"?

To these questions Kissinger replies, correctly, that it was not the practice in those days to make presidential letters public, and that in any case there was nothing secret about Nixon's determination to enforce the Paris agreement by military action if necessary. Both he and Nixon also indignantly deny that they were being cynical or merely looking for a "decent interval." On the contrary, Kissinger was, and remains, convinced that if not for Watergate, Nixon, with the same willingness that he had shown to take the political heat during the Christmas bombing of 1972, would have responded with air strikes to North Vietnamese violations.

I have no difficulty in believing this: it makes sense and follows logically from Nixon's public commitment to achieve a "peace with honor." But finally, of course, would it have made any difference? Even if we had intervened this time, wasn't Hanoi's victory inevitable in the end? Or would the changing foreign policy of China have brought a new factor into play on the side of an independent South Vietnam?

Etc., ad infinitum—interminable, tiresome, tantalizing questions, begetting more questions, and meanwhile, as Kissinger keeps reminding us in his memoirs, you are obliged to act, whether you have satisfactory answers or not.

Or not to act, which is what it came down to in March 1975. You are Gerald Ford, say, and the North Vietnamese, in open violation of the agreement that Kissinger had spent four years negotiating, are coming straight down over the central highlands to the coast and the highway to Saigon. The Soviets, in contemplation of realizing a return—at last—on a very old investment, have built them a pipeline through Laos and Cambodia, emerging at Loc Ninh, a couple of hours from the coast. But now the United States Congress, led by Jack Kennedy's younger brother and Lowell Weicker and Bella Abzug, has informed the notoriously "authoritarian" and "corrupt" Thieu regime (over your veto) that they will get no more help from us. Not a bullet. The South Vietnamese army is demoralized and crumbling, like the French and British in the face of Nazi Germany in June 1940. In a few days our ambassador and his staff will have to run for it, ignominiously, with at best a handful of our Vietnamese friends.

At this point, say, General Vogt, the commander of our air force in Thailand, flies over the area and reports that he has never seen anything like it: enemy tanks, artillery, half-tracks, personnel carriers, bumper to bumper—since there are only a couple of roads capable of carrying this kind of traffic—all the way down to the outskirts of Saigon. After groping around in the jungle for years, and dropping millions of tons of explosives on trees, we have a target. "A turkey shoot," Vogt calls it. We could make those roads look like the Sinai in 1967, after the Israeli air force destroyed Nasser's motorized columns in the desert.

What would you do? Does the congressional interdiction wipe out your responsibility to provide for the security of our people in Saigon? Would you order the air-force commander and the carriers cruising along the coast to wipe out all that congestion on the highways and give the South Vietnamese a chance to pull themselves together? And thereby, in all probability, even if the American public rallied to your support, open up a constitutional crisis as bitter as the one that almost led to the impeachment of Richard Nixon?

I don't know whether such a notion ever crossed Gerald Ford's mind. I doubt it. In any case, it's all behind us now. A great power cannot afford to throw good money after the bad and lose itself in remorse and introspection. . . . Or can it? Should it?

The last letter in *The Palace File* is from Thieu, begging for the help he had been promised again and again. It was never answered.

For all that it is born of Hung's sorrow and Schecter's indignation, their book remarkably keeps its cool. It has the tone and gait of a historical narrative, not of a political tract—recounting lucidly what happened to the government and people of the South after we turned away, which each of us did at different times, of course, depending on who we were and how we were related to the situation. In my case, for example, I quit the Paris delegation late in 1969, after Kissinger had begun holding his secret trysts with Le Duc Tho, and retired from the Foreign Service. During the period covered by *The*

Palace File, I forgot the few words of Vietnamese that I had learned and gradually lost touch with my friends in Saigon.

As a national phenomenon, however, the amnesia that befell us can be dated with some precision: the Paris Accords were signed on January 27, 1973, instituting a cease-fire in place and various political arrangements, including an international supervisory commission in which no one believed. For the North Vietnamese this was merely a phase, albeit an important one, in their famous fight-talk-fight strategy. For Richard Nixon and Henry Kissinger it was a culmination and a release. Planes could now at last be sent to Hanoi to pick up our prisoners, who had been subjected to torture and ignominy not only by the Communists but also by visiting American literati; and by mid-July the last of our combat battalions was gone from the South. On August 15, ignoring warnings that the Paris agreements would have to be enforced, the Congress of the United States decreed that there would be no more funds for American military action of any kind in Indochina.

Richard Nixon, by then, was in irremediable trouble, although impeachment proceedings were still many months away. For Cambodia the worst was yet to come, as it was for Saigon, but the news media would now be shifting their attention elsewhere—to the Middle East, for example, where Egyptian staff officers were once again bent over maps of the Sinai. "Vietnam," in the words of a well-known survivor of Camelot, "could now return to the obscurity it so richly deserved."

What happened thereafter is told—admirably, in my opinion—from a point of view that strikes us as surprising and rather odd for the simple reason that it is South Vietnamese; and to this we have not been accustomed. The effect is to remind us that we have been experiencing the war in a multitude of ways, "in-country," as we used to say, or out, through the pain and bewilderment of our soldiers, or as a quarrel with others and with ourselves—but always or almost always this dimension has been missing: the people about whom or for whom, allegedly, it was fought. For this alone, and quite apart from the hitherto unpublished letters and skillful narration, *The Palace File* deserves an attentive reading.

But there is nothing in *The Palace File* to equal the pathos of Hung's last visit to Washington, as the enemy tanks are closing in on Saigon. Congress is in recess and no one suggests that it might be called back. The idea is absurd. Gerald Ford is playing golf in Palm Springs. Hung wanders down the long empty corridors clutching his letters, which should have been published years ago. Thieu has always refused to publish them or even allude to them because they are marked top-secret and he feared to anger the lords of the Larger Kingdom, his last resort. Now it is too late.

As he walks, Hung encounters two or three departing solons, including the Senator from Massachusetts, younger brother of the President who first committed American troops to South Vietnam. But Teddy is pressed for time, and makes it clear that his celebrated compassion has its limits; he will pay any price, bear any burden, to bring this conversation with Hung to an end.

And then there is Hung's last sad ill-attended press conference which is reported by some surly stringers on remote back pages, if at all. Someone, it seems, thought to ask Henry Kissinger about this obscure Vietnamese who claimed to have some letters which etc., and Kissinger said yes, letters had passed between Nixon and Thieu, but no, there was nothing newsworthy in them (which, although it scandalizes Schecter and Hung, was sadly true in the sense that there had been nothing secret about the promises that we as a nation, speaking through an almost unanimous Congress, were now unwilling to keep, no matter what).

And so it goes. Back in Vietnam, we are overwhelmed with pathetic detail: an incident with some soldiers and a roadblock, a talk with an old peasant woman, desperate attempts to save endangered people and equipment; clues to a situation that we could not deal with honorably and therefore resolved to forget. In this richness of reference and atmosphere the protagonists of *The Palace File* come alive and we begin to recover, curiously, not only the little we knew about these people, our friends and victims, but much that we surmised and lacked the time or wit or patience to understand. And now there is something odd, different, in this effort to remember what we never properly knew. Is there any point to it? The story, after all, ends no less badly than it did before. Only the configuration has changed—and the moral center. It used to be a story about us. Now it is a story about them.

Nineteen sixty-eight was the climactic year of the American war, or more specifically of the American phase of the thirty-year war, in Indochina. This was the year of the Tet offensive, a pyrotechnic display featuring dramatic scenes of fighting within the American embassy compound in Saigon and the unprecedented ferocity of the struggle for Hué, preceded—by barely more than a week—by the onset of the siege of Khesanh. All these actions ended badly, even disastrously, for the Communist attackers on the ground, but they inflicted heavy casualties, terrified the South Vietnamese population, and profoundly affected American morale.

The Communists, as they have since told us, were now deliberately trading what they called the "blood and bones" of their followers, especially of their Southern followers who might in any case prove troublesome after the war, for political advantage in an arena they saw, quite correctly, as far more decisive than Hué or Khesanh. In Washington, the Defense Secretary had resigned, a month after the storming of the Pentagon by antiwar demonstrators; but the main thing was that this was an election year in the U.S., during which much of the Democratic party would behave as if it were already in opposition while Nixon, the Republican candidate, would mysteriously allude to a "secret plan" to end the American involvement—an echo of Eisenhower's "I shall go to Korea" promise of 1952. The North Vietnamese, who would later offend Henry Kissinger by instructing him on U.S. public opinion, could therefore deduce from the campaign posture of both candidates what they had already learned from the Soviet ambassador in Washington: that American policy— just as it had been based after 1963 on a national decision to stay in—would now have to conform to an equal and opposite consensus in favor of getting out.

On the other hand, the American war had given Thieu a victory of sorts: the Vietcong was finished, the delta increasingly secure, the government of the republic alive and in better shape than at any time since the early days of Diem. So Hanoi's problem was to make haste slowly: to accelerate the American departure sufficiently to deny the South time to consolidate its hold on the countryside and prepare for the PAVN's frontal assault; but not to such a point that the Americans, ceasing to take casualties and bearing a much lighter financial burden, would be able to install themselves in a garrison situation, as in Korea, and thus deprive the North of the prize it had sought for so long and at such great cost.

Richard Nixon, presumably, made similar calculations. For us, too, and for our allies, timing was crucial. Each move we made on the ground would have to be balanced against the effects it produced on our troops and at home. During the first five years of the American war our battle deaths had totaled some 16,000. By the end of 1968 the number had dramatically risen to 30,610. Disengagement began in 1969, but Hanoi saw to it that fighting remained heavy, with the result that another 10,000 Americans died in the course of the year. And the fact that we were now on our way out, in addition to affecting military morale, seemed to galvanize the most radical elements of the antiwar movement— those who were in fact pro-war, but on the enemy's side. In May 1970, for example, a few days after the start of a joint U.S.–South Vietnamese incursion into Cambodia, four students at Kent State University in Ohio were shot and killed by National Guardsmen during a demonstration; and all across the country colleges shut down in protest. Still, the Cambodian invasion vastly improved the security of Vietnam's eastern provinces, including the great rice-growing area south of Saigon; and Thieu had reason to be proud of the conduct of his troops.

So it wasn't easy to draw up a statement of profit and loss. In this instance, my old friend Bui Diem, Thieu's ambassador to Washington, drafted a cable to Saigon to warn that Hanoi, on the whole, had come out ahead politically. So he tells us in his memoirs. But Thieu, with his Mandarin Confucian mentality, refused to take the point. The Cambodian action, he thought, was long overdue—as indeed it was.

However that may be, from the onset of the Nixon administration, as Kissinger began his secret talks with Le Duc Tho, our troops were removed from South Vietnam in increments corresponding (we said) to the growing ability of the South to defend itself—but also, obviously, to political calculations and pressures at home. It was the sort of thing we did well, and the process took on a life of its own. From our peak troop strength of 543,400 in the spring of 1969 we went to 24,200 in 1972; and the last of these were gone in the following year.

The ARVN, meanwhile, increased its complement from 820,000 to 1,048,000—an enormous effort, but insufficient to replace the shortfall in numbers and fire-power; and the ARVN had become dependent on certain American command functions—intelligence and communications, especially—that the JGS was still far from being able to replace.

These were technical matters, and most Americans were happy to leave them to the experts. They wanted out, and expected that we would leave in an orderly and honorable way; and this general approval of Nixon's policy as it was understood was repeatedly confirmed by opinion polls and by the landslide Republican victory in the elections of 1972.

For the South Vietnamese, however, everything now hung on a thread. They knew that they could not have come this far without our help; and, having suffered hundreds of thousands of casualties during the preceding decade, they were physically and morally exhausted. Outnumbered, outgunned, with thousands of miles of porous frontiers and seacoast, they found themselves still facing a juggernaut, the PAVN, which could attack at will from sanctuaries in Laos, Cambodia, and North Vietnam, replace its losses from Soviet arsenals, and attack again. They knew that their country, for all the highly publicized faults of the Thieu government, was richer and freer than the North—but of what avail was such knowledge if Enlightened Opinion throughout the world decreed that Hanoi's nationalist credentials were more authentic, since it was Ho Chi Minh who had driven out the French; and if God, in any case, was on the side of the bigger battalions?

To continue to fight under such circumstances, the South Vietnamese had to believe in our ultimate commitment to their survival. This had always been difficult for a variety of reasons, the most obvious of which was that a great many Americans did not believe in it and said so. But of course it was also difficult for the Vietnamese, if not impossible, to interpret the many varieties of opposition to the war. So most of them tended, like Thieu, to shrug the American opposition—Hanoi's hope and comfort—away.

For the Southerners, the core of the problem was elsewhere: *they could not see our interest*, even when our involvement was at its height; and it became increasingly hard for them to grasp as we began to withdraw. The Vietnamese I knew, or more precisely met, in Saigon and a few years later in Paris, were incomparably more sophisticated than the villagers who made up the great mass of the population; yet even they astonished me by their ignorance of our world—which was almost as great as my ignorance of theirs.

The Southern bourgeoisie was composed for the most part of villagers once or twice removed, with bits of property somewhere in the delta or up north; or Chinese merchants with Vietnamese names; or professional people, lawyers, doctors, teachers, and (for some mysterious reason) an inordinate number of pharmacists. They had been to French schools, usually, and had absorbed a little elementary history, but this did not include the doctrine of containment. Obviously, our intentions were not colonial, as some had hoped and others feared; we built no plantations and did no business, except with each other. The great bases we built at Danang, Long Binh, Camranh Bay suggested a strategic interest, but by the early 70's we were turning these over to the government of South Vietnam. Rumors kept cropping up to the effect that oil, or some other natural resource, had been discovered; but none was confirmed.

Of course, there was our rhetoric, and we had certainly put our money where our mouth was, but this still begged the question—especially now that we were leaving—of *why*. Why had we come to save them at such horrendous cost in the first place? Why had we, visibly not the most patient of peoples, adopted a strategy that carefully preserved Hanoi's ability to inflict pain on us and prolong the war? And why, since we had now apparently become embroiled in some obscure but important crisis of our own, *chez nous,* should we continue to concern ourselves with theirs?

I am not talking about peasants, for whom the great thing throughout the centuries of Chinese domination, warring kingdoms, and French colonialism had always been to discern who (in the immediate vicinity) had the "Mandate of Heaven"—i.e., the actual power to recruit their sons and confiscate their rice—but about their city cousins, especially those who had a modicum of education and the prestige that goes with it in Confucian society.

The vast majority of these, including the minority who were or who had been tempted by the NLF, were anti-Communist and anxious to keep Hanoi at arm's length. *"Kaplan-oi,"* I heard them saying. "Is this possible? Are you Americans for real?" And I used to hold imaginary conversations with them, lucidly explaining that the political and military mistakes we had made, appalling as they were, only increased our obligation to set things right; that the American people continued to believe that world peace was threatened if the Communists were allowed to believe that they could extend their empire by military force; and that, as a great power, we could not in any event afford to let the South Vietnamese down, lest we come to be considered more dangerous to our friends than to our enemies.

In fact, however, this subject of our ultimate interest practically never came up, perhaps because it was too important. These people had a way that comes back to me now of tiptoeing around a fateful issue with a sort of superstitious tact. Most, it seemed to me, had simply given up trying to understand. They believed in our commitment, if and when they did, for no rational reason at all: because it was the only alternative to despair. But to carry on they constantly needed reassurance. And in this respect, alas, the *manner* of our withdrawal was the final disaster.

Secrecy is a normal and necessary mode of diplomacy, but in this case it was counterindicated, as a diplomat might put it, because it played precisely into Hanoi's hands. Quite apart from the unsettling effect it had on the South Vietnamese, it was inevitable that the secrecy of the negotiations leading to the Paris Accords would discourage public interest in the United States—especially after the agreement in principle was signed and the haggling about details began. If there was any chance of committing this country to the responsibilities implicit in the Paris Accords—the culmination, after all, of an enormous national effort—it was in using the presidential pulpit to the utmost and insisting that Congress and the media be informed of the entire process, all along the way.

This is easier to say than it would have been to do, given Hanoi's opposition and Nixon's impatience. And no one could foresee in 1969, when Kissinger first slipped into Paris for a rendezvous with Le Duc Tho, what would happen to the Nixon presidency at the beginning of his second term. Yet, to stand the Clausewitzian formula on its head, the peace could only be "a continuation of the war by other means." An agreement with the Communists, *any* agreement with the Communists, would have to be enforced. And this meant that the country had to be prepared for a continuing effort, insignificant in comparison with what we had been doing, but irksome; and, as in South Korea, with no end in sight.

To be sure, the mills of Watergate were now grinding, and it was late in the day to commit this country to anything in Southeast Asia, after ten years of a war conducted so incoherently, beyond the stand-off im-

plied in Nixon's formula: an honorable peace. There
was no public clamor to know what Kissinger was up to
in Paris. It was as if Congress, the press, and the
academic world from which he had so surprisingly come
were relieved to let him rid them of this tiresome
business at last.

Of the negotiations, in any event, nothing or almost
nothing was known until 1970. For once there were no
leaks from the American side. And thereafter, until
Secretary of State Rogers and the Vietnamese foreign
ministers were summoned to Paris for the signing, the
public knew only that Kissinger was conducting talks
with Hanoi on the one hand and with Saigon on the
other. It was understood that the latter, on the whole,
was being at least as stubborn and difficult as the former; and this fed the growing anti-South-Vietnamese
passion that had begun to inhabit certain corners of the
Congress. But the details, excepting those that the
Communists chose to reveal for the purposes of psycho-
logical warfare, remained obscure. For his part, Thieu
never went public with his objections to the form and
content of Kissinger's talks with Le Duc Tho. One can
only speculate about the reasons for his discretion—but
who can doubt now that it was a fatal mistake?

In January 1969, as Kissinger was organizing his new
office in the White House, the magazine *Foreign Affairs*
appeared with an article in which he—writing as a
Harvard professor—makes an elementary point about
negotiations with the Vietnamese:

> To survive, the Vietnamese have had to learn to
> calculate—almost instinctively—the real balance of
> forces. If negotiations give the impression of being
> camouflaged surrender, there will be nothing left
> to negotiate. Support for the side which seems to
> be losing will collapse. Thus, all the parties are
> aware—Hanoi explicitly, for it does not view war
> and negotiation as separate processes; we in a more
> complicated bureaucratic manner—that the *way* ne-
> gotiations are carried out is almost as important as
> *what* is negotiated.

To which one can only say amen. But the newly appointed National Security Adviser then proceeded to deal directly with Hanoi, just as we in the Harriman–Vance mission had conducted "exploratory talks" a year or so earlier. Only, this time, the South Vietnamese were not even briefed after each meeting; for a long time they were not briefed at all. No serious consideration was ever given to Thieu's insistent demand that, since it was the fate of his people that hung in the balance, his government should be directly involved.

And thus, over the next four years, the Republic of Vietnam, which even the Soviets had once been willing to recognize, was delegitimized, in direct contradiction to what we were saying in South Vietnam and to the world, and indeed to all that we had spent so much blood and treasure to assert since 1965—namely, that Saigon was the rightful government of the South and, given the wherewithal, would eventually be able to take care of itself.

To provide the wherewithal we had a program called Vietnamization. In practice it meant that we left behind hundreds of millions of dollars worth of materiel, much of it useless to Thieu's armed forces because they lacked the facilities for repairing and maintaining it, and said in effect: goodbye and good luck and don't hesitate to call. And for the first couple of years or so there was usually someone, however distracted, at the other end of the line. With the materiel went certain training programs, some of them reasonably effective; and at least two or three South Vietnamese divisions were—by 1972—equipped and organized and led in a manner that made them equal if not superior to any units of comparable size that the PAVN could muster. But they were far too few, and the ARVN was fatally weak (after the withdrawal of MAC-V) at the general-staff level.

Meanwhile the Communists, as expected, began violating the cease-fire immediately, just to make their point: small probing actions at first, increasingly bold as they discovered just how far it was possible to go without eliciting a reaction from us. The Soviets were now giving them the full panoply of their equipment, including helicopters and fixed-wing aircraft; and then there was that ominous pipeline; and the reconstruction of their base areas in Cambodia, from which the Khmer Rouge could be unleashed to attack Phnom Penh and the PAVN to move eastward to control the vital centers of the South.

All in good time. By the spring of 1974 it was clear that Hanoi need not worry about going too far, the Congress and the people of the United States being otherwise engaged. The Judiciary Committee of the House of Representatives began its television inquiry into the possible impeachment of Richard Nixon on May 9. Few noticed, two weeks later, when the House voted to gut the budget for military aid to South Vietnam. This was a signal, if any were needed, to both sides.

Still, the war would drag on for another year, until the final spasm which began with the PAVN offensive against Ban Me Thuot on March 10, 1975. Indeed, Hanoi did not anticipate that things would move so swiftly. In January a Northern division had been moved across the river from Cambodia to occupy Phuoc Long— not much of a drive, a few hours, perhaps an afternoon, from my house on Phan Dinh Phung. There was no reaction from our air force and this, when the ARVN began to crumble in the central highlands, must have told the Northerners that they could now drive on to Saigon unimpeded. On the coast, Danang, where our marines had come ashore ten years earlier, fell on March 10. On April 10 President Ford's last pro-forma request for funds was turned down by the House; it was already unlikely that such funds would ever be spent. One last ARVN division held the Communists up before Saigon for a few days, inflicting heavy casualties until its munitions were spent and most of its men were dead. Saigon fell on April 30.

In the last twelve years of Vietnam's thirty-year war, during which we destroyed Diem's republic, which we had helped to create, then encouraged Thieu to set up another that might have survived and even prospered, and finally tired of the whole business and turned it all over to Hanoi, we ourselves had suffered over 300,000 casualties and more than 57,000 dead; inflicted enormous damage on both North and South Vietnam; induced our South Vietnamese allies to hope and fight and suffer even greater—far greater—human losses than our own; spent billions upon billions of dollars in the manner best calculated to distort and inflate our economy for years to come; built a lavish and immensely useful naval base for the Soviets to inherit at Camranh Bay, thus tilting the strategic balance in their favor in the South Pacific; disrupted and almost destroyed civil society and the idea of national service in our own country and—but need I go on? The disaster was and remains incalculable. And yet we turned away from it and went about our business, beginning to forget Vietnam even before it was over.

Amnesia, I am told, is the response of the organism to an intolerable inner trouble. But this is a response that we cannot afford. It deprives us of a vital dimension. Memory, however painful, is better. My old friend Raymond Aron used to say that history, which is after all a form of memory, cannot really help us solve our present problems; we learn nothing from it, he said, but history itself. So much for that old tag that people are forever quoting from Santayana, to the effect that those who do not know history are condemned to repeat it. But this is not to say that it is useless to think about the past. What we choose to remember, and how, is part of the process by which we become what we are.

So now, I would suggest, it is time to remember what we did and failed to do in Vietnam. We cannot be content with the nightmarish fantasies of combat that our novelists and film-makers have given us. They were part of the experience, to be sure. But books like *The Palace File* and Ellen Hammer's *Death in November* remind us that this war was not simply devised as a test of our young manhood or a mindless horror show. There was more to Vietnam than "all that."

BLESSED ARE THE MEEK

G. C. Edmondson

Gary Edmondson first appeared in the science fiction magazines some thirty years ago. He has made a living at writing ever since.

Gary spent much of his time traveling around the country in a home built RV that serves as both house and office. About ten years ago I introduced him to writing with computers, and he installed a word processor in his rig. I keep trying to get him to write a book about that.

I read this story when it first appeared in the old *Astounding Science Fiction*, and for some reason I have always remembered it. In the movie *The Karate Kid* the old sensei, accused of making his student wax cars, paint houses, and scrub floors while giving him no instruction in karate says, "Things not always what they seem."

This is often true.

BLESSED ARE THE MEEK

G. C. Edmondson

The strangers landed just before dawn, incinerating a good li of bottom land in the process. Their machines were already busily digging up the topsoil. The Old One watched, squinting into the morning sun. He sighed, hitched up his saffron robes and started walking down toward the strangers.

Griffin turned, not trying to conceal his excitement. "You're the linguist, see what you can get out of him."

"I might," Kung Su ventured sourly, "if you'd go weed the air machine or something. This is going to be hard enough without a lot of kibitzers cramping my style and scaring Old Pruneface here half to death."

"I see your point," Griffin answered. He turned and started back toward the diggings. "Let me know if you make any progress with the local language." He stopped whistling and strove to control the jauntiness of his gait. *Must be the lower gravity and extra oxygen,* he thought. *I haven't bounced along like this for thirty years. Nice place to settle down if some promoter doesn't turn it into an old folks' home.* He sighed and glanced over the diggings. The rammed earth walls were nearly obliterated by now. *Nothing lost,* he reflected. *It's all on tape and they're no different from a thousand others at any rate.*

Griffin opened a door in the transparent bubble from which Albañez was operating the diggers. "Anything?" he inquired.

"Nothing so far," Albañez reported. "What's the score on this job? I missed the briefing."

"How'd you make out on III, by the way?"

"Same old stuff, pottery shards and the usual junk. See it once and you've seen it all."

"Well," Griffin began, "it looks like the same thing here again. We've pretty well covered this system and you know how it is. Rammed earth walls here and there, pottery shards, flint, bronze, and iron artifacts and that's it. They got to the iron age on every planet and then blooey."

"Artifacts all made for humanoid hands, I suppose. I wonder if they were close enough to have crossbred with humans."

"I couldn't say," Griffin observed dryly. "From the looks of Old Pruneface I doubt if we'll ever find a human female with sufficiently detached attitude to find out."

"Who's Pruneface?"

"He came ambling down out of the hills this morning and walked into camp."

"You mean you've actually found a live humanoid?"

"There's got to be a first time for everything." Griffin opened the door and started climbing the hill toward Kung Su and Pruneface.

"Well, have you gotten beyond the 'me, Charlie' stage yet?" Griffin inquired at breakfast two days later.

Kung Su gave an inscrutable East Los Angeles smile. "As a matter of fact, I'm a little farther along. Joe is amazingly cooperative."

"Joe?"

"Spell it Chou if you want to be exotic. It's still pronounced Joe and that's his name. The language is monosyllabic and tonal. I happen to know a similar language."

"You mean this humanoid speaks Chinese?" Griffin was never sure whether Kung was ribbing him or not.

"Not Chinese. The vocabulary is different but the syntax and phonemes are nearly identical. I'll speak it perfectly in a week. It's just a question of memorizing two or three thousand new words. Incidentally, Joe wants to know why you're digging up his bottom land. He was all set to flood it today."

"Don't tell me he plants rice!" Griffin exclaimed.

"I don't imagine it's rice, but it needs flooding whatever it is."

"Ask him how many humanoids there are on this planet."

"I'm way ahead of you, Griffin. He says there are only a few thousand left. The rest were all destroyed in a war with the barbarians."

"Barbarians?"

"They're extinct."

"How many races were there?"

"I'll get to that if you'll stop interrupting," Kung

rejoined testily. "Joe says there are only two kinds of people, his own dark, straight-haired kind and the barbarians. They have curly hair, white skin, and round eyes. You'd pass for a barbarian, according to Joe, only you don't have a faceful of hair. He wants to know how things are going on the other planets."

"I suppose that's my cue to break into a cold sweat and feel a premonition of disaster." Griffin tried to smile and almost made it.

"Not necessarily, but it seems our iron-age man is fairly well informed in extraplanetary affairs."

"I guess I'd better start learning the language."

Thanks to the spadework Kung Su had done in preparing hypno-recordings, Griffin had a working knowledge of the Rational People's language eleven days later when he sat down to drink herb-infused hot water with Joe and other Old Ones in the low-roofed wooden building around which clustered a village of two hundred humanoids. He fidgeted through interminable ritualistic cups of hot water. Eventually Joe hid his hands in the sleeves of his robe and turned with an air of polite inquiry. *Now we get down to business*, Griffin thought.

"Joe, you know by now why we're digging up your bottom land. We'll recompense you in one way or another. Meanwhile, could you give me a little local history?"

Joe smiled like a well nourished bodhisattva. "Approximately how far back would you like me to begin?"

"At the beginning."

"How long is a year on your planet?" Joe inquired.

"Your year is eight and a half days longer. Our day is three hundred heartbeats longer than yours."

Joe nodded his thanks. "More water?"

Griffin declined, suppressing a shudder.

"Five million years ago we were limited to one planet," Joe began. "The court astronomer had a vision of our planet in flames. I imagine you'd say our sun was about to nova. The empress was disturbed and ordered a convocation of seers. One fasted overlong and saw an answer. As the dying seer predicted, the Son of Heaven came with fire-breathing dragons. The fairest of maidens and the strongest of our young men were taken to serve his warriors. We served them honestly and faithfully. A thousand years later their empire collapsed leaving us scattered across the universe. Three thousand years later a new race of barbarians conquered our planets. We surrendered naturally and soon were serving our new masters. Five hundred years passed and they destroyed themselves. This has been the pattern of our existence from that day to this."

"You mean you've been slaves for five million years?" Griffin was incredulous.

"Servitude has ever been a refuge for the scholar and the philosopher."

"But what point is there in such a life? Why do you continue living this way?"

"What is the point in any way of life? Continued existence. Personal immortality is neither desirable nor possible. We settled for perpetuation of the race."

"But what about self-determination? You know enough astronomy to understand novae. Surely you realize it could happen again. What would you do without a technology to build spaceships?"

"Many stars have gone nova during our history. Usually the barbarians came in time. When they didn't—"

"You mean you don't really care?"

"All barbarians ask that sooner or later," Joe smiled. "Sometimes toward the end they even accuse us of destroying them. We don't. Every technology bears the seeds of its own destruction. The stars are older than the machinery that explores them."

"You used technology to get from one system to another."

"We used it, but we were never part of it. When machines fail, their people die. We have no machines."

"What would you do if this sun were to nova?"

"We can serve you. We are not unintelligent."

"Willing to work your way around the galaxy, eh? But what if we refused to take you?"

"The race would go on. Kung Su tells me there is no

life on planets of this system, but there are other systems."

"You're whistling in the dark," Griffin scoffed. "How do you know if any of the Rational People survive?"

"How far back does your history go?" Joe inquired.

"It's hard to say exactly," Griffin replied. "Our earliest written records date back some seven thousand years."

"You are all of one race?"

"No, you may have noticed Kung Su is slightly different from the rest of us."

"Yes, Griffin, I have noticed. When you return ask Kung Su for the legend of creation. More hot water?" Joe stirred and Griffin guessed the interview was over. He drank another ritual cup, made his farewells and walked thoughtfully back to camp.

"Kung," Griffin asked over coffee next afternoon, "how well up are you on Chinese mythology?"

"Oh, fair, I guess. It isn't my field but I remember some of the stories my grandfather used to tell me."

"What is your legend of creation?" Griffin persisted.

"It's pretty well garbled but I remember something about the Son of Heaven bringing the early settlers from a land of two moons on the back of his fire-breathing dragon. The dragon got sick and died so they couldn't ever get back to heaven again. There's a lot of stuff about devils, too."

"What about devils?"

"I don't remember too well, but they were supposed to do terrible things to you and even to your unborn children if they ever caught you. They must have been pretty stupid though; they couldn't turn corners. My grandfather's store had devil screens at all the doors so you had to turn a corner to get in. The first time I saw the lead baffles at the pile chamber doors on this ship it reminded me of home sweet home. By the way, some young men from the village were around today. They want to work passage to the next planet. What do you think?"

Griffin was silent for a long time.

"Well, what do you say? We can use some hand labor for the delicate digging. Want to put them on?"

"Might as well," Griffin answered. "There's a street-car every millennium anyway."

"What do you mean by that?"

"You wouldn't understand. You sold your birthright to the barbarians."

Editor's Introduction To:

LIMITING FACTOR

Theodore Cogswell

Ted Cogswell used to give himself titles, mostly by ordering return address mailing labels from Grayarc. One proclaimed him a Brigadier General, U.S. Podiatric Corps, Retired. Another proclaimed him the Vicar General of an obscure religious order.

In real life he was a professor of English in a small college; a veteran of the Abraham Lincoln Battalion, International Brigade, in the Spanish Civil War; an excellent science fiction writer who hated to write and never turned out enough stories to live on; the publisher of an amateur magazine called *The Proceedings of the Institute for Twenty First Century Studies,* generally known as *PITSFCS* (which is pronounced just as you suspect it is); and the central figure in a number of bizarre stories, all of which are both true and more exotic than any member of the U.S. Podiatric Corps would suspect.

In a word, Ted was not always what he seemed. Neither are the people in his stories. Empires may be founded by supermen; but there are other ways as well.

LIMITING FACTOR

Theodore Cogswell

The beautiful girl slammed the door shut behind her and for a moment there was silence in the apartment. The blond young man in baggy tweeds looked at the closed door uncertainly, made a motion as if to follow her, and then stopped himself.

"Good boy," said a voice from the open window.

"Who's there?" The young man turned and squinted out into the darkness.

"It's me. Ferdie."

"You didn't have to spy on me. I told Karl I'd break off."

"I wasn't spying, Jan. Karl sent me over. Mind if I come in?"

Jan grunted indifferently and a short stocky man drifted in through the window. As his feet touched the floor, he gave a little sigh of relief. He went back to the window, leaned out, and looked down the full eighty stories to the street below.

"It's a long way down there," he said. "Levitation's fine, but I don't think it will ever take the place of the old-fashioned elevator. The way I look at it is that if Man was intended to fly, he'd have been born with wings."

"Man, maybe," said Jan, "but not superman. Want a drink? I do."

Ferdie nodded. "Maybe our kids will take it as a matter of course, but I just can't relax when I'm floating. I'm always afraid I'll blow a neuron or something and go spinning down." He gave a shudder and swallowed the drink in one gulp. "How did it go? Did she take it pretty hard?"

"Tomorrow will be worse. She's angry now and that acts as a sort of emotional anesthetic. When that wears off, it's really going to hurt. I don't feel so good myself. We were going to be married in March."

"I know," said Ferdie sympathetically, "but if it's any

consolation, you're going to be so busy from now on that you won't have much time to think about it. Karl sent me over to pick you up because we're pulling out tonight. Which reminds me, I'd better call old Kleinholtz and tell him he'll have to find himself a new lab technician. Mind if I use your phone?"

Jan shook his head mutely and gestured toward the hallway.

Two minutes later, Ferdie was back. "The old boy gave me a rough time," he said. "Wanted to know why I was walking out on him just when the apparatus was about ready for testing. I told him I had a sudden attack of itchy feet and there wasn't much I could do about it." He shrugged. "Well, the rough work's done, anyway. About all that's left is running the computations and I couldn't handle that if I wanted to. It's strange, Jan— I've spent a whole year helping him put that gadget together, and I still don't know what it's for. I asked him again just now and the tight-mouthed old son of a gun just laughed at me and said that if I knew which side my bread was buttered on, I'd get back to work in a hurry. I guess it's pretty big. It's a shame I won't be around to see it." He moved toward the window. "We'd better be on our way, Jan. The rest will be waiting for us."

Jan stood irresolute and then slowly shook his head. "I'm not going."

"What?"

"You heard me. I'm not going."

Ferdie went over to him and took him gently by the arm. "Come on now, boy. I know it's hard, but you've made your decision and you've got to stick to it. You can't pull back now."

Jan turned away sullenly. "You can all go to hell! I'm going after her."

"Don't be a fool. No woman is worth that much."

"She is to me. I have been a fool, but I'm not going to be any longer. I was a pretty happy guy before you people came along. I had a job I liked and a girl I loved and the future looked good. If I backtrack fast enough, maybe I'll be able to salvage something. Tell the rest I've changed my mind and I'm pulling out."

The short stocky man went over and poured himself another drink. "No, you're not, Jan. You aren't enough of a superman to be able to forget those poor devils down there." He gestured at the peaceful city that spread out below them.

"There won't be any trouble in our time," Jan said.

"Or in our children's," agreed Ferdie, "but there will be in our grandchildren's and then it will be too late. Once the row starts, you know how it will come out. You've got an extra something in your brain—use it!"

Jan looked out into the night and finally turned to answer. Before he could, an angry voice suddenly boomed inside his head.

"What's holding you up over there? We haven't got all night!"

"Come on," said Ferdie. "We can argue later. If Karl is wound up enough about something to telepath, it must be important. Me, I'll stick to the telephone. What's the point to having a built-in transceiver, if you have to put up with a splitting headache every time you use it?" He stepped to the window and climbed up on the sill. "Ready?"

Jan hesitated and slowly climbed up beside him.

"I'll go talk to Karl, anyway," he said. "Maybe you're right, but it still hurts like hell."

"The head?"

"No, the heart. All set?"

Ferdie nodded. They both closed their eyes, tensed, and drifted slowly up into the night.

Karl was stretched out on the couch with his head in Miranda's lap and a look of suffering on his face. She was gently massaging his temples.

"Next time use a telephone," said Ferdie as he and Jan came in.

Karl sat up suddenly. "What took you so long?"

"What do you mean, so long? An aircab would have got us here a lot quicker, but we're supermen—we've got to levitate."

"I'm not amused," said Karl. "Are you all set?"

Ferdie nodded. "All ties broken and everything prepared for a neat and tidy disappearance."

"And him?" Karl looked narrowly at Jan.

"He's all right."

"Yeah, I'm fine," said Jan.

"Girl and job dumped down the drain. Do you want the details? Ferdie's boss figured he'd be back. He said Ferdie knew which side his bread was buttered on. My girl didn't say anything; she just slammed the door in my face. And now that that's over, if you'll just detail me a female I'll start breeding little supermen for you. How about Miranda? She's one of the elect."

"Climb off it, Jan," Karl said sharply. "We know it wasn't easy, but dramatics won't help."

Jan threw himself sullenly into an overstuffed chair and stared morosely at the ceiling.

Karl pulled himself to his feet and made a quick survey of the room. ". . . thirty-seven, thirty-eight—I guess we're all here. Go ahead, Henry. You've got the floor."

A tall, prematurely gray man began to speak quietly. "It's got to be tonight. There is heavy cloud cover over Alta Pass that goes up to twenty thousand feet. If we're careful, we should be able to take off without detection. I suggest we leave at once. It'll take some time to move the ship out of the cave and we want to be on our way before the weather clears."

"Check," said Karl. He turned to Miranda. "You know your job. The ship will be back to pick up the new crop in ten months or so."

"I still think you should leave somebody else behind," she objected. "I can't listen twenty-four hours a day."

"You're just looking for company," Karl said impatiently. "The unconscious mental signals that mark the *change* go on for a week or more before the individual knows anything is happening. You'll have plenty of time to make contact."

"Oh, all right, but don't forget to send a relief back for me. It's going to be lonely with all of you gone."

Karl gave her a short but affectionate kiss. "O.K., gang, let's go."

The engine room of the ship consisted simply of an oval table with ten bucket seats spaced equidistantly around it. At the moment, only one of them was occupied. Ferdie sat there, his eyes closed and his face pale and tense. As a hand touched his shoulder, he jumped, and for a moment the ship quivered slightly until the new mind took over.

Ferdie ran his hands through his hair and then pressed them against his aching temples. Then he stood up. There was a slight stagger to his walk as he pulled himself up the ladder into the forward observation room.

"Rough shift?" said Jan.

Ferdie groaned. "They're all rough. If I'd known how much work was going to be involved in this superman stuff, I'd have arranged to be born to different parents. You may think there is something romantic about dragging this tin ark through hyperspace by sheer mental pressure, but to me it feels like the old horse-and-buggy days with me as the horse. Mental muscle, physical muscle—what's the difference? It's still plain hard work. Give me an old-fashioned machine where I can sit back and push buttons."

"Maybe this was your last turn at the table." Jan looked out at the gray nothingness on the other side of the observation port. "Karl says we're due to pull out of warp this evening."

"And by the time we look around and find that Alpha Centauri has no suitable planets, it'll be my turn to pull us back in again."

Late that evening, a bell clanged through the ship. A moment later, all ten seats in the engine room were occupied.

"Brace yourself and grab hold," snapped Karl. "This is going to take a heap of twisting."

It did. Three times, figures collapsed and were quickly replaced by those waiting behind them, but at last they broke through into normal space. With a sigh of relief, they all relaxed. Karl reached over and switched on the ship intercom.

"How does she look up there, Ferdie?"

"Alpha Centauri blazing dead ahead." There was a slight pause. "Also there's a small man in a derby hat directly off the starboard bow."

Those in the engine room deserted their posts and

made a mad dash for the forward observation compartment. Ferdie was standing as if transfixed, staring raptly out into space. As Karl came up and grabbed his arm, he pointed with a shaking finger.

"Look!"

Karl looked. A plump little figure wearing a severely cut business suit, high-buttoned shoes, spats, and a derby hat was floating a scant five yards from the observation port. He waved cheerily at them and then opening the briefcase he carried, removed a large sheet of paper. He held it up and pointed to the words lettered on it in large black print.

"What does it say?" demanded Karl. "My eyes don't seem to be working."

Ferdie squinted. "This is insanity."

"It says that?"

"No, I do. It says, 'May I come on board?' "

"What do you think?"

"I think we're both crazy, but if he wants to, I say let him."

Karl made a gesture of assent to the figure floating outside and pointed aft to the airlock. The little man shook his head, unbuttoned his vest, and reached inside it. He twiddled with something for a moment and then disappeared. A split second later, he was standing in the middle of the observation compartment. He took off his hat and bowed politely to the jaw-dropped group.

"Your servant, gentlemen. My name is Thwiskumb— Ferzial Thwiskumb. I'm with Gliterslie, Quimbat, and Swench, Exporters. I was on my way to Fomalhaut on a customer service call when I noted an odd disturbance in sub-ether, so I stopped for a moment to see what would come out. You're from Sol, aren't you?"

Karl nodded dumbly.

"Thought so," said the little man. "Do you mind if I ask your destination?"

He had to repeat the question before he was able to get a coherent answer. Ferdie was the first to recover enough from shock to say anything.

"We were hoping to find a habitable planet in the Alpha Centauri system."

Mr. Thwiskumb pursed his lips. "There is one, but

there are difficulties. It's reserved for the Primitives,
you see. I don't know how the Galactic Council would
view settlement. Of course, the population has been
shrinking of late and there's practically nobody left on
the southern continent." He stopped and thought. "Tell
you what I'll do. When I get to Fomalhaut, I'll give the
Sector Administrator a call and see what he has to say.
And now if you'll excuse me, I don't want to be late for
my appointment. Gliterslie, Quimbat, and Swench pride
themselves on their punctuality."

He was reaching inside his vest again when Karl
grabbed his arm. The flesh felt reassuringly solid.

"Have we gone insane?" begged the leader.

"Oh, dear me, of course not," said Mr. Thwiskumb,
disengaging himself gently. "You're just a few thousand
years behind on the development cycle. The migration
of the Superiors from our home planet took place when
your people were still in the process of discovering the
use of fire."

"Migration?" repeated Karl blankly.

"The same thing you're off on," said the little man.
He removed his glasses and polished them carefully.
"The mutations that follow the release of atomic power
almost always end up in the evolution of a group with
some sort of control over the *terska* force. Then the
problem of future relations with the Normals comes up,
and the Superiors quite often decide on a secret migration to avoid future conflict. It's a mistake, though.
When you take a look at Centauri III, you'll see what I
mean. I'm afraid you'll find it a depressing place."

Placing his derby firmly on his head, he gave a genial
wave of farewell and disappeared.

A wild look was in Karl's eyes as he held up his arms
for silence.

"There's just one thing I want to know," he said.
"Have I or have I not been talking to a small man in a
derby hat for the past five minutes?"

Forty-eight hours later, they pulled away from Centauri
III and parked in free space until they could decide
what they wanted to do. It was a depressed and con-

fused group that gathered in the forward observation compartment to discuss their future.

"There's no use wasting time now talking about what we saw down there," said Karl. "What we've got to decide is whether we're going to push on to other solar systems until we find a planet that will suit our needs, or whether we are going to return to Earth."

A little red-headed girl waved her hand.

"Yes, Martha?" Karl said.

"I think we are going to have to talk about what we saw down there. If our leaving Earth means that we are condemning it to a future like that, we're going to have to go back."

There was an immediate objection from a tense young man in horn-rimmed glasses.

"Whether we go back or ahead will make little difference in our lifetimes, so we can't be accused of personal selfishness if we don't return to Earth. The people it will make a difference to are our descendants. That strange little man who materialized among us two days ago and then vanished is a concrete demonstration of what they can be—if we stay apart and develop the new powers that have been given us. I say the welfare of the new super-race is more important than that of the Ordinaries we left behind!"

There was a short muttering of agreement as he sat down.

"Next?" Karl asked.

Half a dozen people tried to get the floor at once, but Ferdie managed to get recognized.

"I say go back!" he stated. "And since the previous speaker was talking about accusations let me say that I can't be accused of personal bias, either. As far as I'm concerned, I would just as soon spend the next several years cruising around to the far corners to see what's up. But the longer we're gone, the harder it will be to fit ourselves back into normal society.

"Look, we left Earth because we thought it was the best thing for mankind. And when I say mankind, I mean the Normals, the parent race. What we saw down there—" he gestured in the direction of Centauri III—"is dramatic proof that we were wrong. It would seem that a scattering of Superiors is somehow necessary to keep human society from collapsing. Maybe we act as a sort of essential catalyst or something. Whatever it is, we're needed. If we walk out on Man, we'll never be able to live with ourselves in our brave new world."

Karl looked worried. "I think I agree with you," he said, "but if we go back, we'll be dumped into the old problem of future relations again. Right now there are so few of us that if we were found out, we'd be looked upon as freaks. But what's going to happen when our numbers start to shoot up? Any group that has special powers is suspect, and I don't relish the thought of condemning our descendants to a world where they'll have to kill or be killed."

"If worst comes to worst, they can always take off the way we did," replied Ferdie. "But I'd like to point out that migration was the first solution proposed and the one we've given all our attention to. There must be other ways out, if we look for them. We've got to give it a try, anyway." He turned to the young man in the horn-rimmed glasses. "How about it, Jim?"

The other nodded reluctantly. "I'm dubious, but maybe we should go back and make the try you've been talking about." His voice sharpened. "Under one condition, though. If the Normals start to give us any trouble, we get out again!"

"I'll agree to that," said Ferdie. "How about the rest of you?"

The ayes had it.

There was a sound of polite applause from the doorway. Mr. Thwiskumb had returned. "A very wise decision," he said, "very wise. It demonstrates a commendable social maturity. I am sure your descendants will thank you for it."

"I don't know what for," said Karl sadly. "We're robbing them of all the things that you have. Instantaneous teleportation, for example. It's no particular sacrifice for us—we're just starting to develop the powers within us—but it will be for them. I don't know if we are right, asking them to pay such a price."

"What about the other price?" demanded Ferdie. "What about that scrawny grimy gang down on Centauri

III, sitting apathetically in the hot sun and scratching themselves? We also have no right to condemn the Ordinaries to a future like that."

"Oh, you wouldn't be doing that," said Mr. Thwiskumb mildly. "Those people down there aren't Ordinaries."

"What!"

"Dear me, no. They weren't the ones that were left behind. They are the descendants of those who migrated. Those poor devils down there are pure-blooded Superiors. When they ran into the limiting factor, they just gave up."

"Then what accounts for you? You're obviously a Superior."

"That's a very kind thing to say," answered the little man, "but I'm just as ordinary as anyone can be. We're all Ordinaries where I come from. Our Superiors left a long time ago." He chuckled. "It's a funny thing—at the time, we didn't know they were gone, so we didn't miss them. We just went about business as usual. Later, we found them, but it was already too late. You see, the big difference was that we had an unlimited area of development and they didn't. There's no limit to the machine, but there is to the human organism. No matter how much training you have, there is a limit to how loud you can shout. After that, you have to get yourself an amplifier.

"A slight neural rearrangement makes it possible for you to tap and control certain sources of physical energy that aren't directly available to the ordinary man of your planet, but you are still dealing with natural forces . . . and natural organic limits. There is a point beyond which you can't go without the aid of the machine, an organic limiting factor. But after several generations spent in mastering what is inside your heads, rather than struggling for control of the world around you, and the time comes when your natural limits are reached, the very concept of the machine has been lost. Then where do you go from there?"

He waited for an answer, but nobody offered one.

"There is an old story in our folklore," he continued, "about a boy who bought himself an animal somewhat like your terrestrial calf. He thought that if he lifted it above his head ten times a day while it was little, he would build up his strength gradually until he would still be able to lift it over his head when it was a full-grown animal. He soon discovered the existence of a natural limiting factor. Do you see what I mean? When those people down there reached their natural limits, there was no place for them to go but backward. We had the machine, though, and the machine can always be made smaller and better, so we had no stopping point."

He reached inside his vest and pulled out a small shining object about the size of a cigarette case. "This is hooked by a tight beam to the great generators on Altair. Of course I wouldn't, but I could move planets with it if I wanted to. It's simply a matter of applying a long enough lever, and the lever, if you'll remember, is a simple machine."

Karl looked dazed. In fact, everyone did.

"Yeah," he muttered, "yeah, I see what you mean." He turned to the group. "All right, let's get back to the engine room. We've got a long flight ahead of us."

"How long?" asked the little man.

"Four months if we push it."

"Shocking waste of time."

"I suppose you can do better?" Karl inquired belligerently.

"Oh, dear me, yes," said Mr. Thwiskumb. "It would take me about a minute and a half. You Superiors dawdle so—I'm glad I'm normal."

Jan was doing a happy little dance through his apartment when his buzzer rang. He opened the door and Ferdie stepped in.

"I came up on the elevator," he said. "It's a lot easier on the nerves. My, you look pleased with yourself. I know why, too—I saw her coming out of the lobby when I came in. She walked as if she were wearing clouds instead of shoes."

Jan did a little caper. "We're getting married next week and I got my job back."

"I got mine back, too," said Ferdie. "Old Kleinholtz gave me a lecture about walking out on him when work was at its heaviest, but he was too pleased with himself to do more than a perfunctory job. When he took me back into the lab, I saw why. He's finally got his gadget running."

"What did it turn out to be? A time machine?"

Ferdie grinned mysteriously. "Something almost as good. It lifts things."

"What kind of things?"

"Any kind. Even people. Old Kleinholtz had a little set of controls rigged up that he could strap to his chest. He turned the machine on and went flying around the lab like a bird."

Jan's jaw dropped. "The way we do?"

"Just the same, boy. He's found a way to tap the *terska* force. Really tap it, not suck little driblets out, as we do. Another ten years and the Ordinaries will be able to do anything we can do, only better. And a good thing, too. Telepathy gives us headaches, and levitation is a pleasant Sunday afternoon pastime, but hardly something to build a civilization on. As Mr. Thwiskumb said, the machine has no natural limits, so I guess our worries about the future are over. Nobody is going to be unhappy about us being able to fly thirty miles an hour when they can make it instantaneous. Looks like superman is obsolete before he even had a chance to get started."

He stretched his arms and yawned. "Guess I'd better get home and hit the sack. It's going to be a busy day at the lab tomorrow."

He walked over to the open window and looked out.

"Flying home?" asked Jan.

Ferdie grinned and shook his head. "I'm waiting until the new improved model comes out."

Editor's Introduction To:

TRIAGE

William Walling

The news this week tells us of floods in Bangladesh: they have denuded the high ground of trees, and now the low ground floods. There is nothing to eat. Food shipments are urgently needed.

Bangladesh has one of the highest rates of population growth on Earth.

We like to believe we have rational control of our lives, but how much history depends on personal accidents? Henry II of England spent many of his evenings getting drunk with his knights. He does not seem to have been an actual alcoholic. He also suffered from chilblains and piles. Were they especially painful the night that Henry drunkenly muttered "Will no one rid me of this meddlesome priest?" A week later Thomas à Becket, Archbishop of Canterbury, was dead in his cathedral. Henry accepted responsibility for the order he claimed he had never intended to give, and seemed genuinely penitent; but the history of the English church and state was changed forever.

Sometimes, too, what seems coldly rational is not. Robert S. McNamara and his Pentagon "Whiz Kids" attempted to subordinate military strategy and doctrine to a mathematical technique called "systems analysis." The notion was that military judgment was flawed; what was needed was "objective criteria." In practice that meant numbers; and soon a great part of our effort in Vietnam was devoted to collecting statistics. One USAF colonel, examining our efforts against North Vietnam, pointed out a new way to make the attack more effective—and was told "Colonel, you have the wrong idea. We're not trying to destroy targets, we're flying sorties and delivering weapons tonnage." The stories about body counts are too well known to need repeating.

Decisions can and should be rational; but those who make the decisions remain human.

TRIAGE

William Walling

(Tre-áhzh) [*Fr. "sorting"*]. Classification of casualties of war, or other disaster, to determine priority of treatment: Class 1—those who will die regardless of treatment; Class 2—those who will live regardless of treatment; Class 3—those who can be saved only by prompt treatment.

> We have met the enemy, and he is us.
> From Walt Kelly's cartoon strip, *Pogo*.

The man waited with outward patience, standing stiff-backed, knees together, opposite the desk where a nervous male secretary feigned work under his punishing scrutiny. Seemingly quite at ease, the man was tall, forceful in appearance, with a proud aquiline nose, sleek dirty-blond hair, and chill hazel eyes. The wrap-around collar of his pearl-gray jacket was buttoned even though a power brownout had once again paralyzed Greater New York during the night and early morning hours, leaving the anteroom overwarm and stuffy.

The secretary darted occasional furtive looks toward the tall man. At last, their glances crossed. The secretary squirmed. "Sorry . . . for the delay, Mr. Rook. I can't imagine what's keeping her."

"Madame Duiño is busy, Harold." The man folded his

arms. "Don't trouble yourself; pretend that I'm not here."

"Yes, sir." The secretary plunged back into his paperwork. When the intercom buzzed, moments later, he said hastily, "You can go right in now, sir." The inner door eased shut; the secretary looked immensely relieved.

The office of Dr. Victoria Maria-Luisa Ortega de Duiño, Chairperson of the Triage Committee, UN Department of Environment and Population, was as severe and desiccated as the woman herself. A blue-and-white United Nations ensign hung behind her desk on the left; on the right, atop a travertine pedestal, the diorite bas-relief presented to her by Emilio Quintana, Mexico's preeminent sculptor, depicted a stylized version of UNDEP's logo; the globe of Earth, with a set of balanced scales and the motto TERRA STABILITA superimposed across it. A pair of guest chairs hand-crafted of clear Honduras mahogany were adrift upon a sea of wall-to-wall shag the color of oatmeal. Save for an old-fashioned French pendulum clock, and the floor-to-ceiling video panels—now dark—Sra. Duiño's sanctum was enclosed by barren oyster-white walls. Lined damask draperies shrouded a picture window overlooking the East River ninety floors below.

Rook did not take a seat. He chose a spot just inside the door, studying the old woman with an indolent expression.

If aware of the man's presence, Dr. Duiño gave no sign, occupying herself with the sheaf of papers before her on the desktop. Her hair, as short and brittle as her temper, was roached stiffly backward to form a platinum aura; her features were wrinkled, sagging, though her eyes retained the dark and shining luster of youth. Around her frail neck, pendant against the lace mantilla thrown over her shoulders, was a large silver crucifix. In six months and eleven days, Victoria Duiño would celebrate her eighty-eighth birthday. She was the most reviled and detested human on Earth.

"My apologies, Bennett." The old woman looked up at last. "Please sit down. I had not intended to keep you away from your desk so long."

"Quite all right, Victoria." The tall man made it a point to remain standing. "I take it the matter is pressing?"

"No. Not really." She touched a button: a hologram condensed in the largest video tank across the office, allowing them to eavesdrop on a courtroom scene. Now in its penultimate stages, the trial was taking place half a continent away. "I merely wish to assure myself that we were obtaining full PR value from the Sennich Trial," she said. "Have you been following it?"

Bennett Rook turned with leisurely grace. He listened briefly to the defense attorney's final plea. "Alas, no," he said. "Actually, I've been too busy. Is it the gluttony action you mentioned in your memo?"

The old woman made no rejoinder. Her interest in the trial was exclusively political. In her mind, the guilty verdict soon to be handed down was a foregone conclusion. One Nathan Sennich, and a pair of miserable codefendants, had resurrected the ancient sin of gluttony, which reflected but one symptom of an ailing society in her opinion. But, for UNDEP, the trial carried important propaganda overtones; widespread public indignation, fanned by tabloid journalism, had begun to create a welcome avalanche of letters and calls. If UNDEP press releases were to add fuel to the fire, were to milk the sordid affair for all it was worth . . .

"The gall of those swine!" she said. "In a starving world, they dared slaughter and gorge themselves on the roasted flesh of a fawn stolen from Denver's zoo."

Rook's lip curled. His voice was resonant, unruffled. "Grotesque, Victoria. But I can't imagine what's in it for us. In forty-eight hours, or less, the remains of our mischievous gourmands will be fertilizing crops in Denver's greenbelts: or perhaps those of the Denver Zoo itself. Poetic justice, eh?"

"Don't make light of it." A throaty burr crept into Sra. Duiño's voice. "I asked you to get PR cracking on this action. You have ignored my request. We stand to reap a certain amount of public sympathy if trial coverage is properly handled, Bennett."

"We?" The man's brows lifted. "Triage Committee? Nothing could improve our image, Victoria. Day before yesterday, *L'Osservatore Romano* once again referred to you as the 'Matriarch of Death.' PR abandoned all attempts to 'sell' the committee years ago."

"You know perfectly well what I meant," said the old woman tautly. "Bennett, must we always fence? Can't you ever sit down and converse with me sociably?"

Rook smiled an arctic smile. He rocked on his heels, returning her stare with steadfast calm. "There are several matters we shall never see in the same light, Victoria. Nothing personal, you understand; if you want the truth, I rather like you. If I did not, I would tell you so. I am no hypocrite."

"No," she agreed, "you are not a hypocrite. Blunt, perhaps; but not a hypocrite."

He made a slight gesture, turning over the flats of his hands. "Blunt, then, if you will."

Dr. Duiño watched him with unwinking concentration. "I want your cooperation," she said, "not your enmity."

Rook sighed. "I'd rather not discuss it."

"Why not? Are you afraid?"

Rook tensed the least bit. "I'm afraid of nothing. Pardon me; of almost nothing."

"Your use of a qualifier makes me curious."

"My only fear," he said slowly, "is for the continuation of our species."

"And mine, Bennett. But that is what we are laboring so earnestly to ensure."

"To little avail," he said.

"That is not a fair and reasonable statement."

"Oh?" Rook stood firm under her withering gaze, his eyes aglow with patriotic fervor. "You are familiar with this week's global delta, of course."

Victoria Duiño hesitated. "I am. It is most encouraging —less than one-quarter of one percent."

"Bravo!" Rook clapped his hands in genteel emphasis. "Despite our sanctions, proscriptions, lawful executions and extensive triage judgments; despite floods, earthquakes, plagues, and the further encroachment of desertlands upon our remaining arable soil, there are now some twenty-five thousand *more* human beings on Earth than the nine and three-quarter billions we could not feed last week. And you tell me all's right with the world."

Sra. Duiño looked taken aback. After a moment, she said quietly, "Zero population growth will be a reality in one and one-half to three years."

"Too damned little, Victoria—too damned *late*. With sterner measures, we would be on the downslope instead of approaching the crest."

"I am familiar with your views," said the woman. " 'Sterner measures,' as you call them, would have made us less than human. I refuse to subscribe to inhumanity as a cure-all for the world's ills."

"Humane philosophy is a luxury we cannot afford."

"Bennett, Bennett! You are intelligent, industrious, thoroughly dedicated; that is why I selected you from the crowd these many years past. But have you no compassion, no slight twinge of conscience for the dreadful judgments we must pass day after day, month after month, year after year?"

"None," said Rook. "It's an interesting facet of human nature; mortal danger to a single individual—the victim of a mine disaster, or someone trapped in a fire—never fails to stimulate a tidal wave of public sympathy, while similar disasters affecting gross numbers are mere statistics, hardly worth a shrug. We do what must be done. We do it analytically, dispassionately, dutifully. Were it otherwise, there would be no sane committee members."

"I . . . see. And you think me a senile, idealistic old fool who should step aside and allow a younger individual, such as yourself, to chair the committee?"

Bennett Rook stood perfectly still. "Senile? Hardly. Your mind is clear and sharp as ever; you are one of very few who can best me in debate. Idealism I will not answer; I am not qualified. But you are less of a fool than anyone I have ever met. I admire you vastly, respect you enormously, even love you in my own manner, perhaps. Yet, given the opportunity, I would replace you tomorrow."

"Because I am too soft?"

"Because you are too soft," he said.

"Thank you for stopping by, Bennett. May I remind

you once again to prod PR on the Sennich Trial coverage?"

"I'll take care of it immediately," Rook tipped his head; there was nothing sarcastic about his deference. "Good day, Victoria." His eyes were veiled as he left the office.

In silent reflection, Victoria Duiño gazed at the closed door for quite some time before resuming her labors.

And the Egyptians will I give over into the hand of a cruel lord; and a fierce king shall rule over them, saith the Lord, the Lord of hosts.

And the waters shall fail from the sea, and the river shall be wasted and dried up.

(Isaiah 19:4,5)

In midafternoon, the intercom's buzz interrupted Victoria Duiño's train of thought. "Yes, Harold?"

"Cardinal Freneaux is in the anteroom, madame. And your granddaughter is calling—channel sixteen."

She glanced at the clock. "If I am not mistaken, His Eminence made an appointment for three. It is not but two fifty-eight. Surely he will allow me two minutes to indulge my only grandchild."

"Surely he will, madame. I will tell him."

"Thank you, Harold." Keeping one eye and a portion of her attention on a flashing digital readout, Dr. Duiño switched on the vidicom. "Monique, I can't talk very long just now. I trust that you and Stewart are well?"

"Hello, Grandma." The image that formed in the small tube was of a petite, attractive young woman whose dark hair was in disarray. Her eyes were red-rimmed, desperate.

Victoria Duiño straightened in her chair. "What is it, child? What has happened?"

"I've got . . . big troubles, Grandma."

"What sort of troubles? Can I help?"

"Oh, God, I hope so! I . . . doubt it. I just got back from the doctor. I'm . . . in the family way, if you know what I mean."

"Monique!" Sra. Duiño clutched the arms of her chair. "How did this happen? Were you careless?"

"No. I don't know. I . . . took my pills. I never missed. I just don't know, Grandma. Fate, I guess—or bad luck."

After the first flush of emotion had washed through her, Victoria relaxed and began to think. She seized a yellow legal pad and a stylus. "I want to know where you buy your birth-control tablets."

"What? But, Grandma, what does that have to do with—?"

"Never mind, child. Just tell me. I assume you buy them regularly in one specific place?"

"Uh, yes. At Gilbert's Pharmacy here in the arcology complex. But I—"

"Have you any left?"

"A few," said the younger woman. "I think. Yes; a few."

"Send them to me. Mail them this afternoon—special delivery, and insure the package. Address it to Harold Strabough, United Nations Tower, and beneath the address write the initials V.M.L. That will assure prompt attention. I should receive it tomorrow."

"I . . . all right, Grandma. I will. Oh, Stew's so broken up; we would have been approved for parenthood within the year. What can we do?"

"Leave that to me."

"Can you . . . ? Do you think you can do something?"

"I think so, Monique. I want you to be as calm as you can about this. Follow the doctor's instructions verbatim, and let me know at once if any complications arise."

"Grandma, wh . . . what will they do to me—to my baby?"

"Nothing, for the time being," said Dr. Duiño with assurance. "Unauthorized birth is a crime; unauthorized pregnancy is not. We have many months to effect a solution. Don't be afraid."

"Stew's talking kind of wild," said her granddaughter. "He's been raving about running off to Brazil."

"Hum-m-mph! To live in the jungle with the other outcasts, I suppose. Think about that, Monique. Would the Amazon Basin be a fit place for Stewart and yourself to raise an infant? It is a jungle, just now, in more ways than one. You wouldn't last long enough to give birth, let alone build anything more than an animal existence for yourselves."

"Are you sure, Grandma?"

"Absolutely certain," said the old woman. "I am in a position to know. Do exactly as I have advised. I'll call you later in the week when we have more time to chat. Above all, don't despair, my dear. Until later, then."

"God bless you, Grandma. And . . . thank you. I love you."

Seething inside, Victoria switched off the vidicom. She permitted herself the use of an expletive not in keeping with the dignity of her high office, then seized her bamboo cane and rose stiffly to stand upright, her mind whirling. Monique's call had come at a most inopportune moment; she had only seconds to contemplate its ramifications before receiving the Cardinal.

Diminutive and birdlike, she hunched beside the desk, squinting down at the carpet. It was an attack, of course. But from what quarter? She had been the victim of numberless attacks, both political and physical, during her long career. She had survived eleven attempts on her life, attempts ranging from clumsy bunglings like the homemade bomb thrown by that theology student in Buenos Aires, which had permanently impaired the hearing in her right ear, to the ingenious poisoned croissants, four years ago, which had resulted in the death of a loved and trusted friend.

The old woman heaved a sigh, feeling something wither and die inside her. Damn them! There was no time to think about it now. No time. She closed her eyes tightly, washing the residue of Monique's call from her mind, and pressed the intercom button. She hobbled to mid-office, leaning on her cane.

His Eminence Louis Cardinal Freneaux stood framed in the doorway, a wasted figure whose rich robe hung loosely about him. Victoria knew that he made it a point of honor to limit his caloric intake to something commensurate with that of the most deprived member of his vast flock. She respected him for it, and considered him one of the more intelligent churchmen in her acquaintance. Beneath the red skullcap, the Cardinal's eyes were lackluster and sad.

"You are looking very well, my dear," he said.

"Thank you, Louis. At my age, I can't imagine a nicer compliment." She bent stiffly as if to kiss the prelate's ring.

"That . . . is not necessary," he said, withdrawing. "My visit is official, I'm afraid."

Sra. Duiño straightened slowly. "Is it to be like that?"

"Please don't be offended, Victoria."

"I take it the Holy Father is even more displeased with me than usual," she said. "I am truly sorry to have caused him further pain. What is it this time?"

"Egypt."

The old woman nodded once. She turned slowly and stumped toward her desk, motioning the Cardinal to a chair. "Four million inhabitants of the Nile Delta, formerly Class Three, were declared Class One last week. I fear there was little choice: the vote was unanimous."

"Deplorable!" said the Cardinal.

"No one deplored its necessity more than I. Damanhûr, El Mansûra and Tanta, Zagazig, El Faiyûm and El Minya share the fate of numberless villages scattered along the dry gulch that was once a mighty river."

"There are many Coptic Christians in Egypt," said Cardinal Freneaux. "They have petitioned the Holy See for redress."

"Oh?" Victoria's dark eyes flashed. "And why, pray, have they not petitioned the Father and Teacher in Moscow who refuses to allow them to help themselves? More than a decade ago, UNDEP warned of what the Aswan Dam was doing to the Nile. The weight of Lake Nasser upon the land, swollen by spring floods in East Africa, helped create a severe seismic disturbance; the upper Rift Valley developed a subsidiary fracture, and the river found a new path through Nubia to the Red Sea. Today, Cairo is a dusty ruin, as dead and forgotten as the pyramids to the west."

"Rationalization is useless, Victoria." The Cardinal frowned. "We must be practical."

"*Practical*, is it? In modern Egypt, more than three

thousand *fellahin* crowd every remaining square mile of arable land. *Something* had to give, Louis."

The Cardinal coughed apologetically. "Four million . . . somethings," he said in a low voice.

Victoria Duiño reacted as if the Cardinal had slapped her. "That was unkind of you. They are four million helpless human beings; they work and love and have aspirations and laugh together on rare occasions, even as you or I. Unfortunately, they also have appetites. Do you—does the Holy Father—suppose that we *enjoy* our work?"

"Of course not, Victoria."

"Then why does he refrain from exercising whatever influence he has over Eastern Orthodox churchmen inside the Soviet Union? Why can't they aid in making the Kremlin realize that its insensate drive for world domination is literally starving millions? With Soviet help instead of hindrance our triage activities would dwindle significantly."

Cardinal Freneaux made a small sound of disgruntlement. "You know how little public opinion is worth in Russia."

Sra. Duiño silently recited a Hail Mary, allowing her temper to subside. She tapped a stylus on the desktop. "Louis, the impoverished portion of the Third World sprawling across Africa, Asia Minor, and the Arabian Peninsula is a Russian creation; it is perpetuated solely as a political weapon. Soviet-controlled military forces outnumber UN forces two to one; we are powerless to inflict our wills upon the Third World, save for the Indian subcontinent and South America, except as Russia allows. The Great Northern Bear graciously condescends to permit triage judgments rendered wherever and whenever we choose, then points a long propaganda finger and calls us 'murderers of millions.'

"But let us suggest something *beneficial*, such as the Qattara Project, and the Bear immediately exercises his veto. The measure dies without question of recourse."

Cardinal Freneaux looked uncomfortable. "I am not familiar with the project," he dissimulated, hoping against hope to divert the old woman's waxing anger.

"Really?" Victoria's eyes radiated pale fire. She spun

a tickler file, then touched a series of buttons on the video controller. A full-color map of the Middle East formed in the large tank. "Just southwest of Alexandria is El Alamein, a town of some historical significance. Near there, Britain's armored forces turned back those of Nazi Germany in one of the climactic land battles of the Second World War.

"Which is neither here nor there, except that Britain chose that particular site to make her winner-take-all stand for an excellent reason. To the uninitiated, it would have seemed easy for Rommel's *Panzers* to swing out into the open desert, avoiding Montgomery's trap on his drive toward Alexandria and the Suez. Such was not the case; on a larger scale, the area is a corridor much like Thermopylae, and British strategy much like that of the Greeks who stood off the Persian hordes in classical times. You see, Rommel had neither the petrol, nor supplies, to skirt a huge natural obstacle.

"Let your eye drift southward from El Alamein, Louis. See the long crescent marked Qattara Depression? It is a vast sink rather like Death Valley, which lies between the Libyan Plateau and the Western Desert, and is more than four hundred feet below the level of the Mediterranean in most places.

"UNDEP's ecosystems engineers proposed a fifty-kilometer-long canal, excavated by use of 'clean' mini-fusion devices from a point east of El Alamein to the depression. A hydroelectric power station was to have been built on the brink: seventy years would have been required for a large, fan-shaped inland sea to form, stretching from Siwa Oasis near the Libyan border to the foundations of the pyramids at El Giza, with a long neck reaching southward along the Ghard Abu Muharik almost to El Kharga. The Qattara Sea would have altered the climate of the Western Desert, bringing rainfall to the parched, rich soil; in ancient times, much of the region was a garden. Egypt could have reclaimed millions of hectares of arable land, helping to alleviate her perpetual famine.

"The Father and Teacher in Moscow vetoed the proposal out-of-hand." With an abrupt gesture, Victoria switched off the video map. "Pardon me; I did not mean to lecture."

Cardinal Freneaux shifted disquietedly in his chair. "You make it sound so brave and simple. The situation is much more complex. Visionary schemes, such as this Qattara Project—"

"There is nothing 'visionary' about it," she said in an icy tone. "I could name a dozen similar UNDEP proposals vetoed by the USSR."

The Cardinal ran his tongue around his upper lip. He rose and began pacing the office, hands clasped behind his back. "The Church is not blind," he said. "Russia's geopolitical game is far from subtle. Yet the Bear is not to be provoked, Victoria. His Holiness dreads war. Have you any concept of the carnage thermonuclear weapons would wreak among the vast populations of Asia, Africa, Europe, and the Americas?"

"I have indeed; a global holocaust would either extinguish our species, or reduce our numbers to something the Earth could once again tolerate. Triage on a grand scale, Louis."

The Cardinal was aghast. "How can you even *think* such a thing?"

The old woman shrugged. "There are wars, and then there are wars. We are engaged in a global war right this instant, and one of the major battles is taking place in Egypt. If His Holiness refuses to recognize this fact, I am hard-put to explain it."

"I've never heard you speak like this before, Victoria."

Victoria sighed. "I suppose my optimism and diplomacy have begun to wear out, like the rest of me." She searched the Cardinal with her eyes. "No, that isn't true. Louis, we are not winning the war just yet. But, we will—must! There are, after all, only three alternatives left: triage, Armageddon, or a sniveling decline that is certain to end in a whimper."

Cardinal Freneaux remained silent for a time. "Our conversation has wandered far afield," he said. "Victoria, do you consider yourself a good daughter of the Church?"

"You know that I do."

The churchman pondered something invisible which

had obtruded between himself and the old woman. He
cleared his throat. "His Holiness was unusually stern
when he dispatched me on this mission. He instructed
me to plead immediate reclassification of the four million inhabitants of the Nile Delta. He urged me strongly
not to take 'no' for an answer."

Victoria Duiño looked solemn. "Then the stern Father
must discover that he has an equally stern daughter,"
she said. "My answer must be . . . no. Battles are
never without casualties; grain shipments to Egypt have
already halted."

"I warn you; he has spoken of excommunication."

The old woman grew very pale, very calm. "And do
you expect me to be intimidated by such a threat?"

"I do not. I have known you too long."

"I am literally amazed that the Holy Father would
stoop to attack me personally, would choose to threaten
damnation of my immortal soul in order to destroy me
professionally. Were he to carry out this awful threat, it
would mean absolutely nothing to the Triage Committee or its works. Doesn't he realize that?"

"I'm not . . . sure."

Victoria fingered her crucifix. "Louis, what have we
come to? The Church, our Church, has grown quite
permissive on the question of homosexuality, now coun-
tenances therapeutic abortion, even condones euthana-
sia when the pain of life becomes too great for her sons
and daughters to bear, yet obstinately faces away from
the fact that without triage judgments our planet will
never again be a fit environment for the human species."

"Discussion is painful to me. I must ask you for a
definite answer, Victoria."

"You have had it. Tell His Holiness that the Matriarch of Death considers eternal fire a small price to pay
for the work she does, and must continue to do."

The Cardinal's eyes were misted. He bowed. "Then I
will bid you good-bye, my dear Victoria. I sincerely
hope that our next meeting will be more pleasant."

"I hope so."

The causal chain of the deterioration is easily followed
to its source. Too many cars, too many factories, too

much detergent, too much pesticide, multiplying con-
trails, inadequate sewage treatment plants, too little
water, too much CO_2—all can be traced easily to too
many people.

                    Dr. Paul Ehrlich, *The Population Bomb*

Monique's package arrived in late forenoon the following day, Dr. Duiño sent two of the suspect birth-
control tablets to the UN lab for analysis, receiving a
report in less than one hour. Properly stamped with the
infertility symbol, the placebos lacked the chop of any
pharmaceutical house, and were therefore quite illegal.
If found, the seller would be liable to harsh prosecution.

After an evening snack of thin vegetable soup and
soya toast, Sra. Duiño retired to her quarters high on
the two-hundredth floor, feeling roughly battered by
life. She had been attacked from the left and the right,
from above and below.

She pondered Monique's problem all evening, sitting
alone in the cramped two-room suite. She rarely left
the UN Tower nowadays; there would be little purpose
in it. Almost everything that remained in her life was
here: her meager creature comforts, the small chapel
on the twelfth floor where she heard mass and went to
confession—more and more infrequently of late—and
her work.

Sudden nostalgia spun her mind back to the early
days in Argentina when Vicky Ortega, a serious-minded
medical student newly risen from the tumbled shacks
and endemic poverty of a Buenos Aires *barrio,* had
visited the clinic and been lovestruck at first sight of a
young doctor named Enrique Duiño. Love had come in
the blink of an eye, in the macrocosmic slice of eternity
it had taken for the handsome doctor to look at her
infected throat and prescribe three million units of pen-
icillin and bedrest.

Oh, she had pursued him; no mistake about that—
two months of thoroughly premeditated "accidental"
encounters, while her studies went neglected and she
lived in terror of losing him.

But she remembered the miraculous day when she
had led Enrique up a crooked, debris-strewn alley to

the ramshackle lean-to her parents and brothers and sisters called home, the day Enrique had turned his hat brim slowly, nervously in his deft surgeon's hands while he asked her father's permission to make her his bride. Later, mentioning the five children she'd prayed God would allow them to have, Vicky had received the lecture which was to change her life.

In those days, Enrique had been a walking encyclopedia, stuffed with demographic statistics, facts and figures on family planning, on the fantastic rate at which the world's population was doubling, on the coming extinction of fossil fuels, and on and on. They, he had insisted, would have *one* child—two at most. At first, Vicky had been horrified, then resentful, then fascinated.

Their first decade together had been an exciting hodge-podge: the missionary hospital in Bolivia; their studies together in Madrid, and at the Sorbonne, and later in Mexico; finally, the years in America and, somewhat late in life, the birth of young Hector Duiño. That had been the richest, most tranquil period, Victoria reflected. Enrique and she had practiced in San Francisco, and in New York; the boy had grown to manhood almost overnight, so it seemed. And when Enrique's crusading articles won him selection as a delegate to the third International Population Control Convention in New Delhi, she had been so proud, even though her practice had kept her home in New York.

Curiously enough, Enrique had always tended to neglect his own health. When the cholera epidemic erupted, he had refused to be flown home with the majority of other delegates, staying on in India to lend what help he could. The first prognosis from the hospital where they had taken him had been favorable. But Victoria had had an ugly premonition. All her prayers had gone unanswered; her beloved had come home in a plain wooden casket.

The ensuing years of loneliness melted into a blur—long years of struggle and disappointment. She had carried on Enrique's great work, making a nuisance of herself by shouting his message into deaf political ears. But at last—not too late, perhaps; but *very* late—after the Mideast conflagration which all but destroyed Israel and placed the whole of Islam under Russia's thrall, she and the other criers-in-the-wilderness had at last been heard. After much panicking and pointing of fingers, the UN peacekeeping troops had been bolstered and united into a true international armed force. Then— could it be nearly twenty-five years ago?—UNDEP's Triage Committee had been formed. Dr. Duiño had been its first and only chairperson.

The old woman raised withered hands. There were times when she imagined she could see light streaming through the mottled parchment stretched over her bones. Where was pretty little Vicky Ortega now? Submerged in this twist of exhausted flesh, she supposed.

She rose with the aid of her bamboo cane and shuffled to the window. It was after midnight, and fairly clear. She looked up at the few visible stars for a time, then stood gazing far out over the inky wash of the Atlantic into the depths of night.

Two days later, a preliminary report arrived from the UN Intelligence Agents who were investigating the bogus birth-control tablets. The assistant manager of Gilbert's Pharmacy, thirty-third layer, twelfth sector, northwest quadrant of the gargantuan arcology complex where Monique and her husband lived, had recently applied for parenthood. Pressure was brought to bear— and a hint of amnesty if full cooperation were forthcoming. During the ensuing week, the trail led from the pharmacy to a disreputable retired chemist in Cleveland, to a thrice arrested though never convicted Philadelphia dealer in black-market pharmaceuticals, to a drug wholesaler with shady connections in Trenton, and finally to the legman for a prominent Congressman. A second week passed before the UN Intelligence Director called Sra. Duiño and mentioned a name.

"Are you certain?" she asked, stiffening.

"No, madame. There's no way short of a trial to be certain, and I doubt whether the DA would indict upon the sort of evidence we've managed to gather."

"Are you yourself certain?"

"I . . . yes, madame. I myself am quite certain."

"Thank you for all your efforts," she said. "Please make sure your findings remain confidential."

Dr. Duiño snapped off the vidicom and sought her cane. She stumped from the office, startling Harold and three VIP's who were waiting to see her. She rode upward in the private lift, failed to acknowledge everyone who greeted her in the corridor, and spent the remaining afternoon hours closeted with her fellow Triage Committee members behind closed doors.

Late the following day, Victoria entered Bennett Rook's anteroom, breezing past his receptionist unannounced.

The inner office was crowded: Rook was at the chalkboard, running over some statistics with a group of underlings. He telescoped the collapsible pointer he had been using. "Dr. Duiño. To what do we owe this honor?"

"I must speak to you at once in private." She shooed them out with her cane, causing a concerted fumbling for notebooks and other papers. The UNDEP employees filed out, studiously avoiding one another's eyes.

When the door closed behind the last straggler, she said, "Is this room safe?"

"Quite safe, Victoria."

The old woman inspected Rook analytically. "Well, is it to be 'wroth in death, and envy after'? Or will you bargain?"

"Pardon me?"

"Come, come, Rook; bluffing was never your forte. If for some reason I should choose to step down," she said, speaking slowly, distinctly, "will you allow my granddaughter to bear her child in peace?"

"Why, certainly, Victoria. As I once told you, I'm not a hypocrite."

"No," she said, "merely a . . . !" She choked off the gutter term that came to her lips. "May I ask what I have done to you to deserve *this*?"

"Personalities aren't involved," he said. "It's the job—the job you are *failing* to accomplish. You left me no choice."

The old woman swayed, leaning heavily on her cane. Rook moved as if to help her, but she fended him off, saying sharply, "Please keep your hands to yourself."

Settling herself in a chair, Victoria Duiño looked up

at the man, her eyes bright. With measured intonation, she enumerated certain facts concerning an assistant pharmacy manager, a Cleveland chemist, a Philadelphia dealer in pharmaceuticals, a drug wholesaler, and a Congressman's stooge.

Rook was nonplused. "Thorough," he said smoothly. "You've been very thorough, as I anticipated. You realize, of course, that such 'evidence' would never hold up in court."

"No district attorney, judge, or jury will ever hear it."

"Then, how——?"

"Tomorrow morning," directed the old woman sternly, "you will personally arrange official parenthood sanction for my granddaughter and her husband. Spare me the seamy details of how the deed is to be accomplished."

"And . . . if I refuse?"

Victoria's smile was thin, totally lacking in humor— the smile of a canary who has successfully evaded the cat. "I visited with the other seven members of our committee yesterday, Rook. They all seemed quite eager to see things *my* way. Persist in your endeavor, and you will find yourself out on the street, looking in. Discovering another meal ticket might become a serious problem."

Bennett Rook took a moment to digest this information. "Then I suppose you have won," he said at last.

"Yes, I suppose so. As such things are reckoned."

"Do you blame me?" Rook sounded the injured party. "I'm not really an orge, Victoria. You've lived long, worked hard; you've seen the world change into something ill and decrepit. Was it so despicable to try and force you to lay down your burden and rest?"

"It was," she said, "though I don't expect you to understand why. You are not a flesh and blood creature, Rook; no juices of life flow within you. You are cold and rational—both a superb asset, and a potentially terrible liability to triage activities."

"I'll make the necessary arrangements tomorrow," he said.

Victoria Duiño nodded. "Good. Now that we understand one another, I have a bombshell for you; the

Matriarch of Death has at last decided to abdicate. Not, however, because of your foolish blackmail scheme.

"You were correct, Rook: I am indeed old, feeble, and used up. And tired—very tired. You strike at me through my grandchild; His Holiness attacks me through my faith; my name is anathema from Antarctica to Greenland, and all around the world."

"You've managed to amaze me, Victoria."

"Furthermore," she went on, disregarding his incredulous stare, "had you refrained from this silly coup, you might well have been elected Chairperson of the Triage Committee next week. As it is, while eminently qualified, you have proved yourself utterly unworthy."

"Bitter gall." Rook grimaced. "That does sting, Victoria. But don't count me out just yet. I—"

"Hear me, Bennett!" She twisted the cane savagely in her hands. "This will be our final encounter, and I intend to have the last word. I want to clarify something, now and forever; something you *must* comprehend.

"You have repeatedly condemned my triage philosophy as being too lenient, too soft. It is not. Triage is, and has always been, a concession to the inevitable, not premeditated mass-murder. Twenty-five years ago, in the white heat of a new crusade, we set a rather idealistic goal: semi-immediate reversal of runaway overpopulation. We were dismayed to find it not that simple. How can an illiterate Third Worlder, whose single recreation in an otherwise drab existence is sex, be persuaded to remain chaste during his wife's fertile period?

"But now, whether you care to acknowledge it or not, a dim glow brightens the far end of the tunnel. We faced cold facts, long ago, asking ourselves whether it would be wiser to disrupt every socioeconomic system on Earth by seeking a quick solution, or to wage a strategically paced, long-range war. The latter policy is saner, more practical, and far more humanitarian; the ultimate solution may lay farther in the future, but victory is also much more assured.

"I will not live to see even a partial victory; nor, in all likelihood will you, Rook. But my great-grandchild-to-be, whose strange godfather you are, might do so—

if you and the others make the best possible use of the varied technological weapons we will someday have at our disposal: new bio-compatible pesticides, new hybridized grains, reclamation of desertlands, perhaps interplanetary migration.

"As in any war, we will face mini-triumphs and small setbacks, major victories and hideous defeats; we must bear up equally under good fortune and adversity alike. We must take what we have to take, and give what we have to give to re-create a world where my great-grandchild-to-be can enjoy a noble, cheerful life, a world where a gallon of potable water is not a unit of international exchange, where reusable containers are not an article of law, where food is abundant and air is fit to . . ."

Victoria broke off, shaking her head sadly. "I can see that I am wasting breath. Very well; if you choose to have your lesson the hard way, so be it. I wish you luck; you will need all you can get."

The old woman labored to rise. Though he dared not help her, Bennett Rook came forward half a step despite himself. She did not deign to look at him again, making her way slowly to the door, dignity pulled tightly about her like a cloak.

Her mind at peace, Victoria went to her quarters and phoned St. Patrick's Cathedral. She spent two minutes persuading the young priest who buffered all incoming calls that she was indeed who she said she was. Finally, he allowed her to speak to Cardinal Freneaux.

"Oh, Louis, I'm so glad; I was afraid you had already left the city. I called to invite you to have dinner with me."

"Delighted, my dear Victoria." He sounded pleased and surprised. "I had made other plans, but they can be changed."

"This is an occasion," she said. "A UNDEP news bulletin of some importance will be released tomorrow morning. I want you to be the first to know. May I come by for you in an hour, Louis?"

"Fine! That will be fine. I'll look forward to seeing you."

She dressed without haste—the black gown reserved

for formal affairs—and slipped on a diamond bracelet
Enrique had given her many years before. She had
difficulty fastening the clasp of an emerald brooch at
her neck.

When she was ready, she took up a large satin hand-
bag, the fancy black cane with the ivory tip, and called
down to the garage. The electric limousine and its driver,
accompanied by omnipresent UN Security Agents, were
waiting for her outside the tower's staff entrance.

They rode in silence, with the windows rolled up
despite the muggy summer evening. With keen interest,
Victoria watched the defeated multitudes overspilling
the sidewalks; four hours, and more, remained until the
midnight curfew. They crawled west through dense traffic on East 48th Street, turning right at Fifth Avenue.

When the limousine nosed its way into an enormous
queue of hungry supplicants gathered outside St. Patrick's Cathedral, Dr. Victoria Maria-Luisa Ortega de
Duiño crossed herself.

Editor's Introduction To:

HYPERDEMOCRACY

John W. Campbell, Jr.

"Theodore White (among many others) describes the shift in national attitude toward welfare from 'equality of opportunity' to 'equality of result' as a fundamental change. The sponsors of the Civil Rights Act of 1964, with Hubert Humphrey in the lead, had come down adamantly on the side of equality of opportunity—the nation was made color-blind. The wording of the legislation itself expressly dissociated its provisions from preferential treatment. Yet only a year later, speaking at Howard University commencement exercises, Lyndon Johnson was proclaiming the 'next and most profound stage of the battle for civil rights,' namely, the battle 'not just for equality as a right and theory but equality as a result.' A few months later Executive Order 11246 required 'affirmative action.' By 1967, people who opposed preferential measures for minorities to overcome the legacy of discrimination were commonly seen as foot-draggers on civil rights if not closet racists.

"A number of writers have pointed to a combination of two events: the ascendancy of legal stipulation as the only guarantor of fair treatment and the contemporaneous Balkanization of the American population into discrete 'minorities.' "

Charles Murray, *Losing Ground: American Social Policy 1950–1980*

Cicero tells us that the trouble with oligarchy is that the government has too much power; but in a democracy, the brilliant and able have no way to better themselves without destroying the nation.

The United States was founded on a different principle, of *liberty* rather than *democracy* or *equality*.

We forget that at our peril.

John Campbell wrote this editorial in 1958. It could have been written today.

HYPERDEMOCRACY

John W. Campbell, Jr.

So far as I can make out, there is such a thing as an excess of anything you can name. There's the old gag that you can get drunk on water . . . just as you can on land. But it's also true that you can become intoxicated by too much water. Hard to do, of course, but it's a medical fact. Too much oxygen can produce quite a tizzy, too.

Too much truth, unmodified by good sense and understanding, can be destructive, also. The "catty" woman frequently uses truth as her weapon to hurt.

I rather imagine the following comments are going to call forth howls of wrath from a good many sources. Nevertheless, I feel that they constitute painful truths that need to be examined.

I propose for debate the proposition: "The United States is suffering from an acute attack of excessive democracy."

First, it needs to be determined whether or not there can be such a thing as an excess of democracy—too much equality.

The original purpose of the democratic concept was to establish the value of the individual—the right of the Freeman individual to think for himself, and to work for himself, as against the older concept of the individual as an entity owned by the state. The original intent of democracy was to allow the individual to achieve the full development of his individual potentials, unlimited by such arbitraries as aristocracy-of-birth, or other arbitrarily imposed restrictions. That all men were to have equal opportunity to develop their own valuable potentials.

In hyperdemocracy, however, the democratic concept is subtly, and malignantly, shifted to hold that all men should *be* equal—that *individually achieved* developments should be equal.

This is *not* the same thing as equality of opportunity, since it actually imposes an arbitrary limitation on the right of the individual to achieve his maximum potentials. Equality of opportunity, however, is exceedingly hard to demonstrate!

Suppose two individuals, Tom and Dick, are given equal opportunity to develop their individual abilities. Tom winds up a millionaire, and Dick winds up on a skimpy retirement pay. The objective evidence clearly shows that Tom and Dick did not have equal opportunity, doesn't it?

Yes, it does. Tom had superior opportunities; he had the gift of learning very rapidly, so that, exposed to the same information sources, and the same situations Dick was, Tom learned fifteen times as much. Tom, going to the same school Dick did, learned that Columbus discovered America . . . and that Leif Ericson probably landed in Labrador five or six centuries earlier. That various French and Spanish pioneers explored the area of the western United States, but that the Lewis and Clark expedition was more important.

And Dick, having answered the school examinations properly, knew that he had learned what the proper citizen was supposed to learn.

But Tom, having answered the school examinations the same way Dick did, learned something quite different. "It doesn't do much good to open a pathway if people don't want to go there. There's no point in discovering a continent until people need a new continent. There's no use exploring a new territory until people are present to move in, and want a new territory to move into." That was a great help to Tom in later life, when he was organizing the companies and enterprises that made his millions.

Dick had the same opportunities to learn . . . but Tom had an unfair, arbitrary opportunity not given Dick. Something *not* education, but inherent, gave Tom a greater ability to learn from the data offered him.

In hyperdemocracy, inequality of results is considered proof of inequality of opportunity. Inequality of what level of opportunity? Is innate, God-given ability undemocratic? Something to be suppressed, punished, ground out, so that we can have absolute equality?

But this isn't democracy! Democracy implies giving each free individual the right to develop his own talents as best he may—so long as those talents are not destructive to others. (Talented assassins will be suppressed, of course.)

To hold that results must be equal is to violate the central intent of true democracy—that each individual shall have equal opportunity to develop his abilities.

A hyperdemocracy, if such existed, would have the characteristic of seeking to force individuals to conform to an arbitrary norm—neither rising above the "proper" level, nor allowing them to lag below. It would seek to punish individuals who advanced beyond the norm—who showed "undemocratic" superiority of actual ability. It would confuse superior *ability* with superior *opportunity*. It would insist that no individual had any right to marked superiority of achievement—that the true proof of democratic equality of opportunity was equality of results. That innate difference did not, and of a right should not, exist. That anyone who claimed innate differences did exist was undemocratic—and that anyone who demonstrated that such differences existed was criminally undemocratic, and should be punished for his anti-democratic actions.

Lopsided superiority, with compensating hopeless deficiencies, would be tolerable, of course. A Steinmetz, a brilliant cripple, wouldn't be anti-democratic, because, of course, his physical deformity makes him average out not-superior. The genius must be crippled, one way or another, either physically, or mentally, or he is unacceptable in a hyperdemocratic concept. The brilliant scientist must be an oddball of some sort, or he's unacceptable. To suggest that individuals exist who are genuinely, innately superior is, in the hyperdemocratic concept, intolerable.

And I'm defying every rule of our present hyperdemocracy by bringing these propositions into the open. I'm suggesting that there are human beings who have innate, unmatchable-by-education talents of genuine superiority that you haven't got a prayer of achieving—things that neither training, practice, education, or anything else can ever give you or me.

First: A hemophiliac bleeds by reason of a genetic anomaly. It's not due to training, education, or lack of opportunity to learn something. You don't have that defect. Then, with respect to the hemophiliac you have an innate superiority, due to genetic difference—and it is unarguably a survival superiority.

You didn't earn that superiority; it was given you by your ancestors. (They, one might say, earned it.)

In the same way, a Peruvian Indio can play football at 15,000-foot elevation. You can't. Even if you trained for five years, you still wouldn't have the fundamental biochemical adaptations that generations of selective breeding have given the Peruvian. He can use a lower oxygen-tension, and get successful displacement of the CO_2 from his blood. You can't; you never will be able to. It's not learnable. I can't, and don't kid myself that I can.

I saw an article on the biochemical adaptations of the Peruvian Indios in the *Scientific American* a couple of years ago; it was a fine piece of objective reporting . . . down to the last paragraph. In that, the researcher felt forced to specifically state that it was not proper to conclude that it was a genetic superiority—that, in fact, any human baby born and raised at 15,000-foot altitudes would undoubtedly display the same type of adaptation.

That last statement is no doubt true. Their tests showed that an American engineer who'd been living at 14,000 feet for many years was able to perform on their treadmill for only eight minutes; their Indio subjects had worked on it for as long as ninety minutes. If a man in excellent health, after years of adaptation, could manage only eight minutes of work on the treadmill—could a woman survive the period of labor in childbirth? Conclusion: undoubtedly a child born and raised at that altitude would show the Peruvian Indio adaptations. He'd *be* a Peruvian Indio; no woman of other racial stock without those adaptations could bear a child there.

What made the scientist who did that report add that gratuitous—and invalid!—statement that the data did not indicate an innate superiority of altitude adaptation?

In a hyperdemocracy, we don't acknowledge innate differences not correctable by education and training. Not even if we've found one . . . unless we want to raise the wrath of misguided super-democrats. And universities don't, these days, like to annoy the populace.

(How long has it been since an American university raised a real, angry debate by a firm, open statement contrary to popular ideology? The only time our modern, remarkably spineless universities get into controversies is when they get caught in a squeeze between two opposed groups of the populace. The conflicts are never of their own doing! The universities that were, once, the leaders of thought are, today, remarkable for their fast footwork in following public opinion trends.)

It's a self-evident fact that mammalian species can be bred for special characteristics; what men have done with dogs, horses, and other animals is rather incontrovertible evidence that selective breeding can, and does, produce marked variations of type.

Is Man a mammalian species or not?

There are sports, mutants, among other species. Only a hyper-democratic philosophy could maintain that there aren't among men, too!

The essence of hyperdemocracy is the denial of the right to difference—the *denial of individuality*. In that, it is the exact reverse of true democracy; democracy insists on the importance of the rights of the individual. Hyperdemocracy, in essence, says, "The rights of the individual are sacred . . . but there aren't any individuals, because we're all just alike."

"Togetherness" . . . "belonging" . . . "conforming" . . . "adjusting to your environment" . . . these are all denials of the propriety of having individuality.

The United States has, I suggest, fallen for that philosophy, hook, line, and sinker. And it's sinking us. Our educational system is accepting the philosophy of the convoy—"Proceed at the maximum pace of the slowest member"—with disastrous results. "Togetherness" is a fine idea . . . but not when it means slowing down the class to the pace of the high-grade moron that happens to be the slowest member. Mustn't drop the incompetent back a grade; it might damage his precious ego.

Yes? What's the resultant crawl doing to the egos of the stultified bright students?

When a "Social Studies" teacher assigns *three* pages of text, for studying every *two* days, in a sixth-grade class . . . whose precious, incompetent ego is being protected? And at what cost?

And what's with this "Social Studies," anyway? They used to call it Geography, and History, and Civics, make it three courses, and require that the students learn something, or get dropped back a grade.

So its a painful shock to a child to be rejected from his group! So what? If he's earned it, why should not he get a boot in the rear? He's going to get some rugged shocks when he gets out of that educational system!

Or . . . wait, maybe he isn't. They're certainly doing everything possible to make the real world of adult work just as cushioned and protected as that cockeyed educational hothouse. Advancement in a job isn't to be determined by individual ability, but by seniority. It isn't fair to advance a young man over twenty others who've been with the company for a dozen years of faithful service just because the young man happens to be a clear, quick, fruitful thinker, and accomplishes things, is it? Would it be democratic to let a young man develop his individual abilities like that, at the risk of injuring togetherness? No . . . in our adult world of real work, we're rapidly installing the principle our schools have established; each individual must be promoted with his class, incompetence to the contrary notwithstanding.

But the shock is coming just the same. Those nasty Communists in Russia have the idea that they can overtake the United States by setting the pace not at the convoy pace of the maximum speed of the slowest—but at the maximum speed a working quorum can maintain. Hard on the slower ones, of course . . . but it'll be even harder on other nations, won't it?

There seems to be a basic law of the Universe that is correctly and accurately expressed in our Declaration of Independence in saying that among the inalienable rights of Man is the right to the *pursuit* of Happiness. The framers of that document had more sense than our modern educational philosophers; they did *not* say that a man had a right to Happiness.

The law of the Universe seems to be, "You have a right to try anything . . . but that doesn't guarantee the right to succeed!"

From the hyperdemocratic viewpoint, unusual achievement is *de facto* proof of antisocial behavior. It is not proper for any individual to achieve markedly more than his neighbors by ability; only lucky accidents—which could happen to anyone—are tolerable, because they are unearned benefits.

If you doubt that is the present philosophy in the United States, notice how it is embodied in the income tax laws. A "tax" of ninety percent or more is not a tax—it's a confiscatory fine. It's a punitive measure, intended to make the culprit cease and desist. Which any relatively sane individual would, of course, do. The present income tax laws are designed to prevent any individual *earning* by his own productive efforts, any great economic power. Any great economic reward for outstanding ability. He is punished for insisting that he has exceptional talents that *earn* reward—insisting on it by that most obnoxious of all methods, demonstrating the ability.

However, it's not antisocial to get rich by a lucky accident; it's *earning* advantages that's obnoxious. If they accidentally happen to you, that's not antisocial. Therefore the capital gains tax is a true, reasonable tax—about twenty-five percent. Thus if you are lucky, and accidently discover an oil well, and make ten million or so, that isn't *earned* income, and you aren't punished for it. There's only a twenty-five percent capital gains tax.

If, however, you make an invention, and license the invention to many companies, and the invention is of great value so that your royalties amount to $10,000,000 —that's antisocial. It's well-earned income, and is punishable with a ninety percent fine. That's what you get for trying to be smart, instead of merely lucky.

There is, of course, the fact that patents represent an effort to achieve an advantage by being smart, by thinking out problems and devising ingenious solutions. That, obviously, is anti-hyperdemocratic, and would be attacked in a hyperdemocracy.

A patent is a license to sue; it's a government-granted right to a time-limited monopoly, enforceable by the courts.

If the courts show a consistent record of enforcing that monopoly, a consistent record of validating the concept of patents, protecting the inventor, the tendency to violate a patent will be small. But if the courts show an acute disinterest in protecting the inventor's rights, if they usually disallow patents brought before them, patent-violators have little reason to worry, and a strong temptation to violate the inventor's patent.

The record of the United States courts over the last two decades indicates that an inventor can, generally, expect his patent to be invalidated if it is brought to trial. Bringing it to trial is extremely expensive, and offers little probability of eventual reward.

The result is that patents aren't of much value to individuals; only large, well-heeled corporations can afford to use the pressure of legal harassment to make their patents work.

The Department of Justice is equalizing that situation, however. The Bell Laboratories and IBM, two of the greatest industrial research and development organizations, have already been forced, by anti-monopoly suits, to surrender their patent rights. The Justice Department is currently gunning for RCA.

There's a lot of wild hullabaloo about the United

States educational system, currently. Well, the nation is, after all, a democracy in the sense that the votes of the majority determine what shall be done. The clear vote of the majority over the last decades has been "We don't want leaders who show us what we *need;* that's frequently uncomfortable. We want servants who give us what we *want.*"

People *want* the proposition "My little Johnny is just as smart as anybody else, even if he is somewhat of a moron," to be validated. They wanted it, and they got an educational system based solidly on that postulate.

They did not want an educational system based on the proposition, "Those who can't think, can't graduate." That was the type of system we did have. It made a lot of people unhappy. And that's terrible, of course, because most people know that the Declaration of Independence guarantees us the right to Happiness, doesn't it?

No, it doesn't. The right to try *and fail* must be protected just as rigorously as the right to try and succeed.

We've tried to wipe out the right to fail . . . and have very nearly wiped out the right to earned achievement.

I was looking over a current Social Studies textbook; in it there is a recitation of the characteristics that made America great. One that interested me was "Americans Will Try Any Job."

The Pilgrims tackled a big one, when they tackled the howling wilderness of New England . . . and they won. George Washington and his fellow rebels took on the greatest military power of the time, and won. Pecos Bill and Paul Bunyan were willing to tackle anything—as were the cowboys and lumbermen of that era.

The United States of today, however, got the atomic bomb first largely because of a highly arbitrary, authoritarian, one-man decision by Franklin D. Roosevelt—who took an immense chance in tackling that job.

We got pushed into tackling the hydrogen bomb, out of pure fright. We knew that the Russians were taking on the job.

We didn't tackle the satellite problem—we teased it.

You can cite history to show that America is a great,

courageous nation, willing to tackle the big jobs, and fight its way through.

Yes . . . but that's the history of what our *fathers* were. What's the son like? You're not citing *our* achievements when you cite history—you're citing someone else's achievements.

What have we done lately?

That's a big set of oars old Pop carved out; we can't rest on things that size! And it looks like Son is a delicate flower, who must be protected from the cruel shock of getting his ears slapped down when he muffs a job, or being passed over if he's incompetent.

We've gotten so hyperdemocratic, we've gone full circle. The individual's rights are sacred . . . except for the right to be an individual, which is antisocial.

No one has a right to be different. He must be adjusted until he conforms, and appreciates togetherness.

Personally, I can't feel the slightest sense of togetherness with dopes. Nor do I feel I have an inalienable right to inflict my presence on geniuses.

And I don't like hyperdemocracy a bit better than tyranny; each denies the most important of all individual rights—

the right to be an individual!

Editor's Introduction To:

CHAIN REACTION

Algis Budrys

Just before the turn of the century, the United States shouldered aside the doddering Spanish Empire, and liberated Spain's colonies. There was strong sentiment for the immediate annexation of Cuba, but unlike Puerto Rico, Cuba became a sovereign nation.

We also inherited the Philippine Islands; which caused Rudyard Kipling to write:

THE WHITE MAN'S BURDEN

Take up the White Man's burden—
  Send forth the best ye breed—
Go bind your sons to exile
  To serve your captives' need;
To wait in heavy harness
  On fluttered folk and wild—
Your new-caught sullen people,
  Half devil and half child.

Take up the White Man's burden—
  In patience to abide,
To veil the threat of terror
  And check the show of pride;
By open speech and simple.
  An hundred times made plain.
To seek another's profit,
  And work another's gain.

171

Take up the White Man's burden—
    The savage wars of peace—
Fill full the mouth of Famine
    And bid the sickness cease;
And when your goal is nearest
    The end for others sought,
Watch Sloth and heathen Folly
    Bring all your hope to nought.

Take up the White Man's burden—
    No tawdry rule of kings,
But toil of serf and sweeper—
    The tale of common things.
The ports ye shall not enter,
    The roads ye shall not tread,
Go make them with your living,
    And mark them with your dead!

Take up the White Man's burden—
    Ye dare not stoop to less—
Nor call too loud on Freedom
    To cloak your weariness;
By all ye cry or whisper,
    By all ye leave or do,
The silent, sullen peoples
    Shall weigh your Gods and you.

Take up the White Man's burden—
    Have done with childish ways—
The lightly offered laurel,
    The easy, ungrudged praise.
Comes now, to search your manhood
    Through all the thankless years,
Cold-edged with dear-bought wisdom,
    The judgment of your peers!

That poem as much as any other has caused Kipling
to be charged with racism. He self-evidently was guilty,
although he was much less so than most people of his
time. Today, of course, we have eliminated racism.
(There is a Black Caucus in the U.S. Congress, and a
Black Social Worker's Association; there are Black Stu-

dent Unions in most universities. If their white counterparts existed they would, of course, be racist. Meanwhile, Mack Reynolds wrote tellingly of the Black Man's Burden: the obligation of blacks in the United States and Britain to take civilization to Africa. These are all surely anomalies.)

One presumes that in centuries to come, racial differences on Earth will vanish. What, though, will we find between the stars?

CHAIN REACTION

Algis Budrys

I

Dahano the village Headman squatted in the doorway of his hut, facing the early sun with his old face wrinkled in thought. Last night he'd seen omens in the sky.

For good or for bad? Dahano considered both sides of the question. Two days ago, the Masters had made an example of Borthen, his son. They'd ordered him to die, and when he'd died they hung his body on a frame in the slave village square. Dahano'd cut him down last night.

He cremated him in the hollow where generation after generation of villagers had burned. There, on the ashen ground, Dahano'd traced out the old burning-ritual signs and sung the chant. The dirge had been taught to him by his father, from his grandfather and his great-grandfather. It had been remembered faithfully from the old, great days when men had lived as they ought to live. Harsh, constricted in Dahano's dried old throat, the chant had keened up to the sky:

Here is a dead person. Take him, Heaven People—give him food and drink; shelter him. Let him live among you and be one of you forever; let him be happy, let him rest at the end of his day's labor, let him

*dwell in his own house, and let him have broad fields
for his own. Let his well give sweet water, and let his
cattle be fat. Let him eat of the best, and have of the
best, and give him the best of your women to wive.
Here is a dead person. Let him live with you.*

Then Dahano'd told the Heaven People how Borthen
had come to die before his time. In the days when
people lived as they ought to, the reason might have
been any one of many: a weak soul, bad luck that
brought him to drown in a creek or be killed by a wild
beast, or death in war. But since a time gone so long
ago that it came before Dahano's grandfather, there'd
been only one such reason to give the Heaven People:

He was killed for breaking the Masters' law.

Which is not the proper law for people, Dahano'd
added in bitterness and in the slow, nourished anger
his father'd taught him along with the stories of the
times before the Masters.

*Take him, Heaven People. Take him, shelter him, for
I can do no more for him. Let him live among you
forever, for he can no longer live here in the village
with me. Take Borthen up among you—take my only
son.*

In bitterness, in fresh anger and in old, the chant had
gone up. It made no difference that the Masters could
hear Dahano if they wanted to. Anger they let a person
keep, so long as he followed their law. Some day, in
some way, that anger would rise and tear down their
golden city, but the Masters with their limitless power
couldn't help but laugh at the thought.

Perhaps they were right. But last night, as the smoke
of Borthen's pyre rose to mingle his soul with those that
had gone before it into the sky, Dahano'd seen lights
that weren't stars, and faint threads reaching down
toward the Masters' golden city on the plain. It was as
though the souls of all the people who had burned in
funeral hollows behind all the villages were stirring at
last.

So now Dahano sat in his doorway, the last of his
line, waiting until it was time to go out and work in the
hated fields, and wondering if perhaps the golden build-

ings would come crashing down at last, and the Masters die, and the people of the villages be free again.

But it wasn't a new hope with him or with any of the other villagers. Sometimes a person was driven to believe he could overcome the Masters; rage or thoughts turned too long inward clouded his reason. He rebelled; he cursed a Master or disobeyed a command, and then his foolish hope only caused him to be commanded to die, to die, and to hang in the square. Sometimes a person in cool thought wondered how close a watch the Masters kept. He stayed in his hut when the time came to work, or stayed awake at sleeping time in the hope that the Masters didn't see into quite every person's head. These, too, were always proved mistaken and died.

Dahano kept his omens to himself. An old person learns a great deal of patience. And the Headman of a village learns great caution along with his great anger. He would wait and see, as all his life had taught him. He knew a great number of things; the proper ways to live, the ways of keeping his people as safe as a person could, and all the other things he had learned both from what his father had passed on to him and what he had thought out for himself. But most of all, he knew a slow, unquenchable, immovable waiting.

In the hut next door, he heard Gulegath clatter his cookpot noisily back down on the oven. Dahano's expression sharpened and he listened closely, trying to follow the younger person's movements with his ears.

Gulegath was an angry one. All the villagers were angry, but Gulegath was angry at everyone. Gulegath wouldn't listen to wiser persons. He kept to himself. He was too young to realize how dangerous he was. He was often rude, and never patient.

But Dahano was Headman of the village, and every villager was his concern. It was a Headman's duty to keep his people as safe as possible—to keep the village whole, to protect the generations that weren't yet born—in the end, to protect that generation which would some day come and be free. So, every person—even Gulegath—must be kept safe. Dahano didn't like Gulegath. But this was unimportant, for he was Headman first and Dahano second, and a Headman neither likes nor dislikes. He guards the future, remembers the things that must be remembered and passed on, and he protects.

Gulegath appeared in his doorway—a slight, quick-movemented person who seemed younger than he really was. Dahano looked toward him.

"Good day, Gulegath."

"Good day, Headman," Gulegath answered in his always bitter voice, shaping the words so they sounded like a spiteful curse. He was still too young to be a man; coming from his thin chest, the sound of his voice had no depth, only an edge.

Dahano couldn't quite understand the source of that constant, overpowering bitterness that directed itself at everyone and everything. It was almost a living thing of its own, only partly under Gulegath's control. No one had ever injured him. Not even the Masters had ever done anything to him. He'd burned no sons, had never been punished, had never known more sorrow than every villager was born to. This seemed to make no difference to the special beast that went everywhere with him and made him so difficult to live with.

"How soon before we go out to work, Headman?"

Dahano looked up at the sun. "A few more moments."

"Really? They're generous, aren't they?"

Dahano sighed. Why did Gulegath waste his anger on trifles? "I burned my son last night," he said to remind him that others had greater injuries.

Gulegath extended him no sympathy. He'd found a target for his anger—for now. "Some day, I'll burn *them*. Some day I'll find a way to strike fast enough. Some day I'll hang *their* bodies up for me to look at."

"Gulegath." This was coming too close to self-killing folly.

"Yes, Headman?"

"Gulegath, you're still too young to realize that's a fool's attitude. Things like that aren't to be said."

"Is there a person who doesn't think the same way? What difference if I put it in words? Do you think fear is a wise quality?" Gulegath spoke like a person looking deep inside himself. "Do you think a person should give in to fear?"

"It's not that." Slowly—slowly, now, Dahano told himself. A Headman has a duty to his people. His anger can't keep him from fulfilling it. Be patient. Explain. Ignore his lack of respect for you. "No, Gulegath. It's what too much of that kind of talk can do to you. You must try to discipline yourself. A thought once put in words is hard to change. This anger can turn over and over in your mind. It'll feed on itself and grow until one day it'll pass beyond words and drive you into self-destruction. If you die, the village has lost by that much." *If I let you die, I've failed my duty by that much.*

Gulegath smiled bitterly. "Would you grieve for me?" His mouth curled. "Let me believe that some day they'll pay for all this: Get up at a certain time, work in these fields, tend these cattle, stop at a certain time, eat again when the Masters command and sleep when the Masters tell you. Be slaves—be slaves all your aching lives or die and hang in the square to cow the others!" Gulegath clenched his thin fists. "Let me believe I'll end that—let me think I'll find a way and some day burn them in their city. Let me suppose I'll be free."

"Not as soon as that, youngster. No person can rebel against the Masters. They see our thoughts, they come and go as they please, appearing and disappearing as they can. They command a hut to appear and it's there, with beds, with its oven, with a fire in the oven. They command a man to die and he dies. What would you do against persons like that? They aren't persons, they are gods. How can we do anything but obey them? Perhaps your some day'll come, but I don't think you or I will bring it."

"What're we to do, then? Rot year after year in this village?"

"Exactly, Gulegath. Year after year after year. Rot, *save ourselves,* and wait. And hope."

He was thinking of the lights in the sky, and wondering.

II

The particular Master who oversaw this village was

Chugren. He was only a medium-tall person, too heavy for his bones, with a pasty face and red-laced eyes. Dahano had never seen him without a sodden breath or a thickness in his tongue. Any person who wasn't a Master ought to have collapsed long ago under the poisons he seemed to swill as thirstily as a villager gulping water from the bucket in the fields. His visits to the village were only as frequent as they had to be. If he thought very often at all about the village, he was too lazy and too uncaring to come and see to it properly. He contented himself with watching it from his palace among the golden spires of the Masters' city on the plains. Watching it with his drunken, stupored mind.

But this morning he was here. The villagers were just leaving their huts to go to the fields when Dahano saw the Master step out into the middle of the square and stand looking around him.

So, Dahano thought. Last night there were lights in the sky, and today Chugren comes for the first time in months.

The villagers had stopped, clustered in their doorways, and everyone looked impassively at Chugren. Then the Master's gaze reached Dahano, and he beckoned as he always had. "Come over here, Dahano."

Dahano bowed his head. "I hear, Chugren." He shuffled forward slowly, stooping, taking on a slowness and age that were feebler than his own. A slave has weapons against his master, and this was one of them. It seemed like such a trifle, making Chugren wait an extra moment before he reached him. Enough of a trifle so the Master would feel foolish in making an issue of it. But, nevertheless, it was a way of gnawing at the foundation of his power. It meant Dahano was not wholly crushed—not wholly a slave, and never would be.

Finally, Dahano reached Chugren and bowed again. "It is almost time for us to go work in the fields," he muttered.

"It'll wait," Chugren said.

"As the Master wishes." Dahano bowed and hid a thin smile. Chugren was discomfited. Somehow, the slave had scored against the Master once more, simply by reminding him that he was an attentive slave.

"There's time enough for that." Chugren was using a sharp tone of voice, and yet he was speaking slowly. "This village is a disgrace! Look at it—huts falling apart and not a move made to repair them; a puddle of sewage around that broken drain there . . . don't you people do anything for yourselves?"

Why should we? Dahano thought.

"All right," Chugren went on. "If you people can't clean up after yourselves, I suppose I'll have to do it for you. But if it happens again, you'll see how much nonsense I'll tolerate!" He jerked his arm in quick slashes of motion at the huts. He repaired the drain. In a moment, the village looked new again. "There. Now keep it that way!"

Dahano bowed. His twisted, hidden smile was broader. Another victory. It had been a long time since the last time Chugren gave in on the matter of the huts and drains. But he had given in at last, as Dahano had known he must. It was his village, built by him. His slaves had no wish to keep it in repair for him. This was an old, old struggle between them—but the slaves had won again.

He looked up at Chugren's face. "I hear, Chugren." Then he looked more closely.

He couldn't have said what signs he saw in the Master's face, but he had known Chugren for many years. And he saw now that Chugren's hesitant wordings didn't come from a dulled brain. The Master was sober for the first time in Dahano's experience. He sounded, instead, like a child who's not yet sure of all his words.

Dahano's eyes widened. Chugren glanced at him sharply as the Master saw what he knew. Nevertheless, Dahano put it in words:

"You aren't Chugren," he whispered.

The Master's expression was mixed. "You're right," he admitted in a low voice. He looked around with a rueful lift to the corners of his mouth. "I see no one else has realized that. I'd appreciate it if you continued to keep your voice down." The look in his eyes was now both discomfited and unmistakably friendly.

Dahano nodded automatically. He and Chugren stood

silently looking at each other while his brain caught up
with its knowledge.

Dahano was not a person to go rushing forward into
things he understood imperfectly. "Would the Master
condescend to explain?" he asked finally, carefully.

Chugren nodded. "I think I'd better. I think it might
be a good idea, now I've met you. And we might as
well start off right—I'm not your master, and don't
want to be."

"Will you come to my house with me?"

Chugren nodded. Dahano turned and motioned the
other villagers out into the fields. As the crowd broke
up and drifted out of the square, glancing curiously at
the Master and the Headman, Chugren followed Dahano
toward his hut. Gulegath brushed by them with a pale
look at the Master, and then they were in the hut, and
Dahano took a breath. "You don't want to be our Master?" His hands were trembling a little bit.

"That's right." It was odd to see Chugren's features
smile at him. "Your old Masters are gone for good. My
men and I took their places last night. As soon as
possible, we're going to set you people completely
free."

Dahano squatted down on the floor. It was Chugren's
voice and face, though nothing like Chugren's manner.
He studied the person again. He saw Chugren, dressed
in Chugren's usual loose, bright robe, with his dough
coloring and pouched eyes. And under them was a
sureness and firm self-possession quite different from
the old Master's drunken, arbitrary peevishness. Dahano
was not sure how all this could be—whether this was
somehow a trick, or somehow an illusion, or where this
false Chugren had come from. But he knew he would
find out if he had patience.

"I saw lights in the sky last night. Was that you?"

Chugren looked at him with respect. "You've got
sharp eyes, Headman. We had to take the screen down
for an instant so we could get through—but, still, I
didn't think anyone would spot us."

"Screen?"

"I'd better start at the beginning." Chugren made
chairs for them, and when they were both sitting, the

Master leaned forward. "I wish I knew how much of this will come through. I've been trying to build up a vocabulary, but there are so many things we have and do that your people don't have words for."

Dahano was curious. How could that be? There was a word for everything he knew. It was possible there were words he hadn't learned—but, no words at all? He mulled the idea over and then put it away. There were more important things to busy himself with.

Chugren was still preoccupied with that problem. "I wish I could explain all this directly. That'd be even better. But that's out, too."

Dahano nodded. This part was understandable to him. "The Masters told us. Their minds are made differently from ours. They could not even see into ours clearly unless we were angry or excited."

"You're not organized to send messages direct. I know. We used to think it was our instruments, but we ran into it no matter how we redesigned."

"Instruments?"

Chugren pulled up the sleeve of his robe. Strapped to his upper arm were two rows of small black metal boxes. "We weren't born Masters. We use machines—like a person uses a mill instead of a pestle to grind his grain—to do the things a Master does with his mind. Only we can do them better that way. That's how we were able to surprise your Masters last night and capture them."

Dahano grunted in surprise.

"You see," Chugren said, "there aren't any Masters and slaves where I and my men come from. Any man can be a Master, so no one can enslave anyone else. And of what conceivable use is a slave when you can have anything you want just by making it?"

Dahano shook his head. "We have thought on that."

Chugren's nod was grim. "We thought about it, too. We've been watching this world from our . . . our boat . . . for weeks. We couldn't understand what your Masters wanted. They didn't eat your grain or cattle, they didn't take you for personal servants—they never took you to their city at all. Not even your women. Why, then?"

"For pleasure. We thought on it for a long time, and there is no other answer." Dahano's eyes were sunk back in their sockets, remembering Borthen's body hanging on its frame in the village square. "For pleasure."

Chugren grimaced. "That's the conclusion we reached. They won't come back here . . . re-education or no re-education . . . sick or well, Dahano—ever."

Dahano nodded to himself, staring off at nothing. "Then it *is* true—you're here to free us."

"Yes." Chugren looked at him with pity in his eyes. "You've gotten out of the habit of believing what a Master tells you, haven't you?"

"If what he says is not another of his commands, yes. But I don't think you are like our Masters."

"We're not. We come from a world called Terra, where we have had masters of our own, from time to time. But not for a long time, now. We're all free, and one of the things a free man does is to pass his freedom on to anyone who needs it."

"Another world?"

Chugren spread his hands. "See? There are some things I can't explain. But— You see the stars in the sky. And you see the sun. Well, this world is part of your sun's family. All those stars you see are suns, too—so far away that they look little. But they're as big as yours, and each of them has worlds in its family, some of them pretty much like yours. Some of them have people living on them. We have a boat that lets us travel from one to another."

Dahano thought about that. When he decided he had it clear in his mind, he asked: "Other people. Tell me—what do you look like when you don't resemble Chugren? Do you look like us? Does everyone?"

Chugren smiled. "Not too different. I can show you." He stood up and touched his arm to his body. His robe flowed into different colors and two parts, one of which loosely covered his legs and hips while the other hugged his upper body, leaving his arms bare. He changed his face, and the color of his hair and eyes.

He was shorter than the usual person, and the shape of his ears and eyes was odd. His hands were too broad.

He looked a good deal like a usual person or Master, except that he was possibly physically stronger, for he looked powerful. Not too different.

Still, Dahano said, "Thank you," rather quickly. It was unsettling to look at him, for anyone could see at a glance that he was not born of any female person on this world.

The Terran nodded in understanding, and was Chugren again. "You see why I didn't come here as myself?"

Dahano could picture it. The villagers would have been frightened and upset. More than that, they would never have dared listen to him.

But there was something else Dahano wanted to clear up. He returned to his point: "Other worlds and other people. Tell me, have you ever been to the world where our Heaven People live?"

"Heaven People?" Chugren frowned, and Dahano knew he was trying to grasp the meaning from his mind.

"The souls of our dead persons," Dahano explained. "I had thought at first that you might be one of them, but I can see you aren't. I thought perhaps, in your boat, you might have visited them." He stopped himself there. A person does not inflict his grief on those who have no share in it.

But his mind had welled up, and Chugren saw his thought. He shook his head slowly. "No, I'm sorry, Dahano. I didn't meet your son."

Dahano looked down. "At least there will be no more." He thought of all the persons who had burned because of the Masters, and all the souls that had gone into the sky. Somewhere, on one of those worlds Chugren spoke of, there were many persons who had waited for this day to come. It was good to know that they had a home much like this world, which only the Masters had spoiled. It was good to know that some day his own soul would be there with them, and that he would be with his son again.

He remembered the long hours with Borthen, passing on to him the old ways he had learned from his father—the ways of having land of a person's own, and a house, and cattle; the remembered things, saved and kept whole from the days before the Masters were here, coming suddenly from their one village in the faraway mountains.

Many things had been lost, but they were only unimportant things that would be of no use; persons' names, and the memory of persons' lives. A person lived, died, and his sons remembered him for their lives, but then he began to fade, and his grandsons might never remember him.

The important things had lived on. Dahano knew that had been a great effort. There were always persons who were willing to let themselves forget, and simply live out what lives they had. But always there were persons who would not forget; who waited for the day when the villagers could claim the world for their own again, and need to know how to live without anyone's commanding them.

So, in all the villages, fathers taught their sons, and the sons remembered.

Dahano's face wrinkled in grief as he thought of his dead son. Borthen had remembered—perhaps too well. He had still been a young man, with a young man's fire in his blood. So he tested Chugren's power, and Chugren—the old Chugren—had commanded him to die for not tending the cattle properly.

Two more days—two more days of patience, Borthen, and I would have my son. I would not be alone. Some day you would have been Headman.

Dahano raised his eyes slowly. There were things to be done, and he was Headman in this village.

"What are you going to do?" he asked Chugren. "Are you going to make us all Masters?"

Chugren shook his head. "No. Not for a long time. And then it's going to be your own people who make themselves Masters. That's why, at first, we weren't going to let you know that anything had happened to Chugren and his fellows. What do you think would happen if we simply went to all the villages and told the people they were free?"

"If you went as you really are?"

"Yes."

"The people would be frightened. Many of them wouldn't know what to do. And afterwards I don't think they'd be happy."

"They'd know somebody came down from the sky and simply gave them their freedom."

Dahano nodded. "It would never be their freedom. It would be a gift from someone else who might come to take it back some day."

"That's why we've got to go slowly. Today Chugren came to this village and cleaned it up. In a few days, he'll come back and do something else to make things better. One by one, the old Masters' rules will be eliminated, and in a few months, everyone will be free. Some people will wonder what made the Masters change. But it won't have been sudden, and in a few generations, I think your people will have invented a hero who made the Masters change." Chugren smiled. "You, perhaps, Dahano. And then one day the Masters will go away, and their city'll burn to the ground, and that'll be the end of it."

"We'll be free."

"You'll be free, and you'll have your pride. You'll grow, you'll learn—a little faster than you might have, perhaps, and you'll spend less time on blind alleys, I can promise you—and when you have grown enough, you'll be Masters. Without more than a friendly hand to help. I don't think you'd really like it if we gave you everything, and so left you with nothing."

"A friendly hand—yes, Chugren." Dahano stood up. "That's all my people want." He felt his back straighten, and his head was up. "No more commands. No more Masters coming to give orders. No more working in fields which do not belong to anyone, doing what you do not wish to."

"I promise you that, Dahano."

"I believe you."

Chugren smiled. "On my world, friends clasp hands."

"They do the same here."

They stepped toward each other, their arms outstretched, and shook hands.

III

It was three days later, again in the early morning, when Chugren returned to the village square. Dahano, waiting in his doorway, saw the surprise on the faces of the villagers waiting to go out to the fields. None of the Masters had ever come this often. As Chugren beckoned to him and Dahano moved forward, none of the villagers made a sound.

They might not know what was happening, Dahano thought, but they could feel it. Freedom had an excitement that needed no words to make itself known.

He stopped in front of Chugren and bowed. "I hear, Chugren," he said, a faint smile just touching the corners of his mouth too lightly for anyone but Chugren to see.

"Good," Chugren answered harshly. Only Dahano saw the twitch of his eyelids. "Now—it's almost time for the next planting. And this time you're going to do it right. You're wearing out the land, planting the same fields year after year. Furthermore, I want to see who the lazy and stupid ones among you are. I want every family in this village to take a plot of ground. I don't care where—take your pick—as long as it's fresh ground. The plot has to be large enough to support that family, and every family will be responsible for its work. It's not necessary to follow the old working hours, so long as the work's done. Nobody will work anyone else's plot. If a person dies, his plot goes to his oldest son. Is that clear?"

Dahano bowed deeply. "I hear, Chugren. It will be done."

"Good. See to it."

"I hear."

"If the plot is too far away from the person's house, I will give him a new house so he doesn't waste his time walking back and forth. I'll have no dawdling from you people. Is *that* clear?"

"I hear, Chugren." Dahano bowed again. "Thank you," he whispered without moving his lips. Chugren grunted, winked again, and went away. Dahano turned back toward his hut, careful not to show his joy.

They were free of the fields. In every village this morning, the Masters had come and given their particular village this freedom, and the days of getting up to go to work at the Masters' commands were over.

There was a puzzled murmur coming from the crowd of villagers. One or two persons stepped forward.

"Headman—what did he mean? Aren't we to go out this morning?"

"You heard what he said, Loron," Dahano answered quietly. "We're to pick out plots of our own, and he'll give us houses to go with them."

"But, Headman—the Masters have never done this before!" The villagers were clustering around Dahano now, the bewildered ones asking him to explain, the thoughtful ones exchanging glances that were slowly coming alight.

It was one of those—Carsi, who'd never bent his head as low as some of the others—who shouted impatiently: "Who cares what or why! We're through with herding together in these stables. We're through with plowing Chugren's fields, and *you* can stay here and talk but *I'm* going to find my land!"

Dahano stepped into his hut with a lighter heart than he ever remembered, while outside the villagers were hurrying toward their huts, a great many of them to pack up their bundles and set out at once. Then he heard Gulegath stop in the doorway and throw his bitterness in before him.

"I think it's a trick!"

Dahano shrugged and let it pass. In a few weeks, the youngster would see.

"I suppose you think it's all wonderful," Gulegath pressed on. "You forget all of his past history. You discard every fact but the last. You don't stop to see where the poison lies. You bite into the fruit you think he's handed you, and you say how good it tastes."

"Do you see what his trick is, Gulegath?" Dahano asked patiently.

"If there's no trick," Gulegath answered, "then there's only one other explanation—he's afraid of us. Nothing else fits the evidence as I see it. He sees that his days are almost over, for some mysterious reason, and he's trying to buy his life. Somehow, that seems ridiculous to me."

"Perhaps," Dahano answered shortly. He didn't like Gulegath's gnawing at him like this. "But in the meantime, will you please go out and see where the new plots are, so I'll know where my village is?"

Grow older soon, Gulegath, Dahano thought. How much can my patience stand? How much longer will I have to watch you this closely? Grow wiser, or even these Masters might not let you.

He thought of telling Gulegath all of the truth. It might help. But he decided against it. If he told him, the youngster would surely react in some unsettling manner.

IV

Dahano sat in his doorway, looking out at the great empty spaces where the village huts had been, and beyond them at the old fields losing their shape under the rain that had been pounding them steadily for hours each day. That, too, was not by accident, he guessed.

He looked around. Here and there the old huts were still standing—or rather, new houses stood where families had decided to stay. Straight roads stretched out in the directions of the farms.

Dahano smiled to himself. This is freedom, he thought. New, large houses, each set apart. The cattle barn gone, and the herds divided. The granaries taken away, and each house with its own food store until the new farms can be harvested.

And that is the best freedom of all. We have houses, but we would sleep in the open. We have food, but we would go hungry. Chugren has given us our last new lengths of cloth, but we would go naked. For we have freedom—we have our land that no one can take from us, and we live without the Masters' laws.

It was true. They did. Even so soon, though Chugren and the other "Masters" still came and went among them, playing out their parts before they let go the reins entirely, already there were many people who had lost their fear of them. The old ways were coming back, even before the "Masters" withdrew. From everywhere, Gulegath and all of Dahano's other messengers brought him the same news. All the villages were spreading out, the homesteads dotting the green face of the plains, and there were persons plowing out new ground almost at the foot of the golden city that had always stood alone before. The villagers had remembered. The fields were planted and the wells were dug as their great-grandfathers had done, and the people drew their strength from the land.

In my lifetime, he thought. I see it in my lifetime, and when my soul goes to the Heaven People's world, I will be able to tell them we live as people ought to.

He raised his head and smiled as he saw Chugren step into the road in front of his house.

"Chugren."

"Good day, Headman." Chugren wiped his hand over his forehead, taking away perspiration. "I've had a busy day."

A clot of excitement surged through Dahano's brittle veins. He knew what Chugren was going to tell him.

"How so?"

Chugren smiled. "I don't suppose this'll be any great surprise. I went out and inspected all the homesteads from this village. All I have left to do are these few here, and that'll be that. I found fault in every case, was completely disgusted, and finally said that I had no use for lazy slaves like these. I said I was tired of trying to get useful work out of them, and from now on they'd have to fend for themselves—I wasn't going to bother with them any longer."

Dahano took a breath. "You did it," he whispered.

Chugren nodded. "I did it. It's done. Finished. You're free."

"And the same thing happened in all the other villages?"

"Every last one of them."

Dahano said nothing for a few moments. Finally, he murmured: "I never quite believed it until now. It's all over. The Masters are gone."

"For good."

Dahano shook his head, still touched by wonder, as a man can know for months that his wife will give him a child but still be amazed when it lies in his hands. "What are you going to do now?"

"Oh, we'll stay around for a while—see if we've missed anything."

"But you won't give orders?" Dahano asked quickly.

Chugren laughed gently. "No, Headman. No orders. We'll just watch. Some of us will always be around, keeping an eye out. You'll never have any wars that come to much, and I don't think you'll have cloudbursts washing out your crops too often, but we'll never interfere directly."

Dahano had thought he was prepared for this day. But now he saw he was not. While there had been no hope, he had been patient. When things were growing better every day, he could live in confidence of tomorrow. But now he had what he longed for, and he was anxious for its safety.

"Remember—you gave your promise." He knew he sounded like a nervous old man. "Forgive me, Chugren— but you could take all this back in the time of a heartbeat. I . . . well, I'm glad none of my people know as much."

Chugren nodded. "I imagine there are times when a person would just as soon not know as much as he does." He looked directly into Dahano's eyes. "I gave my promise, Headman. I give it again. You're free. We've given our last command."

They reached out and shook hands.

"Thank you, Chugren."

"No one could have seen what the Masters were doing and let it go on. You don't owe me any special thanks. I couldn't have lived with myself if I'd seen slavery and not done my best to wipe it out."

They sat together silently in the doorway for a few moments.

"Well, I don't imagine we'll be seeing very much more of each other, Headman."

"I'm sorry about that."

"So am I. I have to go back to Terra and make my report on this pretty soon."

"Is it far?"

"Unbelievably far, even for us. Even with our boat's speed, it'll be months before I'm home. We sent the boat back with your old Masters, for example. It won't return for another ten days, though it started straight back. It may be a year before word comes of how well your old Masters are taking their re-education. Probably, I'll come back with it."

"I'm an old man, Chugren. I may not see you then."

"I know," Chugren said in a low voice. "We've never found a way to keep a person from wearing out. What're you going to do 'til then? Rest?"

Dahano shook his head. "A person rests forever when he joins the Heaven People. Meanwhile, my village needs its Headman. There are many things only a Headman can do."

"I suppose so." Chugren stood up. "I have to go finish up these last homesteads," he said regretfully. "Good-by, Headman."

"Good-by, my friend," Dahano answered.

V

It was a week later. Dahano sat with the sun warming his body. His stomach was paining him to some extent—yesterday it had pained him less—and the sun felt good.

I'm old, he thought. *An old man without too many sunny days left for him. But in these past days, I've been free.*

It's good to be Headman where people live the way they ought to live; the way our fathers told us, the way their fathers told them, the way people never forgot in spite of everything the Masters did to us. It's good to know we'll live this way forever.

He shifted the length of cloth wrapped around his hips. It was good cloth Chugren'd given them. It ought to last a long time.

He looked up as he heard Gulegath come up to him. "Headman."

"Yes, Gulegath?"

Gulegath was frowning. "Headman—Chugren's over

at Carsi's house. He's giving Carsi's wife orders on how to live."

Dahano pushed himself to his feet, half-afraid and half-angry at Gulegath for making a mistake of some kind. "I want to see for myself." He walked in the direction of Carsi's house as quickly as he could, and Gulegath came after.

It was true. As he came to Carsi's house, he heard Chugren arguing with Terpet, the woman. Dahano's face and insides twisted. He was afraid and unwilling to think what this could be. He wondered what could have happened.

Frightened, he came quickly into the front room and saw Terpet standing terrified against one wall, clutching her small daughter and staring wide-eyed at Chugren as the Master stood in front of her, his face angry.

Dahano peered at Chugren, but it was still the different Chugren, not the old Master. Except that he was acting exactly the way the old Master used to. While Gulegath stayed warily in the doorway, Dahano moved forward.

"I told you last time," Chugren was saying angrily. "Do you *want* your daughter to be crippled? I told you what she needed to eat. I explained to you that eating nothing but that doughcake and those plants was making her sick. I explained how to prepare them and give them to the girl. And you said you'd do it. That was two days ago! Now she's getting worse, and you're still feeding her the same old way!"

Drawing himself up, Dahano stepped between them. "This is my duty, Chugren," he snapped. He felt no further fear. He knew nothing but disappointment and anger at Chugren's betrayal of his word.

Chugren stepped back. "I'm glad you're here, Dahano," he said. "Maybe you can get through to this woman. She's letting that little girl get sick—deliberately. I told her what to do, but she won't listen to me."

For the moment, Dahano turned his back on Chugren. "Terpet!" he said sternly. "Is your daughter sick?"

The woman nodded guiltily, looking down at her

feet. "Yes, Headman." The little girl stared up at Dahano, hollow-eyed.

"How long has she been sick?"

"A week or two," Terpet mumbled.

"Where is your man?"

"In the fields. Working."

"Does he know she's sick?"

Terpet shook her head. "She's asleep when he goes out and comes home. She sleeps a lot."

"I'm your Headman. You should have told me."

"I didn't want to bother you." The woman kept shifting her eyes away from him.

"If somebody's sick—particularly if a child is sick—I *must* be told! Didn't your mother teach you the old ways?"

Terpet nodded.

"Did Chugren come here two days ago? Did he see the girl was sick? Did he tell you what food to give her?"

"Yes."

"Why didn't you tell me *that?*"

"He . . . he wasn't angry, last time. He just gave me the plants, and he told me to give them to Theva instead of the *shuri* greens."

"What did you do with the plants?"

"I . . . I took them. He's a Master, and I didn't want to get him angry. When he was gone, I threw them away. He wanted me to give them to Theva without . . . without cooking them."

"*Raw?*"

"Yes."

Dahano turned around quickly, shocked. "That was a terrible thing to do!" He felt the beginnings of desperation. "Chugren, you have no right to tell this woman what to do. You're no longer to come giving orders. You're no longer to tell us what to eat. You gave me your word!"

"I—" Chugren looked like a man who had just seen a new plowshare crack. "But . . . Dahano . . . that baby's well on her way to rickets! She'll be a cripple. And look at this place—" He pointed into the next room. "*Smell* it!"

Dahano's temper strained at his self-control. "She keeps her milk cow in there. How do you want it to smell? Do you expect a woman with a sick child to clean every day?"

"She's got a cattle shed."

"The next room is closer. She can milk the cows without having to go out of the house and leave her child."

"You can get sick and die from things like this! That cow could go tubercular. And there's a sickness called anthrax. Do you know how a person dies from that? He gets running sores in his flesh, he burns up with fever, and finally he dies out of his head, with his body full of poisons. Or if you get it from the air—which is probably what'll happen here—the sores are in your lungs. Do you think that's a good thing to have happen? To a little girl like that!" Chugren was very close to shouting.

"Did you think we'd forgotten?" Dahano snapped back. "Do you think you can tell us stories like that and make us forget how a person should live? What're these 'rickets' and 'anthrax' things? Names to frighten ignorant people with? A person's either whole and strong or isn't. He either lives or dies according to the nature of things. He eats what people have always eaten, when you—*Masters!*—will let him. He keeps his homestead and house the way a person ought to. You mustn't use these silly arguments to once again tell us how to live, what to eat, how and where to keep our cattle." Dahano felt a terrible helplessness. "You mustn't!"

"Listen, Dahano, there's nothing congenitally wrong with that child! It's the food she's given! If her mother would give her some of these other things to eat—or if she took her out in the sun more often . . ."

"If Terpet can eat the food, so can the girl. And the sun's too strong for young children. It hurts their heads and burns their brains. Now, that's the end of this matter. If you're not going to give orders any more, then don't give orders any more!"

Chugren took a deep breath. "All right!" He turned around abruptly, growling something that sounded like "So now I'll have to personally concentrate Vitamin D in her. Every day." He jerked his head in disgust and went away.

Dahano turned back to Terpet, conscious that his chest was heaving. "Very well. That's taken care of. I'll be back in a week to see the child."

The woman nodded, still trembling, and Dahano's voice grew gentler. "I'm sorry I had to shout. He made me angry. I hope Theva gets better. But you must try to remember how a person ought to live. It's been a long time since we last had our freedom. We must live properly, for if we don't we won't deserve to keep it."

The woman had calmed a little. "Yes, Headman," she whispered.

"In a week, then." He walked out of the house, with Gulegath trailing beside and a little behind him. He walked head-down, trying to puzzle out what had happened.

"They meant it when they promised to leave us alone. I know they did. Why should they be playing this game with us? They had us under their thumbs. They let us go, but now they're bothering us again. If Chugren's doing it here, the rest of them are doing the same in the other villages." He shook his head, conscious of Gulegath just beside him, thinking of how the youngster was being made to look foresighted through no virtue of his own. "But there's nothing we can do. We depend on the honesty of their promise. If they're going to make us slaves again, there's no stopping them. But— why? It makes no *sense!*"

He waited for Gulegath's bitter comments, knowing that they would express his own mood as well as the youngster's. But Gulegath, inexplicably enough, sounded thoughtful:

"I . . . don't know," the youngster murmured. "You're right. It makes no sense—that way." Dahano felt peculiarly disappointed. "I wonder," Gulegath went on, mostly to himself. "I wonder . . . he didn't sound so much like a person whose commands have been disobeyed. He sounded, instead, like a father who can't get his stupid child to understand something important—" Gulegath seemed wrong-headedly determined not to take his opportunity for saying "I told you so."

Somehow, this angered Dahano more than anything else could have done.

What kind of dedicated perversity was this? he thought in exasperation. Couldn't the youngster abide to *ever* agree with his Headman? Hadn't he been the one who hated the Masters so much? Then why was he defending them now? What kind of knot did he have in the threads of his thinking?

"When I want bad advice," Dahano snapped, "I'll find it for myself."

Gulegath, busy with his wonderings, barely grimaced, as though a bug had flown against his cheek for a brief moment and then gone on.

Dahano scowled at being so ignored. Then he walked on stiffly, trying to understand just what kind of complicated scheme the new Masters might be weaving. But it wouldn't come clear no matter how hard he tried.

The pain in his belly was worse than ever. He walked along, his mind churning, trying to ignore the teeth gnawing at his stomach.

He had realized, in the days that followed, that the only thing to do was wait and see. There was no other way. He heard more stories that his runners brought from other villages. Everywhere it was the same. The Masters were constantly poking and prying, trying to bully people into following their orders again.

They turned up at house after house, not only telling persons what to eat but how to drink, too. They took away people's cattle wells, and sometimes their house wells, too, if they had them. True enough, the Masters gave them new wells—but they were strange, overly-deep things a man couldn't use a well-sweep with. The Masters gave them long ropes wound around a round log with a handle to turn, but that was no way to get well water. It was a needless time-waster. A person could see no sense in the new wells, which were often far away from the cattle, when the old ones had been closer and much easier to use. Many persons waited until the Masters were gone again and then re-dug proper wells.

It made no difference that the Masters used words like "cholera" and "typhoid" to justify themselves. These were meaningless things, and meanwhile a person's life was made that much harder. Was this the freedom they'd promised?

And furthermore, no one was sick. A number of people began to get sick, for one reason or another, but they always grew strong in their souls and well again after the first signs had shown themselves. So Dahano was puzzled. What were the Masters so incensed about?

He could only go about his Headman's duties day by day, and calming his people as well as he could, as though his freedom might still be there tomorrow. But the contentment of it was gone, and he grew short-tempered with strain while the fire in his stomach gave him no rest.

Dahano had just returned home after attending to a spoiled child when Chugren came into his doorway.

"May I come in, Headman?" the Master asked tiredly. His shoulders were slumped, and his eyes were rimmed pink with sleeplessness.

"Please yourself," Dahano growled, sitting in a corner with his arms folded across his belly. "I thought you were leaving last week."

Chugren made a chair and dropped into it. "The ship came back, all right. No word yet on your old Masters' progress, but I wonder, now, what that report'll be like. And I'm staying here indefinitely. Dahano, I don't know what to do."

"That's a peculiar thing for a Master to say."

Chugren's mouth quirked. "I don't want to be a Master."

"Then go away and leave us alone. What more do you want from us?"

"I . . . we don't want anything from you. Dahano, I'm trying to find an answer to this mess. I need your help."

"What," asked Dahano bitterly, "does the Master ask of his slave?"

For a second, Chugren was blazing with frustrated anger. Dahano's lip lifted at one corner as he saw it. Good. These Masters were inexperienced in the peculiar weapons only a slave could use. Then Chugren's head dropped and, in its own way, his voice was bitter, too.

"You're not going to give an inch. You're going to go right on killing yourselves."

"No one's dying."

"No thanks to you. Do you know none of us are doing anything any more but spot-checking you people for diseases and dietary deficiencies? You're scattered from blazes to breakfast and we're forced to hop around after you like fleas." Chugren looked at Dahano's robe. "And it looks like we're going to have to extend the public health program, too. Don't you ever wash that thing? Have you any idea of what a typhus epidemic would do to you people? You haven't got an ounce of resistance to any of these things."

"Another mysterious word. How many of them do you know, Master? I have no other robe. How can I wash this one? Is it any of your concern whether I do or not?"

"Well, *get* another robe!"

"I need fiber plants to grow. And I'm only one man with no one to help him—with no son. My field has to grow food. What's it to you—what's it to me?—if my clothes're dirty while I'm a healthy person with food in the house? A person first feeds himself. Then he worries about other things."

"Do you want me to get you another robe?"

"No! I'm a free person. I don't need your charity. You can force more cloth on me, but you can't make me wear it—unless you want to break your word completely."

Chugren beat his fist down at the air. "It's not charity! It's an obligation! If you take responsibility for someone—if you're so constituted that you're equipped for responsibility—then there's nothing else you can do. But I'm not getting through to you at all, am I?"

"If my Master wishes to teach me something, I can't stop him."

"The Devil you can't. You've gone deaf."

"Chugren, this is fruitless. Say what you want from me and I'll have to do it."

"I'm not here to force you into anything! I'm not your Master . . . I don't want to be your Master. Sometimes I wish I'd never found this place."

"Then go away. Go away and leave us alone. Leave us alone to live the way we want—the way people ought to live."

Chugren shook his head tiredly. "We can't do that, either. You're our tarbaby. And I don't know what we're going to do with you. Bring your old Masters back, maybe, with apologies. You're their tarbaby, too, and they've had more experience. The way you're scattered out—the incredible number of things you don't know—this business of following you around one by one, trying not to step on your toes but trying to keep you alive, too—it's more than we can take."

Dahano stood up straight. "Leave us alone! We don't want you sneaking around us. People should be free— you said that yourself. Don't come to me talking nonsense! Either we're your slaves, and you're a liar, or we're free and we don't want you. We just want to live the way people ought to live!"

Chugren's eyes were widening. "Dahano," he said in a strange voice, "what were you doing tonight?"

"I was attending to a spoiled child. Every Headman's duties include that."

Chugren looked sick. "What do you mean by a spoiled child?"

"You've seen it in my head. It was a child born double. It had divided in two and split its soul. Neither half was a whole person."

"What did you do with them?"

"I did what's done with all spoiled or weak children. They aren't people."

"You killed those twins?"

"I killed it."

Chugren sat wordless for a long time. Then he said: "All right, Dahano. That's the end."

VI

It was early morning in the village. Dahano stood in his doorway, looking out at the houses clustered tightly around the square. Between the closely-huddled walls, he could look out to the slope beyond the village where the fields he hated were stretched furrow on furrow, waiting to be worked.

Today the houses were smaller, he saw. The cattle would be back in their long shed, no man's property again. Chugren'd said he'd do it if Dahano didn't get the villagers to keep them out of the houses.

Dahano's lip curled. A slave has his weapons. Among them is defiance where the blame could be spread so wide the Master couldn't track it down. If Chugren asked, he could always say he'd told everyone. He couldn't be blamed if no one'd listened. It became everybody's fault.

It was only when one distinct person rebelled that an example could be made. There'd be none of those as long as Dahano was Headman. The village would lose as few people as possible. It would stay alive, save itself, wait—for generations, patiently, stubbornly, always waiting for the day when people could live as they ought to, in freedom.

He saw Chugren step into the middle of the square, and he stiffened.

"Dahano!"

"I hear, Chugren," Dahano muttered. He shuffled forward as slowly as he thought the Master would tolerate. He saw that Chugren was haggard. Dahano sneered behind his wooden face. Debauching himself in the comforts of his golden city, no doubt. None of the Masters ever came near the villages unless they absolutely had to, any more. "I hear." Liar. Tyrant.

"I took the cattle back."

Dahano nodded.

"That was the last of your freedoms."

"As the Master wishes."

Chugren's mouth winced with hurt. "I didn't like doing it. I don't like any of these things. I don't like penning you up in this village. But if I've got to watch you all, every minute, I've got to have you in one place."

"That's up to the Master."

"Is it?"

"What orders do you have for today, Master?"

Chugren reached out uncertainly, like a man trying to hold a handful of smoke. "I don't have any, Dahano. I was hoping this last thing— I'm trying to get something across to you. One last time— You were *dying*, Dahano. When we moved you back here, we saw little animals living in your stomach—"

Coldly, Dahano saw that Chugren actually did seem troubled. Good. Here was something to remember; one more way to strike back at the Master.

"All right, then," Chugren murmured. "It seems we're no smarter than your old Masters. Go out in the fields and raise your food." He turned and walked away, and then he was gone.

Dahano smiled thinly and went back to his hut. But he found Gulegath waiting.

The sight of the youngster was almost too much for Dahano to bear. As he saw that Gulegath himself was furious, Dahano almost lost control of the dignified blankness that was a Headman's only possible expression. What *right* had this young, perversely foolish person to be as angry as that? He wasn't Headman here. He wasn't old, with his hope first fanned and then drowned out in a few terrible days. He wouldn't ever know how close they'd all come to freedom, and how inexplicably they had lost it again.

"Well, Dahano—" Dahano saw the nearer villagers stiffen as the youngster called him by his name. "Well, Dahano—so we're slaves again."

"Do you mean that's my fault?" This was almost too far—almost too much for a person to say to him.

"You're Headman. You're responsible for us all." Dahano saw that all of Gulegath's anger—all his bitterness—were out of their flimsy cage and attacking only one man and one thing. For the first time, he saw a man in Gulegath's eyes. He saw a man who hated him.

"Can I defy the Masters?" There was a growing crowd of villagers around them.

"Can you *not* defy the Masters? Can you, somewhere, find the intelligence to try and work *with* them? You *stubborn*, willful old man! You won't change, you won't learn, you won't ever stop beating your head against a wall! Did it ever occur to you to learn anything about them? Did you ever try to convince them they could take the wall down?"

That was too far and too much.

"Are you questioning your Headman? Are you questioning the ways we have lived? Are you saying that the things we have held sacred, the things we have never permitted to die, are worthless?"

Gulegath's face was blazing. "I'm saying it!"

From a great distance within himself—from a peak of anger such as he had never known, Dahano spoke the ritual words no Headman in the memory of people had been forced to speak. But the words had been remembered, and told from father to son, down through the long years against this unthinkable day.

"You are a person of my village, but you have spoken against me. I am your Headman, and it is a Headman's duty to guard his village, to keep it from harm, and to remember the things of our fathers which have made us all the persons we are. Who speaks against his Headman speaks against himself."

The persons nearest Gulegath took his twisting arms and held him. They, too, had never heard these words spoken in real use, but they had known they must be today.

Suddenly, Gulegath's anger had gone out of him. Dahano felt some animal part of himself surge up gleefully as he saw Gulegath turn pale and weakly helpless. But he also saw the immovable clench in his jaw, and the naked anger as strong as ever in his eyes despite the fear that was rising with it.

"Kill me, then," Gulegath said in a high, desperate voice. "Kill me and dispose of all your troubles." Desperate it was—but it was unwavering, too, and Dahano's hands reached out for Gulegath's thin neck with less hesitation than they might have.

"A person is his village, and a village is its Headman. So all things are in the Headman, and no person can be permitted to destroy him, for he is the entire proper world.

"I do this thing to keep the village safe." His old hands went around Gulegath's throat. Gulegath said nothing, and waited, his eyes locked, with an effort, on Dahano's.

Chugren came back, and they were flung apart by his shoulders and arms, as though the Master had forgotten he had greater strengths.

"Stop that!"

The villagers fell back. Dahano got to his feet, wiping the dust of the ground out of his eyes. Gulegath was watching the Master carefully, uncertain of himself but certain enough to stand straight and probe Chugren's face. Chugren looked at Dahano.

"The Master commands," Dahano muttered.

"He does." Chugren looked sideward at Gulegath. "Why didn't you ever call attention to yourself before?"

Gulegath licked his lips. "I tend to save my bravery for times when it can't hurt me."

Dahano nodded scornfully. Gulegath had only rebelled in words. He'd been nothing like Borthen—for all that Borthen was needlessly dead.

"Times when it can't hurt you, eh? What about this time?"

Gulegath shrugged uncomfortably. "There's a limit, I suppose."

Chugren grunted. "I think we'll be keeping you. And thanks for the answer." Sudden pain came into his face. "And quite an answer it is, too."

"Answer?"

Chugren swung back toward Dahano. "Yes. So you know the proper ways to live, do you? You know how a person should keep his house, and work his ground, and grow his food, do you?"

The villagers were still.

"There are other worlds." Chugren drew himself up, touched his chest, and began to speak. His words rolled over the village in a voice of thunder.

"You're going to a far land, all of you. We can't stand

the sight of you any more. We're going to send you to a place where you can live any way you please, and we'll be rid of you."

There was a swelling murmur from the villagers.

"What kind of place, Chugren?" Dahano demanded. "Some corner where we cannot ever hold up our heads— some corner from which we can never rise to challenge you?"

Chugren shook his head. "No, Headman. A world exactly like this. If we can't find one that fits, then we'll change one to suit. There'll be plains like these, and soil that'll accept your plants, and fodder for your cattle."

"I don't believe you."

"Suit yourself. We're going to do it."

Now Dahano, once again, couldn't be sure of what to think.

Gulegath touched Chugren's arm. "What's the catch?"

"Catch?"

"Don't sidestep. If that was the whole answer, you could reach it by simply leaving us alone here."

Chugren sighed. "All right. The day'll be one hour shorter."

Dahano frowned over that. One hour shorter? How could that be? A day was so many hours—how could there be a day if there weren't hours enough to fill it?

He preoccupied himself with this puzzle. He failed to understand what Gulegath and Chugren were talking about meanwhile.

"I . . . see—" Gulegath was saying slowly. "The plants . . . they'll grow, but—"

"But they won't ripen. Unless the villages move nearer the equator. And if that happens, nothing will be right for the climate—neither the houses, nor the clothes, nor any of the things your people know. But we won't move them. We won't change them. And all the rules will almost work."

Dahano listened without understanding. How could simply moving to another place change the kind of house a person needed?

Gulegath was looking down at the ground. "A great many people will die."

"But to a purpose."

"Yes, I suppose."

"What else can we do, Gulegath? We can't push them. They'll have to change of themselves." Chugren put his arm around Gulegath's shoulders. "Come on," he said like a man anxious to get away from a place where he has committed murder.

Gulegath shook his head. "I think I'll stay." He looked around at the villagers. "I seem to want to go with them."

"They'll kill you. We won't be around to stop them."

"I think they'll be too busy."

Chugren looked at him for a long moment. Then he took a deep breath, started a gesture, and went away.

Gulegath looked around again, shook his head to himself, and then walked slowly back toward his hut. The villagers moved slowly out of his way, mystified and upset by something they saw in his face.

Dahano looked after him. So you think you'll be Headman after me, he thought. You think you'll be the new Headman, in the new land.

Well, perhaps you will. If you're clever enough and quick enough. I don't know—there's something you seem to know that I don't—perhaps you'll make another error so I can kill you for it. I wish—

I don't know. But you'll pay your price, no matter what happens. You'll learn what it is to be Headman. And you won't have the words of your fathers to help you, because you've never listened.

Dahano began walking across the square, ignoring the villagers because he had nothing to say to them. He thought of what it would be like, the day they would all be filing aboard the Masters' sky boats, carrying their belongings, driving their cattle before them, and he thought back to the night he'd looked up and seen lights in the sky.

Omens. For good or for bad?

Editor's Introduction To:

EARTHMAN'S BURDEN

Morton Klass

"Good government is no substitute for self-government," cried the subject nations of the American, British, and French Empires.

One presumes they were right.

EARTHMAN'S BURDEN

Morton Klass

His first sensation was of lying on something soft; his second was of a bright light close above him, its glare felt even through his tightly shut eyelids. His third sensation was of time having passed—a great deal of time.

"I'm dead," Arthur Morales said aloud, and opened his eyes.

"You *were* dead," a deep, familiar voice answered beside him. "You have been dead for three days, but you are alive now, my friend."

Weakly, Arthur Morales turned his eyes away from the bright light and tried to focus on the furred, grotesque face of Jhumm, the viceroy of the Trogish galactic empire.

"What . . . where—" Morales tried to sit up, and discovered he was too weak. Numbly, he fell back, and a remembered blackness spread like a blanket over his mind, shutting out the world.

At the final moment of consciousness, he remembered a voice. It was the voice of a human, of a man he respected but whose name escaped him for the moment. The voice said: *"You're a traitor, Morales. The worst traitor who ever lived. You're planning to sell out the whole human race—"*

Arthur Morales shuddered, and buried his mind in the blackness of unconsciousness.

He was alone in the room when he awoke the second time. Carefully, without moving his head more than was absolutely necessary, he stared about him at the room. Although he had never been in it before, his practiced, anthropologist's eyes recognized the furnishings as Trogish, rather than that of the race native to the planet.

Morales smiled wryly. The Earthmen had been here four weeks, and he was the only one who had cared enough to notice the differences. The Trogish liked reds and browns, and sharp-angled, hard furniture. Though their buildings were made of the native iridescent plastic, there was none of the usual coruscation, but rather a sedate nimbus of softened light bathing the abodes of the galactic rulers, and setting their buildings off—for those who had the wit to see—from the gayer constructions of the native San Salvadorans.

San Salvador—Morales writhed internally as he remembered with what pomp Commander O'Fallon had planted the flag of the first interstellar exploration party; with what posturing O'Fallon had named the third planet of Sirius, envisioning himself a second, and greater Columbus! And then the discovery that Earth had not established its first extrasolar dominion, but had instead stumbled on a distant, minor outpost of a tremendous galactic empire!

Cautiously, Morales tried to raise his head. Dizziness swept over him, and he gave up the attempt. What had Jhumm said earlier? *You have been dead for three days—*

It came back to him, then. O'Fallon had shot him. In

the back, after that argument in the Earthmen's quarters, when Morales had turned away in anger and announced his intention of going to the Trogish and revealing the plans of the humans. And Pedersen, Morales' best friend, had stood over the dying anthropologist and pronounced the last judgment of humanity . . .

The door in the far wall dilated and someone came in. Even in the semi-darkness, Morales could make out the gangling, heavily furred figure of a Trogish. Amber light blossomed suddenly in the walls, and Morales recognized Kulihhan, son of Jhumm, and the viceroy's only assistant on San Salvador.

"How are you feeling, Arthur?" Kulihhan inquired, bending over him.

Morales smiled weakly. "More alive than dead, I guess," he said. "Where are my friends?"

The young Trogish squatted gracefully beside the anthropologist. "The spaceship of your friends left yesterday," he said. "My father didn't want to put you under the revivifying machines until after they had gone."

He paused, as if debating something within himself. Then he asked, "Why did they kill you, Arthur? You don't have to tell us if you don't want to, but both my father and I are very curious."

Why? Morales knew why, but how do you tell an alien your own kind have passed judgment on you and booted you out of their species? They'd called him a traitor—good old Pete Pedersen had said it—but he wasn't one yet. His answer to Kulihhan could make him one—it was as easy as that.

But it was different now. It was one thing to watch O'Fallon striding up and down on the packed-earth floor of the San Salvadoran house. It was one thing to hear O'Fallon's rasping, gravelly voice: "I'm ordering you all to be more cautious from now on. That goes especially for you, Morales! You've been spending too much time alone in the homes of the natives, studying their eating habits or whatever—"

"I've been collecting data on the customs of the San Salvadorans! That's part of my job as anthropologist of this expedition. I have to do it alone. San Salvadorans believe in privacy at mealtime, and it's been hard enough for me to get permission to visit them then. They're peaceful, agricultural folk, for the most part. What possible danger could there be?"

"That's just it!" O'Fallon's fear had been in his eyes. "I don't know, and I'd rather not find out! Oh, it's not the native tubs of lard I'm afraid of, but their masters, the Trogish. Those boys control the galaxy, remember, and they had to be tough to do that. We know they've got some fancy machinery—language-teachers, antigravity rafts, and the like. Probably a lot of stuff we haven't seen yet."

O'Fallon had paused and gestured for the men to gather close around him. "Look, men—we'll be leaving in a couple of days. We've got to go back to Earth and warn them what the human race is up against—"

"And just what is that, commander?" Morales had wanted to know.

"A galactic empire, you fool! A super-race that thinks it can relegate Earth to the position of a tenth-rate possession!"

Oliphant snickered.

Commander O'Fallon nodded approvingly. "That's right, Harvey—they'll have another think coming in a few years. But we've got to be careful. The Trogish are older, and more advanced, than we are. Probably more numerous, too. And if any of their subject people are willing to fight for them—"

"Wouldn't worry about that," said Oliphant. "From what I could see, the Trogish have to do all the work themselves. The San Salvadorans won't help any more than they have to. The natives raise their crops and work a few hours a year in the factories. The rest of the time, they play their weird music or sculpt or sit around and talk. Jhumm and his son handle all the planetary and interplanetary distribution. But the Trogish'll be trouble enough, when it comes to a fight."

"I wouldn't be so sure of that," Pedersen put in thoughtfully. "I've talked with a couple of San Salvadorans, myself. You hear about the trouble the Trogish have keeping to a shipping schedule? Or about the way they loused up last year's building project? Seems that Jhumm, the big cheese around here, forgot to—"

"What are you getting at, Pedersen?" O'Fallon demanded impatiently.

"Why, just that the Trogish are incompetent," the geologist told him. "If they mess things up that way in peacetime, they would probably do the same in war. You know—mixups in ammunition shipments, warship equipment in need of repair, and so on. It figures."

Kulihhan broke in suddenly on Morales' thoughts. "From your silence, Arthur, I assume you would prefer not to answer my question."

Morales focused his eyes on the furred face of the young Trogish. *Answer the question,* he thought. *Tell him the other humans went home to prepare Earth for a war with the Trogish. Tell him you were opposed to the war, so O'Fallon shot you.*

The anthropologist cleared his throat uncertainly. "It . . . it's not an easy question to answer, Kulihhan. I broke some important rules of human behavior, so they killed me."

Kulihhan waved a four-fingered, furred hand deprecatingly. "Oh, I understood that, of course. It was obvious they didn't kill you for the amusement your death might afford them. But why punish you that way? If you committed some infringement on the human code, wasn't it apparent that you were in need of either instruction or treatment, depending on whether you were aware of what you were doing or not? Destruction, after all, is such a waste of a sentient creature—"

Morales shrugged. "It was a pretty serious infringement, I have to admit. Look, Kulihhan, could we talk about it tomorrow? I'm getting sleepy again."

The Trogish rose to his feet immediately. "Forgive me, my friend. I should have remembered how weak you are."

He started for the door, then stopped. "My father asked me to apologize for him. He couldn't drop in to visit you this evening because of his work. But he hopes to have a free day tomorrow, if he can get everything cleared up tonight, and he would like to spend it with you, if you feel up to it."

Morales nodded, and Kulihhan went out, dimming the lights behind him.

The anthropologist sank back and closed his eyes wearily. He knew that for the hard-working Trogish, a day off was a jealously guarded thing. For ten San Salvadoran days or more, Jhumm would spend long hours supervising quotas of food and machinery production, attempting to meet both the needs of San Salvador and the other planets in the galaxy. Then would come the one day on which Jhumm could sit in the garden with his wire scrolls and his computers and pursue his favorite subject, a development of the unified field theory which none of the humans had been capable of comprehending. Kulihhan, too, cherished his rare workless days, for he was a poet, though the language machines, which had given the humans as complete a knowledge of Trogish and San Salvadoran as it had given the Trogish a knowledge of English, hadn't been able to pass on sufficient understanding of Trogish symbolism and abstraction to make their poetry comprehensible.

And yet here was Jhumm prepared to give up his precious day to the company of a human!

The more he thought about it, the more Morales was convinced that Pedersen and O'Fallon and the rest were wrong: the Trogish were not just a conquering race, as the Persians, Romans, and Zulus had been on Earth; there was something more to the Trogish overlordship of the galaxy.

Morales believed that now. It was not uncertainty on that score that had made him give Kulihhan an equivocal answer, but a desire to think matters out more carefully before he made the final, irrevocable, treasonable announcement to the Trogish. For one thing, how would the Trogish react to the news that the barbarian newcomers on Earth planned to challenge their hegemony?

Superior race though the Trogish might be, their only answer might be to destroy the upstart planet. Morales doubted that: Kulihhan's comments on execution might certainly be considered proof enough of the Trogish attitude, but Morales had to be sure.

It was bad enough that the humans had been so

positive of the logic of their own position. There was the argument which had preceded his death—

"The Trogish had it too good for too long," Pedersen pronounced flatly. "They've grown soft. Now it's our turn."

Morales stared at his friend with contempt. "You're going to cheer for the greater glory of the Earth empire?" he demanded. "What's happened to Pete Pedersen the pacifist? Back in college you used to say, 'War is evil. Nothing can be achieved by beating somebody's brains in. If might doesn't make right in personal matters, it certainly doesn't in international affairs—' "

"This is different, Artie," Pedersen interrupted. "Humans shouldn't fight each other, but that doesn't mean they should knuckle under to aliens. And I refuse to shed any tears for the Trogish. They're arrogant—they treat the San Salvadorans like inferiors, refusing to give them any say in their own government or even in their own economy. The Trogish are conquerors, and the only future for conquerors is to be conquered in turn.

"Besides, I don't think an Earth conquest would be so bad for the galaxy. We're not what we once were. I'll bet that a triumphant Earth would teach formerly subjugated peoples like the poor benighted San Salvadorans to stand up for themselves. There's no reason why an Earth-directed confederation couldn't be based on democratic principles."

"With men like O'Fallon here in command? You know very well he's thinking about the loot he can drag home. You're a bigger fool than he is, Pete!"

"And what are you, Morales?" Commander O'Fallon asked evenly. "Pedersen and I may not agree on every point, but we know which side we're on. Which side are you on, Morales?"

Arthur Morales took a deep breath. He was surprised to discover that his forehead was bathed with perspiration. "I'm not on anyone's side," he said slowly. "I don't see why there has to be sides. Commander O'Fallon, if this is a scientific expedition—as it set out to be—you have no right to force me to make such decisions. I'll take your orders in times of danger, but I'm not a soldier or a spy or an empire-builder. I intend to conduct investigations which are in accordance with my field of science. That's all I am qualified or commissioned to do, and that's all I care to do."

"In other words," Oliphant said, "you're agin' us."

"If it comes to that—yes!" Morales couldn't stop the words rushing from his lips, and suddenly he realized that he didn't want to. "I'm against conquest; I'm against destruction—and I don't care who's doing it! There's no reason to believe that a Trogish galactic empire means what it would mean in Earth terms. Maybe it's to the advantage of Earth to submit to the direction and leadership of a more advanced people. I don't know—but I do know that I'm not going to help you start a war with an unoffending race! If you go back thinking the way you do, you'll incite Earth to war! There'll be no backing out, nothing ahead for the whole human race but—"

"And just what do you intend to do about it?" Commander O'Fallon asked.

"I'm going to see Jhumm!" Morales snapped. He turned on his heel and started for the door. "I'm going to warn the Trogish that there are barbaric Earthmen on this expedition who can only think in terms of bloodshed. I'm going to ask them to help me stop you, and to get some sort of sane message back—"

Morales had just reached the doorway when he heard the explosion. Absently, he stared at the rotund San Salvadoran sculptor on the other side of the wide dirt street, who was crawling like a red slug over an unfinished, nonobjective granite statue. The anthropologist's knees grew numb as he tried to comprehend the smashing blow on the back he had just received. He stumbled and went down, twisting so that he landed on his back.

The pain increased agonizingly, and so did the numbness. It seemed to be affecting his vision. He could barely make out the smoking pistol in O'Fallon's right hand.

"You . . . shot me—" he whispered, striving to understand, and bitterly unhappy that he could not.

Pete Pedersen stepped forward and stood over Morales. His voice came thinly over the black gulf that had suddenly opened up before Morales' eyes. "You're a traitor, Morales. The worst traitor who ever lived. You're planning to sell out the whole human race—"

Morales twisted on his narrow cot in the Trogish viceroy's spare room. He moaned and threw a weak hand up over his eyes to shut out the dim light and the accusing voice in his mind. The arm brushed wetness and he knew that he was weeping.

Jhumm was waiting in the garden when Morales came out the next morning. The anthropologist had awakened to discover a bowl of food beside his bed. He had an appetite too, he was pleased to discover, and when he had finished the oatmeal—could it have been that?—he felt strong enough to get out of bed.

The Trogish was listening to a scroll and clacking away at the keys of his computer, but he removed his earphone and looked up courteously when Morales appeared in the doorway.

"Ah, my friend," Jhumm said, rising to his feet, "I see you are recovering from your illness."

"From my death, you mean." Morales stepped to the side of the Trogish and breathed deeply of the perfumed, warm air. "It's good to be alive again. Jhumm," he went on awkwardly, "I don't know how one expresses gratitude for what you've done for me."

Sure you do, Morales told himself silently. *Just tell him why they killed you. Anybody would consider that payment enough.*

Jhumm raised a protesting hand. "Please, my friend! There is no need to thank me. I am most happy the revivifying machines did their work properly. We Trogish are not good mechanics, you know. Two hundred robots are out of commission on our north continent spaceport. Everything is in chaos up there—but enough of this!" He put a furred arm around Morales' shoulder.

"You are alive again, my friend, and I have a free day, and this is after all a period of rejoicing for all the Trogish in the galaxy who can spare the time from their work!"

"Rejoicing? Why?"

Jhumm's wide-eyed face registered surprise, and he was about to answer when a rotund San Salvadoran waddled into the garden.

"Greetings, Jhumm!" the red-skinned, hairless creature pronounced, raising a double-jointed arm. "I understand that all went well with the Earthmen. I have come to proffer my congratulations!"

Jhumm wiggled his flopping ears happily. "Thank you," he said. "And my thanks, too, to all of your people for bearing with us so patiently in these last difficult years."

Morales was startled. The San Salvadoran was speaking in the Trogish language, and Morales had assumed up until now that no native was capable of that feat. At least, none had ever attempted it before in the presence of any Earthman. Oliphant and the others, as well as Morales, had remarked on the studied San Salvadoran indifference to their rulers. In return, the Trogish had always treated their subjects with a dignified reserve, speaking to them only when it seemed absolutely necessary.

And now here was a San Salvadoran speaking Trogish, and Jhumm was wriggling with happiness!

A sudden, irrational suspicion burgeoned in the anthropologist's mind. "Jhumm," he said, stepping forward, "do you know why I was killed?"

The tall Trogish turned. "To prevent you from warning us of an impending attack by Earth, of course."

Morales swallowed hard.

"You knew that?" he whispered. "And yet you let them go?"

The San Salvadoran waddled to Morales' side. He looked up at the human earnestly. "You must not grieve over that which cannot be changed, human," he said in his own sibilant language, and Morales became more confused then ever.

For four weeks the humans had tried in every conceivable way to get on speaking terms with the natives. But the San Salvadorans had answered every inquiry as briefly as possible and then returned to their own pursuits. It had been decided, finally, that the San Salvadorans were either too bucolically stupid or too subjugated to be able to respond intelligently. But this native, for some obscure reason, was offering his sympathy to Morales!

Then, suddenly, the anthropologist became aware that Jhumm was speaking.

". . . We didn't exactly know why they'd killed you, yet it wasn't hard to figure out. We were quite certain O'Fallon, your commanding officer, disapproved of the Trogish empire and had dreams of destroying it. When he killed you, the inference was that you refused to go along with him."

The tall Trogish played absently with the keys of his computer. "As for our letting them go, knowing they planned to persuade Earth to attack us," he went on, "I'm afraid I have a confession to make. Not only have we been aware of this plan, but we've been hoping desperately that nothing would happen to change the Earthmen's minds!"

"But . . . but why? Earth *will* attack, you know. They'll be back just as soon as a warfleet can be constructed. Unless you think your empire is impregnable—"

"Oh, don't worry about that," Jhumm said airily. "It's not. Our warships have been rusting hulks for almost a thousand years, and we probably couldn't operate them properly even if we knew how to put them back in shape, which we don't. No, Earth will attack us, and that will be the end of the Trogish empire, and I thank the ancient gods of my people that I am alive to see this happen."

The San Salvadoran whistled with amusement. "I appreciate how you must feel, Jhumm. And speaking for all of us on this planet, it couldn't have happened to a more deserving race!"

Morales clutched a throbbing head. "I don't understand," he muttered.

In a patient, almost lecture-room tone, the Trogish went on. "For close to two thousand years, Arthur, the Trogish have administered to the needs of the galaxy. That's long enough. We've paid our price of admission to the status of a mature, civilized race. We want to be able to concentrate at last on the more important things—

basic philosophy, the arts, science, and the general ordinary enjoyment of living. A race which has to worry about the multitudinous details of a three-billion-planet galactic civilization just hasn't the time for those things. I want to be a mathematician—and it looks like I'm going to get the chance!"

"But there will be bloodshed . . . warfare—" Morales protested.

"Not if we don't put up a fight," Jhumm told him. "And we won't. Nobody will. As soon as the Earth warships appear, we'll surrender and turn the reins of galactic rule over to them. Then we'll go about our own business, and let Earth run things, while we sit home thankfully on our own world. That's what the Pikux did to us, and before them the—"

"You mean the entire galaxy will just relax and allow Earth to take over?"

The Trogish viceroy wiggled his ears contentedly. "That's right. The galaxy is a smoothly running affair, you see. All it needs is a few individuals on each planet to keep things moving. Isn't it fair that the youngest, most backward species be given the job? After all, someone has to do it, and the older races obviously can do much more important things. Besides, it helps the newcomers to mature. After a few centuries, they begin to realize that what they thought was an empire is more on the order of being interstellar bookkeepers and clerks. But they weren't forced into anything—they demanded the job, and now they're stuck with it."

Morales began to chuckle crazily. "What happens if they up and quit?"

"They won't. None of us do. By the time they realize it fully, they've matured to the point where they can accept their position at the bottom of the galactic heap. Then it's a matter of waiting for a new race to come boiling up off a planet, demanding control of the galaxy."

"So for the next thousand years or so, Earthmen will be nothing but administrators, technicians—janitors?"

The San Salvadoran rippled its skin sympathetically. "Yes, human, that is the way it must be. The rest of us will help out occasionally, after a while, but only if we want to."

*   *   *

A thought occurred to Morales. "What happens to me?"

"That's up to you," Jhumm told him. "I'm afraid we can't permit you to meet up with Earthmen again. Not because we want to keep the future a secret—they wouldn't believe you, anyway. But because you're supposed to be dead, and they'll get curious about the revivification process. They'll learn it eventually, of course, but there's an established pattern to galactic conquest, and we mustn't disturb it."

The Trogish stared down at his computer thoughtfully for a moment. "How would you like to travel from planet to planet on the supply ships, visiting the different peoples? Every planet has its own culture, you know, and they're all interesting."

The young anthropologist nodded violently, so overwhelmed that he could not speak.

"You would? Good! It would take more than your own lifetime, even if we extend it to the full limit of our ability, to visit them all. It will even be many hundreds of Earth-years before full Earth administration is established over the entire galaxy. The Trogish will have to maintain interim control until then, but as long as it's interim, we won't mind."

"Oh, that reminds me!" the San Salvadoran broke in. "The planting season for this continent is upon us again, Jhumm. How many of *shasiss* beans are we to set our robots to planting this year?"

"My son is working on that problem right now," Jhumm said. "He will announce the quota as soon as he knows the figures himself." He pointed at the half-dilated door of the house, through which Kulihhan, the assistant Trogish viceroy on San Salvador, could be seen dimly, working furiously at his desk, almost buried beneath a mound of papers.

Editor's Introduction To:

BLOOD BANK

Walter M. Miller, Jr.

As empires age, they become more civilized. This may result in sheer decadence, but it won't be called that. For whatever reason, though, the empire won't be able to recruit many legionnaires from its heartland.

That leaves no choice but to recruit from the frontier areas; places with younger and more dynamic cultures; places where honor may be more important than life.

BLOOD BANK

Walter M. Miller, Jr.

The colonel's secretary heard clomping footsteps in the corridor and looked up from her typing. The footsteps stopped in the doorway. A pair of jet-black eyes bored through her once, then looked away. A tall, thin joker in a space commander's uniform stalked into the reception room, sat in the corner, and folded his hands stiffly in his lap. The secretary arched her plucked brows. It had been six months since a visitor had done that—walked in without saying boo to the girl behind the rail.

"You have an appointment, sir?" she asked with a professional smile.

The man nodded curtly but said nothing. His eyes

flickered toward her briefly, then returned to the wall. She tried to decide whether he was angry or in pain. The black eyes burned with cold fire. She checked the list of appointments. Her smile disappeared, to be replaced by a tight-lipped expression of scorn.

"You're Space Commander Eli Roki?" she asked in an icy tone.

Again the curt nod. She gazed at him steadily for several seconds. "Colonel Beth will see you in a few minutes." Then her typewriter began clattering with sharp sounds of hate.

The man sat quietly, motionlessly. The colonel passed through the reception room once and gave him a brief nod. Two majors came in from the corridor and entered the colonel's office without looking at him. A few moments later, the intercom crackled, "Send Roki in, Dela. Bring your pad and come with him."

The girl looked at Roki, but he was already on his feet, striding toward the door. Evidently he came from an unchivalrous planet; he opened the door without looking at her and let her catch it when it started to slam.

Chubby, elderly Colonel Beth sat waiting behind his desk, flanked by the pair of majors. Roki's bearing as he approached and saluted was that of the professional soldier, trained from birth for the military.

"Sit down, Roki."

The tall space commander sat at attention and waited, his face expressionless, his eyes coolly upon the colonel's forehead. Beth shuffled some papers on his desk, then spoke slowly.

"Before we begin, I want you to understand something, commander."

"Yes, sir."

"You are not being tried. This is not a court-martial. There are no charges against you. Is that clear?"

"Yes, sir."

The colonel's pale eyes managed to look at Roki's face without showing any contempt. "This investigation is for the record, and for the public. The incident has already been investigated, as you know. But the people are aroused, and we have to make a show of some kind."

"I understand, sir."

"Then let's begin. Dela, take notes, please." The colonel glanced at the papers before him. "Space Commander Roki, will you please tell us in your own words what happened during patrol flight Sixty-one on fourday sixmonth, year eighty-seven?"

There was a brief silence. The girl was staring at the back of Roki's neck as if she longed to attack it with a hatchet. Roki's thin face was a waxen mask as he framed his words. His voice came calm as a bell and clear.

"The flight was a random patrol. We blasted off Jod VII at thirteen hours, Universal Patrol Time, switched on the high-C drive, and penetrated to the ten-thousandth level of the C'th component. We re-entered the continuum on the outer patrol radius at thirty-six degrees theta and two-hundred degrees psi. My navigator threw the dice to select a random course. We were to proceed to a point on the same co-ordinate shell at thirty theta and one-fifty psi. We began—"

The colonel interrupted. "Were you aware at the time that your course would intersect that of the mercy ship?"

The girl looked up again. Roki failed to wince at the question. "I was aware of it, sir."

"Go on."

"We proceeded along the randomly selected course until the warp detectors warned us of a ship. When we came in range, I told the engineer to jockey into a parallel course and to lock the automatics to *keep* us parallel. When that was accomplished, I called the unknown freighter with the standard challenge."

"You saw its insignia?"

"Yes, sir. The yellow mercy star."

"Go on. Did they answer your challenge?"

"Yes, sir. The reply, decoded, was: Mercy liner Sol-G-6, departure Sol III, destination Jod VI, cargo emergency surgibank supplies, Cluster Request A-4-J."

Beth nodded and watched Roki with clinical curiosity. "You knew about the Jod VI disaster? That twenty thousand casualties were waiting in Suspendfreeze lockers for those supplies?"

"Yes, sir. I'm sorry they died."

"Go on with your account."

"I ordered the navigator to throw the dice again, to determine whether or not the freighter should be boarded for random cargo inspection. He threw a twelve, the yes-number. I called the freighter again, ordered the outer locks opened. It failed to answer, or respond in any way."

"One moment. You explained the reason for boarding? Sol is on the outer rim of the galaxy. It doesn't belong to any cluster system. Primitive place—or regressed. They wouldn't understand our ways."

"I allowed for that, sir," continued the cold-faced Roki. "I explained the situation, even read them extracts of our patrol regs. They failed to acknowledge. I thought perhaps they were out of contact, so I had the message repeated to them by blinker. I know they got it, because the blinker-operator acknowledged the message. Evidently carried it to his superiors. Apparently they told him to ignore us, because when we blinked again, he failed to acknowledge. I then attempted to pull alongside and attach to their hull by magnetic grapples."

"They resisted?"

"Yes, sir. They tried to break away by driving to a higher C-level. Our warp was already at six-thousand C's. The mass-components of our star cluster at that level were just a collapsing gas cloud. Of course, with our automatic trackers, they just dragged us with them, stalled, and plunged the other way. They pulled us down to the quarter-C level; most of the galaxy was at the red-dwarf stage. I suppose they realized then that they couldn't get away from us like that. They came back to a sensible warp and continued on their previous course."

"And you did what?"

"We warned them by every means of communication at our disposal, read them the standard warning."

"They acknowledge?"

"Once, sir. They came back to say: This is an emergency shipment. We have orders not to stop. We are continuing on course, and will report you to authority upon arrival." Roki paused, eyeing the colonel doubtfully. "May I make a personal observation, sir?"

Beth nodded tolerantly. "Go ahead."

"They wasted more time dodging about in the C'th component than they would have lost if they had allowed us to board them. I regarded this behavior as highly suspicious."

"Did it occur to you that it might be due to some peculiarity in Sol III's culture? Some stubbornness, or resentment of authority?"

"Yes, sir."

"Did you ask opinions of your crew?"

A slight frown creased Roki's high forehead. "No, sir."

"Why not?"

"Regulation does not require it, sir. My personal reason—the cultural peculiarities of my planet."

The barb struck home. Colonel Beth knew the military culture of Roki's world—Coph IV. Military rank was inherited. On his own planet, Roki was a nobleman and an officer of the war-college. He had been taught to rely upon his own decisions and to expect crisp, quick obedience. The colonel frowned at his desk.

"Let's put it this way: Did you *know* the opinions of the crew?"

"Yes, sir. They thought that we should abandon the pursuit and allow the freighter to continue. I was forced to confine two of them to the brig for insubordination and attempted mutiny." He stopped and glanced at one of the majors. "All due apologies to you, sir."

The major flushed. He ranked Roki, but he had been with the patrol as an observer, and despite his higher rank, he was subject to the ship commander's authority while in space. He had also been tossed in the brig. Now he glared at the Cophian space commander without speaking.

"All right, commander, when they refused to halt, what did you do?"

"I withdrew to a safe range and fired a warning charge ahead of them. It exploded in full view of their scopes, dead ahead. They ignored the warning and tried to flee again."

"Go on."

Roki's shoulder lifted in the suggestion of a shrug. "In

accordance with Article Thirty of the Code, I shot them
out of space."

The girl made a choking sound. "And over ten
thousand people died on Jod VI because of you—"

"*That will do, Dela!*" snapped Colonel Beth.

There was a long silence. Roki waited calmly for
further questioning. He seemed unaware of the girl's
outburst. The colonel's voice came again with a forced
softness.

"You examined the debris of the destroyed vessel?"

"Yes, sir."

"What did you find?"

"Fragments of quick-frozen bone, blood plasma, various bodily organs and tissues in cultured or frozen
form, prepared for surgical use in transplanting operations; in other words, a complete stock of surgibank
supplies, as was anticipated. We gathered up samples,
but we had no facilities for preserving what was left."

The colonel drummed his fingers. "You said 'anticipated.' Then you knew full well the nature of the cargo,
and you did not suspect contraband material of any
kind?"

Roki paused. "I suspected contraband, colonel," he
said quietly.

Beth lifted his eyebrows in surprise. "You didn't say
that before."

"I was never asked."

"Why didn't you say it anyway?"

"I had no proof."

"Ah, yes," murmured the colonel. "The culture of
Coph IV again. Very well, but in examining the debris,
you found no evidence of contraband?" The colonel's
distasteful expression told the room that he knew the
answer, but only wanted it on the record.

But Roki paused a long time. Finally, he said, "No
evidence, sir."

"Why do you hesitate?"

"Because I still suspect an illegality—without proof,
I'm afraid."

This time, the colonel's personal feelings betrayed
him in a snort of disgust. He shuffled his papers for a

long time, then looked at the major who had accompanied the patrol. "Will you confirm Roki's testimony,
major? Is it essentially truthful, as far as you know?"

The embarrassed officer glared at Roki in undisguised
hatred. "For the record, sir—I think the commander
behaved disgracefully and insensibly. The results of the
stoppage of vitally needed supplies prove—"

"I didn't ask for a moral judgment!" Beth snapped. "I
asked you to confirm what he has said here. Were the
incidents as he described them?"

The major swallowed hard. "Yes, sir."

The colonel nodded. "Very well. I'll ask your opin-
ions, gentlemen. Was there an infraction of regulations?
Did Commander Roki behave as required by Space
Code, or did he not? Yes or no, please. Major Tuli?"

"No direct infraction, sir, but—"

"No *buts!* Major Go'an?"

"Uh—no infraction, sir."

"I find myself in agreement." The colonel spoke directly at Dela's note pad. "The ultimate results of the
incident were disastrous, indeed. And, Roki's action
was unfortunate, ill-advised, and not as the Sixty-Star
Patrol would approve. Laws, codes, regulations are made
for men, not men for regulations. Roki observed the
letter of the law, but was perhaps forgetful of its spirit.
However, no charge can be found against him. This
investigating body recommends that he be temporarily
grounded without prejudice, and given thorough physical and mental examinations before being returned to
duty. That brings us to an end, gentlemen. Dela, you
may go."

With another glare at the haughty Cophian, the girl
stalked out of the room. Beth leaned back in his chair,
while the majors saluted and excused themselves. His
eyes kept Roki locked in his chair. When they were
alone, Beth said:

"You have anything to say to me off the record?"

Roki nodded. "I can submit my resignation from the
patrol through your office, can't I, sir?"

Beth smiled coldly. "I thought you'd do that, Roki."
He opened a desk drawer and brought out a single

sheet of paper. "I took the liberty of having it prepared for your signature. Don't misunderstand. I'm not urging you to resign, but we're prepared to accept it if you choose to do so. If you don't like this standard form, you may prepare your own."

The jet-eyed commander took the paper quickly and slashed his name quickly across the bottom. "Is this effective immediately, sir?"

"In this case, we can make it so."

"Thank you, sir."

"Don't regard it as a favor." The colonel witnessed the signature.

The Cophian could not be stung. "May I go now?"

Beth looked up, noticing with amusement that Roki—now a civilian—had suddenly dropped the "sir." And his eyes were no longer cold. They were angry, hurt, despairing.

"What makes you Cophians tick anyway?" he murmured thoughtfully.

Roki stood up. "I don't care to discuss it with you, colonel. I'll be going now."

"Wait, Roki." Beth frowned ominously to cover whatever he felt.

"I'm waiting."

"Up until this incident, I liked you, Roki. In fact, I told the general that you were the most promising young officer in my force."

"Kind of you," he replied tonelessly.

"And you could have been sitting at this desk, in a few years. You hoped to, I believe."

A curt nod, and a quick glance at Beth's shoulder insignia.

"You chose your career, and now you don't have it. I know what it means to you."

A tightening of the Cophian's jaw told the colonel that he wanted no sympathy, but Beth continued.

"Since this is the oldest, most established, most static planet in the Cluster, you're out of a job in a place where there's no work."

"That's none of your business, colonel," Roki said quietly.

"According to my culture's ethics it *is* my business,"

he bellowed. "Of course you Cophians think differently. But we're not quite so cold. Now you listen: I'm prepared to help yóu a little, although you're probably too pig-headed to accept. God knows, you don't deserve it anyway."

"Go on."

"I'm prepared to have a patrol ship take you to any planet in the galaxy. Name it, and we'll take you there." He paused. "All right, go ahead and refuse. Then get out."

Roki's thin face twitched for a moment. Then he nodded. "I'll accept. Take me to Sol III."

The colonel got his breath again slowly. He reddened and chewed his lip. "I did say galaxy, didn't I? I meant . . . well . . . you know we can't send a military ship outside the Sixty-Star Cluster."

Roki waited impassively, his dark eyes measuring the colonel.

"Why do you want to go *there*?"

"Personal reasons."

"Connected with the mercy ship incident?"

"The investigation is over."

Beth pounded his desk. "It's crazy, man! Nobody's been to Sol for a thousand years. No reason to go. Sloppy, decadent place. I never suspected *they'd* answer Jod VI's plea for surgibank supplies!"

"Why not? They were *selling* them."

"Of course. But I doubted that Sol still had ships, especially C-drive ships. Only contribution Sol ever made to the galaxy was to spawn the race of Man—if you believe that story. It's way out of contact with any interstellar nation. I just don't get it."

"Then you restrict your offer, colonel?" Roki's eyes mocked him.

Beth sighed. "No, no—I *said* it. I'll do it. But I can't send a patrol ship that far. I'll have to pay your way on a private vessel. We can find some excuse—exploration maybe."

Roki's eyes flickered sardonically. "Why not send a diplomatic delegation—to apologize to Sol for the blasting of their mercy ship."

"Uk! With YOU aboard?"

"Certainly. They won't know me."

Beth just stared at Roki as if he were of a strange species.

"You'll do it?" urged Roki.

"I'll think it over. I'll see that you get there, if you insist on going. Now get out of here. I've had enough of you, Roki."

The Cophian was not offended. He turned on his heel and left the office. The girl looked up from her filing cabinets as he came out. She darted ahead of him and blocked the doorway with her small tense body. Her face was a white mask of disgust, and she spoke between her teeth.

"How does it feel to murder ten thousand people and get away with it?" she hissed.

Roki looked at her face more closely and saw the racial characteristics of Jod VI—the slightly oversized irises of her yellow-brown eyes, the thin nose with flaring nostrils, the pointed jaw. Evidently some of her relatives had died in the disaster and she held him personally responsible. He had destroyed the ship that was on its way to casualties.

"How does it feel?" she demanded, her voice going higher, and her hands clenching into weapons.

"Would you step aside please, Miss?"

A quick hand slashed out to rake his cheek with sharp nails. Pain seared his face. He did not move. Two bright stripes of blood appeared from his eye to the corner of his mouth. A drop trickled to the point of his chin and splattered down upon the girl's shoe.

"On my planet," he said, in a not unkindly tone, "when a woman insists on behaving like an animal, we assist her—by having her flogged naked in the public square. I see personal dignity is not so highly prized here. You do not regard it as a crime to behave like an alley cat?"

Her breath gushed out of her in a sound of rage, and she tore at the wounds again. Then, when he did nothing but look at her coldly, she fled.

Eli Roki, born to the nobility of Coph, dedicated to the service of the Sixty-Star Cluster, suddenly found

himself something of an outcast. As he strode down the
corridor away from Beth's office, he seemed to be walking into a thickening fog of desolation. He had no home
now; for he had abdicated his hereditary rights on Coph
in order to accept a commission with the SSC Patrol.
That, too, was gone; and with it his career.

He had known from the moment he pressed the
firing stud to blast the mercy freighter that unless the
freighter proved to be a smuggler, his career would be
forfeit. He was still morally certain that he had made no
mistake. Had the freighter been carrying any other
cargo, he would have been disciplined for *not* blasting
it. And, if they had had nothing to hide, they would
have stopped for inspection. Somewhere among Sol's
planets lay the answer to the question—"What else was
aboard besides the cargo of mercy?"

Roki shivered and stiffened his shoulders as he rode
homeward in a heliocab. If the answer to the question
were "Nothing," then according to the code of his planet,
there was only one course left to follow. "The Sword of
Apology" it was called.

He waited in his quarters for the colonel to fulfill his
promise. On the following day, Beth called.

"I've found a Dalethian ship, Roki. Privately owned.
Pilot's willing to fly you out of the Cluster. It's going as
an observation mission—gather data on the Sol System.
The commissioners vetoed the idea of sending a diplomatic delegation until we try to contact Solarians by
high-C radio."

"When do I leave?"

"Be at the spaceport tonight. And good luck, son. I'm
sorry all this happened, and I hope—"

"Yeah, thanks."

"Well—"

"Well?"

The colonel grunted and hung up. Ex-Commander
Roki gathered up his uniforms and went looking for a
pawn shop. "Hock 'em, or sell 'em?" asked a bald man
behind the counter. Then he peered more closely at
Roki's face, and paused to glance at a picture on the
front page of the paper. "Oh," he grunted, "you. You
wanta sell 'em." With a slight sneer, he pulled two bills

from his pocket and slapped them on the counter with a contemptuous take-it-or-leave-it stare. The clothing was worth at least twice as much. Roki took it after a moment's hesitation. The money just matched the price tag on a sleek, snub-nosed Multin automatic that lay in the display case.

"And three hundred rounds of ammunition," he said quietly as he pocketed the weapon.

The dealer sniffed. "It only takes one shot, bud—for what *you* need to do."

Roki thanked him for the advice and took his three hundred rounds.

He arrived at the spaceport before his pilot, and went out to inspect the small Dalethian freighter that would bear him to the rim of the galaxy. His face clouded as he saw the pitted hull and the glaze of fusion around the lips of the jet tubes. Some of the ground personnel had left a Geiger hanging on the stern, to warn wanderers to keep away. Its dial indicator was fluttering in the red. He carried it into the ship. The needle dropped to a safe reading in the control cabin, but there were dangerous spots in the reactor room. Angrily he went to look over the controls.

His irritation grew. The ship—atly named the *Idiot*— was of ancient vintage, without the standard warning systems or safety devices, and with no armament other than its ion guns. The fifth dial of its position-indicator was calibrated only to one hundred thousand C's, and was redlined at ninety-thousand. A modern serviceship, on the other hand, could have penetrated to a segment of five-space where light's velocity was constant at one hundred fifty thousand C's and could reach Sol in two months. The *Idiot* would need five or six, if it could make the trip at all. Roki doubted it. Under normal circumstances, he would hesitate to use the vessel even within the volume of the Sixty-Star Cluster.

He thought of protesting to Beth, but realized that the colonel had fulfilled his promise, and would do nothing more. Grumbling, he stowed his gear in the cargo hold, and settled down in the control room to doze in wait for the pilot.

*   *   *

A sharp whack across the soles of his boots brought him painfully awake. "Get your feet off the controls!" snapped an angry voice.

Roki winced and blinked at a narrow frowning face with a cigar clenched in its teeth. "And get out of that chair!" the face growled around its cigar.

His feet stung with pain. He hissed a snarl and bounded to his feet; grabbing a handful of the intruder's shirt-front, he aimed a punch at the cigar—then stayed the fist in midair. Something felt wrong about the shirt. Aghast, he realized there was a woman inside it. He let go and reddened. "I . . . I thought you were the pilot."

She eyed him contemptuously as she tucked in her shirt. "I am, Doc." She tossed her hat on the navigation desk, revealing a sloe-cropped head of dark hair. She removed the cigar from her face, neatly pinched out the fire, and filed the butt in the pocket of her dungarees for a rainy day. She had a nice mouth, with the cigar gone, but it was tight with anger.

"Stay out of my seat," she told him crisply, "and out of my hair. Let's get that straight before we start."

"This . . . this is *your* tub?" he gasped.

She stalked to a panel and began punching settings into the courser. "That's right. I'm Daleth Shipping Incorporated. Any comments?"

"You expect this wreck to make it to Sol?" he growled.

She snapped him a sharp, green-eyed glance. "Well listen to the free ride! Make your complaints to the colonel, fellow. I don't expect anything, except my pay. I'm willing to chance it. Why shouldn't you?"

"The existence of a fool is not necessarily a proof of the existence of two fools," he said sourly.

"If you don't like it, go elsewhere." She straightened and swept him a clinical glance. "But as I understand it, *you* can't be too particular."

He frowned. "Are you planning to make *that* your business?"

"*Uh*—uh! You're nothing to me, fellow. I don't care *who* I haul, as long as it's legal. Now do you want a ride, or don't you?"

He nodded curtly and stalked back to find quarters. "Stay outa my cabin," she bellowed after him.

Roki grunted disgustedly. The pilot was typical of Daleth civilization. It was still a rough, uncouth planet with a thinly scattered population, a wild frontier, and growing pains. The girl was the product of a wildly expanding tough-fisted culture with little respect for authority. It occurred to him immediately that she might be thinking of selling him to the Solarian officials—as the man who blasted the mercy ship.

"Prepare to lift," came the voice of the intercom. "Two minutes before blast-off."

Roki suppressed an urge to scramble out of the ship and call the whole thing off. The rockets belched, coughed, and then hissed faintly, idling in wait for a command. Roki stretched out on his bunk, for some of these older ships were rather rough on blast-off. The hiss became a thunder, and the *Idiot* moved skyward— first slowly, then with a spurt of speed. When it cleared the atmosphere, there was a sudden lurch as it shed the now empty booster burners. There was a moment of dead silence, as the ship hovered without power. Then the faint shriek of the ion streams came to his ears—as the ion drive became useful in the vacuum of space. He glanced out the port to watch the faint streak of luminescence focus into a slender needle of high-speed particles, pushing the *Idiot* ever higher in a rush of acceleration.

He punched the intercom button. "Not bad, for a Dalethian," he called admiringly.

"Keep your opinions to yourself," growled Daleth Incorporated.

The penetration to higher C-levels came without subjective sensation. Roki knew it was happening when the purr from the reactor room went deep-throated and when the cabin lights went dimmer. He stared calmly out the port, for the phenomenon of penetration never ceased to thrill him.

The transition to high-C began as a blue-shift in the starlight. Distant, dull-red stars came slowly brighter, whiter—until they burned like myriad welding arcs in the black vault. They were not identical with the stars of the home continuum, but rather, projections of the same star-masses at higher C-levels of five-space, where the velocity of light was gradually increasing as the *Idiot* climbed higher in the C-component.

At last he had to close the port, for the starlight was becoming unbearable as its wave-length moved into the ultra-violet and the X-ray bands. He watched on a fluorescent viewing screen. The projective star-masses were flaring into supernovae, and the changing continuums seemed to be collapsing toward the ship in the blue-shift of the cosmos. As the radiant energy increased, the cabin became warmer, and the pilot set up a partial radiation screen.

At last the penetration stopped. Roki punched the intercom again. "What level are we on, Daleth?"

"Ninety thousand," she replied curtly.

Roki made a wry mouth. She had pushed it up to the red line without a blink. It was O.K.—if the radiation screens held out. If they failed to hold it, the ship would be blistered into a drifting dust cloud.

"Want me to navigate for you?" he called.

"I'm capable of handling my own ship," she barked.

"I'm aware of that. But I have nothing else to do. You might as well put me to work."

She paused, then softened a little. "O.K., come on forward."

She swung around in her chair as he entered the cabin, and for the first time he noticed that, despite the close-cropped hair and the dungarees and the cigar-smoking, she was quite a handsome girl—handsome, proud, and highly capable. Daleth, the frontier planet, bred a healthy if somewhat unscrupulous species.

"The C-maps are in that case," she said, jerking her thumb toward a filing cabinet. "Work out a course for maximum radiant thrust."

Roki frowned. "Why not a least-time course?"

She shook her head. "My reactors aren't too efficient. We need all the boost we can get from external energy. Otherwise we'll have to dive back down for fuel."

Worse and worse!—Roki thought as he dragged out the C-maps. Flying this boat to Sol would have been a feat of daring two centuries ago. Now, in an age of finer ships, it was a feat of idiocy.

*   *   *

Half an hour later, he handed her a course plan that would allow the *Idiot* to derive about half of its thrust from the variations in radiation pressure from the roaring inferno of the high-level cosmos. She looked it over without change of expression, then glanced at him curiously, after noting the time.

"You're pretty quick," she said.

"Thank you."

"You're hardly stupid. Why did you pull such a stupid boner?"

Roki stiffened. "I thought you planned to regard that as none of your business."

She shrugged and began punching course-settings into the courser. "Sorry, I forgot."

Still angry, he said, "I don't regard it as a boner. I'd do it again."

She shrugged again and pretended a lack of interest.

"Space-smuggling could be the death of the galaxy," he went on. "That's been proven. A billion people once died on Tau II because somebody smuggled in a load of non-Tauian animals—for house pets. I did only what history has proven best."

"I'm trying to mind my own business," she growled, eyeing him sourly.

Roki fell silent and watched her reshape the radiation screen to catch a maximum of force from the flare of energy that blazed behind them. Roki was not sure that he wanted her to mind her own business. They would have to bear each other's presence for several months, and it would be nice to know how things stood.

"So you think it was a stupid boner," he continued at last. "So does everyone else. It hasn't been very pleasant."

She snorted scornfully as she worked. "Where I come from, we don't condemn fools. We don't need to. They just don't live very long, not on Daleth."

"And I am a fool, by your code?"

"How should I know? If you live to a ripe old age and get what you want, you probably aren't a fool."

And *that*, thought Roki, was the Dalethian golden rule. If the universe lets you live, then you're doing all right. And there was truth in it, perhaps. Man was born with only one right—the right to a chance at proving his fitness. And that right was the foundation of every culture, even though most civilized worlds tried to define "fitness" in terms of cultural values. Where life was rough, it was rated in terms of survival.

"I really don't mind talking about it," he said with some embarrassment. "I have nothing to hide."

"That's nice."

"Do you have a name—other than your firm name?"

"As far as you're concerned, I'm Daleth Incorporated." She gave him a suspicious look that lingered a while and became contemplative. "There's only one thing I'm curious about—why are you going to Sol?"

He smiled wryly. "If I told a Dalethian that, she would indeed think me a fool."

Slowly the girl nodded. "I see. I know of Cophian ethics. If an officer's blunder results in someone's death, he either proves that it was not a blunder or he cuts his throat—ceremonially, I believe. Will you do that?"

Roki shrugged. He had been away from Coph a long time. He didn't know.

"A stupid custom," she said.

"It manages to drain off the fools, doesn't it? It's better than having society try and execute them forcibly for their crimes. On Coph, a man doesn't need to be afraid of society. He needs only to be afraid of his own weakness. Society's function is to protect individuals against unfortunate accidents, but not against their own blunders. And when a man blunders, Coph simply excludes him from the protectorate. As an outcast, he sacrifices himself. It's not too bad a system."

"You can have it."

"Dalethian?"

"Yeah?"

"You have no personal anger against what I did?"

She frowned at him contemptuously. "Uh-uh! I judge no one. I judge no one unless I'm personally involved. Why are you worried about what others think?"

"In our more highly developed society," he said stiffly, "a man inevitably grows a set of thinking-habits called 'conscience.'"

"Oh—yeah." Her dull tone indicated a complete lack of interest.

Again Roki wondered if she would think of making a quick bit of cash by informing Solarian officials of his identity. He began a mental search for a plan to avoid such possible treachery.

They ate and slept by the ship's clock. On the tenth day, Roki noticed a deviation in the readings of the radiation-screen instruments. The shape of the screen shell was gradually trying to drift toward minimum torsion, and assume a spherical shape. He pointed it out to Daleth, and she quickly made the necessary readjustments. But the output of the reactors crept a notch higher as a result of the added drain. Roki wore an apprehensive frown as the flight progressed.

Two days later, the screen began creeping again. Once more the additional power was applied. And the reactor output needle hung in the yellow band of warning. The field-generators were groaning and shivering with threatening overload. Roki worked furiously to locate the trouble, and at last he found it. He returned to the control cabin in a cold fury.

"Did you have this ship pre-flighted before blast-off?" he demanded.

Her mouth fluttered with amusement as she watched his anger. "Certainly, commander."

He flushed at the worthless title. "May I see the papers?"

For a moment she hesitated, then fumbled in her pocket and displayed a folded pink paper.

"Pink!" he roared. "You had no business taking off!"

Haughtily, she read him the first line of the pre-flight report. " 'Base personnel disclaim any responsibility for accidents resulting from flight of Daleth Ship—' It doesn't say I can't take off."

"I'll see you banned from space!" he growled.

She gave him a look that reminded him of his current status. It was a tolerant, amused stare. "What's wrong, commander?"

"The synchronizers are out, that's all," he fumed. "Screen's getting farther and farther from resonance."

"So?"

"So the overload'll get worse, and the screen'll break down. So you'll have to drop back out of the C-component and get it repaired."

She shook her head. "We'll chance it like it is. I've always wanted to find out how much overload the reactor'll take."

Roki choked. There wasn't a chance of making it. "Are you a graduate space engineer?" he asked.

"No."

"Then you'd better take one's advice."

"Yours?"

"Yes."

"No! We're going on."

"Suppose I refuse to let you?"

She whirled quickly, eyes flashing. "I'm in command of my ship. I'm also armed. I suggest you return to your quarters, passenger."

Roki sized up the situation, measured the determination in the girl's eyes, and decided that there was only one thing to do. He shrugged and looked away, as if admitting her authority. She glared at him for a moment, but did not press her demand that he leave the control room. As soon as she glanced back at the instruments, Roki padded his rough knuckles with a handkerchief, selected a target at the back of her short crop of dark hair, and removed her objections with a short chopping blow to the head. "Sorry, friend," he murmured as he lifted her limp body out of the seat.

He carried her to her quarters and placed her on the bunk. After removing a small needle gun from her pocket, he left a box of headache tablets in easy reach, locked her inside, and went back to the controls. His fist was numb, and he felt like a heel, but there was no use arguing with a Dalethian. Clubbing her to sleep was the only way to avoid bloodier mayhem in which she might have emerged the victor—until the screen gave way.

The power indication was threateningly high as Roki activated the C-drive and began piloting the ship downward through the fifth component. But with proper adjustments, he made the process analogous to freefall, and the power reading fell off slowly. A glance at the C-maps told him that the *Idiot* would emerge far beyond the limits of Sixty-Star Cluster. When it re-entered the continuum, it would be in the general volume of space controlled by another interstellar organization called The Viggern Federation. He knew little of its culture, but certainly it should have facilities for repairing a set of screen-synchronizers. He looked up its capital planet, and began jetting toward it while the ship drifted downward in C. As he reached lower energy-levels, he cut out the screen altogether and went to look in on Daleth Incorporated, who had made no sound for two hours.

He was surprised to see her awake and sitting up on the bunk. She gave him a cold and deadly stare, but displayed no rage. "I should've known better than to turn my back on you."

"Sorry. You were going to—"

"Save it. Where are we?"

"Coming in on Tragor III."

"I'll have you jailed on Tragor III, then."

He nodded. "You *could* do that, but then you might have trouble collecting my fare from Beth."

"That's all right."

"Suit yourself. I'd rather be jailed on your trumped-up charges than be a wisp of gas at ninety-thousand C's."

"Trumped up?"

"Sure, the pink pre-flight. Any court will say that whatever happened was your own fault. You lose your authority if you fly pink, unless your crew signs a release."

"You a lawyer?"

"I've had a few courses in space law. But if you don't believe me, check with the Interfed Service on Tragor III."

"I will. Now how about opening the door. I want out."

"Behave?"

She paused, then: "My promise wouldn't mean anything, Roki. I don't share your system of ethics."

He watched her cool green eyes for a moment, then chuckled. "In a sense you *do*—or you wouldn't have said *that*." He unlocked the cabin and released her, not trusting her, but realizing that the synchronizers were so bad by now that she couldn't attempt to go on without repairs. She could have no motive for turning on him—except anger perhaps.

"My gun?" she said.

Again Roki hesitated. Then, smiling faintly, he handed it to her. She took the weapon, sniffed scornfully, and cocked it.

"Turn around, fool!" she barked.

Roki folded his arms across his chest, and remained facing her. "Go to the devil," he said quietly.

Her fingers whitened on the trigger. Still the Cophian failed to flinch, lose his smile, or move. Daleth Incorporated arched her eyebrows, uncocked the pistol, and returned it to her belt. Then she patted his cheek and chuckled nastily. "Just watch yourself, commander. I don't like you."

And he noticed, as she turned away, that she had a bump on her head to prove it. He wondered how much the bump would cost him before it was over. Treachery on Sol, perhaps.

The pilot called Tragor III and received instructions to set an orbital course to await inspection. All foreign ships were boarded before being permitted to land. A few hours later, a small patrol ship winged close and grappled to the hull. Roki went to manipulate the locks.

A captain and two assistants came through. The inspector was a young man with glasses and oversized ears. His eyebrows were ridiculously bushy and extended down on each side to his cheekbones. The ears were also filled with yellow brush. Roki recognized the peculiarities as local evolutionary tendencies; for they were shared also by the assistants. Tragor III evidently had an exceedingly dusty atmosphere.

The captain nodded a greeting and requested the ship's flight papers. He glanced at the pink pre-flight, clucked to himself, and read every word in the dispatcher's forms. "Observation flight? To Sol?" He addressed himself to Roki, using the interstellar Esperanto.

The girl answered. "That's right. Let's get this over with."

The captain gave her a searing, head-to-toe glance. "Are you the ship's owner, woman?"

Daleth Incorporated contained her anger with an effort. "I am."

The captain told her what a Tragorian thought of it by turning aside from her, and continuing to address Roki as if he were ship's skipper. "Please leave the ship while we fumigate and inspect. Wohr will make you comfortable in the patrol vessel. You will have to submit to physical examination—a contagion precaution."

Roki nodded, and they started out after the assistant. As they entered the corridor, he grinned at Daleth, and received a savage kick in the shin for his trouble.

"Oops, sorry!" she muttered.

"Oh—one moment, sir," the captain called after them. "May I speak to you a moment—"

They both stopped and turned.

"Privately," the captain added.

The girl marched angrily on. Roki stepped back in the cabin and nodded.

"You are a well-traveled man, E Roki?" the bushy-browed man asked politely.

"Space has been my business."

"Then you need no warning about local customs." The captain bowed.

"I know enough to respect them and conform to them," Roki assured him. "That's a general rule. But I'm not familiar with Tragor III. Is there anything special I should know before we start out?"

"Your woman, E Roki. You might do well to inform her that she will have to wear a veil, speak to no man, and be escorted upon the streets at all times. Otherwise, she will be wise to remain on the ship, in her quarters."

Roki suppressed a grin. "I shall try to insure her good behavior."

The captain looked defensive. "You regard our customs as primitive?"

"Every society to its own tastes, captain. The wisdom of one society would be folly for another. Who is qualified to judge? Only the universe, which passes the judgment of survival on all peoples."

"Thank you. You are a wise traveler. I might explain that our purdah is the result of an evolutionary peculiarity. You will see for yourself, however."

"I can't *guarantee* my companion's behavior," Roki said before he went to join Daleth. "But I'll try my best to influence her."

Roki was grinning broadly as he went to the patrol vessel to wait. One thing was certain: the girl would have a rough time on Tragor if she tried to have him jailed for mutiny.

Her face reddened to forge-heat as he relayed the captain's warning.

"I shall do nothing of the sort," she said stiffly.

Roki shrugged. "You know enough to respect local customs."

"Not when they're personally humiliating!" She curled up on a padded seat in the visitor's room and began to pout. He decided to drop the subject.

Repairing the synchronizers promised to be a week-long job, according to the Tragorian inspector who accompanied the *Idiot* upon landing. "Our replacements are standardized, of course—within our own system. But parts for SSC ships aren't carried in stock. The synchronizers will have to be specially tailored."

"Any chance of rushing the job?"

"A week *is* rushing it."

"All right, we'll have to wait." Roki nudged the controls a bit, guiding the ship toward the landing site pointed out by the captain. Daleth was in her cabin, alone, to save herself embarrassment.

"May I ask a question about your mission, E Roki—or is it confidential in nature?"

Roki paused to think before answering. He would have to lie, of course, but he had to make it safe. Suddenly he chuckled. "I forgot for a moment that you weren't with Sixty-Star Cluster. So I'll tell you the truth. This is supposed to be an observation mission, officially—but actually, our superior sent us to buy him a holdful of a certain scarce commodity."

The captain grinned. Graft and corruption were apparently not entirely foreign to Tragor III. But then his grin faded into thoughtfulness. "On Sol's planets?"

Roki nodded.

"This scarce commodity—if I'm not too curious—is it surgibank supplies?"

Roki felt his face twitch with surprise. But he recovered from his shock in an instant. "Perhaps," he said calmly. He wanted to grab the man by the shoulders and shout a thousand questions, but he said nothing else.

The official squirmed in his seat for a time. "Does your federation buy many mercy cargoes from Sol?"

Roki glanced at him curiously. The captain was brimming with ill-concealed curiosity. Why?

"Occasionally, yes."

The captain chewed his lip for a moment. "Tell me," he blurted, "will the Solarian ships stop for your patrol inspections?"

Roki hesitated for a long time. Then he said, "I suppose that you and I could get together and share what we know about Sol without revealing any secrets of our own governments. Frankly, I, too, am curious about Sol."

The official, whose name was WeJan, was eager to accept. He scrawled a peculiar series of lines on a scrap of paper and gave it to Roki. "Show this to a heliocab driver. He will take you to my apartment. Would dinner be convenient?"

Roki said that it would.

The girl remained in her quarters when they landed. Roki knocked at the door, but she was either stubborn or asleep. He left the ship and stood for a moment on the ramp, staring at the hazy violet sky. Fine grit sifted against his face and stung his eyes.

"You will be provided goggles, suitable clothing, and an interpreter to accompany you during your stay," said WeJan as they started toward a low building.

But Roki was scarcely listening as he stared across the ramp. A thousand yards away was a yellow-starred mercy ship, bearing Solar markings. The most peculiar thing about it was the ring of guards that surrounded it.

They apparently belonged to the ship, for their uniforms were different from those of the base personnel.

WeJan saw him looking. "Strange creatures, aren't they?" he whispered confidentially.

Roki had decided that in the long run he could gain more information by pretending to know more than he did. So he nodded wisely and said nothing. The mercy ship was too far away for him to decide whether the guards were human. He could make out only that they were bipeds. "Sometimes one meets strange ones all right. Do you know the Quinjori—from the other side of the galaxy?"

"No—no, I believe not, E Roki. Quinjori?"

"Yes. A very curious folk. Very curious indeed." He smiled to himself and fell silent. Perhaps, before his visit was over, he could trade fictions about the fictitious Quinjori for facts about the Solarians.

Roki met his interpreter in the spaceport offices, donned the loose garb of Tragor, and went to quibble with repair service. Still he could not shorten the promised-time on the new synchros. They were obviously stuck for a week on Tragor. He thought of trying to approach the Solarian ship, but decided that it would be better to avoid suspicion.

Accompanied by the bandy-legged interpreter, whose mannerisms were those of a dog who had received too many beatings, Roki set out for Polarin, the Tragorian capital, a few miles away. His companion was a small middle-aged man with a piping voice and flaring ears; Roki decided that his real job was to watch his alien charge for suspicious activities, for the little man was no expert linguist. He spoke two or three of the tongues used in the Sixty-Star Cluster, but not fluently. The Cophian decided to rely on the Esperanto of space, and let the interpreter translate it into native Tragorian wherever necessary.

"How would E Roki care to amuse himself?" the little man asked. "A drink? A pretty girl? A museum?"

Roki chuckled. "What do most of your visitors do while they're here?" He wondered quietly what, in particular, the *Solarian* visitors did. But it might not be safe to ask.

"Uh—that would depend on nationality, sir," murmured Pok. "The true-human foreigners often like to visit the Wanderer, an establishment which caters to their business. The evolved-human and the nonhuman visitors like to frequent the Court of Kings—a rather, uh, peculiar place." He looked at Roki, doubtfully, as if wondering about his biological status.

"Which is most expensive?" he asked, although he really didn't care. Because of the phony "observation mission papers," he could make Colonel Beth foot the bill.

"The Court of Kings is rather high," Pok said. "But so is the Wanderer."

"Such impartiality deserves a return. We will visit them both, E Pok. If it suits you."

"I am your servant, E Roki."

How to identify a Solarian without asking?—Roki wondered as they sat sipping a sticky, yeasty drink in the lounge of the Wanderer. The dimly lighted room was filled with men of all races—pygmies, giants, black, red, and brown. All appeared human, or nearly so. There were a few women among the crewmen, and most of them removed their borrowed veils while in the tolerant sanctuary of the Wanderer. The Tragorian staff kept stealing furtive glances at these out-system females, and the Cophian wondered about their covetousness.

"Why do you keep watching the strange women, E Pok?" he asked the interpreter a few minutes later.

The small man sighed. "Evidently you have not yet seen Tragorian women."

Roki had seen a few heavily draped figures on the street outside, clinging tightly to the arms of men, but there hadn't been much to look at. Still, Pok's hint was enough to give him an idea.

"You don't mean Tragor III is one of those places where evolution has pushed the sexes further apart?"

"I do," Pok said sadly. "The feminine I.Q. is seldom higher than sixty, the height is seldom taller than your jacket pocket, and the weight is usually greater than your own. As one traveler put it: 'short, dumpy, and dumb.' Hence, the purdah."

"Because you don't like looking at them?"

"Not at all. Theirs is our standard of beauty. The purdah is because they are frequently too stupid to remember which man is their husband."

"Sorry I asked."

"Not at all," said Pok, whose tongue was being loosened by the yeasty brew. "It is our tragedy. We can bear it."

"Well, you've got it better than some planets. On Jevah, for instance, the men evolved into sluggish spidery little fellows, and the women are big husky brawlers."

"Ah yes. But Sol is the most peculiar of all, is it not?" said Pok.

"How do you mean?" Roki carefully controlled his voice and tried to look bored.

"Why, the Vamir, of course."

Because of the fact that Pok's eyes failed to move toward any particular part of the room, Roki concluded that there were no Solarians in this place. "Shall we visit the Court of Kings now, E Pok?" he suggested.

The small man was obviously not anxious to go. He murmured about ugly brutes, lingered over his drink, and gazed wistfully at a big dusky Sanbe woman. "Do you suppose she would notice me if I spoke to her?" the small interpreter asked.

"Probably. So would her five husbands. Let's go."

Pok sighed mournfully and came with him.

The Court of Kings catered to a peculiar clientele indeed; but not a one, so far as Roki could see, was completely inhuman. There seemed to be at least one common denominator to all intelligent life: it was bipedal and bimanual. Four legs was the most practical number for any animal on any planet, and it seemed that nature had nothing else to work with. When she decided to give intelligence to a species, she taught him to stand on his hind legs, freeing his forefeet to become tools of his intellect. And she usually taught him by making him use his hands to climb. As a Cophian biologist had said, "Life first tries to climb a tree to get to the stars. When it fails, it comes down and invents the high-C drive."

Again, Roki looked around for something that might be a Solarian. He saw several familiar species, some horned, some tailed, scaled, or heavily furred. Some stumbled and drooped as if Tragorian gravity weighted them down. Others bounced about as if floating free in space. One small creature, the native of a planet with an eight-hour rotational period, curled up on the table and fell asleep. Roki guessed that ninety percent of the customers were of human ancestry, for at one time during the history of the galaxy, Man had sprung forth like a sudden blossom to inherit most of space. Some said they came from Sol III, but there was no positive evidence.

As if echoing his thought, Pok suddenly grunted. "I will never believe we are descended from those surly creatures."

Roki looked up quickly, wondering if the small interpreter was telepathic. But Pok was sneering toward the doorway. The Cophian followed his tipsy gaze and saw a man enter. The man was distinguished only by his height and by the fact that he appeared more human, in the classical sense, than most of the other customers. He wore a uniform—maroon jacket and gray trousers— and it matched the ones Roki had seen from a distance at the spaceport.

So this was a Solarian. He stared hard, trying to take in much at once. The man wore a short beard, but there seemed to be something peculiar about the jaw. It was—predatory, perhaps. The skull was massive, but plump and rounded like a baby's, and covered with sparse yellow fur. The eyes were quick and sharp, and seemed almost to leap about the room. He was at least seven feel tall, and there was a look of savagery about him that caused the Cophian to tense, as if sensing an adversary.

"What is it you don't like about them?" he asked, without taking his eyes from the Solarian.

"Their sharp ears for one thing," whispered Pok as

the Solarian whirled to stare toward their table. "Their nasty tempers for another."

"Ah? Rage reactions show biologic weakness," said the Cophian in a mild tone, but as loud as the first time.

The Solarian, who had been waiting for a seat at the bar, turned and stalked straight toward them. Pok whimpered. Roki stared at him cooly. The Solarian loomed over them and glared from one to the other. He seemed to decide that Pok was properly cowed, and he turned his fierce eyes on the ex-patrolman.

"Would you like to discuss biology, manthing?" he growled like distant thunder. His speaking exposed his teeth—huge white chisels of heavy ivory. They were not regressed toward the fanged stage, but they suggested, together with the massive jaw, that nature might be working toward an efficient bone-crusher.

Roki swirled his drink thoughtfully. "I don't know you, Bristleface," he murmured. "But if your biology bothers you, I'd be glad to discuss it with you."

He watched carefully for the reaction. The Solarian went gray-purple. His eyes danced with fire, and his slit mouth quivered as if to bare the strong teeth. Just as he seemed about to explode, the anger faded—or rather, settled in upon itself to brood. "This is beneath me," the eyes seemed to be saying. Then he laughed cordially.

"My apologies. I thought to share a table with you."

"Help yourself."

The Solarian paused. "Where are you from, manthing?"

Roki also paused. They might have heard that a Cophian commander blasted one of their ships. Still he didn't care to be caught in a lie. "Sixty-Star Cluster," he grunted.

"Which sun?" The Solarian's voice suggested that he was accustomed to being answered instantly.

Roki glowered at him. "Information for information, fellow. And I don't talk to people who stand over me." He pointedly turned to Pok. "As we were saying—"

"I am of Sol," growled the big one.

"Fair enough. I am of Coph."

The giant's brows lifted slightly. "Ah, yes." He in-

spected Roki curiously and sat down. The chair creaked
a warning. "Perhaps that explains it."

"Explains what?" Roki frowned ominously. He disliked overbearing men, and his hackles were rising.
There was something about this fellow—

"I understand that Cophians are given to a certain
ruthlessness."

Roki pretended to ponder the statement while he
eyed this big man coldly. "True, perhaps. It would be
dangerous for you to go to Coph, I think. You would
probably be killed rather quickly."

The angry color reappeared, but the man smiled
politely. "A nation of duelists, I believe, military in
character, highly disciplined. Yes? They sometimes serve
in the Sixty-Star Forces, eh?"

The words left no doubt in Roki's mind that the
Solarian knew who had blasted their ship and why. But
he doubted that the man had guessed his identity.

"I know less of your world, Solarian."

"Such ignorance is common. We are regarded as the
galactic rurals, so to speak. We are too far from your
dense star cluster." He paused. "You knew us once.
We planted you here. And I feel sure you will know us
again." He smiled to himself, finished his drink, and
arose. "May we meet again, Cophian."

Roki nodded and watched the giant stride away. Pok
was breathing asthmatically and picking nervously at his
nails. He let out a sigh of relief with the Solarian's
departure.

Roki offered the frightened interpreter a stiff drink,
and then another. After two more, Pok swayed dizzily,
then fell asleep across the table. Roki left him there. If
Pok were an informer, it would be better to keep him
out of the meeting with the patrol officer, Captain
WeJan.

He hailed a cab and gave the driver the scrap of
paper. A few minutes later, he arrived before a small
building in the suburbs. WeJan's name was on the
door—written in the space-tongue—but the officer was
not at home. Frowning, he caught a glimpse of a man
standing in the shadows. It was a Solarian.

Slowly, Roki walked across the street. "Got a match, Bristleface?" he grunted.

In the light of triple-moons, he saw the giant figure swell with rage. The man looked quickly up and down the street. No one was watching. He emitted a low animal-growl, exposing the brutal teeth. His arms shot out to grasp the Cophian's shoulders, dragging him close. Roki gripped the Multin automatic in his pocket and struggled to slip free. The Solarian jerked him up toward the bared teeth.

His throat about to be crushed, Roki pulled the trigger. There was a dull *chug*. The Solarian looked surprised. He released Roki and felt of his chest. There was no visible wound. Then, within his chest, the incendiary needle flared to incandescent heat. The Solarian sat down in the street. He breathed a frying sound. He crumpled. Roki left hastily before the needle burned its way out of the body.

He hadn't meant to kill the man, and it had been in self-defense, but he might have a hard time proving it. He hurried along back alleys toward the spaceport. If only they could leave Tragor immediately!

What had happened to WeJan? Bribed, beaten, or frightened away. Then the Solarians *did* know who he was and where he was going. There were half a dozen men around the spaceport who knew—and the information would be easy to buy. Pok had known that he was to meet with WeJan, and the Solarian had evidently been sent to watch the captain's quarters. It wasn't going to be easy now—getting to Sol III and landing.

What manner of creatures were these, he wondered. Men who supplied mercy cargoes to the galactic nations—as if charity were the theme and purpose of their culture—yet who seemed as arrogant as the warriors of some primitive culture whose central value was brutal power? What did they really want here? The Solarian had called him "manthing" as if he regarded the Cophian as a member of some lesser species.

The Solarians were definitely different. Roki could see it. Their heads were plump and soft like a baby's, hinting of some new evolutionary trend—a brain that could continue growing, perhaps. But the jaws, the

teeth, the quick tempers, and the hypersensitive ears—
what sort of animal developed such traits? There was
only one answer: a nocturnal predator with the instincts
of a lion. "You shall get to know us again," the man had
said.

It spelled politico-galactic ambitions. And it hinted at
something else—something that made the Cophian
shiver, and shy away from dark shadows as he hurried
shipward.

Daleth Incorporated was either asleep or out. He
checked at the ship, then went to the Administration
Building to inquire about her. The clerk seemed
embarrassed.

"Uh . . . E Roki, she departed from the port about
five."

"You've heard nothing of her since?"

"Well . . . there was a call from the police agency, I
understand." He looked apologetic. "I assure you I had
nothing to do with the matter."

"Police! What . . . what's wrong, man?"

"I hear she went unescorted and unveiled. The police are holding her."

"How long will they keep her?"

"Until some gentleman signs for her custody."

"You mean I have to sign for her?"

"Yes, sir."

Roki smiled thoughtfully. "Tell me, young man—are
Tragorian jails particularly uncomfortable?"

"I wouldn't know, personally," the clerk said stiffly.
"I understand they conform to the intergalactic 'Code of
Humanity' however."

"Good enough," Roki grunted. "I'll leave her there
till we're ready to go."

"Not a bad idea," murmured the clerk, who had
evidently encountered the cigar-chewing lady from
Daleth.

Roki was not amused by the reversal of positions, but
it seemed as good a place as any to leave her for
safekeeping. If the Solarians became interested in him,
they might also notice his pilot.

He spent the following day watching the Sol ship,

and waiting fatalistically for the police to come and question him about the Solarian's death. But the police failed to come. A check with the news agencies revealed that the man's body had not even been found. Roki was puzzled. He had left the giant lying in plain sight where he had fallen. At noon, the Solarian crew came bearing several lead cases slung from the centers of carrying poles. They wore metal gauntlets and handled the cases cautiously. Roki knew they contained radioactive materials. So that was what they purchased with their surgibank supplies—nuclear fuels.

Toward nightfall, they loaded two large crates aboard. He noted the shape of the crates, and decided that one of them contained the body of the man he had killed. Why didn't they want the police to know? Was it possible that they wanted him free to follow them?

The Sol-ship blasted-off during the night. He was surprised to find it gone, and himself still unmolested by morning. Wandering around the spaceport, he saw WeJan, but the man had developed a sudden lapse of memory. He failed to recognize the Cophian visitor. With the Solarians gone, Roki grew bolder in his questioning.

"How often do the Solarians visit you?" he inquired of a desk clerk at Administration.

"Whenever a hospital places an order, sir. Not often. Every six months perhaps."

"That's all the traffic they have with Tragor?"

"Yes, sir. This is our only interstellar port."

"Do the supplies pass through your government channels?"

The clerk looked around nervously. "Uh, no sir. They refuse to deal through our government. They contact their customers directly. The government lets them because the supplies are badly needed."

Roki stabbed out bluntly. "What do you think of the Solarians?"

The clerk looked blank for a moment, then chuckled. "I don't know, myself. But if you want a low opinion, ask at the spaceport cafe."

"Why? Do they cause trouble there?"

"No, sir. They bring their own lunches, so to speak.

They eat and sleep aboard ship, and won't spend a thin galak around town."

Roki turned away and went back to the *Idiot*. Somewhere in his mind, an idea was refusing to let itself be believed. A mercy ship visited Tragor every six months. Roki had seen the scattered, ruined cargo of such a ship, and he had estimated it at about four thousand pints of blood, six thousand pounds of frozen bone, and seven thousand pounds of various replaceable organs and tissues. That tonnage in itself was not so startling, but if Sol III supplied an equal amount twice annually to even a third of the twenty-eight thousand civilized worlds in the galaxy, a numbing question arose: where did they get their raw material? Surgibank supplies were normally obtained by contributions from accident victims who lived long enough to voluntarily contribute their undamaged organs to a good cause.

Charitable organizations tried to secure pledges from men in dangerous jobs, donating their bodies to the planet's surgibank in the event of death. But no man felt easy about signing over his kidneys or his liver to the bank, and such recruiters were less popular than hangmen or life insurance agents. Mercy supplies were quite understandably scarce.

The grim question lingered in Roki's mind: where did the Sol III traders find between three and five million healthy accident victims annually? Perhaps they made the accidents themselves, accidents very similar to those occurring at the end of the chute in the slaughterhouse. He shook his head, refusing to believe it. No planet's population, however terrorized by its rulers, could endure such a thing without generating a sociological explosion that would make the world quiver in its orbit. There was a limit to the endurance of tyranny.

He spent the rest of the week asking innocent questions here and there about the city. He learned nearly nothing. The Solarians came bearing their peculiar cargo, sold it quickly at a good price, purchased fissionable materials, and blasted-off without a civil word to anyone. Most men seemed nervous in their presence, perhaps because of their bulk and their native arrogance. When the base personnel finished installing the syn-

chronizers, he decided the time had come to secure
Daleth Incorporated from the local jail. Sometimes he
had chided himself for leaving her there after the
Solarians had blasted-off, but it seemed to be the best
place to keep the willful wench out of trouble. Belat-
edly, as he rode toward the police station, he wondered
what sort of mayhem she would attempt to commit on
his person for leaving her to fume in a cell. His smile
was rueful as he marched in to pay her fine. The man
behind the desk frowned sharply.

"Who did you say?" he grunted.

"The foreign woman from the Dalethian Ship."

The officer studied his records. "Ah, yes—Talewa
Walkeka the name?"

Roki realized he didn't know her name. She was still
Daleth Incorporated. "From the Daleth Ship," he
insisted.

"Yes. Talewa Walkeka—she was released into the
custody of Eli Roki on twoday of last spaceweek."

"That's imposs—" Roki choked and whitened. "I am
Eli Roki. Was the man a Solarian?"

"I don't recall."

"*Why don't you?* Didn't you ask him for identification?"

"Stop bellowing, please," said the official coldly. "And
get your fists off my desk."

The Cophian closed his eyes and tried to control
himself. "Who is responsible for this?"

The officer failed to answer.

"*You* are responsible!"

"I cannot look out for all the problems of all the
foreigners who—"

"Stop! You have let her die."

"She is only a female."

Roki straightened. "Meet me at any secluded place of
your choice and I will kill you with any weapon of your
choice."

The official eyed him coldly, then turned to call over
his shoulder. "Sergeant, escort this barbarian to his
ship and see that he remains aboard for the rest of his
visit."

The Cophian went peacefully, realizing that violence
would gain him nothing but the iron hospitality of a

cell. Besides, he had only himself to blame for leaving her there. It was obvious to him now—the contents of the second crate the Solarians had carried aboard consisted of Talewa Walkeka, lately of Daleth and high-C. Undoubtedly they had taken her alive. Undoubtedly she was additional bait to bring him on to Sol. Why did they want him to come? *I'll oblige them and find out for myself*, he thought.

The ship was ready. The bill would be sent back to Beth. He signed the papers, and blasted off as soon as possible. The lonely old freighter crept upward into the fifth component like a struggling old vulture, too ancient to leave its sunny lair. But the synchros were working perfectly, and the screen held its shape when the ascent ceased just below red-line level. He chose an evasive course toward Sol and began gathering velocity.

Then he fed a message into the coder, to be broadcast back toward the Sixty-Star Cluster: *Pilot abducted by Solarians; evidence secured to indicate that Solarian mercy-merchandise is obtained through genocide*. He recorded the coded message on tape and let it feed continuously into the transmitters, knowing that the carrier made him a perfect target for homing devices, if anyone chose to silence him.

And he knew it was a rather poor bluff. The message might or might not be picked up. A listening ship would have to be at the same C-level to catch the signal. Few ships, save the old freighters, lingered long at ninety-thousand C's. But if the Solarians let him live long enough, the message would eventually be picked up—but not necessarily believed. The most he could hope for was to arouse curiosity about Sol. No one would care much about the girl's abduction, or about his own death. Interstellar federations never tried to protect their citizens beyond the limits of their own volume of space. It would be an impossible task.

Unless the Solarians were looking for him however, they themselves would probably not intercept the call. Their ships would be on higher C. And since they knew he was coming, they had no reason to search for him. At his present velocity and energy-level, he was four months from Sol. The mercy ship on a higher level, would probably reach Sol within three weeks. He was a sparrow chasing a smug hawk.

But now there was more at stake than pride or reputation. He had set out to clear himself of a bad name, but now his name mattered little. If what he suspected were true, then Sol III was a potential threat to every world in the galaxy. Again he remembered the Solarian's form of address—"manthing"—as if a new race had arisen to inherit the places of their ancestors. If so, the new race had a right to bid for survival. And the old race called Man had a right to crush it if he could. Such was the dialectic of life.

Four months in the solitary confinement of a spaceship was enough to unnerve any man, however well-conditioned to it. He paced restlessly in his cell, from quarters to control to reactor room, reading everything that was aboard to read and devouring it several times. Sometimes he stopped to stare in Daleth's doorway. Her gear was still in the compartment, gathering dust. A pair of boots in the corner, a box of Dalethia cigars on the shelf.

"Maybe she has a book or two," he said once, and entered. He opened the closet and chuckled at the rough masculine clothing that hung there. But among the coarse fabrics was a wisp of pale green silk. He parted the dungarees to stare at the frail feminine frock, nestled toward the end and half-hidden like a suppressed desire. For a moment he saw her in it, strolling along the cool avenues of a Cophian city. But quickly he let the dungarees fall back, slammed the door, and stalked outside, feeling ashamed. He never entered again.

The loneliness was overpowering. After three months, he shut off the transmitters and listened on the space-frequencies for the sound of a human voice. There was nothing except the occasional twittering of a coded message. Some of them came from the direction of Sol.

Why were they letting him come without interference? Why had they allowed him to transmit the message freely? Perhaps they wanted him as a man who knew a great deal about the military and economic resources of the Sixty-Star Cluster, information they would need if they had high ambitions in space. And perhaps the message no longer mattered, if they had already acquired enough nuclear materials for their plans.

After a logical analysis of the situation, he hit upon a better answer. Their ships didn't have the warp-locking devices that permitted one ship to slip into a parallel C with an enemy and stay with that enemy while it maneuvered in the fifth component. The Solarians had proven that deficiency when the "mercy ship" had tried to escape him by evasive coursing. If their own ships were equipped with the warp lockers, they would have known better than to try. They wanted such equipment. Perhaps they thought that the *Idiot* possessed it, or that he could furnish them with enough information to let them build it.

After several days of correlating such facts as he already knew, Roki cut on his transmitters, fanned the beam down to a narrow pencil, and directed it toward Sol. "Blind Stab from Cluster-Ship *Idiot*," he called. "Any Sol Ship from *Idiot*. I have information to sell in exchange for the person of Talewa Walkeka. Acknowledge, please."

He repeated the message several times, and expected to wait a few days for an answer. But the reply came within three hours, indicating that a ship had been hovering just ahead of him, beyond the range of his own out-moded detectors.

"Cluster-Ship from Sol Seven," crackled the loudspeaker. "Do you wish to land on our planet? If so, please prepare to be boarded. One of our pilots will take you in. You are approaching our outer patrol zone. If you refuse to be boarded, you will have to turn back. Noncooperative vessels are destroyed upon attempting to land. Over."

There was a note of amusement in the voice. They knew he wouldn't turn back. They had a hostage. They were inviting him to surrender but phrasing the invitation politely.

Roki hesitated. Why had the man said—"destroyed upon attempting to land?" After a moment's thought, he realized that it was because they could not destroy a ship while maneuvering in the fifth component. They could not even stay in the same continuum with it, unless they had the warp-locking devices. A vague plan began forming in his mind.

"I agree conditionally. Do you have Talewa Walkeka aboard? If so, prove it by asking her to answer the following request in her own voice: 'List the garments contained in the closet of her quarters aboard this ship.' If this is accomplished satisfactorily, then I'll tentatively assume intentions are not hostile. Let me remind you, however, that while we are grappled together, I can rip half your hull off by hitting my C-drive—unless you're equipped with warp-locking devices."

That should do it, he thought. With such a warning, they would make certain that they had him aboard their own ship as a captive before they made any other move. And he would do his best to make it easy for them. Two or three hours would pass before he could expect an answer, so he began work immediately, preparing to use every means at his disposal to make a booby trap of the *Idiot*, and to set the trap so that only his continued well-being would keep it from springing.

The *Idiot's* stock of spare parts was strictly limited, as he had discovered previously. There were a few spare selsyns, replacement units for the calculator and courser, radio and radar parts, control-mechanisms for the reactors, and an assortment of spare instruments and detectors. He augmented this stock by ruthlessly tearing into the calculator and taking what he needed.

He was hard at work when the answer came from the Sol Ship. It was Daleth's voice, crisp and angry, saying, "Six pair of dungarees, a jacket, a robe, and a silk frock. Drop dead, Roki."

The Solarian operator took over. "Expect a meeting in six hours. In view of your threat, we must ask that you stand in the outer lock with the hatch open, so that we may see you as we grapple together. Please acknowledge willingness to cooperate."

Roki grinned. They wanted to make certain that he was nowhere near the controls. He gave them a grumbling acknowledgment and returned to his work, tearing into the electronic control-circuits, the radio equipment, the reaction-rate limiters, and the controls of the C-drive. He wove a network of inter-dependency throughout the ship, running linking-circuits from the air-lock mechanisms to the reactors, and from the communication equipment to the C-drive. Gradually the ship became useless as a means of transportation. The jets were silent. He set time clocks to activate some of the apparatus, and keyed other equipment by relays set to trip upon the occurrence of various events.

It was not a difficult task, nor a long one. He added nothing really new. For example, it was easy to remove the wires from the air-lock indicator lamp and feed their signal into a relay section removed from the calculator, a section which would send a control pulse to the reactors if the air-locks were opened twice. The control pulse, if it came, would push the units past the red line. The relay sections were like single-task robots, set to obey the command: "If *this* happens, then push *that* switch."

When he was finished, the six hours were nearly gone. Pacing restlessly, he waited for them to come. Then, noticing a sudden flutter on the instruments, he glanced out to see the dark hulk slipping through his radiation screen. It came to a stop a short distance away.

Roki started the timers he had set, then donned a pressure suit. Carrying a circuit diagram of the changes he had wrought, he went to stand in the outer lock. He held open the outer hatch. The beam of a searchlight stabbed out to hold him while the Sol ship eased closer. He could see another suited figure in its lock, calling guidance to the pilot. Roki glanced up at his own grapples; they were already energized and waiting for something to which they could cling.

The ships came together with a rocking jerk as both sets of grapples caught and clung. Roki swung himself across a gravityless space, then stood facing the burly figure of the Solarian. The man pushed him into the next lock and stepped after him.

"Search him for weapons," growled a harsh voice as

Roki removed his helmet. "And get the boarding party through the locks."

"If you do that, you'll blow both ships to hell," the Cophian commented quietly. "The hatches are rigged to throw the reactors past red line."

The commander, a sharp-eyed oldster with a massive bald skull, gave him a cold stare that slowly became a sneer. "Very well, we can cut through the hull."

Roki nodded. "You can, but don't let any pressure escape. The throttles are also keyed to the pressure gauge."

The commander reddened slightly. "Is there anything else?"

"Several things." Roki handed him the circuit diagram. "Have your engineer study this. Until he gets the idea, anything you do may be dangerous, like trying to pull away from my grapples. I assure you we're either permanently grappled together, or permanently dead."

The Solarian was apparently his own engineer. He stared at the schematic while another relieved Roki of his weapon. There were four of them in the cabin. Three were armed and watching him carefully. He knew by their expressions that they considered him to be of a lesser species. And he watched them communicate silently among themselves by a soundless language of facial twitches and peculiar nods. Once the commander looked up to ask a question.

"When will this timer activate this network?"

Roki glanced at his watch. "In about ten minutes. If the transmitter's periodic signals aren't answered in the correct code, the signals serve to activate C-drive."

"I see that," he snapped. He glanced at a burly assistant. "Take him out. Skin him—from the feet up. He'll give you the code."

"I'll give it to you now," Roki offered calmly.

The commander showed faint surprise. "Do so then."

"The Cophian multiplication tables is the code. My transmitter will send a pair of Cophian numbers every two minutes. If you fail to supply the product within one second, a relay starts the C-drive. Since you can't guarantee an exactly simultaneous thrust, there should be quite a crash."

"Very well, give us your Cophian number symbols."

"Gladly. But they won't help you."

"Why not?"

"Our numbers are to the base eighteen instead of base ten. You couldn't react quickly enough unless you've been using them since childhood."

The Solarian's lips pulled back from his heavy teeth and his jaw muscles began twitching. Roki looked at his watch.

"You have seven minutes to get your transmitter set up, with me at the key. We'll talk while I keep us intact."

The commander hesitated, then nodded to one of the guards who promptly left the room.

"Very well, manthing, we will set it up temporarily." He paused to smile arrogantly. "You have much to learn about our race. But you have little time in which to learn it."

"What do you mean?"

"Just this. This transmitter—and the whole apparatus—will be shut down after a certain period of time."

Roki stiffened. "Just how do you propose to do it?"

"Fool! By waiting until the signals stop. You obviously must have set a time limit on it. I would guess a few hours at the most."

It was true, but he had hoped to avoid mentioning it. The power to the control circuits would be interrupted after four hours, and the booby trap would be deactivated. For if he hadn't achieved his goal by then, he meant to neglect a signal during the last half-hour and let the C-ward lurch tear them apart. He nodded slowly.

"You're quite right. You have four hours in which to surrender your ship into my control. Maybe. I'll send the signals until I decide you don't mean to co-operate. Then——" He shrugged.

The Solarian gave a command to his aides. They departed in different directions. Roki guessed that they had been sent to check for some way to enter the *Idiot* that would not energize a booby circuit.

His host waved him through a doorway, and he found himself in their control room. A glance told him that their science still fell short of the most modern cultures. They had the earmarks of a new race, and yet Sol's civilization was supposedly the oldest in the galaxy.

"There are the transmitters," the commander barked. "Say what you have to say, and we shall see who is best at waiting."

Roki sat down, fingered the key, and watched his adversary closely. The commander fell into a seat opposite him and gazed coolly through narrowed lids. He wore a fixed smile of amusement. "Your name is Eli Roki, I believe. I am Space Commander Hulgruv."

A blare of sound suddenly came from the receiver. Hulgruv frowned and lowered the volume. The sound came forth as a steady musical tone. He questioned the Cophian with his eyes.

"When the tone ceases, the signals will begin."

"I see."

"I warn you, I may get bored rather quickly. I'll keep the signals going only until I think you've had time to assure yourselves that this is not a bluff I am trying to put over on you."

"I'm sure it's not. It's merely an inconvenience."

"You know little of my home planet then."

"I know a little."

"Then you've heard of the 'Sword of Apology.'"

"How does that—" Hulgruv paused and lost his smirk for an instant. "I see. If you blunder, your code demands that you die anyway. So you think you wouldn't hesitate to neglect a signal."

"Try me."

"It may not be necessary. Tell me, why did you space them two minutes apart? Why not one signal every hour?"

"You can answer that."

"Ah yes. You think the short period insures you against any painful method of persuasion, eh?"

"Uh-huh. And it gives me a chance to decide frequently whether it's worth it."

"What is it you want, Cophian? Suppose we give you the girl and release you."

"She is a mere incidental," he growled, fearful of choking on the words. "The price is surrender."

Hulgruv laughed heartily. It was obvious he had other plans. "Why do you deem us your enemy?"

"You heard the accusation I beamed back to my Cluster."

"Certainly. We ignored it, directly. Indirectly we made a fool of you by launching another, uh, mercy ship to your system. The cargo was labeled as to source, and the ship made a point of meeting one of your patrol vessels. It stopped for inspection. You're less popular at home than ever." He grinned. "I suggest you return to Sol with us. Help us develop the warp locks."

Roki hesitated. "You say the ship *stopped for inspection?*"

"Certainly."

"Wasn't it inconvenient? Changing your diet, leaving your 'livestock' at home—so our people wouldn't know you for what you really are."

Hulgruv stiffened slightly, then nodded. "Good guess."

"*Cannibal!*"

"Not at all. I am not a man."

They stared fixedly at one another. The Cophian felt the clammy cloak of hate creeping about him. The tone from the speaker suddenly stopped. A moment of dead silence. Roki leaned back in his chair.

"I'm not going to answer the first signal."

The commander glanced through the doorway and jerked his head. A moment later, Talewa Walkeka stepped proudly into the room, escorted by a burly guard. She gave him an icy glance and said nothing.

"Daleth—"

She made a noise like an angry cat and sat where the guard pushed her. They waited. The first signal suddenly screeched from the receiver: two series of short bleats of three different notes.

Involuntarily his hand leaped to the key. He bleated back the answering signal.

Daleth wore a puzzled frown. "Ilgen times ufneg is hork-segan," she muttered in translation.

A slow grin spread across Hulgruv's heavy face. He

turned to look at the girl. "You're trained in the Cophian number system?"

"Don't answer that!" Roki bellowed.

"She *has* answered it, manthing. Are you aware of what your friend is doing, female?"

She shook her head. Hulgruv told her briefly. She frowned at Roki, shook her head, and stared impassively at the floor. Apparently she was either drugged or had learned nothing about the Solarians to convince her that they were enemies of the galaxy.

"Tell me, Daleth. Have they been feeding you well?"

She hissed at him again. "Are you crazy—"

Hulgruv chuckled. "He is trying to tell you that we are cannibals. Do you believe it?"

Fright appeared in her face for an instant, then disbelief. She stared at the commander, saw no guilt in his expression. She looked scorn at Roki.

"Listen, Daleth! That's why they wouldn't stop. Human livestock aboard. One look in their holds and we would have known, seen through their guise of mercy, recognized them as self-styled supermen, guessed their plans for galactic conquest. They breed their human cattle on their home planet and make a business of selling the parts. Their first weapon is infiltration into our confidence. They knew that if we gained an insight into their bloodthirsty culture, we would crush them."

"You're insane, Roki!" she snapped.

"No! Why else would they refuse to stop? Technical secrets? Baloney! Their technology is still inferior to ours. They carried a cargo of hate, our hate, riding with them unrecognized. They couldn't afford to reveal it."

Hulgruv laughed uproariously. The girl shook her head slowly at Roki, as if pitying him.

"It's true, I tell you! I guessed, sure. But it was pretty obvious they were taking their surgibank supplies by murder. And they contend they're not men. They guard their ships so closely, live around them while in port. And he admitted it to me."

The second signal came. Roki answered it, then began ignoring the girl. She didn't believe him. Hulgruv appeared amused. He hummed the signals over to himself—*without mistake*.

"You're using polytonal code for challenge, monotonal for reply. That makes it harder to learn."

The Cophian caught his breath. He glanced at the Solarian's huge, bald braincase. "You hope to learn some three or four hundred sounds—and sound-combinations—within the time I allow you?"

"We'll see."

Some note of contempt in Hulgruv's voice gave Roki warning.

"I shorten my ultimatum to one hour! Decide by then. Surrender, or I stop answering. Learn it, if you can."

"He can, Roki," muttered Daleth. "They can memorize a whole page at a glance."

Roki keyed another answer. "I'll cut it off if he tries it."

The commander was enduring the tension of the stalemate superbly. "Ask yourself, Cophian," he grunted with a smile, "what would you gain by destroying the ship—and yourself? We are not important. If we're destroyed, our planet loses another gnat in space, nothing more. Do you imagine we are incapable of self-sacrifice?"

Roki found no answer. He set his jaw in silence and answered the signals as they came. He hoped the bluff would win, but now he saw that Hulgruv would let him destroy the ship. And—if the situation were reversed, Roki knew that he would do the same. He had mistakenly refused to concede honor to an enemy. The commander seemed to sense his quiet dismay, and he leaned forward to speak softly.

"We are a new race, Roki—grown out of man. We have abilities of which you know nothing. It's useless to fight us. Ultimately, your people will pass away. Or become stagnant. Already it has happened to man on Earth."

"Then—there *are* two races on Earth."

"Yes, of course. Did apes pass away when man appeared? The new does not replace the old. It adds to it, builds above it. The old species is the root of the new tree."

"Feeding it," the Cophian grunted bitterly.

He noticed that Talewa was becoming disturbed. Her eyes fluttered from one to the other of them.

"That was inevitable, manthing. There are no other animal foodstuffs on Earth. Man exhausted his planet, overpopulated it, drove lesser species into extinction. He spent the world's resources getting your ancestors to the denser star-clusters. He saw his own approaching stagnation on Earth. And, since Sol is near the rim of the galaxy, with no close star-neighbors, he realized he could never achieve a mass-exodus into space. He didn't have the C-drive in its present form. The best he could do was a field-cancellation drive."

"But that's the heart of the C-drive."

"True. But he was too stupid to realize what he had. He penetrated the fifth component and failed to realize what he had done. His ships went up to five-hundred C's or so, spent a few hours there by the ship's clock, and came down to find several years had passed on Earth. They never got around that time-lag."

"But that's hardly more than a problem in five-space navigation!"

"True again. But they still thought of it in terms of field-cancellation. They didn't realize they'd actually left the four-space continuum. They failed to see the blue-shift as anything more than a field-phenomenon. Even in high-C, you measure light's velocity as the same constant—because your measuring instruments have changed proportionally. It's different, relative to the home continuum, but you can't know it except by pure reasoning. They never found out.

"Using what they had, they saw that they could send a few of their numbers to the denser star-clusters, if they wanted to wait twenty thousand years for them to arrive. Of course, only a few years would pass aboard ship. They knew they could do it, but they procrastinated. Society was egalitarian at the time. Who would go? And why should the planet's industry exhaust itself to launch a handful of ships that no one would ever see again? Who wanted to make a twenty thousand year investment that would impoverish the world? Sol's atomic resources were never plentiful."

"How did it come about then?"

"Through a small group of men who didn't *care* about the cost. They seized power during a 'population rebellion'—when the sterilizers were fighting the euthanasiasts and the do-nothings. The small clique came into power by the fantastic promise of draining off the population-surplus into space. Enough of the stupid believed it to furnish them with a strong backing. They clamped censorship on the news agencies and imprisoned everyone who said it couldn't be done. They put the planet to work building ships. Their fanatic personal philosophy was: 'We are giving the galaxy to Man. What does it matter if he perishes on Earth?' They put about twelve hundred ships into space before their slave-structure collapsed. Man never developed another technology on Sol III. He was sick of it."

"And *your* people?"

Hulgruv smiled. "A natural outgrowth of the situation. If a planet were glutted with rabbits who ate all the grass, a species of rabbits who learned to exploit other rabbits would have the best chance for survival. We are predators, Cophian. Nature raised us up to be a check on your race."

"You pompous fool!" Roki snapped. "Predators are specialists. What abilities do you have—besides the ability to prey on man?"

"I'll show you in a few minutes," the commander muttered darkly.

Daleth had lost color slowly as she listened to the Solarian's roundabout admission of Roki's charge. She suddenly moaned and slumped in a sick heap. Hulgruv spoke to the guard in the soundless facial language. The guard carried her away quickly.

"If you were an advanced species, Hulgruv—you would not have let yourself be tricked so easily, by me. And a highly intelligent race would discover the warp locks for themselves."

Hulgruv flushed. "We underestimated you, manthing. It was a natural mistake. Your race has sunk to the level of cattle on earth. As for the warp locks, we know their principles. We have experimental models. But we could short-circuit needless research by using your design.

We are a new race, new to space. Naturally we cannot do in a few years what you needed centuries to accomplish."

"You'll have to look for help elsewhere. In ten minutes, I'm quitting the key—unless you change your mind."

Hulgruv shrugged. While Roki answered the signals, he listened for sounds of activity throughout the ship. He heard nothing except the occasional clump of boots, the brief mutter of a voice in the corridor, the intermittent rattling of small tools. There seemed to be no excitement or anxiety. The Solarians conducted themselves with quiet self-assurance.

"Is your crew aware of what is happening?"

"Certainly."

As the deadline approached, his fingers grew nervous on the key. He steeled himself, and waited, clutching at each second as it marched past. What good would it do to sacrifice Daleth and himself? He would succeed only in destroying one ship and one crew. But it was a good trade—two pawns for several knights and a rook. And, when the Solarians began their march across space, there would be many such sacrifices.

For the last time, he answered a signal, then leaned back to stare at Hulgruv. "Two minutes, Solarian. There's still time to change your mind."

Hulgruv only smiled. Roki shrugged and stood up. A pistol flashed into the commander's hand, warning him back. Roki laughed contemptuously.

"Afraid I'll try to take your last two minutes away?"

He strolled away from the table toward the door.

"Stop!" Hulgruv barked.

"Why? I want to see the girl."

"Very touching. But she's busy at the moment."

"What?" He turned slowly, and glanced at his watch. "You don't seem to realize that in fifty seconds—"

"We'll see. Stay where you are."

The Cophian felt a sudden coldness in his face. Could they have found a flaw in his net of death?—a way to circumvent the sudden application of the *Idiot*'s C-drive, with its consequent ruinous stresses to both ships? Or had they truly memorized the Cophian symbols to a one-second reaction time?

He shrugged agreeably and moved in the general direction of the transmitter tuning units. There was one way to test the possibility. He stopped several feet away and turned to face Hulgruv's suspicious eyes. "You are braver than I thought," he growled.

The admission had the desired effect. Hulgruv tossed his head and laughed arrogantly. There was an instant of relaxation. The heavy automatic wavered slightly. Roki backed against the transmitters and cut the power switch. The hum died.

"Ten seconds, Hulgruv! Toss me your weapon. Shoot and you shatter the set. Wait and the tubes get cold. *Toss it!*"

Hulgruv bellowed, and raised the weapon to fire. Roki grinned. The gun quivered. Then with a choking sound, the Solarian threw it to him. "Get it on!" he howled. "*Get it on!*"

As Roki tripped the switch again, the signals were already chirping in the loud-speaker. He darted aside, out of view from the corridor. Footsteps were already racing toward the control room.

The signals stopped. Then the bleat of an answer! Another key had been set up in the adjoining room! With Daleth answering the challenges?

The pistol exploded in his hand as the first crewman came racing through the doorway. The others backed out of sight into the corridor as the projectile-weapon knocked their comrade back in a bleeding sprawl. Hulgruv made a dash for the door. Roki cut him down with a shot at the knee.

"The next one takes the transmitter," he bellowed. "Stay back."

Hulgruv roared a command. "Take him! If you can't, let the trap spring!"

Roki stooped over him and brought the pistol butt crashing against his skull, meaning only to silence him. It was a mistake; he had forgotten about the structure of the Solarian skull. He put his foot on Hulgruv's neck and jerked. The butt came free with a wet *cluck*. He raced to the doorway and pressed himself against the wall to listen. The crewmen were apparently having a parley at the far end of the corridor. He waited for the next signal.

When it came, he dropped to the floor—to furnish an unexpected sort of target—and snaked into view. He shot twice at three figures a dozen yards away. The answering fire did something to the side of his face, blurring his vision. Another shot sprayed him with flakes from the deck. One crewman was down. The others backed through a door at the end of the corridor. They slammed it and a pressure seal tightened with a rubbery sound.

Roki climbed to his feet and slipped toward a doorway from which he heard the click of the auxiliary key. He felt certain someone was there besides Daleth. But when he risked a quick glance around the corner, he saw only the girl. She sat at a small desk, her hand frozen to the key, her eyes staring dazedly at nothing. He started to speak, then realized what was wrong. Hypnosis! Or a hypnotic drug. She sensed nothing but the key beneath her fingers, waiting for the next challenge.

The door was only half-open. He could see no one, but there had been another man; of that he was certain. Thoughtfully he took aim at the plastic door panel and fired. A gun skidded toward Daleth's desk. A heavy body sprawled across the floor.

The girl started. The dull daze left her face, to be replaced with wide-eyed shock. She clasped her hands to her cheeks and whimpered. A challenge bleated from the radio.

"Answer!" he bellowed.

Her hand shot to the key and just in time. But she seemed about to faint.

"Stay on it!" he barked, and dashed back to the control room. The crewmen had locked themselves aft of the bulkhead, and had started the ventilator fans. Roki heard their whine, then caught the faint odor of gas. His eyes were burning and he sneezed spasmodically.

"Surrender immediately, manthing!" blared the intercom.

Roki looked around, then darted toward the controls.

He threw a damping voltage on the drive tubes, defocused
the ion streams, and threw the reactors to full emission.
The random shower of high-speed particles would spray
toward the focusing coils, scatter like deflected buck-
shot, and loose a blast of hard X-radiation as they pep-
pered the walls of the reaction chambers. Within a few
seconds, if the walls failed to melt, the crewmen back of
the bulkhead should recognize the possibility of being
quickly fried by the radiant inferno.

The tear gas was choking him. From the next compartment, he could hear Daleth coughing and moaning.
How could she hear the signals for her own weeping?
He tried to watch the corridor and the reaction-chamber
temperature at the same time. The needle crept toward
the danger-point. An explosion could result, if the walls
failed to melt.

Suddenly the voice of the intercom again: "Shut it
off, you fool! You'll destroy the ship."

He said nothing, but waited in tense silence, watching the other end of the corridor. Suddenly the ventilator fans died. Then the bulkhead door opened a crack,
and paused.

"Throw out your weapon first!" he barked.

A gun fell through the crack and to the floor. A
Solarian slipped through, sneezed, and rubbed his eyes.

"Turn around and back down the corridor."

The crewman obeyed slowly. Roki stood a few feet
behind him, using him for a shield while the others
emerged. The fight was gone out of them. It was strange,
he thought; they were willing to risk the danger of the
Idiot's C-drive, but they couldn't stand being locked up
with a runaway reactor. They could see death coming
then. He throttled back the reactors, and prodded the
men toward the storage rooms. There was only one
door that suggested a lockup. He halted the prisoners
in the hallway and tried the bolt.

"Not in there, manthing!" growled one of the Solarians.

"Why not?"

"There are—"

A muffled wail from within the compartment interrupted the explanation. It was the cry of a child. His
hand trembled on the bolt.

"They are wild, and we are weaponless," pleaded the Solarian.

"How many are in there?"

"Four adults, three children."

Roki paused. "There's nowhere else to put you. One of you—*you* there—go inside, and we'll see what happens."

The man shook his head stubbornly in refusal. Roki repeated the order. Again the man refused. The predator, unarmed, was afraid of its prey. The Cophian aimed low and calmly shot him through the leg.

"Throw him inside," he ordered tonelessly.

With ill-concealed fright for their own safety, the other two lifted their screaming comrade. Roki swung open the door and caught a brief glimpse of several human shadows in the gloom. Then the Solarian was thrown through the doorway and the bolt snapped closed.

At first there was silence, then a bull-roar from some angry throat. Stamping feet—then the Solarian's shriek—and a body was being dashed against the inside walls while several savage voices roared approval. The two remaining crewmen stood in stunned silence.

"Doesn't work so well, does it?" Roki murmured with ruthless unconcern.

After a brief search, he found a closet to lock them in, and went to relieve Daleth at the key. When the last signal came, at the end of the four hours, she was asleep from exhaustion. And curled up on the floor, she looked less like a tough little frontier urchin than a frightened bedraggled kitten. He grinned at her for a moment, then went back to inspect the damage to the briefly overloaded reactors. It was not as bad as it might have been. He worked for two hours, replacing fused focusing sections. The jets would carry them home.

The *Idiot* was left drifting in space to await the coming of a repair ship. And Daleth was not anxious to fly it back alone. Roki set the Solarian vessel on a course with a variable C-level, so that no Sol ship could track them without warp lockers. As far as Roki was concerned the job was done. He had a shipful of evidence and two live Solarians who could be forced to confirm it.

"What will they do about it?" Daleth asked as the captured ship jetted them back toward the Sixty-Star Cluster.

"Crush the Solarian race immediately."

"I thought we were supposed to keep hands-off non-human races?"

"We are, unless they try to exploit human beings. That is automatically an act of war. But I imagine an ultimatum will bring a surrender. They can't fight without warp lockers."

"What will happen on Earth when they do surrender?"

Roki turned to grin. "Go ask the human Earthers. Climb in their cage."

She shuddered, and murmured, "Some day—they'll be a civilized race again, won't they?"

He sobered, and stared thoughtfully at the star-lanced cosmos. "Theirs is the past, Daleth. Theirs is the glory of having founded the race of man. They sent us into space. They gave the galaxy to man—in the beginning. We would do well to let them alone."

He watched her for a moment. She had lost cockiness, temporarily.

"Stop grinning at me like that!" she snapped.

Roki went to feed the Solarian captives: canned cabbage.

Editor's Introduction To:

HERE, THERE BE WITCHES

Everett B. Cole

The Philosophical Corps has the task of guarding young cultures and allowing them to develop without killing themselves.

Arthur C. Clarke's Law states: "Any sufficiently advanced technology is indistinguishable from magic." Commander A-Riman of the Philosophical Corps has good reason to know this.

HERE, THERE BE WITCHES

Everett B. Cole

Commander Kar Walzen looked up from his desk as Hal Carlsen came in.

"I'm told you had some trouble with my Operations Officer."

Carlsen shook his head. "No real trouble, sir. He wanted to schedule us for a C.A. assignment. I explained to him that I had an assignment that would take some time. Suggested that he pick one of the regular Criminal Apprehension teams to handle it."

The Sector Criminal Apprehension Officer frowned. "You refused an assignment, then. Right?"

"No, sir. I simply explained to Captain Koren that my detachment would be tied up for a while. His assignment would be delayed if he waited for us to get back."

"That constitutes a refusal in my book. Now, let's get this clear right at the start. You and your people are not a bunch of prima donnas. You've turned in some good assignments, but you were sent to C.A. to work, not to go hareing off any time you happened to feel like it. Is that clear?"

"Sir, we have a Philosophical Corps assignment. It came in through Sector this morning. According to our orders, it takes priority."

"Nonsense! You're assigned to me." Walzen exhaled loudly and regarded the junior officer angrily.

Carlsen reached into his tunic and took out a folded sheaf of papers. He pulled one off and extended it. "You should have received a copy of this, sir. I gave one to the captain."

Walzen grabbed the sheet, scanning it. Finally, he threw it down and reached for his communicator switch.

"I'll get this rescinded and set those people straight once and for all. Now you get back to Operations. Get your instructions from Captain Koren. I want to see a completed operational plan on this desk not later than tomorrow morning." He rapped at the communicator switch.

"You may go."

Carlsen hesitated for a few seconds, then went out to the outer office and sat down. The clerk looked at him curiously.

"You need something, sir?"

Carlsen shook his head. "No. The commander'll be wanting to see me in a few minutes. No point in making him wait."

The clerk looked doubtful. "Yes, sir."

Carlsen sat back and relaxed. A low murmur came from the inner office. Walzen's voice raised almost to a shout.

"I tell you, I can't perform my mission if my people are going to be constantly pulled out of service for some errand." The murmur went on. Carlsen waited.

There was a harsh, grating sound and Walzen's door

slammed open. The commander strode out, glaring at his clerk.

"Get Mr. Carlsen back in here on the double."

He turned, then saw Carlsen.

"Oh. You're still here, eh? Come inside."

The commander slammed down in his chair and looked up angrily.

"Headquarters tells me that assignment of yours has priority. Now I won't go against definite orders. Never have, and never will. So you can go ahead this time. But let me tell you this: Next time you sneak over my head to the front office, I'm going to see to it that your career in the Stellar Guard is short, brutal, and nasty. Is that clear?"

Carlsen nodded, waiting.

"How long is this little junket of yours going to take?"

"It's hard to say, sir. We've got the Exploratory team's field notes, but we've no idea what sort of detailed situations we may run into."

Walzen snorted. "Bunch of amateurs! I'll give you a week. Then I'll expect you to report back for duty. And I'm going to tell you once again. Don't you ever again try going over my head so you can take one of these little vacations. Understand?"

Hal Carlsen looked into the viewsphere as his scouter floated toward distant foothills. He examined the valley below, occasionally changing magnification as features of interest caught his attention.

In the remote past, water running from newly formed mountains had raged across the land, cutting a path for itself as it raced toward the sea. Now, it had cut its channel, shifted course time after time, and at last had come to be a peaceful, elderly stream, meandering lazily at the center of a wide valley.

Occasional cliffs along the ancient river course marked water lines of old. But in most places, erosion had caused the cliffs to become sloping bluffs which rose to a table-land above.

Even the mountains had weathered, to become tree-clad hills, and their sediment had paved the water-carved valley. Hedgerows divided the fertile land into fields and pastures. Tall trees grew on the river bank, their roots holding the soil to inhibit the river from further changes in course. Clusters of buildings dotted the valley floor and narrow roads connected them to one another and to a main highway which roughly bisected the valley's width.

Carlsen examined a craggy cliff speculatively, then shrugged. *Could have been times when the sea came up here. Might be what's left of a gulf, at that,* he told himself. *But right now, it's people I'm interested in, not historical geology.*

A winding road led up the face of the cliff to a castle gate. Carlsen looked at it thoughtfully, then glanced at his range markers. It was just about at his own altitude and fairly close. He reached for the manual override, then shook his head. Just ahead was a large town at the head of the valley. He could look into the castle later.

Beast-drawn carts were making their jolting way along the road below and as the ship passed over one of them, Carlsen tapped the controls, slowing to the speed of the cart. He increased magnification and studied the man and his draft animal.

The driver was a youngish man, dressed in a sort of faded yellow smock and wide, short pantaloons. Thongs wrapped around his ankles supported a boardlike sole and gave his feet some protection. He was obviously humanoid and Carlsen could see no significant difference between him and the basic homo sapiens type. He nodded.

Just about have to be, he told himself. *It's a geomorphic planet. Who else would you expect to find?* He turned his attention to the draft beast.

The creature was a slate gray. Carlsen estimated its mass at nearly a thousand kilograms. The body was relatively short and fat, supported on blocky legs. The neck was long, the muzzle shovel-like. Carlsen tilted his head. Might be a herbivorous reptile? He increased magnification, then shook his head. No, there was scanty, coarse body hair. Lines ran from the cart to a system of straps at the animal's shoulders. The beast plodded gracelessly, occasionally stretching its long neck aside to tear a bit of herbage from the growth at the roadside.

*   *   *

Carlsen turned his attention back to the driver, then reached out and focused his psionic amplifier. For a few seconds, he sat in concentration, then he abruptly snapped a switch.

Gloch! None of my business. That's no kind of research.

The driver moved uneasily, then looked upward. He searched the sky then shook his head uncertainly and returned his attention to his beast and the rutted road before him.

Carlsen's hand darted out, bringing the ship down until it hovered close over the cart.

Interesting, he murmured. *This guy knows there's something up here.* He glanced at a cluster of meters and shook his head.

No trace of radiation shield leakage and at this speed there's not a chance of concussion. He examined the man curiously. *He's got to be a sensitive,* he decided. *I think I'll just record this guy for a while.*

Again, the driver squirmed uneasily and looked up and behind him. For a moment, he faced directly at Carlsen, who flipped a casual salute.

Hi, chum, he laughed. *If you can see anything here, you've got something new in the way of eyesight. But how about looking the other way for a while? I don't want you to get curious about insects that pop out of nowhere. And I don't want to use a full shielded spyeye. Haven't got an oversupply of those.* His hand poised over a switch.

The driver shook his head again, rubbed a hand over his eyes, and finally faced forward, muttering to himself.

Carlsen flicked up the psionic amplification.

Wysrin Kanlor, the man was saying, *you're as crazy as that Mord claims. There's got to be something up there. Something big. But all I can see is sky.*

Carlsen took his hand from the switch and looked thoughtfully at the man. At last, he opened a wall cabinet, took out a stubby cylinder, and opened its access port. For a few minutes, he busied himself in making adjustments, then he snapped the port shut. The cylinder faded from view, and he opened a drawer under the console and shoved the invisible object inside. He swung around and watched a small viewscreen as the instrument approached, hovered before the driver, then focused.

Locked on, Carlsen said. *I'd say it's worth it. If I don't get anything else, I'll get a good line on language and dialect from the way he talks to himself.* He lifted ship, pointed its nose toward the town, and switched to the auto pilot.

For a while, he studied the details of narrow, winding streets as the ship slowly circled. Then he eased down over the central plaza and set the auto pilot to hold position.

At one side of the open space, a blackened area surrounded a thick, charred post. Several short lengths of chain, terminated by heavy cuffs, dangled from ringbolts. Nearby, a cart bearing a new post had pulled up and men were unloading tools. Carlsen frowned.

Now just what have we here? he muttered. He snapped on the psionics and focused on one of the workmen.

For an instant, there was a picture of flames rising about the post. A human figure twisted and moved frantically. There was a mixed sense of vicious pleasure, deep guilt, and suppressed skepticism. Then the man's thoughts became crisply businesslike. Vocalized thought came through clearly.

"All right, you two," he ordered. "Let's be at it. This stick's got to be set sometime today. Man says they're going to be needing it."

The workers went about their duties mechanically, paying no attention to their surroundings and showing no suspicion of awareness of the watcher above them. Carlsen frowned in distaste.

Public executions, he decided. *Pretty savage about it, too.* He examined the buildings surrounding the plaza, then flicked at a series of switches. A swarm of beetlelike objects appeared, then swung about the plaza, dispersed, and disappeared through openings in the various buildings. Carlsen rotated a selector, examining the viewsphere. Finally, he stopped to study an interior view. The telltale was high on the wall.

The high-ceilinged room was almost square. Rough stone walls were partly hidden by draperies. Overhead, rough rafters formed a grid in the plaster of the ceiling. At one end of the room, on a raised part of the stone flooring, a group of men sat behind a heavy table. Carlsen looked at them curiously.

Two were enveloped in drab, gray robes whose texture belied their apparent austerity. Both wore ornate rings and one had a heavily jeweled amulet.

Bet there's some mighty nice tailoring under those robes, Carlsen told himself. He looked at the other three men.

They were richly dressed, their clothing bearing small resemblance in either cut or material to the coarse cloth worn by the farmer and the workmen. They were leaning forward, listening attentively to the robed man with the jeweled amulet.

The telltale was too small to handle psionic overtones. For a time, Carlsen listened to the man's harangue, then he turned and got out another stubby cylinder.

I need to know what this fellow's thinking about, he told himself. *What he's saying may make sense to those people, but it's so far from reality, I can't get much out of it.*

He locked the spyeye to the telltale, launched it, and waited till it was in position. The beetle was clinging to a fold in one of the drapes.

Better anchor this thing to the ceiling, I'd say. No one'll stumble over it there. He snapped switches and sat watching the presentation.

"I get it," he finally said aloud, "but I don't get the sense. Demons! Sorcery, yet! And this bum's actually more than half convincing these guys, even though he doesn't really believe much of it himself." He leaned back.

"Well, maybe I'll get something to collate with this from the rest of the team."

He grabbed a lever switch and held it back.

"Cisner?"

"Here, Chief." A tanned face appeared in one of the screens.

"Got anything yet?"

"Yes, sir. I've bugged a sort of palace down this way. Got a spyeye or two around town, too." The man shrugged. "Chief, some of these people are nothing but psycho. And the local archduke is the worst of the bunch. He's been so badly suckered, he eats . . . Chief, you'll have to see the whole run to believe it."

Carlsen nodded. "I think I know what you mean. Demons. Sorcery. Witches who prey on their neighbors?"

"That's it, sir. Couple of these vultures don't believe the guff they're selling, but a couple more do. They're all pushing it, though. People? Some of 'em swallow it whole, some of 'em aren't so sure and a few of them think it's a bunch of bunk. But no one's got the nerve to ask foolish questions."

"Well, get full coverage. I think we'll have to do something about this. Out." Carlsen hesitated, then pushed the switch again.

"Waler?"

Another face appeared.

"I've caught a kind of university, Chief. Lecturer was giving them the lowdown on demonology." Waler grinned lopsidedly. "This guy's really sold. He's even had wild dreams of his own. He's got some sort of intestinal parasite. Pretty toxic and he's subject to delirious nightmares." He frowned.

"He's a good talker, but some of his students still aren't sure. They're just wondering how they can learn all the patter and get by their examinations."

"Oh, me! Every culture needs leaders like that! Any of them psionically sensitive?"

"Yeah. Several of 'em. They're the skeptics."

"Makes sense. Look, Waler, see if you can get spyeyes in some of the other lecture rooms. Try to psi bug a few student hangouts, too."

"Will do, sir. Oh, they don't have lecture rooms. These profs do their teaching at their homes, most of them. Few use rooms in some tavern."

"So bug their homes and the taverns. Got enough eyes?"

"Couple dozen."

"Should do it. Incidentally, I've picked up some of

that same stuff here in Varsana. There's a theocratic Chief Examiner named pen Qatorn. He hasn't been here too long, but he's got the locals scared to death and he's holding trials. Well, we'll see what else we get. Then we can figure out what we have to do, if anything. Out."

Wysrin Kanlor abruptly reined up his mount and sat staring at a patch of wide leaves, sickly yellow against the deep green of the field.

Lizard weed, he growled. *I knew I should have checked up here before.* He looked at the patch, estimating its size, then headed his beast back to the barn.

It'll take a while to burn that patch out, he mused. *It'll be no town fair for me today, or maybe tomorrow, either.* He gathered tools, hitched the *garn* to a water wagon, and drove back.

The weeds burned furiously at first, then became a mass of smoldering embers. A thick, yellow column of smoke rose into the still air, spread, then drifted lazily away. Kanlor leaned on his shovel, watching. There had been a few bad moments when the drenching he had given the grass had failed and the blaze had threatened to leap out into the pasture, but fast work with the shovel had prevented disaster. Fortunately, the weeds hadn't reached maturity, so no flaming seeds had sprung out. And he'd seen no trace of the vicious *yarlnu* lizards. He looked back at his herd, which had drifted away from the blaze.

Well, none of them are on the ground. I guess the patch wasn't ripe enough for 'em to try eating it. He moved his shoulders uneasily, then waved a hand by his face. For a few days past, something had been nearby—something that kept watching him closely. But he had never been able to see— He looked about, then up into the clear sky. There was nothing. He shrugged, then looked across the fields at another column of smoke. Black mixed with the yellow.

Delon Mord's place. Looks as though he had to burn, too. He studied the smoke column critically. *It's spread and he's got a grass fire.* He looked at the glowing embers behind him, then busied himself in putting them out.

Finally, he drove the water wagon away from a black mass of mud and lifted his saddle from it.

It would be well to ride over and see if Mord needed help. In this dry season, a grass fire out of control could spread and destroy several farms. He saddled the *garn* and swung up. In fact, given a wind, the whole plateau could become a sea of flame.

By the time Kanlor got to Mord's property, several other farmers had arrived. The fire was blazing across a pasture and flames were licking at the trees on a hedgerow. Men were filling buckets and passing them to wet down the foliage. A few men were hurriedly throwing dirt on advancing flames. Kanlor grabbed his shovel from a saddlebag and joined them.

Delon Mord had been rushing about, shouting directions at the fire fighters. He dashed up to Kanlor and seized his arm.

"Never mind that," he shouted. "There's plenty of men here. Go over and help those fellows on the buckets. Those are valuable trees."

Kanlor shrugged him off. "Why don't you help them, then? An overseer's just what we don't need right now. It's your fire, so why not help put it out?"

Mord backed away. "Gotta be somebody takes charge."

Kanlor threw another shovelful on the flames before him. "Well, take charge somewhere else and quit pestering me. I'm busy."

Mord looked angrily at him, started to speak, then dashed away to scream advice at the bucket brigade.

At last, the fire was contained and burned itself out. A pasture had been burned out completely and most of an adjoining field was a waste of smoking ash, but the danger of widespread fire was over. Men put away their tools and gathered in groups. One bent down to crumble soil between his fingers.

"Dry," he commented. "All the farms are drying out this season. Else we get some rain, we'll have thin crops this year. And I hate to think of burning out any more weed patches." He looked at Kanlor. "You don't seem to be having any trouble, though. Your place is green as in a good year."

Kanlor nodded. "It's those wells of mine," he said. "I run water on my fields when the rains fail."

The other shrugged. "Yeah, sure. Nice for you, but who else has all that water to spare?"

"You could dig more wells."

"Oh, to be sure. I've nothing but time. And who's to do my regular farm work while I spend my days heaving dirt?"

"My father and I did it," Kanlor said quietly, "several years ago."

"Yeah." The man turned away. "That was several years back. It's right now I've a family to feed." He kicked at the ground. "Besides, how am I to know I'll have your luck and hit water every time I dig?"

Kanlor watched the man walk away. *We didn't*, he remembered. *There're quite a few dry holes we filled in. And it's precious little time we spent in the village, too.* He walked toward his *garn*, then turned as he heard Mord's loud voice.

"It's just not fair," the man was saying. "I come out to the pasture day after day and there's nothing amiss. Then this morning, there's this big weed patch. Bunch of lizards in it, too." He waved an arm. "Look, bull's dead of a lizard bite. Two cows all bloated up from eating the filthy leaves, I'll probably lose them, too. And then this fire runs wild. How's a man to . . ."

Kanlor turned away and climbed into his saddle. He looked back at the group wearily. It took time, he knew, for lizard weed to grow. And it took more time for the poisonous *yarlnu* to find a patch and nest in it. He looked back at the scanty stand of grain in what was left of Mord's field. The man's voice carried to him.

"I tell you, it's black sorcery. Witchcraft, that's what it is—a spell on this land of mine."

Kanlor rapped his heels into the *garn's* side. *Of course*, he said to himself. *Sorcery! Evil spells! This past year, there's more and more talk of it. No man really believes the tales till he needs an alibi. When a man lets his fields go, spends his time chasing about the village, goes to every fair down at Varsana, then it's a black spell that causes his farm to go down.* He turned his face toward his own holdings.

*   *   *

Moren pen Qatorn, Chief Examiner for the Duchy of Varsan, leaned forward and cupped his chin in his hands.

"And you say this man has cast repeated spells in your neighborhood?"

Delon Mord looked up at him eagerly. "Yes, my lord. Why only a few days ago, he caused a large patch of lizard weed to grow in my pasture overnight. And somehow, by a black spell, he brought *yarlnu* lizards to infest it." He drew his mouth into a downward curve and spread his hands.

"My cattle were poisoned and one bitten. They died, to my great loss."

"And you say it was this"—pen Qatorn glanced at his secretary's notes—"Wysrin Kanlor who caused this misfortune to you?"

Mord nodded eagerly. "Oh, to be sure, sir. Soon after I started burning the patch off, Kanlor made as if to burn weed on his own property. It was right after that when my fire blazed up and fired the whole field." He peered at the Examiner cunningly.

"They say this is the way the sorcerers work. They take something like that which they would destroy, and—"

Pen Qatorn sighed impatiently. "Yes, yes. We are quite familiar with the workings of black magic. We know about these hopelessly damned sorcerers, and with the demons who are their masters." He looked down sternly.

"This, then, is your story? To be sure, you weren't a bit remiss in the husbandry of your fields? Perhaps you could have been a bit careless in guarding that your flames should not spread?"

"Oh no, sir!" Mord shook his head. "I am careful to look over my fields daily, and to do that which is needful. There was no weed before that morning."

"I see." Pen Qatorn smiled sardonically. "And this, of course, is the only proof you have to show Kanlor's sorcery?"

"Oh no, sir. There is yet more. All this year, my fields and my neighbors' fields have been dry and the crops scant. Only Kanlor's fields remain rich on the whole plateau. His crops are good and his cattle fat. Thus, he will command a high price for his produce while the rest of us grow poor."

"Ah, yes. This may well merit investigation. And you, I believe, are asking just compensation for these losses you claim were caused by the man's sorcery?"

"Yes, my lord." Mord nodded eagerly. "These spells I tell you of have caused me grievous loss."

"I understand. Well, we shall see." Pen Qatorn raised his head and nodded portentiously. "You may go for now. Perhaps we may call upon you later for further evidence." He waved a hand in dismissal, then turned to his secretary.

"What about this man Kanlor?" he asked in a low voice. "Have you anything on him?"

The secretary nodded. "Information is at hand, my lord. Our original survey showed this might be a man to look up." He smiled and flipped a paper from the stack before him.

"Kanlor has five fields and a pasture, not far from the duke's High Keep. His crops have been good for several seasons back. Man's unmarried and lives alone." The man paused, examining the sheet.

"The duke would pay well for those fields, sir. Kanlor has good wells on them—the only really good wells for several farms around. Oh, yes, there's another thing. He's literate. Dropped from the university when his parents died."

"I see. A fit subject for investigation, then. Tell me, is the man well liked in his village?"

The secretary shook his head. "He lives on his farm. Most of his neighbors seem to be a bit envious of him. No one but this Mord has actually made any accusation, but it's obvious that few tears would be shed if misfortune overtook Kanlor."

"Interesting. And what about Mord?"

"Slovenly farmer, sir. Neglects his fields, though he does manage to scratch out a living and pay his bills. Frequents the tavern and spends a lot of time at the fairs. He lives in the village."

"Married?"

The secretary tilted his head. "Yes, and he has a pair of scrawny children as well. But the man has a certain popularity. He's no brawler and he has a ready wit. The villagers are tolerant of him and the tavern crowd follows his lead."

The Chief Examiner got to his feet. "I find that this information against the man Kanlor has merit," he said loudly. "We shall pursue an inquiry and bring him before this tribunal shortly." He looked at the local judges, who had moved a bit apart.

"Subject, of course, to any comments you gentlemen might have," he added.

The three men looked uneasily at each other, then turned to face the Chief Examiner.

"We are of the same opinion as your lordship," one said.

Pen Qatorn nodded curtly. "Very well, gentlemen, we shall meet tomorrow after lunch to consider any further information that may come to light. We may, perhaps, question the man Kanlor at that time." He threw a stern glance at the guardsmen who flanked the judicial table.

"Surely, we shall question the man no later than the second day." He rose and strode from the room.

The secretary followed pen Qatorn to a small room, then closed the door and turned to his chief.

"How about this Mord?" he asked. "He's asking compensation."

Pen Qatorn smiled. "And for a long list of claims, I have no doubt. Oh, I think we can allow him a bit for his losses," he decided. "And you might do a little inquiring as to the value of his holdings." He pursed his lips.

"You know, it's a serious crime to make false claim. Too, this informant has been associated with the suspect Kanlor for some time and he shows a certain knowledge of magic himself. It might be well to inquire closely into his activities."

The secretary nodded, then backed away and went through the door. Outside, he shook his head, smiling.

Old fox, he said to himself. *He never misses a thing.*

Going or coming, he's got them. He fingered one of his gold rings as he went through an archway, to pace across a small courtyard.

An inconspicuous brown beetle had been perched on a curtain. It flew silently to him and concealed itself in a fold of his clothing.

For a time, he was no more than a free mind, floating in a shapeless void with neither identity nor feeling. Then there was pain. At first, a tiny, hesitant ache insinuated itself. Then it grew to become a throbbing flood of agony. He tried to move a hand, but something held it behind him and the effort made the blinding throb become more acute. He breathed deeply and red flames stabbed at chest and side.

A flood of evil-smelling water poured over him and he jerked his head back. His eyes opened. Now, he remembered. He was Wysrin Kanlor. He had been in a field when guardsmen had come for him, and dragged him from his *garn*. He could remember no words, but there had been kicks and blows, then nothingness.

Dazedly, he looked about at vaguely seen rafters, then at a huge, fat man who towered over him and finally reached down to drag him to his feet.

"Come along, witch," the man ordered. "The Examiner, pen Qatorn, would have words with you." He jerked on a chain and Kanlor's head throbbed as a leash pulled at his neck. He stumbled after his captor.

They went through an arch, then turned. Kanlor's eyesight was clearing and he could see men in somber robes who sat at a table above him. The man in the middle spoke.

"Your name is Wysrin Kanlor. Is this true?"

"Yes. But why—"

"Silence! I shall ask the questions. You have but to answer—and truthfully."

The big man slashed the back of his hand across Kanlor's face.

"And address the Examiner as 'his lordship,'" he ordered.

Kanlor swayed dizzily, then recovered his balance.

The Examiner continued. "And for how long have you been delving into black sorcery?"

Kanlor's eyes widened. "But I—"

Again the hard hand slammed at his face.

"Answer. Don't try to evade his lordship's questions."

"I ask you again, Wysrin Kanlor," the Examiner said sternly, "how long have you been a witch?"

"Your lordship, I have never been a witch."

The Examiner frowned. "The man is reluctant," he commented. "He answers, but his answers mean nothing. He has yet to learn the value of truth. Sir Executioner, perhaps you might instruct him?"

The large man nodded. "Thumbscrews," he ordered.

There was a movement behind Kanlor, then he felt something being clamped to his right thumb. Pressure was swiftly exerted and raging pain shot up his arm. He barely choked back a scream.

Pen Qatorn looked at him coldly. "You have been using black sorcery to the damage of your neighbors. For how long have you done this? Five years? Six?"

Kanlor stared at him silently. Pen Qatorn watched for a moment, then continued.

"We shall come back to that again. Why did you become a witch?"

There was a jerk at Kanlor's hand and the pressure on his thumb increased. A clamp was placed on his other thumb and tightened. His mouth flew open in shocked disbelief. This, he told himself, simply was not happening. It was a horrible dream. He . . .

The pressure was abruptly increased and a scream started to well from his throat. He clamped his lips fiercely shut. It was no dream and nothing he could say would help. He stared silently at the Examiner. Pen Qatorn frowned.

"How did you become a witch? What was done at that time? Who is your evil master?" He paused.

More clamps were fastened to Kanlor's fingers and tightened. His hands throbbed and the muscles of his arms tightened and cramped.

"Well, will you answer? How long have you been a witch?"

Kanlor drew a shuddering breath, then closed his

eyes. Pen Qatorn glared at him, then turned to his
secretary.

"Let it be noted that the man is taciturn," he remarked. He looked back at Kanlor.

"Oh, have no doubt. You shall answer these questions," he said coldly. "These and more. It will but take
time." He moved his hand.

"Take him to the torture chamber. There, he may
realize the error of his ways."

The Executioner jerked at the leash, forcing Kanlor
to follow. They went through a hall and down a short
flight of steps, to come out into a large room. On the
walls hung tongs, pincers, branding irons and other
implements unfamiliar to Kanlor. The Executioner
glanced around for a moment, then jerked his captive
toward the center of the room, signing to a pair of
assistants.

Overhead, a pulley was fastened to the rafters. A
thick rope had been threaded through it and hung, its
ends tied to a ring set in the floor. An assistant untied
one end of the rope, then went to Kanlor and secured it
to his wrist bonds. He slipped the other end from the
ring and pulled on it till Kanlor was forced to bend
over. The other assistant looped the free end of the
rope through the ring again and took up the slack. They
stood, eyeing their chief.

The Executioner nodded. "Take him up a bit."

The assistants hauled away and Kanlor swung a meter
above the floor. A knot was tied, securing the rope end
to the ring and again, the assistants watched their chief,
who smiled approvingly at them.

"Very good," he said. He looked at Kanlor.

"Now, we are just ordinary men," he said reasonably,
"who have to do our job. We have no real desire to do
you hurt, or to cause you needless pain." He smiled
disarmingly. "In fact, we really don't like to do it. Why
don't you be a good fellow? Let me bring his lordship
here so you can answer his questions. It will make it
easier for all of us. Your hurts will be tended and we
won't have to go to great efforts. How about it?"

Momentarily, the thought entered Kanlor's mind that

the man might be right. Perhaps he should simply answer. Then he remembered the questions. He could do himself no good, however he spoke. He closed his eyes, ignoring the fat man.

"Well, I tried." The Executioner sighed resignedly. "We shall leave you in the rafters for a time. You may consider and think of what you will tell the Examiner when he again deigns to consider you." He waved a hand.

"Pull him up, boys," he ordered. "We'd as well go out for a bite to eat." He turned toward the steps.

Wysrin Kanlor was no weakling. Long hours of work with shovel, hay hook, and flail had given him powerful arm and shoulder muscles. He found that he could support his weight even in this unaccustomed position. For a while, he even thought he might be able to pull his body between his arms, swing himself up, and somehow undo the ropes with his teeth. Maybe he might be able somehow to escape. But there simply wasn't space for his body to pass between his arms. Blood rushed to his head and he was forced to give up the effort and to dangle, breathing heavily.

His shoulders began to ache with the strain, then the muscles of his chest added their complaints. Time passed and the ache became a numbing sea of pain. He breathed in agonized gasps, dimly wondering how many eternities he had been up here, and how many more long eons it would be before he was taken down.

He tried to focus his eyes on the stone floor, but the flagstones blended into a blurred, gray mass. Agony spread over his entire upper body, then even his legs began to cramp.

And still he hung from the pulley, gasping through wide-open mouth and wondering how long it might be before his shoulders would tear loose to drop him to the floor below.

At last, he stopped even wondering and simply hung, submerged in formless pain.

Dimly, as from a long distance, he heard footsteps. The rope vibrated. Suddenly he was falling, only to stop with a violent jerk that tore muscles and tendons. A startled scream forced its way from him.

"The man is not truly dumb, your lordship," said a voice. "Perchance he can answer your questions now."

"Your name? Come, fellow, give your name." The second voice was imperious.

Kanlor managed to open his eyes.

"Please," he croaked. "Let me down."

"Later. You have questions to answer now. Come, now, what is your name?"

"Kanlor. Wysrin Kanlor. It hurts!"

"Never mind whining. Just answer. How long have you been a witch? Five years?"

"I'm not a—"

"Fellow, we've been most forbearing with you. Now if you persist in your refusal to answer, we will have to put you to the torture. Once again, how long have you been a witch?"

Kanlor closed his eyes. Talking did no good and it took too much effort. Perhaps if he hung here for long, his heart would stop. The peace of death would be better than long periods of suffering.

"The man is still taciturn. Indicate to him what may lie ahead should he persist in his silence."

Kanlor felt liquid being poured over his head. A rag was roughly wiped over his face. He could feel a chill on his back as some of it trickled down his spine. A torch was brought near and suddenly, his head and shoulders were enveloped in flame. Desperately , he held his breath, refusing to let out the screams that fought to be released—holding back sudden madness that tore at him.

The flare died as the alcohol burned out. Cold salt water was dashed over him and every nerve screamed in outrage.

All at once, he was coldly, clearly sane and aware. He had seen people burned over large parts of their bodies. They never survived. He would never again walk the fields; this, he knew.

But they'll get little satisfaction, he told himself fiercely. *I may not live, but I can die silent*.

Dimly, he heard question after question. He sealed his lips, holding one all-encompassing thought. *Silence!*

At last, he was taken down and bedded in some straw, only to be awakened for more questions. Someone explained to him the ways of witches.

"So, you see, you will be giving away no secret," he was told. "We only wish that you may purge yourself of your sin."

He lost all track of time. Questioners hammered at him. Variations of torture were tested. At times, he lost consciousness, only to be roused by buckets of cold water. There came a time when he was unsure as to whether he was speaking or not.

And there were other times when he wondered if perhaps he had, by some force of his desires, caused drought, raging flames in neighbors' fields, death of cattle.

At last, he realized vaguely that he was being supported by two men and taken to the open air. There were many people. He was chained, then left alone.

Then flames and smoke surrounded him and he waited for an end. It would be relief. He fainted.

Carlsen watched the viewscreen as relayed recordings flashed across it. His hands flicked over the editing controls as he alternately speeded and slowed the presentation. Suddenly, he straightened and brought the presentation to normal speed. This one was recent.

He watched as the victim was stretched on a rack, then listened as unanswered questions were asked. He glanced at the data panel and shook his head furiously.

That was less than an hour ago!

Abruptly, he snapped the recorders off and turned to his flight controls.

I've had it! It's not all that far to Varsana. The devil with concealment. Let 'em hear a good, solid sonic boom. Might give 'em something to worry about.

The ship leveled off at two thousand meters and streaked toward the town at the head of the valley. Ahead and below, the plaza came into view and Carlsen kicked up magnification, then swore and threw the ship into a screaming dive.

*   *   *

Pen Qatorn stood before the wide door of the House of Questioning and watched as Kanlor was fastened to the execution post.

"This," he said, "is a stubborn witch. Not a word from him. May there be few like that."

His secretary nodded. "Yes, sir, but there is yet this man Mord. Perhaps he may tell us of other suspects."

Pen Qatorn cleared his throat. "Well, at least, we're well rid of this Kanlor." He waved a hand curtly at the Executioner and pitched his voice to the right judicial tone.

"Let the flames rise," he called, "that they may purify the duchy of this evil one."

The burly Executioner tossed a torch, then reached for another. Faggots and brushwood smoked and flamed.

Then there was confusion. The plaza shook to a loud explosion. A blast of wind raged briefly. The fire, fanned into sudden fury, flew toward the spectators, who beat frantically at suddenly flaming clothing. The confusion became panic. Coughing and screaming, the crowd became a terrorized mob that stampeded wildly through the streets.

Unbelievingly, pen Qatorn stared at the chaos. At last, he recovered his thoughts and looked toward the execution pole. Something was . . . somehow, the captive was being released. The Examiner started to dash forward, then cringed away as pale blue flame washed over the flagstones toward him.

Chief Surgeon Palken was just snapping his communicator off as Carlsen came in. He looked up, then spread his hands.

"I don't know how the man does it," he said. "Know who that was?"

"Commander Walzen?"

"Right. How did you know? Well, anyway, he's demanding things. First, he wants that primitive you brought in today. Next, he wants you to report to him immediately. Says he knows you must be in the hospital area and I'd better find you." He smiled wryly. "You've got me nicely in the middle."

"At this time of night?"

Palken nodded. "At this time of night! He's scream-ing for blood. Says he's going to get that primitive out of here and back to his own planet a little sooner than possible."

"That's a man he's talking about," Carlsen said softly. "His name is Kanlor and if he goes back to his own planet, he's going to be burned as a witch. How is he, by the way? That's what I came up here to find out."

"Physically, he's coming along nicely. You people did an excellent first-aid job on him. Psychologically, though, I'm not so sure. Pretty traumatic. Thinks he's dead—or should be."

"Yes, sir. Well, that'll be a nice headache for the Corps rehabilitation people, I guess. I certainly am not about to release him to C.A. He's part of a Corps mission and I haven't even got off to a good start with it yet."

Palken shook his head sorrowfully. "Now I know I'm in the middle," he complained. "I've worked with our Corps Commander A-Riman and he's about the last man in the Federation I want to mix with. On the other hand, Commander Walzen's no lily, either. He's got something on half the people on this base."

"Oh?"

"That's right. You know, almost everyone's left a body buried somewhere. The good commander seems to know where each one is, and just how to dig them up." Palken shrugged. "I think he keeps a special file—a large one."

"I see. Well, I don't think he's found any of mine yet. He'd have used one already." Carlsen looked down at Palken's desk. "I'll report to him right away, of course. There's one thing, though, sir."

"What's that?"

"Please keep several of your people that aren't in the commander's files around Kanlor from now on out. If I lose him, Corps Commander A-Riman'll fry me like a doughnut."

Palken looked after him as he walked out of the office.

Yeah, he said happily, *after he's rendered me out for*

the grease. He reached for his communicator switch, then changed his mind and hurried out to the corridor.

The clerk finally looked expressionlessly at Carlsen. "You can go in now, sir." He watched as Carlsen went through a door, then turned his attention to his records, smiling derisively.

That's one wise guy who's going to be a tame pussycat when he comes out of there.

Carlsen stepped toward the desk, then stood, waiting.

Commander Kar Walzen took his time about affixing his signature to some papers, carefully put them in appropriate file folders, then looked up and regarded him coldly, slowly inspecting him. Finally, he spoke.

"I understand you landed on a newly discovered primitive planet and interfered with native affairs. Is that correct?"

"There is a dangerous trend in—"

"I asked you a question. Did you, or did you not, make planetfall and take a native off planet?"

"Yes, sir. I did. But—"

"Well, at least I'm glad you have the sense not to deny obvious facts. Now, did you cause a panic and injure some natives?"

Carlsen stiffened. "Sir, you have obviously gained access to my report. It was under confidential seal, addressed to Philosophical Corps Command. This is in violation of regulation— "

"Never mind quoting regulations. Remember this. I'm a staff officer assigned to this sector. I'm not half a galaxy away, I'm here. And you're here. Now, I'm going to review every report that goes out of my branch. And they don't go out until I have approved them. I cautioned you about trying to go over my head to Sector. I've seen your records, yes. And I didn't like what I saw." He drew a long breath and stared angrily at Carlsen.

"I didn't want a Philosophical Corps detachment in the first place. You and your crew of so-called specialists were crammed down my throat and I never liked it. I tried to make the best of it and put you to some use, but it's no good. I can't see much difference between you and your do-gooders and a bunch of thrill-happy drones and I don't like drones. I don't like any kind of criminal activity and your actions have that same unsavory smell. I'm telling you now, I won't tolerate any further such activity so long as you're under my command.

"I'm still going to be fair about this. I'll give you a chance to explain yourself. Why did you go in as you did? Were there any signs of outside interference with the culture?"

Carlsen shook his head. "That culture was endangering itself," he said. He held up a hand as the commander started to speak.

"Sir, I'm sorry, but my detachment is *not* under your command nor am I. We are assigned to act in coordination with your branch and we've leaned over backward in actually taking missions that should have been done by your teams. But—"

"You're assigned here. I'm the Criminal Apprehension Officer for this sector and you are just one of the junior officers in my jurisdiction. And don't try to quote regulations to me! I've read 'em. Now I'm going to order you—"

Again, Carlsen's hand went up, palm forward. "Commander, we are not directly under your command. You know it and I know it. I intend to take my team back and clean up the situation we found. If you have any further comments, I'd suggest you take them up with the Sector Commander for referral to my Corps Command. Right now, sir, with your permission, I'm going over to Headquarters, where I shall make sure that my report is forwarded immediately. If necessary, I shall get the duty officer to contact the Sector Commander directly."

Commander Walzen was a large man. He got to his feet and strode close, to tower over the junior officer. Fists clenched at his sides, he stared down threateningly.

"All right. For the moment, I'll assume you're not directly under my command. I should put you in confinement and prefer charges. But I won't do that just yet. I shall write up those same charges and put them through channels. Meantime, you'll remain on duty and your report will be forwarded."

He raised a fist and slammed it into his other hand.

"I will say this, though. I want you to write up a full, detailed operational plan and then take that crew of yours back and clean up the mess you made. I'm not going to waste the time of any of my own people in bailing you out. I'm not going to tell you how to do this cleanup but I want it done and done in a hurry. Is that clear?"

"Quite, sir." Hal Carlsen snapped a salute and strode from the office. He closed the door with forced gentleness and looked back.

Brother, he murmured. *I'm glad the detachment is on "detached." If that is a typical C.A. officer, they need to do a lot of housecleaning.*

Carlsen examined the cliffs as he approached.

Come to think of it, they do look like the remains of an ancient seashore.

People, you jerk, he reminded himself, *not geology. A full operational plan that idiot wanted! Hah! We've got things roughed in, but I won't know the details till the job's done.* He frowned.

Wonder if the Old Man'll bail me out. That guy's sure to use that for a "direct order" charge. And he is a senior officer.

The communicator screen lit.

"Chief?"

"Go ahead, Waler."

"I suppose you know, you've made the local pandemonium."

"Oh? How's that?"

"Just picked up a lecture. Seems there must've been at least a hundred people saw you pick that guy out of Varsana. You're twenty meters tall, got six or eight extra arms, and poison dripping from every fang. You kicked the fire all over town, clawed down a building or two and breathed fire and poison all over the Chief Examiner, his clerk, and three local judges. They're martyrs now. Then you picked this poor witch up. Jerked him off the pole, chains and all, then tore him into little bits and scattered the pieces so far they haven't found a trace yet."

"*Wow!* And I didn't think they'd have time for a good look." Carlsen grinned, then sobered. "Look, Waler, we've got to get rid of that story before it grows up and has pups."

Waler shook his head. "Might have to take a demonology lecturer or so along with it, sir."

Carlsen shrugged resignedly. "Well, if it comes down to it, the civilization can stumble along without them." He stroked his chin. "Maybe next time around, they'll have a chance to be useful citizens. Just don't hurt them any more than you have to."

He snapped off the communicator and reached for the wall panel. It would take at least two spyeyes for this job, he decided. In fact, three would be better.

Duke Khathor par Doizen, Protector of Varsan and the High Marches, looked at the plump man at his right.

Another Examiner, he sighed to himself, *and full of his convictions and duties. Well, at least, he's one who likes good food and wine. That other fellow made a man uneasy every time he touched a cup.* He lifted his wine cup and sipped.

"It is to be hoped, Sir Examiner," he said, "that you may be able to clear our duchy of all evil in short order."

A servant had just filled Examiner Dorthal Kietol's cup. He set it on the table and turned away. No one noticed that the liquid wavered and rippled more than was normal.

Kietol seized the cup, drank, smacked thick lips, then drank more deeply. He moved his heavily jowled jaw appreciatively.

"An excellent vintage, my lord," he commented. He swayed a trifle in his chair, blinked, and shook his head uncertainly, then looked through squinted eyes at the duke.

"You were saying?"

The duke frowned. "I was speaking of this evil that has come to our duchy," he said. "We hope it will soon be rooted out."

Kietol wagged his head, then drained his cup. He slammed it to the table and waved expansively.

"Nothing to fear," he said loudly. "We'll burn 'em all. Get all the money." He squinted at the duke cunningly.

"Got lots of fat merchants, hey? Rich farmers, too." Again, he wagged his head. "That pen Qatorn, he was a smart one. Good records and we have 'em. Lots of money here." He weaved, then threw his arms out. "We'll get 'em. Burn 'em all."

Par Doizen set his cup down carefully, regarding the Examiner searchingly.

"Yes," he admitted slowly. "Witches should burn. But what's this about merchants and rich farmers? And what of the demon? Isn't there a chance he might return?"

Kietol's head had dropped to his chest. He lifted it with a jerk. "Whazzat? Oh. Witches are rich. Rich are witches." Again, he jerked his head up. "Oh. Huh? Demon? Ha, I know about that. Never any demon. No demons. Just a little storm, y'know. *Whoosh!* Fire blows all over. No such thing as demon." He squinted at the duke, his head weaving uncertainly.

"You're a smart man, Khator, smart. Oughta know better. Demons something for the mob, y'know? Scare 'em good. Then we get the money, see? Duke gets land, College of Examiners gets big, see what I mean?" His head rolled and he put his arms on the table and slumped over. He snored.

His secretary had been sitting down the table, watching in consternation. He got to his feet.

"Why, they've bewitched the Examiner himself," he cried. "We must get an exorcist at once!"

The duke looked thoughtfully at the snoring man by him, then got to his feet and looked down the length of the table.

"They teach that demons and witches have no power against the ordained, or even against men of the law," he said slowly. "But there! I can't argue the point. I know little about demons. But I do know drunks. And this man is drunk. I've also found that men are prone to speak their true thoughts when they are as drunk as this." He pointed to the Examiner, then looked up.

"But I, your Protector, have had little wine. I am not at all drunk. And I say this. No more shall property be confiscated, whatever the charge. Trials may be and shall be held, to be sure, but only on proper and legal representation. And I shall have an officer present to see that none is unduly mistreated. Those who would confess shall stand alone and cry their misdeeds without constraint. Those who will not confess shall be convicted only upon proper presentation by reputable witness. And finally, no more excessive fees shall be paid to guards and executioners, nor shall they feed at the expense of the accused." He looked sternly at his clerks.

"Let this be inscribed for our signature and posted on the morrow." He swung to face the Examiner's secretary.

"You may escort your master to his bed chamber," he ordered. "When he has become sober, you may tell him of this, our edict." He sat down.

In the absence of the guest of honor, the banquet was soon over. Par Doizen made his way to his chambers and perched on the edge of his bed. He sat for a while, thinking, then pulled at a bell cord.

A clerk came in. "Your lordship?"

"That edict I announced. Is it ready?"

The clerk nodded. "I have a fair copy for your hand, my lord. A copy has gone out by courier to the printers."

"Before my signing?"

"My lord, you sounded most urgent. It is late and the printers must have time for their work."

"Yes. I must have been a little tipsy myself. Well, it's said. Let the man go. Every important man in the duchy was listening and I'll be damned if I'll eat my words." He pulled an intricate signet from his belt pouch and held it out.

"And, Kel."

"My lord?" The clerk was inking the signet.

"Go to the Captain of my Guard. Tell him to rally as many men-at-arms as he can find. We may need them. No, better yet. Tell him to report to me immediately and in person."

*   *   *

Hal Carlsen smiled contentedly as he watched the viewsphere. Examiner Kietol was moving about his chambers dispiritedly, picking up belongings and throwing them into a chest.

"I tell you, I couldn't have been drunk," he was saying. "I haven't been drunk these many years, since I was a mere student. And on only three cups of wine? Three, I tell you. Now how could any man get drunk on a tiny sup like that?"

His secretary shook his head. "I don't understand it, sir. You looked drunk. You acted drunk. And sober, you would never have spoken so. I don't know."

Kietol wagged his head, then winced. "I know," he admitted. "I don't remember, but I've been told what I said. And the next morning! By my faith—such as I now have left, you understand—I can still feel that headache!" He slammed the lid of the chest shut.

"Well, that's the last of it. Let's go down and make our way out of this accursed duchy as fast as we may, while the duke still has the grace to protect us on our journey."

Carlsen laughed. *Well*, he told himself, *it'll be a while before any Examiner dares show up around here*. He snapped the communicator on.

"Cisner?"

"Here, sir. Chief, you just wouldn't believe it unless I ran the whole take for you. They're burning 'em five or ten at a time down here. This bunch of vultures have gone wild. They're getting filthy rich and the archduke is getting a good slice, too. He's cheering them on." Cisner paused.

"Look, Chief, the old boy's got a nephew who's the heir apparent. Young fellow. Doesn't think much of the whole thing. Never goes to executions unless his uncle makes him. Can't I just wait till he isn't there and then dive in? I could get the whole mob with one blast."

"Not only no, but hell no!" Carlsen shook his head decisively. "Once is a great plenty. I'll admit I blew my top and we're on the way to covering it up. But if we do it again, we'll stir up a real mess. Varsana's looking good right now, but another blast'd have the duke wondering and maybe changing his mind." He looked thoughtful.

"You say the nephew is the heir apparent and he's against the Examiners. That right?"

"Yes, sir. And when he hears about Varsana, he'll feel even more strongly. But right now, he's keeping awfully quiet. The Examiners are getting wise to him and they're beginning to think about sneaking him into one of their torture chambers some night. He knows it and he's getting scared. That's another thing, Chief. I—"

"I told you, Cisner, no!" Carlsen held up a hand. "Look, why don't you slip a spyeye into the archduke's bed chamber? You might get an idea."

"But, Chief. He holds conferences there. I've got—" Cisner looked confused, then suddenly smiled wolfishly. "Oh! Yes, sir! I'll get right on it."

"Out." Carlsen turned away, then tapped the switch again.

"Waler?"

"Still working, Chief. I got an assist from your way, though. Peddler's caravan just drifted into town. They're talking all over the taverns about the drunk Examiner over in Varsana. Incidentally, what happened to that guy, sir?"

"Oh, just a little drug I whipped up. Made him look drunk and feel awfully truthful."

"Oh. Maybe I could use some of that, too. Well, anyway, I don't know why these peddlers came running over here so fast, or how they got their story prettied up so well, but it's a big help."

Carlsen chuckled. "Let's say they got a little push," he said. "Incidentally, they ran off with one of my spyeyes. How about picking it up?"

"Will do. Oh, there's another thing. Remember that demonology lecturer I reported on? The one with the nightmares? I tried to poke him around a little during a lecture, and . . . honest, Chief, I didn't punch at him hard at all, but he went into convulsions. Raved a bit, then died off right in front of about twenty students."

"Not so good." Carlsen frowned. "I suppose that's all over the taverns, too?"

"Within an hour." Waler shrugged. "But there's a switch. He was Doctor Big Authority and he's the guy that'd sold everyone on the idea that no demon or witch had any power around either a law official or a member of a recognized order. And that, they wanted to believe, so it stuck. It's practically an article of faith. But that only leaves one explanation for what happened to him. He must have been struck down for fibbing." Waler smiled deprecatingly.

"I sort of helped out on that idea. It seemed to tie in pretty well with the peddlers' stories."

"Oh. So it's not so bad after all. Well, keep after it."

"Yes, sir. Out."

Carlsen turned to stare at his flight controls.

One down. One possible—maybe two. Waler seems to have things going his way. Of course, there's Wenzel and Pak, down at Holy City, but they're just getting a nice start. He massaged the back of his neck.

I think I'll go back to the cruiser and start correlating this stuff.

The room was littered with scraps of tape and scribbled notes that had missed the disposal unit. Carlsen inspected the floor, then sighed and started scooping up the debris. At least the whole thing was up to date, in order, and stored in memory units. It included everything of any significance from the original data. He looked around at the communicator panels. Of course, there were a couple of loose ends, but— He walked over to the communicator.

"Cisner?"

"Here, Chief. Mission accomplished. Request permission to return."

"Oh? What about your archduke?"

"That's why I want to come in, sir. You may want to eat me up and make me pay for one each transponder, surveillance shielded." Cisner managed to look woeful.

"I musta goofed my preventive maintenance on that spyeye. It blew its power unit just a few hours after I slipped it into the old boy's bedroom. Practically no explosion and no serious fusing, but it scattered neutrons all over the place."

"Anyone get burned?"

"Just the archduke, sir. He'd gone to bed. Must have taken almost a thousand roentgens. It's lucky those walls were pretty heavy. They made good shielding and no one else got hurt. His nephew took over and he's flat refusing to give the Examiners any cooperation. That Varsana story got down here and he's following the pattern." Cisner laughed.

"They tried a couple of trials, but they didn't go so well. First one, an Executioner tried to slip a thumb-screw onto the accused and one of the duke's guards fed him his teeth. The Chief Examiner tried to rule that the things didn't constitute torture and the Captain of the Guard offered to let him try a couple on, just for size."

Carlsen looked thoughtful. "Of course, you didn't have a thing to do with that?"

"Oh, no, sir." Cisner looked innocent. "I was just observing, sir."

"Naturally, I believe you. But remember, the memory units pick up all the impulses."

Cisner looked apologetic. "Well, you know how it is, sir. A guy sometimes hopes a little."

"See?" Carlsen laughed. "Now that's what I'd call confession without torture. How about the pieces of that blown-up eye?"

"All policed up, sir. I'll turn in the wreckage soon's I get back."

"Fair enough. Maybe we can call it operational loss. Out." Carlsen depressed another switch. "Wenzel?"

"Reporting, sir. They're having a big trial here. Seems the Bursar for the College of Examiners has come up awfully short. He can't account for what happened to about three quarters of the year's take."

Carlsen shook his head. "Even the most ethical organizations will hire a thief now and then, I guess. Any trace of the loot?"

"No, sir. He just won't talk. The High Priest is just about fed up with the whole thing. He's about to decide they've been hunting the wrong people." Wenzel paused.

"But Pak and I've got a little problem, Chief. We just found a lot of odds and ends lying around in the scouter. Place looks like a junkyard in distress. What shall . . . Hey, Chief. We got a visitor!"

"A what?"

"There's something nosing around here. Something pretty big, too. I'll swear somebody just peeled our screens back like a banana and took a real good look. Pak's got the detectors working overtime and we can't get a thing except a damn strong shield."

"Hang on. I'll bring the cruiser down and open him up. Out."

A third voice broke in. "Never mind, Carlsen. I'm coming your way now." The panel flickered and a sharp-featured face looked out.

Carlsen jumped. "Yes, sir! Welcome aboard, sir." He depressed switches. "Philcor Seven. Immediate recall. And make it fast."

Corps Commander A-Riman strode around the room, then perched on the edge of a desk.

"On the whole, I'd say you people have done an acceptable job so far. You've got a few rough edges left, but at least you've definitely stopped what could have been a disastrous massacre of psionics." He looked back at the computer reflectively.

"You know, there have been civilizations that have eliminated virtually all of their parapsychological potential. Every one of them has had serious trouble. Development's always one-sided and there's the danger of complete self-destruction. That's happened, too." He shrugged.

"You've prevented that here—at least for the present. Of course, it could flare up again. We'll have to work out something to prevent that." He looked at Carlsen expectantly.

"I'll have to think that one over, sir." Carlsen hesitated.

"One question. I did disobey a direct order back there at base. No operational plan, and I was ordered to turn one in."

"An order issued by competent authority, in the legal performance of duty?"

"Well . . . I didn't think so at the time, sir."

A-Riman nodded. "Neither did I when I heard about it." He smiled. "I had a little conference with some people before I came out here. Commander Walzen's decided to forget about any charges. I would suggest, though that you remember the experience. You actually were guilty of an entrapment."

"Sir?"

"That's right. You let him push you and your people when you first reported in. It gave him the idea he could do anything he wanted to. Then, when you got your back up, he was surprised, hurt, and jolly well peeved about it. Worms aren't expected to turn, you know." A-Riman waved a hand.

"But that's over. Now you've got another problem. What are you going to do about that man you sent to Rehabilitation?"

"Me, sir?"

"He's your man. You picked him up. Obviously, you can't just drop him back at his farm again. And you can't turn him loose in the Federation and tell him to make his own way. Do you want to enlist him in your detachment?"

"He'd need an awful lot of training."

"Yes. I'd estimate at least six standard years. It could stretch out to ten. Meantime, you'd be short a man. We do have some limitations, you know."

Carlsen dropped into a chair. "I've got a good crew. I'd hate to lose any of them."

"Any suggestions?"

Carlsen rubbed his temple, frowning. Suddenly, he jumped up.

"Commander, would it be possible to train this man for a fixed assignment right here? He already knows his own culture, and we certainly could use an observer on this planet." He strode across the floor.

"Anything out of the ordinary, we'd know about it right away. We could check on him periodically. Keep him supplied. Maybe brief him now and then."

The commander smiled. "Just the one man?"

"Well, maybe he could use some help, sir. But—"

"That's what I was waiting for. Now, your job is to

pick up a few suitable recruits—people you are sure will fit in. They'll be trained and sent back to you, then you can put them to work." The smile widened.

"We've got a special training area for just this sort of thing, you see. There are quite a few native guardians in the galaxy, but no detachment commander ever hears about them until he comes up with the idea and asks for some. That's when he gets promoted. Congratulations, Lieutenant."

Carlsen stared at him, then suddenly started to laugh.

"Something is funny, Lieutenant?"

Carlsen forced his face back into serious lines.

"Sorry, sir," he choked out. "But it really is ironic. These people were about to institute a full dress massacre of psionics. And they'd have killed off a lot of non-psionics, as well. They were perverting their entire culture—maybe setting it up for destruction in the future. And all this was just to stamp out an imaginary cult of witches. Now, they're going to have real witches with real powers around. And they won't even know they exist."

A-Riman regarded him for a minute, shaking his head. Then he chuckled.

"That's one for you, Carlsen. Now here's one for their side. You're going to be on the job to see that these are *good* witches."

Editor's Introduction To:

THE BUZZ OF JOY

Phillip C. Jennings

The fall of Empire generally produces a dark age. We know of several in human history. One came after the collapse of the Minoan/Mycaenean imperial civilization, which fell so far that writing itself was lost—indeed, we have only recently been able to read one of their languages, Linear B, and we still cannot read two of the others. This first dark age came about after the fall of Troy and continued until well after 800 B.C.

The great Dark Ages came after the fall of Rome, and lasted for seven hundred years.

We have not yet experienced a third, and we can only speculate on how long that might last. We do know this: books are widespread. So are computers. Technical artifacts abound. No matter how complete the destruction, some will remain to be found, and used . . .

THE BUZZ OF JOY

Phillip C. Jennings

It was an age lavished with antiquities, rich with stories from Before the Flood, Before the Breakdown, Before the War, Before the Deathwinter, Before the Starfall . . . yet with this abundance of disaster-punctuated eras, and all the artifacts they'd left behind, it had grown harder, not easier, to master the art of chronology, and a superfluity of relics bred general incuriosity.

On the southern verge of the forest of Geel Dubhar a leftover road ran east and west, between one distant ruin and another. Useless! Travelers were obliged to trudge two days more, through rolling farm country, before striking the modern carriageway, which angled off toward Haust, capital of Yain.

Fat as a bumblebee, the Thraxum Motors Cherry II biplane droned to deliver Senator Ramnis across Yain's breadth to the free town of Westhaven where (the True God willing), a Zealand cog might steam him beyond reach of the false god U Gyi. Farms and old roads were mere left-horizon landmarks to the errant senator, whose zigzag course avoided areas of habitation.

Yet gods are cunning, and plan ahead. U Gyi and the senator had been allies last year, in Merica's nip-and-tuck war against INFOWEB, whose single weapon was an orbiting boomstar.

"Well then," U Gyi thought (once the victory had been sufficiently applauded), "where soars one boomstar, why not another? I will listen to the skies, those astral beeps and whistles."

The same god who loved to catalog long strings of DNA spent months deciphering the come-hither of an eight-hundred-year-old weapon. It was this beamed particle generator U Gyi now angrily invoked to smite the wicked.

The weapon smote, and reported back, but its message was a hoax. The boomstar was ludicrously underpowered, its mirrors and fatigued cells pitted into spacejunk. Senator Ramnis' Model II Cherry failed to explode, much less disintegrate. Haloed by a mischief-working electrical corona, the engine merely coughed and died. The plane turned into an inept glider and began to lose altitude. Ramnis peered this way and that, swore distractedly, and waggled the craft away from Geel Dubhar's tangled treetops to find a place to land.

Before taking off, the senator had dreamed a pilot's memories to learn the art of flight, but Earth's umpteenth rennaissance was less than two decades old, and Thraxum Motors had only been in the aircraft business these last six years. There wasn't much emergency experience to draw on; just one desperate landing in the Flinthills of Ye, terminating in a forward somersault.

Now too the Cherry's wheels touched, balked, and pitched the biplane forward. It poised grandly tail-high, then crashed onto its back on the washboard surface of the ancient road.

Ramnis woke in a small, high bed, in a room given to garishly painted wooden furniture. A young girl stood gazing at him, brown of skin, stocky, and utterly bald. Ramnis groaned. "Do you speak Inglish?"

The girl fled, shouting, "Mravi, Mravi!" The one she summoned might have been her older sister: a few inches taller, fleshier, otherwise identical. "You'll have to lie still for a few days," Mravi told him. "Keep your leg elevated so the swelling can go down."

"I take it from your expression that my features lack their usual charm. Where am I? Are there telephones here? Subway connections?"

"No." The girl-woman blushed. "We are modern in Yain, but for these farms: the dominion wants us to give them up. They will not invest in us, because soon there will be food factories in all the cities."

"And you? Will you go the modern way?"

"Some of us are modern enough to wonder whether we can fix your airplane's engine and use it for our purposes. Sir, you must know that your room and care do not come free."

"If there's anything to salvage, go ahead."

Ramnis spent three bedridden days in meditation, stroking his lordly moustachios. Some of his thoughts were small—how to get to Westhaven now that his plane was useless to him. Yet he wondered if U Gyi had not done him a favor by shooting him down. Perhaps he should contact Yain's dozen senators, and build a coalition against this runamok godling.

And plunge the Five Dominions into war?

In the old days wars had been productive. The war against Lord Pest liberated the ancient Library of Knowledge, full of fabulous Twentieth Century lore. After Lord Pest turned to piracy, a cabal of adventurers managed to discover INFOWEB, blackmail the gods, and use their powers to crush Pest's evil.

But surely no more unplumbed secrets remained to be discovered. Society was having more than enough trouble digesting the present feast. Any future war, fought with boomstars and food additives and turtlesong, battle armor and tinglers—such a war might bring about the utter collapse of the Five Dominions and the umpteenth downfall of civilization.

What to do? And why? Senatorial government was not so long established in Merica of the Five Dominions that anyone felt great loyalty to it, not even the senators. Ramnis called himself "senator" because "king" seemed a preposterous title for a monarch whose thousand subjects rantipoled about a crumbling arcopolis. "Senator" enhanced his dignity, as it debased the dignity of U Gyi, god of Bue Gyi and the Hills of Moon, manufacturer of U Gyi's Immortality Tonic, foremost geneticist of the known world and primate of the Redemptorist Cult.

Ramnis shook his head. It was a risk to reverse himself on the appropriations bill. He'd paid the price, but in time U Gyi would simmer down, if he wasn't pushed into a confrontation. This might be a good time to lie low and take off on a time-killing jaunt, as those with his Soul-dancer background were wont to do. "Where am I?" he asked, the next time young Mravi came into the room. "Tell me the local legends."

"Legends? You're ninety kloms north of Haust, in farm country. We are not a fantastical people; we raise crops and pay our taxes."

Ramnis's brown eyes twinkled. "Are there no witches? No pickaroons in the woods? No deathdog hordes? Do the wily Juju-folk never come to trade?"

Mravi shook her solemn head. "I would like to see a Juju. Is it true they have pointed tongues?"

Ramnis smiled mysteriously, and spoke again. "If you were to hike forth in search of curiosities, where would you go?"

His nurse frowned. "Our religion speaks against frivolity and indiscipline. Ah well—there's Haust, but that would interest me more than you. Or you might try walking down the road."

"To what?"

"Just a moment." Mravi departed and returned. "You can see—" she began.

"Not unless I sit up."

She helped him with his pillows and handed him the map. "It doesn't show our road going through the forest, but it did once, centuries ago, and here at what would be the terminus—three dots, signifying a ruined city. Maybe you can read the name."

"It's written too small, and the ink's faded. 'Parthansad?' "

Mravi shook her head. "That doesn't sound like our language. All this region was once part of the Empire of Dhuinunn. The ruins are—"

"—Those of an indigenous people, conquered by your Dhuini ancestors!"

"You read too many romances," Mravi retorted primly. "The dominions are overburdened with cults and factions, races and layers of history, with false gods to flavor the brew. From coast to coast the peoples of Merica are in two parts: the infatuated, who whore off to the cities after memory-dreams and roadsters, cheap factory food, and computer-spawned marvels. We are the others, who exercise caution and prudence . . ."

"Ah, but I'm a Souldancer, and it's my religion always to be infatuated. Yet cities hold no charm. With the subways tying them together, they'll soon be all alike. No, I'd be more inclined to trek westward toward this place . . ." He squinted again. " 'Purthant?' "

"On that knee?"

"If I might buy a horse . . ."

"Senator Ramnis, you were rescued and brought here, with your clothes and satchel. There was no money."

"Someone stole my poke. One of your pious farmers."

"Of course you deserve credit, the more so since I'm sure you're right about the theft, but we're a bit cut off up here, and . . ."

"I see. Well then, how long do I have to work to earn my horse?"

At first Ramnis was given light work: milking cows,

shelling peas, picking plums, and hunting mushrooms. When his knee proved itself the flatpursed king was led to other labors: picking rocks, stacking hay, and splitting wood. These tasks exhausted him; he no longer tried to coax laughter from the mirthlessly sincere Mravi.

August ended. He helped harvest the wheat, and brought dried sheaves to the threshing-floor.

The ordeal was endurable, but for the visits of two grim middle-aged ladies: psaliches of the Panhe religion, who mistrusted his attitude and deemed him a bad influence. Though Yain was an advanced and scientific dominion, Panhe was the prevailing faith, and it was probably the remonstrations of these wandering busybodies that persuaded Ramnis's masters to speed him on his way a month before harvest was done.

And so, leading a swaybacked twelve-year-old mare, Senator Ramnis whistled westward, past one farm and then another, until he entered the forest. Footpaths and deer trails carried him along a slightly ditched ridge; all that remained of the thoroughfare that once connected—Perlanta? to—Onturs?

The journey took three days. The forest gave way to wind-shaken grasses, cropped now and again by herds of bison. The old road grew more obscure, then less. It crossed the modern thoroughfare to the twin cities of Shasch-Kaippa. Ramnis ignored the crossing. Continuing west, his shoulders hunched against a gentle rain, he noticed that the road was now in excellent repair. Indeed, the dominion government had put up signs: "Portland – Interpretive Center – 10 kloms."

"Portland?" The name sounded Inglish. Twice before the dominions of Merica had been dominated by Inglish-speaking peoples; Ramnis wondered whether this ruined city might not be a relic of remote antiquity indeed.

The Interpretive Center was built of stout wooden beams and planks, and surrounded by gardens on three sides. Ramnis pounded the door to no avail; then suddenly a lean gentleman arose from the shrubbery to his left, a soiled blade in his gloved hand. The senator stepped back. "Magnificent roses," he commented, always the diplomat.

"Aren't they? This place is heaven for roses, and for slugs as well. Come in. Here's our guest register . . ."

Ramnis followed the man inside and studied the room. "Is this Portlandish architecture?"

The lean man unstrung his green gardener's apron. On his head he set an official-looking skullcap with the letters "D.A.A." embroidered in a semi-circle.

"Exotic, isn't it?" he answered. "Though not much different from any other Twentieth Century city. Of course, this is a guess—the ruins, however extensive, are altogether crumbled. The ancients used materials of no real durability."

The senator frowned. "So I won't see much by wandering."

"Oh, some excavations here and there . . . Before the archeologists came you'd have never known this was once a place of note."

"Ah? The holy city of some cult? The capital of an empire?"

"More than that, and less," the gardener responded cryptically. "Would it help if I told you that Portland continued to exist for centuries following the Great Collapse?"

"No." Ramnis shook his head, and tiny drops showered off his drooping hat-brim. "Unless you allude to some unknown weapon, by which they resisted the incursions of the Dhuini—"

"Oh, they fell to our Dhuini ancestors, but I do in fact allude to an unknown weapon; sufficient to repel the Yooth of Califerni, the Albartian Canucks, the Leninish hordes— Sir, have you ever heard of the Buzz of Joy?"

"The Buzz of Joy!" Ramnis's face transformed, awe dissolved in ignorance. "Uh, I can't say I have."

His informant raised an eyebrow. "We have pamphlets. In a year or two we might even show a film. I've written to Regal Cinematics, to get a crew out to do a one-reeler on the subject, and they sound interested."

"No doubt." Ramnis hung up his garrick and hat, and plucked a brochure from the heap. "Do you get many visitors?" he asked.

"Dozens," the man responded. "You'll excuse me? My garden—"

The senator nodded, his mind already drifting into the streets of ancient Portland, where barbed-wire barricades blocked the advance of the perfidious Yooth of Californi. Mysterious coiled antennae rose from towers to the right and left—as the Yooth charged, roaring on their mechanical steeds, power surged up the coils and the Buzz of Joy hazed the air in front of them. The Yooth reached the protected zone, guffawed with laughter, spasmed, and tumbled from their two-wheelers, their chests heaving helplessly with mirth as blood coursed from their torn limbs . . .

Such were the images suggested by the pages in Ramnis's hand, published by the Dominion of Yain, Department of Antiquities and Art—Please Refrain from Littering.

Ramnis stroked his moustachios. All he had to do was to find a pair of coiled antennae—no, not really. The antennae were the fruit of an artist's imagination. What he was looking for might as easily be an archetypal Black Box.

Ramnis moved to a second room and studied a plaster model of old Portland. Areas staked by archeologists were flagged in red. If the farmers of Yain were disciplined and methodical, how much more so were its scientists, whose digs boxed the city—without, however, yet penetrating to its heart.

The senator lacked the resources to compete with these others, whose peripheral work was clearly intended to yield barrier-relics of the Buzz of Joy. No, he was a Souldancer, and his ways were different. He would assume that the Buzz radiated like a protective dome, outward from some central height, and lo! Such heights were not hard to find. Here was one, once the acropolis of a cult of healers.

Arbitrarily, Ramnis chose that hill. He would go there, trusting in luck. Luck had made him king, and then senator; why shouldn't luck provide him with the Buzz of Joy?

On his way the senator picked up a stick and used it to hack laboring and puffing, up the slopes of the hill.

His horse balked just short of the crest, and Ramnis tethered her before clambering to the top, where he wandered among titanic trees, kicking at lichenous rocks.

He returned to find that the mare had cropped all the bushes within reach, exposing a damp concrete-lined passage. Spiders had webbed the black interior, and windblown leaves had caught and decomposed, adding by increments to a humic muck that now half-blocked the adit. The stench was heavy. Perhaps a bear had recently used the place as her den, and died . . . a very fat bear.

So this was the fruit of Souldancer luck! Ramnis used his stick to clear a way and squeeze inside. It began to rain again, the gentlest of showers, but he was protected now; he might even light a firestick. Perhaps the flame would also help purify this putrid air!

He opened the packet, popped at a firestick, and it caught—WHOOMP! The force of the fireball blew Senator Ramnis from the passage into the flank of his horse, who whinnied in terror. At the sound of a second, greater explosion the mare reared and pulled her reins free, prevented from galloping off only by the shaking of the earth beneath her hooves.

There must have been a third detonation, so titanic that the senator's senses failed him. Ramnis found himself spread-eagled against the trunk of a tree, watching as a large section of hilltop tipped inwards and sank. A squarish crater was formed. Mammoth trees swayed from the vertical, groaned, and toppled, crashing together. The rain-misted air grew thick with flying dirt, leaves, and shards of bark, while pale flames belched in syncopation with rumbles from underground.

The soft rain rinsed the air and beat back intermittent gouts of fire. The worst was over. The senator coughed, stood forward and brushed his mired garrick.

Embedded among the central roots of one tumbled forest giant was a thing of metal, once rectangular, perhaps larger and certainly more elaborate than a bedframe. Those lumps—could they be axles? Was this the relic of an ancient Portlandish road machine? Ramnis stumbled close. The vehicle had had a body once, but it

had rusted, leaving just this skeleton, through which he
could see . . .

Yes, indeed. The archetypal Black Box.

A week later, and a thousand kloms away, Ramnis
faced a tall polychromatic statue. U Gyi's game had
grown increasingly subtle, and the senator deliberated
before raising his staff of office to smash the plaster
image of the false god. As the object tumbled, the
watchers melted away. The skies darkened. Lightning
strobed as the roof opened. Among these distractions
Ramnis was clearheaded enough to notice the floor was
elevating, carrying him story by story into low clouds.

Light blitzed around the senator; then the brilliance
faded and the glow grew constant. It had a source.
Strong winds tore at the fog and he found himself
treading up a long, wide hall towards a tiny U Gyi,
seated on his throne. The god's guards, genetically tailored to monkey-size, fell in and flanked him as he
approached.

"What an unexpected surprise," U Gyi said, patting
his damp forehead with an embroidered sleeve.

"That I'm still alive?" the senator asked.

"Oh, dear. I was afraid you'd be tiresome about that
airplane episode. If you expect me to apologize—"

"Nice place you've got here," Ramnis remarked. "I
suppose you'd like to keep it."

"Ah? Ah! A threat! You'd risk war?"

"No, and yet in my travels I've made some discoveries
—here, I've come to give you this."

Ramnis set the black box on the steps before U Gyi's
throne. The godling tried and failed to mask his curiosity. "Very well, what is it?"

"A weapon. Harmless without its power source. The
ancients of Portland used it to defend their city. It
worked against the Yooth of Califerni, the Albartian
Canucks—against everyone except the Dhuini, who
turned out to be immune."

"The founders of the Empire of Dhuinunn!"

"The same. Their descendants inhabit the dominion
of Yain. Your Divinity, has it occurred to you that they
might harbor ambitions to revive their Empire?"

The tiny godling's finger rummaged thoughtfully in one of his oversized ears. "I suspect everyone of everything, and I am often right."

"And perhaps you've noticed that the folk of Yain are absolutely incapable of humor? Not once during my stay among them could I get one to smile—but I'm trying your patience. Your Divinity, this box contains a weapon known as the Buzz of Joy. This weapon can render any of us helpless with laughter. Any of us, that is, *except* the people of Yain, whose scientists are busy right now trying to find this thing I'm about to give you—"

"Indeed! And why am I your beneficiary?"

"Because you're clever enough to discover the principle behind this Buzz, and reverse it. I urge you to do so. If the elders of the Dominion of Yain have fielded archaeologists, then they've hired physicists and neurologists as well, and those others might soon make an independent discovery."

U Gyi smiled a toothy smile. "*Reverse* it? I've heard of people rendered helpless with laughter, but never helpless with gloom!"

"Isn't that what we call depression? Your Divinity, I see two armies stalemated in the field: ours rolling on the ground in paroxysms of glee, while the forces of Yain stand, sighing at the futility of existence, too listless to advance. Will you help maintain the balance of powers? Once you've built a Buzz of Gloom—"

"I could use it anywhere, against anyone!"

Ramnis shook his head. "I doubt it. The Buzz of Joy bred a folk incapable of humor. You might use the Buzz of Gloom, but if you do, in time you'll endow the world with a race of irrepressible jokesters, people incapable of taking things seriously, people who laugh at pretentious gods and senators—"

U Gyi turned pink. "People, in other words, very like yourself!"

Ramnis bowed. "Myself, at my worst. Your Divinity, forgive me, but I *do* hope this evens the score between us. Let us be allies again, lest in our squabbles we ignore our foes—for in Yain and elsewhere, our poor excuse for democracy has subtle enemies."

U Gyi pursed his lips. "Your absence unsettled many of my erstwhile friends. I begin to think it's bad luck to kill senators. Very well, Senator Ramnis, you have my promise, and my thanks for your thoughtful gift. Return to your kingdom with my blessing, and know that I shall try to be a better god in the future."

Two years later, when the governor of Yain took his battle-armored, tingler-wielding militia into the field, the scene was not altogether as Senator Ramnis had imagined. Yain's secret weapon, the Buzz of Joy, intersected U Gyi's Buzz of Gloom, creating a neutral zone. In that zone the forces of four dominions clashed with those of only one, the self-styled Second Empire of Dhuinunn, which collapsed later that afternoon. Once more the forces of righteousness prevailed, a little weary, perhaps, of staving off the enemies of representative democracy two or three times a decade. Sometime soon, somebody would unearth the ultimate something . . .

But for now, thanks to Senator Ramnis's Souldancer luck: so far, so good.

Editor's Introduction To:

SECOND CONTACT

W. R. Thompson

". . . the idea that an authoritarian political system must collapse because it cannot provide a decent life for its citizenry can only occur to a democrat. When we reason this way about the Soviet empire, we are simply ascribing democracy's operational rules and attitudes to a totalitarian regime. But these rules and attitudes are signally abnormal, and, as I said earlier, very recent and probably transitory. The notion that whoever holds political power must clear out because his subjects are discontented or dying of hunger or distress is a bit of whimsy that history has tolerated few times in real life. Although they are forced by the current fashion to pay lip service to this cumbersome idea, nine out of ten of today's leaders are careful not to put it into practice; they even indulge themselves in the luxury of accusing the only true democracies now functioning of constantly violating the precept. But then, how could totalitarian rulers break a social contract they've never signed?

"As things stand, relatively minor causes of discontent corrode, disturb, unsettle, paralyze the democracies faster and more deeply than horrendous famine and constant poverty do the Communist regimes . . ."

Jean François Revel, *How Democracies Perish*

Most of the ancient writers on political science believed that cycles were inevitable. Societies grow, flourish, and decay, as do most other organisms. Some societies last longer than others, but all are doomed to eventual collapse.

This view was accepted well into the Renaissance and after. The notion of progress, of continual growth and improvement, onward and upward *per omnia seculae seculorum,* is quite recent.

It is also unproved.

SECOND CONTACT

W. R. Thompson

There was going to be a war.

The Neutral Zone wasn't part of the Republic, not yet, but we sent patrols into it all the time. Our scout teams let us know if any invaders or bandits were near our borders, and the presence of our forces intimidated most troublemakers. Equally important, the patrols protected the people who lived between us and the barbarian kingdoms. Everyone deserves some security in this life; that's why governments exist.

The people in this commune hadn't had any safety. The raiders had encircled them and attacked, overrunning the hamlet before it could defend itself. A few of the local folks had died fighting, but it didn't look as if they'd drawn blood. Footprints showed that the attackers had marched north, taking the survivors with them—as slaves, or worse.

"They were Weyler's men," Colonel Washington said, holding up an arrow he'd found. "See the tip, Mr. Secretary? And the 'feathers'? Nobody else makes arrows like this."

"I know, Colonel." I took the arrow and studied it, not because I could learn anything from it, but because I wanted to stall. The arrow was a hand-turned wooden dowel, given its point on a pre-Collapse pencil sharpener. The feathers had been cut from old soft-drink cans, and laced to the shaft with sinew.

"Maybe Weyler's bully-boys didn't do this," I said. I was clutching at straws. "Other bandits might have bought the arrows from him, or taken them as booty."

"That's possible, sir," Washington said. His tone said he put more faith in the Easter Bunny, and he was right. Nobody sells weapons these days; the buyers are liable to turn around and kill you with them. If anyone had defeated and robbed some of Weyler's men, our spies would have heard.

Just the same, I wanted to believe that the raiders were nomads. The Republic might ignore that, but if they were locals, we would soon be at war with them— and I didn't want to see the Republic fall into another war. That may sound like an odd attitude for a Secretary of War, but my attitude was the reason I'd joined the Structuralist Party and accepted this post.

"Colonel!" One of Washington's scouts signaled us from the edge of an orchard. "We've got something, sir."

Washington and I walked into the orchard. It was a straggling, threadbare clump of apple trees. There was a large empty patch in the center of the grove, and a carved wooden pole had been driven into the dirt.

"A pagan war totem," Washington said in distaste. He pulled it from the ground, looked it over and handed it to me. "And these are Weyler's marks."

"So they are." Triple flames were carved in the soft wood, the same symbol Weyler's men paint on their chests and leather shields. The top of the pole had been carved into the nightmare shape of an Alien's head.

The face mocked us. Human civilization had folded up at its first contact with other worlds, it seemed to say. What made us think we could revive civilization? Weyler had chosen that symbol deliberately, to remind us how fragile our culture was, and how certain he was of ultimate victory.

I couldn't delay forever. We would have to go home and inform the Legislature. They would debate, but in the end they would declare war. I wish I could say I was entirely unhappy at the prospect.

*   *   *

The Legislature meets once a month, in the Forum Building: a barnlike structure which can seat up to five hundred people. It cost us a lot to build the Forum, both in material and work hours, but nobody begrudges the expense. A government body has to meet somewhere—and as anyone in the Republic can tell you, this is *our* government.

That doesn't always make it pleasant.

I was sitting on the stage, rather than on the main floor with the other Legislators. Colonel Washington stood at the podium in front of the speaker's chair, where he was winding up his testimony. He stood at parade rest, seemingly unfazed by the hostile faces in the amphitheater. "By the time the burial detail had finished tending to the dead villagers, the sun was setting. We scouted the area, determined that no hostile forces remained nearby, and made camp. The next day we returned to Northfort. That's all."

The questioning began at once, as several legislators rose to their feet. The speaker pointed her gavel at one of them. "The chair recognizes Gwen Parsons."

"Thank you, Madam Ryan." The leader of the Expansion Party gave the speaker a polite nod—solely out of deference to her position. Kate Ryan is the leader of my party, and the EPs don't like the fact that we outnumber them three to two.

At the moment Parsons seemed pleased, as well she might. I had gone on this scouting trip as an observer, but my actions—or lack of them—could give the Expansionists the leverage they needed to take control of the government.

Parsons faced the Colonel and raised her voice. "Colonel, by your estimate the raiders took over fifty captives. What became of them?"

Washington's brown face remained inscrutable. "This was obviously a slaving raid. The only possible conclusion is that the villagers were taken to Weyler's territory."

"Why didn't you pursue the raiders?" Parsons demanded. The acid in her voice surprised me at first. Aside from being one of the Founders, and the man who helped defeat the Aliens, he's the head of our militia. The Expansionists favor the use of military force to extend our domain; Parsons couldn't want to offend the Colonel.

My surprise lasted perhaps two seconds. Parsons wasn't attacking Colonel Washington; she was after *me*—and the Structuralists, through me.

"I had several reasons for not giving pursuit," Washington said. "By my estimate, the raiders had a full day's start on us. By the time we could have caught up with them, they would have been deep within Weyler's territory. I had a force of eight scouts, one automatic rifleman, and a limited supply of ammunition. I would have faced forty raiders, in addition to probable reinforcements. A rescue attempt would have been suicide."

"But you might have freed those hostages." An approving murmur answered Parsons, and some of my fellow Structuralists nodded agreement. I couldn't hold that against them. I wasn't sure myself that restraint had been the right move.

"I considered that, ma'am," the Colonel said. "I also considered that a battle might have killed many of the people we wanted to save—and that the outlanders would rather kill slaves than free them. In addition, I have standing orders to remain in the Neutral Zone."

Parsons shifted her attack. "You had an observer on this patrol. Didn't Secretary Woodman have anything to say about your decision?"

"Ma'am, I didn't consult him. Civilian observers have no place in making tactical decisions."

"This particular civilian is also the Secretary of War," Parsons countered. "That also makes him your superior. Why didn't he countermand your orders?"

Ryan rapped her gavel on the bench. "Madam Parsons, that question is out of order."

Parsons looked at her. "May I address it to Mr. Woodman?"

"Yes." Ryan nodded for me to take Washington's place.

Before the Collapse, I'm sure, the podium would have had a hot, bright light focused on it. We don't have such luxuries, but I felt as hot and naked as if I'd been pinned under a spotlight. Parsons eyed me for a moment as I stood at the podium. "Mr. Woodman, why didn't you countermand the Colonel's orders?"

"I don't countermand common sense," I told her bluntly. "And I have no authority to order the colonel to leave the Neutral Zone. I'm not empowered to start wars; that's the Legislature's duty."

That gave the EP chief pause—briefly. "Perhaps . . . but Weyler has *de facto* started a war—and a raid, even if it failed, would have shown our determination to revive civilization. That's the goal of both our parties, no matter how much we disagree on techniques."

Ryan rapped her gavel again. "Please, madam, no speeches during questioning."

"My apologies, madam." Even at this distance I could see the sardonic touch to her smile. "My point is that the outlanders invaded the Neutral Zone and took slaves. So far all this government has done is to bury the dead. Mr. Woodman, what *do* you propose to do?"

She had me—and the Speaker, and the whole Structuralist Party—neatly trapped with that question. "As Secretary of War, I'll follow the government's decisions. As a legislator and citizen, I favor any solution which will stop the raids—without endangering the Republic."

"Ah, yes." Parson's voice was just this side of a sneer. "I have no further questions, Madam Ryan—but I would like to make a motion." The other legislators sat down at once. The EPs sat to let their boss make her motion; our people sat because there was no point in stalling—and perhaps because a good many of them agreed with what was coming.

Parsons looked around the Forum, spoke in formal tones. "Madam Speaker, fellow legislators. In view of the Weyler raid, I move that we vote to declare war on Weyler, depose him and annex his lands."

Ryan sighed, a sound I could barely hear from where I stood. "Are there any objections?" she asked, and then waited through a stony silence. "Very well, the motion carries. We will vote after debate tomorrow. This body is dissolved for twenty-four hours."

That gave me one day to stop a war.

*   *   *

I drink at the Crushed Alien for two reasons: the view and the food.

The inn has a dining terrace which overlooks my home district. Zone Twenty-nine isn't much to see, by day or night, but I'm fond of it. The main attraction is the chemical plant, which produces everything from fertilizer through medicine and gasoline to gunpowder . . . all in inadequate amounts, I'll concede; but the output grows every year. Right now it produces enough to help support a nation of two million people, in a section of land that used to be Illinois.

The food? It's nothing fancy, which is a virtue. A lot of tavern cooks like to improvise pre-Collapse dishes, especially things that remind us oldsters of fast foods and other lost delights. That's not for me, thank you; I lost too much in the Collapse to dredge up old memories.

A tavern is also a good place for a politician to do business. An office intimidates some people, especially when they have to face you across a desk. Shooting the breeze over stew and ale is another matter, as long as you remember that nothing you hear is trivial—not to the voter who's saying it.

Pete Bodo, a farmer on the western edge of my zone, was bending my ear. "I don't care about this war talk," he said. "Either Weyler throws in the towel, or we stomp him. Either way, it's all going to happen a couple hundred miles from here. Besides, I have other problems."

Collapse or no Collapse, midwesterners are isolationists at heart. I gave him an encouraging nod. "It's not the water pumps again, is it?"

"Naw. You really got engineering straightened out on that." He set his mug down on the table. "Someone in my neck of the woods is shooting cats. I lost two of my best ratters this past month."

"I see." Rats don't just eat crops, although farmers like Bodo have had granaries ruined by them. The bubonic plague which decimated the East Coast after the Collapse was spread by rats, and no one forgets that. Cats are our first line of defense against rats. "Do you suspect anyone?"

"Naw. All I know is, it's someone with a .410 shotgun." He pulled a brass casing from a pocket and gave it to me. "Found this on the road, fifty yards from one of my dead ratters."

I looked at the shell, and wished that we could afford the luxury of a police department and detectives. We were lucky to have as little crime as we did—or perhaps it wasn't luck. I'd read somewhere that vigorous, pioneering cultures have little crime. "A small gauge like this can't be too common," I said. "Maybe I can find out who bought it."

"Good. Well, I thank you, Tad." We shook hands and he left.

I doubt it occurred to Bodo that finding his cat-killer would take a lot of my time. He was a dawn-to-dusk, light-of-the-moon farmer, the sort who thinks that no other farmer works half as hard as he does, and that all non-farmers are idle hands. Well, this would give me an excuse to nose around my zone and see how things stood.

I was almost finished eating when Gwen Parsons joined me. "Hello, Mr. Secretary," she said, seating herself.

"Mulch that, Gwen," I said. I suppose her formality was a way of apologizing for the debate, as if I might have taken it personally. Well, I *might* have, but I couldn't afford that. If I could convince *her* that a war was a bad idea, I'd gladly forget it. "What brings you out here?"

"You, of course." Gwen has the sort of face and voice that make everything she says sound deadly serious. "You know how the vote will go tomorrow, of course."

I nodded. "I'm still willing to act as though you might win anyway."

She acknowledged the hit with a crooked smile. "Tad, in the unlikely chance that we win, would you consider staying on as our Secretary of War?"

I decided not to fence with her. "You don't have your own choice lined up?"

"I do," Gwen said. "But there are two good reasons to keep you. One, we traditionally have a coalition government during a war. Two, it always takes a month for a new appointee to learn the ropes. We're not going to wait a month to attack."

"Ah." Passions can cool in a month. She'd want to attack Weyler while everyone was fired up over the raid.

" 'Ah,' nothing, Tad," she said. "We have guns, poison gas, cannon, even aircraft. Weyler has bows and arrows, and so forth. Yet he's just provoked us. He expects a war with us—and no one starts a war with the idea that they're going to lose."

"He can't win."

"You're certain?"

I stared at the horizon for a long while. The sun had just set, and a few electric lights came on here and there: at the chemical plant, along the Main Concourse, atop the towers of the radio station. Most of the lights were decoration, but they helped show off our accomplishments.

"He *can't* win," I repeated. "We have the technology, the numbers, the organization—and the *will*. If we fight, we can grind his kingdom into a pulp."

Gwen rested her hands on the terrace table. "But you don't want to fight."

"It's wasteful. Expensive. It takes as many work hours to build a cannon as it does to make a tractor. A soldier can't spend his time teaching or smelting iron. We're trying to rebuild civilization; every resource we divert from that delays the job."

"So you want to toe the Structuralist line." She tilted her head back and looked at the sky. " 'Make war only in self defense; let the barbarians join us when they see the virtues of civilization.' "

I nodded. "Coercion doesn't work—the victims always resent it. The Republic is expanding nicely as it is. In a few more years, Weyler's people will be with us."

"Yes—after a few years of living with slavery, superstition, and Weyler's version of monarchy. What sort of citizens will they be then? If we don't act fast . . ." Her voice trailed off. She craned her head and looked straight up. "Aw, nuts."

I looked and saw it, right on the zenith: the feathery shape of a fusion flame, drifting across Earth's sky like a lazy comet. The Alien ship itself was a silver pinpoint at the head of the drive flame.

After a quarter of a century the Aliens had returned.

I'd known that the Aliens were real when the tabloid papers all declared they were a CIA-created hoax.

Marcia, my first wife, had been beside herself ever since the Alien drive flame was spotted decelerating into the Solar System. Now that I was convinced, she could stop quibbling over a trivial point and get down to some serious arguing. It was going to be the biggest event in our history, she said; even if the visitors forced us to take some strong medicine, they would do it with benevolence and in our best interests.

After a while I'd come to enjoy her optimism. As the UFO neared Earth, the news and entertainment media were filled with gloom and uncertainty. Along with some idiotic speculation on invasion and conquest from space, there was a lot of conjecture about possible dangers to our culture. In the space of two months I heard about every primitive culture which ever collapsed in the face of a superior civilization.

After all the media hype, *Scented Vine*'s arrival in Earth orbit was almost an anticlimax. There'd been an accident on board, they informed us, and they'd stopped here to make repairs. *Scented Vine* was a cargo ship, going from one unimportant star to another. It had been a long, rough trip, and the Aliens (they never told us what they called themselves) wanted to take shore leave.

We believed them. It was disappointing to know that our first contact was brought on by a leaky fuel line, but there was no helping that. Shore leave wasn't the scientific, diplomatic, and cultural exchange everyone had envisioned, but it was better than nothing. Like South Sea islanders greeting a Yankee whaler, we welcomed them to our shores.

After a month I noticed that things were—not different, perhaps, but certainly not right. The Aliens were all over the TV, naturally, doing and saying colorful things. We weren't learning much about them, but they were learning a lot about us, especially our faults and foibles. They never had any suggestions on how to improve ourselves—they would never dream of upset-

ting the development of aboriginal cultures, they said—
but they made plenty of disparaging comments, in the
form of innocent questions. Had we ever thought about
what would happen if we used those nuclear weapons
we had developed? Our cults intrigued them, but why
did we allow our shamans and priests to participate in
serious political decisions?

The questions were not new, but hearing them from
outsiders gave them a weight they had never had before. Our answers were neither new nor good, and they
did not impress the Aliens, who made it clear that even
by primitive standards we were fairly inept. The media
echoed and amplified their remarks, until it seemed
everyone was wondering if humanity was good for anything at all.

There were other things, worse things. One of *Scented
Vine*'s crew, the doctor, had agreed to spend an afternoon with a team from the World Health Organization.
It broke the appointment when, on the way into New
York, it spotted an astrologer's shop. While the WHO
scientists cooled their heels the Alien had its horoscope
cast. The networks gave the proceedings full coverage,
and interviewed a variety of soothsayers on the technical problems of tailoring astrology to fit an Alien's birth.
Someone with a pseudo-Gypsy name was blathering
about planetary influences and the Zodiac when the
Alien emerged from the shop. It announced its satisfaction with our sophisticated magic.

What happened next *was* news. A TV preacher came
roaring out of the crowd, shouting about blasphemy and
iniquity, vowing to smite the Beast. That was when we
learned about the zapper. The preacher and a half-
dozen sight-seers went down in convulsions, overcome
by perfect bliss. One camera showed the televangelist's
face as he dropped. For the first time in memory his
fixed, money-making smile looked genuine. The next
day he preached a brief, disjointed sermon on the Nir-
vana of the zapper.

It didn't take long for the chaser movement to begin.
Within a month tens of thousands of people around the
world were looking for the Aliens; when the creatures
showed up the chasers would provoke the Aliens into

zapping them. To the Aliens it was just another picturesque native activity, one they indulged without interest or sympathy.

More than American society was falling apart. Russia, Red China, Japan, Western Europe, India—no country could keep them out; they landed their shuttlecrafts where they pleased, and everywhere the Aliens turned up they created problems. Things became especially bad in the Soviet Union. Maybe the Soviets thought we were behind their troubles, or maybe they thought we had made a deal with the Aliens. All I know is that five months after the first Alien landing the President ordered a creeping mobilization of American forces. I was a reservist and I was called up, which took me away from home at the height of the Collapse.

I doubt that the full history of World War Three will ever be known. All I saw of it came one midnight in Kansas. I'd been in the Fort Riley Officers' Club, watching the "Tonight" show. The guest host began one of the stock routines, the one about the Native Chief and the Drunken Sailor, at which point I walked out. The audience knew who the characters symbolized, but I couldn't laugh with them. I went outside to smoke a cigarette.

The Soviets must have fired first. I saw the meteor trails of the warheads and rockets as they came in from the north, heading for our missile silos. SAC was on the ball that night, and I saw a pair of our MX missiles take off. Then warheads and missiles began exploding. Somewhere high over the Atlantic, *Scented Vine* was having target practice.

The next day the Aliens apologized for interfering with our tribal dispute, and explained that our fight would have endangered the Aliens among us. I don't know how many people heard their broadcast; things had become hectic, and panic evacuations and riots were running everywhere. The government's authority crumbled overnight. The close call with Armageddon had been bad enough, but the Aliens' casual intervention left the government looking ridiculous, like a naughty boy who'd just had his slingshot confiscated by his mommy. The federal government disintegrated within days. The Soviets held out for a full week before falling themselves. I suppose some governments survived a bit longer, until the growing chaos overwhelmed them.

I understood how those South Pacific natives felt, when their women became disease-ridden whores, and their men turned into alcoholics, and strange gods replaced their old faiths. Like them, we'd been helpless in the face of a superior culture. The fact that we'd seen it coming only made it worse.

For a while I thought that my wife and child were all right. After all, no A-bombs had gone off anywhere. Even when I heard about the widespread food riots, the raiders and vigilantes, I assumed that Marcia and our baby would pull through. It wasn't until my infantry unit disbanded and I went home that I learned otherwise. I don't want to remember that.

I saw the group of Aliens shortly after that, playing with a group of chasers. One of the Aliens had a zapper, while the others carried human rifles. They took turns, zapping and shooting their prey at random. The chasers didn't seem to care; their addiction was that powerful. I don't want to remember that, either.

I drifted for a while—and then I found the Colonel.

"I expect them to land near us," Colonel Washington said the next day. His voice, normally as flat as stale water, had an odd animation in it now. Eagerness for battle, perhaps, although I couldn't say. I've worked with the Colonel since before the foundation of the Republic, and I know next to nothing about him . . . aside from the fact that he gives the impression it is best to know nothing of him.

Gwen, the speaker, and I were the only ones in the room with him as the Colonel described the situation. "We have electric power, lights, and a radio service— and no reason to think that anyone else on Earth has our level of technology."

"We haven't picked up any radio signals," I agreed. Our radio service exists to serve the Republic's communication needs, but ever since it started, our techs have tried to contact other people out there. Being the only enclave of civilization in a darkening world is a lonely feeling. Hearing from other people would have been as welcome a morale boost as anything I can name.

"We can assume that the Aliens have already detected *our* signals," the Colonel said. "They must make an excellent beacon. Unless they land at random, they will want to investigate them. And us."

Speaker Ryan sighed. "In that case, we should plan for the worst. Colonel, can we repel an Alien landing?"

"I see no choice."

She looked impatient. "That doesn't answer my question."

The Colonel shrugged. "I have no idea of how this Alien ship is armed, or why it is here. The *Scented Vine* was a cargo ship; its crew carried only light hand weapons. We had no defense against them."

"We had you, Colonel," I said.

I wondered what the look on his face meant. "I believe my final assault surprised the Aliens. I cannot know. The worst case I can imagine is that this ship is a punitive expedition, here to punish us for fighting *Scented Vine*'s crew. They could be heavily armed."

"In which case, we fight," the Speaker said. "You're correct, Colonel, we have no choice about that. The question is, what will we do if they show up and *don't* attack? That could be just as dangerous."

"No!" Gwen smacked a hand on the conference table. "This isn't 1997. We won't collapse the way the old world did when those monsters showed up—we *can't*. Madam Speaker, if they attack, we fight. If they decide to play tourist again, we tell them to screw themselves."

" 'Indulge in self-impregnation,' " the Colonel said. "Their translating machines didn't handle idioms very well."

"Whatever," Gwen said. "There's no danger of a repeat of 1997, so we've no cause to worry about it. The war with Weyler is our real problem. Now—"

A courier interrupted her. The young man came in, gave the Speaker a note and left. "Weyler's shown up at Coalville," she said.

I felt alarmed; Coalville supplies most of our energy. Gwen looked equally alarmed; if Weyler's men had done any serious damage there, then we had just lost more than a war. "What's the situation?" Washington asked.

"They came under a white flag," Ryan said. "Weyler, a small bodyguard, and some of his flunkies. He'll be here in a couple of days. He wants to negotiate a settlement."

"He can negotiate an unconditional surrender," Gwen said promptly.

"He won't do that," Washington said.

Gwen shrugged. "Then let's shoot the bastard, and let his successor surrender. Madam Speaker—"

"Cut it out, Gwen."

"Kate, we cannot afford to negotiate with Weyler." She jabbed the tabletop with a finger. "It's exactly what he wants: to be seen dealing with us as an equal. That'll give him a lot of prestige with the other warlords."

"We've negotiated with his kind before," I said.

"But we've always called the shots," Gwen said. "We've *forced* them to negotiate, and to give up everything we wanted. We've always used 'peace talks' to emphasize our supremacy. Let's not forget that."

"No one has forgotten," Washington said.

"Good." Gwen looked at him. "Colonel, what's the best course of action?"

Don't ask me what he thought before he answered. "The best course of action is for me to follow the orders I receive. If—"

The last time any of us had heard that noise had been when the last Alien shuttlecraft had lifted from Earth. It was a low, insistent throb, and it made the window-panes vibrate. It got louder for a moment, then cut off abruptly.

Kate Ryan got up and looked out the window. "There's a force-field dome on top of Signal Hill."

Gwen joined her at the window. She spoke with the aplomb that had placed her in charge of the Expansionist Party. "Ah. So there is. Now, what are we going to do about Weyler?" That "we" wasn't presumption on Gwen's part; "we" were now a *de facto* coalition government.

Ryan turned away from the window. "We'll wait for

Weyler to arrive. That will give us time to plan." She sighed. "I hope."

"We don't need time to plan," Gwen said. "We already know what to do."

I was at home, having breakfast, when Weyler's entourage arrived. I thanked the courier who brought me the note, closed the door and went back to the table. "Is it bad news?" Janie asked.

"Weyler's here." I put the note away and went back to eating.

"There's nothing about *them?*" Michael asked.

"No, the Aliens are still inside their bubble. Pass the salt?"

"Does anyone know when they'll come out?" Janie asked. "There's a lot of uncertainty, Tad. The Exchange was a madhouse yesterday. Wheat and corn prices have gone up twenty percent since they landed."

"The Aliens haven't announced any plans," I told her. After twenty-two years, I've learned not to soft-soap my wife. She can pin me down with the same ruthless ease she uses on the trading floor. "Colonel Washington has brought in two platoons to watch them, but they're going to give Weyler's tribe most of their attention."

She nodded. "Is the Colonel staying in town?"

"For the duration, sweets."

"Can he handle the Aliens?"

"Ma, he's the *Colonel*." Like most teenage boys, our youngest child has a tendency toward hero-worship. "Of course he can take them again!"

"Right." I finished my apple juice and got up. "I should get down to the Concourse now."

Signal Hill is the highest hill in the Capital City region. Back in the early days, you could see the entire Republic from its peak, so we mounted some heliographs up there and used it to flash messages everywhere. Now that damned Alien bubble was sending its own message to everyone within sight.

That sight depressed me as much as the uncertainty. Had they come back to finish the job the *Scented Vine* had begun? Back in 1997 the Aliens had destroyed Terran civilization with the deftness of a karate expert splitting a log. For all anyone knew, they derived artistic satisfaction from wrecking alien cultures. There was no telling what to expect.

The uncertainty was a killer for me. I'd lost everything in the Collapse, and so had Janie. Only the birth of the Republic, and the plans to restore civilization, had given us the confidence to start new lives. Things could never be the same, but we believed they would get better again.

Now it was 2024, we had our first grandchild, and what in hell could we expect next?

I was halfway to the Concourse when I saw Washington. I hurried to catch up with him; he has a quick, marching walk which discourages company. "I've arranged a campground for the savages on the north slope of Signal Hill," he told me. "If they make trouble, we can contain them with one platoon."

"And the Aliens?" I puffed.

"We now have three platoons nearby, plus a mortar team and four aircraft. That's all we can spare."

"How are things in the Neutral Zone?"

"Tense, Mr. Secretary. My scouts report that all of the local warlords are mobilizing. They expect the Aliens to destroy us and allow them to move in."

"Then they're in for a disappointment." Gwen Parsons joined us. "Colonel, could you slow down, please?"

"Certainly, ma'am." He slowed and I caught my breath.

"Thanks. We shouldn't let Weyler think we're in a hurry to see him."

A good point, that. "Are you ready to slit his throat?" I asked.

"That would backfire," the Colonel said. "Before Weyler left home, his shamans made a few convenient prophecies. If he dies here, even from natural causes, we'll take the blame."

"And he'll become a martyr?" Gwen sighed in resignation. "Oh, well."

The Colonel had given the savages a good place for a bivouac—good for us, that is. The ground was flat, with rises on all sides, and he had stationed a squad at each corner of a square. If the savages acted up, they'd die in the crossfire.

I had to wonder if Weyler wanted that. I'll never
know if the man was insane or sincere, but he gave
every sign of believing his paganisms. If he died here,
he might become the kind of symbol that could unite
the other outlanders against us in war. We could handle
them one at a time, but not *en masse*.

The Colonel, Gwen, and I walked into Weyler's camp,
under the eyes of our sentries. First and foremost, the
camp stank. Sanitation was something Weyler's people
had forgotten. They'd pitched a few lean-tos, to house
their leader and his counselors. It looked like the dozen
warriors who'd escorted them would sleep out in the
open.

Outlanders. They were all male, of course. They
wore uncured animal hides and warpaint, but the thing
that got my attention was their necklaces. Each one was
made of human finger bones, taken from killed enemies, supposedly as a magical way of retaining the
enemy's strength.

Gwen seemed unmoved by that sight, or by the
variety of knives, spears, and arrows the warriors carried. She glanced at all of them, then gave one a frankly
female look that said *you might not be too bad in the
hay, if we got you cleaned up*. Bless her for that; her
look disconcerted them more than anything I could
have said.

Weyler crawled out of his lean-to and approached us.
I was surprised to see how old he was—about sixty, I'd
say. Few outlanders live beyond their late twenties;
even in the Republic, where we have plenty of food and
some medicines, sixty years is quite an age—I should
know; I'm pushing it myself. He looked ascetic rather
than scrawny, with whipcord muscles under the tan and
dirt. His eyes gleamed as he paused to look at the force
field. No doubt their arrival was a new factor in his
plans, but not one that would upset them.

He looked at us with contempt. "The weaklings of
the New Renaissance. The people who would rebuild
the old world and repeat its blunders. We have come to
talk to your ruler."

"She's busy judging a beauty pageant," Gwen said.

"You're a bit late to enter, but we can hold a spot for you and your chorus line in next year's contest."

The warriors shifted around uneasily. None of them looked old enough to remember chorus lines and beauty pageants, but they couldn't miss her mockery, and they weren't used to this treatment.

Only Weyler maintained any dignity. "We will wait. We have far more time than you." He turned and looked at the force field bubble. "The Dark Gods have numbered your days." He looked to Washington and spoke before Gwen could respond. "And is the beloved hero ready to fight them again?"

"I am," Washington said.

Weyler smiled cynically. "Will it matter to you if you win or lose? No, let it pass." Abruptly he returned to his lean-to.

We walked away, but I waited until we were out of earshot before speaking. "Were you trying to provoke him?" I asked Gwen.

"No," she said. "The absurdity got to me. Weyler's a grown man! He taught college before the Collapse. Now he talks like he believes that 'Dark Gods' granola, and he acts as if he has generations of tradition behind his noble-savage act."

"He might believe it," I said. "A lot of people cracked up during the Collapse."

"Fine. How are we supposed to negotiate with a lunatic?"

The Colonel chuckled. I'd always wondered what that would sound like, but the noise was much drier than I could have expected. "That was a common diplomatic problem even before the Collapse."

Gwen looked annoyed. "If he's really nuts, then that's all the more reason to blow him away—discreetly, of course. The sooner we free his 'tribe' from him, the better."

"We cannot simply liberate his people," the Colonel said, as we walked into his company base—a fancy name for a brace of tents, I'll admit. "If we try to bring them into the Republic, they will not cooperate."

"Colonel, they're savages," Gwen said. "Look at

Weyler's men. If we gave them half a chance, they'd join us in half a second."

Washington shook his head. "My agents have tried to get them to defect. It hasn't worked because they're no longer 'nothing but savages.' Weyler has very carefully, and very thoroughly, indoctrinated his people with a new set of beliefs."

Gwen made a noise of disgust. "They *believe* that simpleminded trash about Dark Gods and magic?"

"They do," Washington said. "The mind that thought it up is anything but simple. He, Weyler, has created a mythology in which science is magic—a very weak magic. The Dark Gods destroyed the old civilization by appearing in the guise of a super-scientific race from the stars, and destroying us with stronger magic."

I shook my head. I didn't doubt the Colonel—understanding the outlanders was a big part of his job—but that was hard to swallow. "Colonel, a lot of Weyler's people were born long before the Collapse. How can they swallow that mulch? They know what science is."

"Do they know?" he asked. "Did they ever know?"

Another good point. Hell, even before the Collapse a lot of people thought of science as a kind of magic. I had no cause to act surprised if Weyler's savages were more open about it.

"There is another point," Washington said. "Weyler uses ritual to condition his people into the viewpoint of savages. He encourages slavery and vendettas to counteract the ideals of civilization. Human sacrifice is a prime example—when a victim is killed, the participants must either feel guilt over a murder, or see the act as a legitimate, even moral deed."

"So to live with their consciences, they have to become savages," I said. Gwen made a small noise; she shared my disgust.

"Indeed." Looking oddly unsettled, the Colonel excused himself and went into his tent. Gwen and I left the camp, heading back to the Concourse. "You met the Colonel in '97," Gwen said. "How well do you know him?"

"How well does anyone know him?" I asked. "He went to West Point, and he fought in Central America for a year—he was wounded and spent some time in Walter Reed. He's one of the Founders. Beyond that, I don't even know his first name. He keeps to himself. Why do you ask?"

"Remember what Weyler said back there? About whether it would matter if the Colonel won or lost to the Aliens? What in hell did that mean?"

"You've got me," I said. "I suppose he was just trying to confuse the issue." Gwen nodded ruefully, said good-bye and went her own way.

I'm a better politician than she is; she hadn't realized I was lying. I know Washington a little better than anyone else; I know his secret. An Alien zapped him during the Battle of Chicago.

The Battle, in which we threw the Aliens back into space, was as lopsided as the devil. On our side, we had a scratch regiment from the Eighty-second Airborne Division, supported by National Guard tanks and artillery, and reservists such as myself. The Aliens had their landing craft, their force-shield and anti-meteor weapon—and one zapper.

The force field deflected most of our small-weapons fire, while the meteor ray vaporized our bombs and shells as they came in. The shield had effectively unlimited power, and once we ran out of bombs and shells, our soldiers had to go in on foot, pitting M-16s against a zapper. No wonder most of them mutinied.

The zapper is a gentle weapon, which works by stimulating the pleasure center of a brain—any brain, Alien, human, or animal. On the one hand, as one of the Aliens explained, their race considered it barbaric to kill or injure other life-forms, no matter how primitive. On the other hand, a blast of pure pleasure can immobilize an attacker as effectively as death; no one can function during the ultimate orgasm. On the other hand (the Aliens have three), they had no idea that humans could become addicted to the zapper.

Everyone learned about that quickly. The zapper left its victims unconscious, to awake with the memory of ecstasy corroding their souls. All that the victims could think about was repeating the experience. Most chasers died of thirst, because drinking water distracted them from the pursuit of the Aliens.

The Colonel wasn't immune to its effects. At the climax of the Battle I saw him walk toward the Alien lander, when everyone else was either running or hiding. I was hiding behind a pile of concrete, and hoping that the zapper couldn't work through it. It was all I could do to peek over the rubble, and see the Colonel fall in convulsions as he was zapped.

I saw him get up and stagger toward the Alien with the zapper. I *know* he was hit again; I heard the zapper's burring noise, and I felt the pleasant sensation of its backlash. Before the monster could fire a third time, he was on top of it. The Colonel grabbed the Alien and slammed it against the pavement, killing it and wrecking the zapper. We'll never know how the other Aliens felt about that; they bugged out then. We saw *Scented Vine*'s drive flame pushing it out of Earth orbit that night.

Maybe Washington's ability to withstand the zapper isn't surprising. His will power is fierce; he held his unit together throughout the Collapse. Lesser men did the same thing, and went on to become petty warlords; the Colonel turned his force into a servant of the Republic and civilization.

Did the experience change the Colonel? I couldn't say. Even before the Battle I had found this mythic-warrior reserve impenetrable. One thing was certain: I couldn't mention any of this to Gwen. Aside from being an intolerable breach of the Colonel's privacy, it would demoralize her, and everyone else, to learn that our national hero was a victim of the zapper.

It didn't do anything for my morale to know that—or to realize that Weyler knew it.

The Aliens came out of their lander that afternoon. They wore suits identical to those of *Scented Vine*'s crew. The garments were said to be puncture-proof, which would prevent the spread of any micro-organisms in either direction. They had a mirror-like anti-laser coating that made it difficult to look at them. Three of them stood inside the haze of the force field, while one moved downhill toward the Concourse and the Forum. Soldiers and outlanders watched it silently, while the Colonel, Gwen, and I went out to speak to it.

I was there more through curiosity than necessity. The Colonel could assess their military potentials better than I could, and the only real plan the government had was to stall for time. Still, I was interested in the things.

Come, let us be honest. I wanted to see how Colonel Washington reacted. If he was hooked on the zapper, I wanted to know now.

The Alien recognized us as a delegation. It stopped in front of us and touched its translator plate. "I wish to visit your leader." The machine sounded as emotionless as the Colonel.

"She's taking the day off," Gwen said.

"My business with her is most urgent."

Gwen shrugged. "If she thought she had urgent business with you, she'd have shown up for work today."

"I wish to discuss the affair of the *Scented Vine*. I am convinced your leader finds this important."

I glanced at the Colonel. His face looked as blank as the Alien's gold visor. He'd noticed the zapper in its holster, along with other devices on the Alien's waistband, but it didn't hold his attention. At least, that's the way it seemed to me.

"Our leader has other things on her mind," Gwen said. "If you want to make an appointment, I think she can work you into her schedule sometime next week."

There was a long pause, and I wondered what was going on inside that helmet. "I will agree to an appointment," the Alien said at last.

"Fine. Speaker Ryan will see you Monday at noon."

"That is acceptable." The Alien spun around and went back to its lander. It walked gracefully, I'll admit; the three legs and three arms moved with a dancelike rhythm.

"Interesting," the Colonel said, as we walked back downhill. "It seemed almost desperate to see the Speaker."

" 'Almost,' nothing," I said. "I'd say it *was* desperate. Not to mention diplomatic."

"It wasn't diplomatic," Gwen said. "Patient, maybe. *Stinking Weed*'s crew never accepted any sort of a delay, remember? That thing tolerated an unavoidable delay, nothing more. I wonder why?"

"It is not here to help us," Washington said. "If it was here to help undo the damage of their last visit, it would have said so."

"So they want something from us," I concluded. As conclusions went, that stank. What did we have that could interest the Aliens? Judging by the looks on their faces, Gwen and the Colonel were as much in the dark as I was.

"I see that the Dark God confounded you," Weyler said. He'd crept up behind us, as quiet as a cat but less welcome.

"Not at all," Gwen said. "It just made an appointment to see Speaker Ryan next week. You should do the same thing, Weyler, although I doubt she'll invite *you* to lunch."

His eyes glinted angrily. "So it confounded you after all."

"It almost sold us the Brooklyn Bridge," Gwen said cheerfully. "Weyler, why don't you walk up to one of those ugly bastards and tell it about your 'Dark Gods' silliness? Or get some of your clowns to pray to them—up close, where they can smell you?"

"The Dark Gods are not mocked!" he said, and stalked away.

Washington's eyes followed him. "I'd better speak to my men," he said. "They have orders to watch him at all times."

"Don't be too hard on them," Gwen said. "Weyler lives like an animal. He knows how to slither around."

"And my men are supposed to know how to follow him." The Colonel left.

I looked Gwen over as we walked down the Concourse. "Gwen, have you got something personal against Weyler?"

"You mean, why am I acting this way?" She shook her head. "Tad, I lost my husband and children to raiders. Maybe I wouldn't hate Weyler so much if he was just a savage, but he's deliberately working to tear apart what's left of civilization. He's no better than the Aliens."

"Is that any reason to bait him?" I asked. "Or them? If you can't be hypocritical enough—"

"I could," she said, and frowned thoughtfully. "But I won't. Treating them seriously is a mistake; it gives them credibility. I think we would have been all right if we'd laughed at those walking milk stools in '97. Don't ask me why we didn't. Well, we both have work waiting for us. Catch you later."

She left me alone with my thoughts. Gwen might provoke either the Aliens or Weyler into doing something dangerous, but politically she was making the right move. If the Republic survived both the Aliens and Weyler's plans, she'd come up smelling like a rose. If we collapsed, well, nothing would matter any more.

I went back to my office. Between Zone Twenty-nine and my War Department work, I had plenty to do. Mobilization was on my mind; if we were going to have a war, I wanted it done as efficiently as possible. There were reports of more incidents in the Neutral Zone; bands of raiders were probing everywhere, no doubt at Weyler's behest. They couldn't hurt us, but they tied down a considerable fraction of the Army.

One thing became obvious: mobilization was going to delay the Mesabi project. For the past twenty-seven years, all of our metals have come from salvage. Old cars, old plumbing, old wiring—there was plenty of scrap left after the Collapse, and so far it had met our needs. However, our industry was growing exponentially now, and we needed other sources. That meant reopening the iron mines in the Mesabi ranges, in upper Minnesota. Almost worked out in the last century, they still held enough ore to last us for decades.

That project was going on hold, I decided. The Mesabis were way outside our territory, and the expedition would have required at least a battalion of infantry for proper security—two battalions, once full-scale mining got under way. The Republic had a toehold on Lake Michigan, so we could reach the Mesabis without going overland, but the people up there were hostile to outsiders. We'd lost half our scouts to them.

We couldn't spare any soldiers now, which was a blow to our overall reconstruction plans. There would be repercussions; industry would suffer, employment would drop, farm outputs would decrease—hell. We'd muddle through, the way we always have, but I wouldn't like it.

You can understand why I was in a bad mood when the Alien waltzed into my office. My secretary was out to lunch, so the first warning I had came when I heard the thing's splayed feet tapping on the floor. It wasn't the one I'd met on the Concourse; the tool belt was different, and the zapper was holstered differently. "Have a seat," I said maliciously. "I'll be with you in a moment."

"Misunderstanding," its translator said. "Anatomy is not compatible with human seating. Regrets at declining implied hospitality. Name, Dzhaz."

"Name, Woodman." Odd. No Alien had ever given its name to a mere human before. While it stood in front of my desk, I picked up a letter and started reading it. The note came from Pete Bodo, who told me that he'd found his cat-killer. A twelve-year-old boy on a neighboring farm was now supplying Bodo with a month of free labor. He thanked me for talking to the salesman who recalled selling the shotgun shells to one of his neighbors. Case closed.

I put the letter down and stared at my visitor. I had the feeling that the thing was uncomfortable. Perhaps I was just projecting human body language onto the Alien, but it kept shifting around in an interminable string of small movements. Fidgeting? Perhaps. "Now, what can I do for you?"

"Assignment, to observe routine of perceived leader or semi-leader. Correct status, request made with ritual polite-words?"

I think it was trying to say "please," certainly another first for an Alien. "I'm a member of the Legislature," I said. "I share the leadership with a large number of people."

"'Legislature,'" Dzhaz repeated, as if taking a note. "Implies democratic or republican governing system. Permission, observe daily routine?"

"Why not?" I said. A soldier appeared in the door

behind it, and I made a quick, casual gesture: everything's fine. I hoped it was. If that Alien really was nervous, it might reach for its zapper and cut loose.

It waited a moment before answering. Maybe the Aliens have trouble understanding that a question can be an answer. Finally Dzhaz touched the letter from Bodo. "Request, nature of document?"

"It's the conclusion of an important criminal matter," I said. "A farmer had two cats killed by a naughty child. I helped find the miscreant."

"This rates as important?"

I mulled that over. I'd meant to bamboozle the monster, but now that I thought of it— "Yes, I'd say so."

The Alien took one of the doohickeys from its belt and held it in front of its visor. "Statement of fact," Dzhaz said. "Statement of fact." I saw subdued lights race across part of the object, and I decided it was a lie detector.

Well, even Aliens have a right to be puzzled when a politician tells the truth. It dawned on me then that I was going to play everything straight with the monster. *Scented Vine*'s crew had treated humanity like a bunch of savages—devious, shifty, untrustworthy. No doubt this thing had the same attitude, in which case a little candor might trip it up.

"Request, explanation of importance?"

"Well . . . aside from a cat's value as a ratter, there's the nature of the crime." I held up the letter, and a quick blip of light told me the Alien had recorded it. "A child enjoyed taking a gun and killing animals. Now he's being punished—"

"Request, brutalizing child is acceptable act?"

"*Disciplining* a child is acceptable," I said. "The boy might have decided that killing people is fun, too. Aside from paying for the damage he's done, he's also learning not to do things like that."

It fiddled with one of its instruments, a thing that looked like frozen quicksilver. "Request, importance of this to you?"

"I represent Bodo in the Legislature—" I stopped, feeling that didn't cover everything. "I represent society as well. The child wasn't fully responsible for his acts, so it was up to society—myself, Bodo, and the boy's family—to intervene."

"Request, explain why society must intervene?"

I wondered if it had a point to its questions. "No society can tolerate members who work against the society's best interests—"

"Request, attitude includes dissent?"

"Dissent is generally in society's interest," I said. That was a damned peculiar question; didn't the Alien understand the difference between dissent and disorder? "How reliable is your translator?"

Dzhaz touched its three hands together. "Uncertain. Use is made of records purchased from *Scented Vine* crew. Reliability perhaps not total, but adequate. Request, dissent is considered beneficial?"

"It's a good way of catching mistakes before they get out of control. Was that a serious question?" It sounded like something that might have been asked in the Kremlin, or the Nixon White House. I wouldn't have expected it from a star-traveler, no matter how non-human it was.

"All requests made for information,"

"That's what the *Stinking Weed*'s crew told us," Gwen said, striding into my office. The look on her face was murderous.

The golden visor turned to her. "Name of earlier ship, *Scented Vine*."

"A rose by any other name," Gwen said, seating herself. "What in hell do you want here, monster?"

"Information, related to social degeneration, this planet."

"What's it to you?" she asked coolly.

"We are academicians. Topic of social collapse rates primary attention in many portions of culture. Hence, information sought."

"Why?" Gwen's face darkened. "So you can write a thesis? Title, *How it Feels to Have Bug-Eyed Monsters Bugger Your World?*"

I made a quick gesture, motioning for silence. The Alien's fidgeting had increased, and now I was certain it was a case of nerves. Gwen's hostility was plain, and I didn't doubt that the Alien's instruments could inter-

pret human emotions for the creature. It might run
amok with its zapper—or just stop talking. In either
case, I wouldn't learn why it was here. "You didn't
come all this way just to learn why we fell."

"Incorrect. As stated, object is to study social collapse."

"You're too late to study anything," Gwen told Dzhaz.
"The damage was done before the *Stinking Weed* left.
They could give you the whole story."

"Incorrect. They could only describe their activities.
Self-evident that they could not describe pre-arrival or
post-departure events. *Scented Vine* crew merely—"
The translator chopped off suddenly. I heard a faint
grinding noise from inside its helmet. Alien speech?
Probably it was talking to its friends. "I will now return
to shuttlecraft."

Gwen shut the door behind it after it left. "Did you
learn anything, Tad?"

"I'm sure I did." The Alien's interests were real
headscratchers. "They're interested in more than the
Collapse. That one wanted to watch me at work—"

"And you let it?"

"Was I supposed to stop it?" I asked her. "Gwen,
we're not in the Forum now, so quit campaigning. I
talked to it about Bodo's cats. It asked me some
questions—basic, simple ones."

"That has a familiar ring," Gwen said.

I nodded. The questions asked by *Scented Vine*'s
crew had helped spark the Collapse. There'd been a
bored, arrogant indifference to their questions then,
when they asked us why we used *such* primitive technology, or why our behavior was *so* barbaric. Such
things, spread over international TV and radio, did
little for the human race's pride. And yet—

"There was something different here," I told Gwen.
"This one acted as if it was trying to get to the bottom
of something. I think my answers puzzled it."

She didn't look pleased. "It may be trying a new
approach to destroying us. Tad, I've always felt that
Scented Vine trashed us on purpose, to destroy potential rivals to their species. These monsters must be here
to check up on the job, and to tidy up loose ends."

"Such as the Republic." I caught myself drumming

my fingers on my desk, something I do when I've got a tough problem on my mind. Gwen's theory fit the facts, but only if we were wrong about certain things. The Aliens could blast us back to the Stone Age, using their anti-meteor beam to destroy a few critical facilities. Despite their claims, *Scented Vine*'s crew had had no compunctions about killing. Certainly the Collapse had led to some five billion deaths over the past quarter century, as most of Earth sank back to the subsistence level, and certainly the Collapse was their doing. The blood was on their hands. Given that, why would our current visitors destroy us the hard way? The facts just didn't jibe.

There was a polite knock at the door, and Washington entered. "You wanted to see me now, Mr. Secretary," he said, standing at parade-rest.

"Yes, I wanted to go over the new mobilization plans." I nodded at the window, in the general direction of Signal Hill. "We're still following Plan Seven, but we never laid any contingency plans for *this*. How much more time will you need to prepare?"

"One week," he said. "The forces watching Weyler and the Aliens are our 'fire brigade'—our emergency reserve," he explained to Gwen. "It will take a week to mobilize their replacements."

"We can afford that week," Gwen said. "How long do you think we'll need to defeat Weyler?"

"I don't think it's possible," he said, a statement that left Gwen looking as surprised as I felt. "The situation has changed."

"Because of the Aliens?" I asked.

"No, sir, the change preceded their arrival." He looked to Gwen. "Ma'am, I said that Weyler has indoctrinated his people."

"What's that got to do with anything?" she said. "They may believe his mumbo-jumbo now, but once we toss him out and send in our educators—"

"The same things were said about Vietnam and Nicaragua," Washington said. "The more I think about it, the more I'm convinced that the situation here is similar. Weyler has given his people a set of beliefs which explains the world; part of the explanation is that the

Republic is a source of evil. An invasion will reinforce this belief."

"We'd defeat ourselves," I said. "Is that your point?"

"Not if our attack was impressive enough," Gwen said doggedly.

"Weyler knows enough to engage us in a guerrilla war," the Colonel said. "I fought in one for a year, in Nicaragua. Even against Stone Age weapons, we would take heavy casualties." He paused, and I got the impression that he was debating something with himself. "We would end up killing many of the people we wish to help."

Gwen looked somber. "That's always the case, Colonel," she said. "We're out to help all of them, even the ones who fight us. It's a choice between prolonged savagery and brief bloodshed—"

"Unending bloodshed is now on the list," he said, surprising me. I've never known him to interrupt anyone. "In Nicaragua, we found ourselves battling a large part of the population. We never knew who was on our side and who was not. I rose from second lieutenant to colonel because the guerrillas concentrated on the officers—and many of them found it impossible to stay alert at every moment."

"But you survived," Gwen argued, "And with your experience, you could avoid the mistakes made down there—"

"My experience," the Colonel said. "For the most part, I learned how to avoid combat. Everyone who wanted to survive did that. It held down casualties, but it was no way to win a war. As for the action I did see . . ." His voice trailed off and an introspective look showed on his face.

He started speaking again, as impassively as ever. "On my last day in Nicaragua, I was in a troop truck with a dozen other men, on the way to the airport. The communists hated the idea of any Americans leaving their country alive, so they made a last-minute attack on us. When the truck stopped at an intersection, a guerrilla ran up behind us with a grenade—"

"Please stop," Gwen said suddenly.

The Colonel ignored her. "I estimate he was ten years

old. No doubt one of his parents gave him the grenade. That was common, because a large part of the population had been indoctrinated to fight at all costs. A military victory would have required genocide, you see, which would have been counterproductive."

"So that's when you were wounded," I said inanely.

"I was not wounded. I shot the guerrilla before he could throw the grenade. A medical officer learned about the incident when I returned stateside, and I was subjected to a psychiatric examination. I was confined to the psychiatric wing of Walter Reed for observation." His voice remained as matter-of-fact as ever. "It was the military's opinion that the things I did to survive were insane, even though I was following orders."

Gwen looked rattled. "But—but they decided you were all right eventually—"

"No, ma'am, I went AWOL from the hospital. I always felt my confinement was a mistake, being a decision made by people who had never been in combat and refused to understand the situation."

I felt my skin crawling. "So when you rejoined the Army—"

"The Collapse was well under way, Mr. Secretary. I knew no one could check on me, and there was a need for my skills." He checked his old wind-up watch. "I should return to my headquarters now."

"Okay." I nodded weakly and he left. My head was buzzing. This explained so much about the man, I thought. Small wonder that he had isolated himself from people. I couldn't imagine how he endured the loneliness that required.

"No wonder he keeps to himself," Gwen said quietly. "He couldn't afford to have anyone learn that—and neither can we."

"Is that all you can think about?" I asked. Granted, it would devastate everyone to learn that our national hero was a ruthless killer and an escaped lunatic, but the Colonel hadn't been speaking merely to unburden what was left of his conscience. "He was warning us not to start this war."

"I know. I just don't want to think about that right now." Gwen was slumping wearily in her chair, and for the first time I realized that she had as many gray hairs as I do. "It's times like this that I can't see why I went into politics."

"You and me both." I forced myself to consider our alternatives to the war. Attack was out, not if it would embroil us in a war we couldn't win . . . and produce more casualties like Washington. The hell of it was that we couldn't back down, which would demoralize our own people while encouraging more outlander attacks. Merely defending our borders wasn't enough, either. With our limited resources, it was either expand or die.

Facing our lack of options, it took me a moment to notice an odd rhythmic sound floating through my office window. The Aliens? I wondered, getting up. I couldn't see anything odd atop Signal Hill. The force field looked steady.

Gwen had noticed it, too. "That sounds like chanting," she said. "We'd better see if Weyler's up to something."

He was. We went down to the Concourse, where Weyler and half his men had arrayed themselves. Weyler himself sat cross-legged on the grass beside the boulevard, while his men formed a semicircle on the asphalt. They were chanting *ottar-idle, hai! ottar-idle, hai!*, over and over at the top of their lungs, while shuffling their feet in an odd step, left, left, right, and swinging their spears in the air. Several of our soldiers were watching them, baffled by the sight, while a crowd of spectators gathered. And then I saw the Alien.

Dzhaz had been on its way back to the shuttlecraft when the savages had blocked its path. Don't ask me why the beast didn't go around them. All I can think of is that it stopped to observe another quaint native activity, and then found itself surrounded by a horde of humans, cutting it off from its friends.

As I approached Dzhaz I knew it was scared. Nothing we or the savages had could cut its suit, but the shiny garment wouldn't protect it from impacts or crushing. I wanted to defuse the situation before its nerve broke and it reached for its zapper.

The Colonel must have had the same idea. I saw him push through the crowd, approaching the monster from its other side. I was slightly ahead of him, and I got to the Alien while he was forcing his way between two spear carriers. Then Weyler shrieked out something and his men lunged with their spears.

The Alien went for its zapper and my mind went into overdrive. Hundreds of people had gathered here. A few indiscriminate shots would turn many of them into chasers. Old as I am, I was on top of the monster before it could take aim.

The first thing I remember is something sharp digging into my ribs as we fell over. I had landed on top of Dzhaz, and something on its tool belt was poking my side. It bucked and tried to heave me aside as I clutched its arm and with both hands, trying to break its grip on the zapper.

I heard a frantic chittering inside its helmet, untranslated but a cry for help. A fainter scrabbling answered it, and I knew what it was saying. *The evil eye! Show the savage your face!* A silvery hand appeared and pushed the visor back.

It almost worked. I'd seen Alien faces before, but never like this, never as a writhing mass inside a clear plastic bubble. We rolled over and the Alien was on top of me, but I kept my grip. I could tell it wasn't as strong as a human; the arm inside the suit felt thin, almost skeletal. I held on with one hand and reached for the zapper with the other.

Two other hands clawed at mine. Without thinking I pulled one away. I saw the third one take the zapper. I had enough time to yell in horror as it took aim at me. A wave of pleasure roared through me, and I gloried in it even as it threw me into a convulsion. It faded, and in a last moment of sanity I knew the zapper had sunk its hooks in my soul. Then there was darkness and nightmares.

The Alien scientists wanted a new tool to destroy other worlds. They'd decided to improve the zapper, and they'd drafted me to help them. They had me trapped in the back of an old Army truck, and every so often they zapped me. They kept changing the settings on the weapon, so that it stimulated a different part of my brain. At each trial I felt loss, agony, misery, and painful new emotions that I hope will never earn names.

I woke up with the sour taste of vomit in my mouth. I was in my bed at home, naked under the blanket. I had a dim memory of my sphincters letting go, and another memory of Janie bathing me. I felt light-headed as I sat up.

"He's awake!" Janie came into the room and stopped just inside the door. "Tad? Are you all right?"

I croaked out something that sounded like yes. There was a pitcher of water on the nightstand. I rinsed out my mouth and tried again. "I'm fine. How long was I out?"

"S-since yesterday."

"Yesterday?" That had an unreal sound. I felt like I'd been out for days. This must have been harder on Janie, though. Her bloodshot eyes and puffy face meant she'd done a lot of crying.

I reached out and touched her face. She's almost my age, but I suddenly realized that she carries the years better than I do. Her face has character. Beauty. I was amazed to find that, after twenty-plus years of marriage, I could look at her face and still feel that I was seeing it for the first time.

I was hugging her and wishing I had the strength for a lot more when it hit me. "Janie. The zapper. It didn't get to me."

I felt her tense. She must have thought I was crazy. "Tad, Tad—"

"I know what happened," I said. "It hit me, but I don't want it again."

She pulled back and looked at me. "You mean that."

I nodded vigorously and my head swam. "It didn't hook me."

"Maybe it wasn't on full force." Janie was still afraid of what had happened to me. "Maybe it was broken."

"No, I caught the full thing." I laughed nervously. "It just wasn't that good."

"You were scared of it," she said, trying to convince herself that I was all right after all. "You've had decades to immunize yourself that way."

"Yes." I didn't believe it, though. There was nothing

special about me. How had I resisted addiction? Washington had done it, but he— No, I cut off that line of thought. It wasn't fair to him to say he was crazy, and it ducked the issue as well.

Janie was drained, physically and emotionally. I doubt she'd slept at all last night. I put her to bed, then dressed and went into the kitchen for some food. Michael came out of his room. "You all right, Dad?"

"Just hungry." I hugged him, hating that scared look on his face, hating the thought that I might have lost my family a second time. Was that what had saved me?

We had breakfast. I found that all the foods had strong, vivid flavors; the backlash of the zapper had sharpened my tastes—or maybe my close call with madness had done that. I ate day-old bread, dried fruits, and apple juice, and I felt like a gourmet with each mouthful. I looked out the kitchen window and admired the sky, which was filling with rain clouds that I might otherwise have found depressing. I could smell the rain coming, along with a heavy petroleum odor from the chemical works. Amazing, the number of things you can find to appreciate.

I sent Michael off to school and started on a second course. Washington appeared at my front door as I was finishing up. "It's good to see you back in health, Mr. Secretary," he said. "There have been some developments since yesterday."

That was the Colonel, I thought, as we went into the front room. Business as usual, no matter what. He sat down, although he held himself with parade-ground erectness. His eyes looked tired; it was obvious that Janie wasn't the only one to have spent a sleepless night. "Have the Aliens done anything?"

"They've withdrawn to their shuttlecraft. The Speaker has told them that they may not carry zappers among us. They have made no reply yet."

"They'll accept," I said suddenly. "Count on it. They want something from us badly enough to do that."

"I agree. However, I don't think they'll leave their lander again until after Weyler and his group are gone. The Aliens feel menaced by them."

"Tell them to get in line with the rest of us." I looked at him. "Weyler arranged that attack."

"Obviously. I think he hoped to turn as many of our people as possible into chasers." He looked pleased. "Your actions made that impossible. By the time the Alien finished with you, the spectators had fled out of the zapper's range."

That gave me a good feeling, the sort you can't get from a zapper or anything else. "I think he wanted something else, Colonel. Weyler didn't signal for the attack until *after* you were inside his ring of warriors. The purpose must have been to have the Alien zap you. If you were incapacitated, or changed into a chaser, we'd lose our best soldier. It would blow morale to hell, too."

He nodded at the logic. "It fits with the remark he made the other day. Evidently Weyler knows I have been zapped before. I suppose you weren't the only witness at the Battle of Chicago. No matter. It is obvious that neither of us are addicted."

"No." I had a sudden qualm. What would I do the next time I saw an Alien with a zapper? I hoped I'd never have to find out. "What's Weyler done lately?"

"After the attack a runner arrived from his homeland. He sent a messenger back a while later. I've no idea what the message said."

"Ditto. Whatever it was, it'll take a couple of days for it to reach his home." I shook my head. "There's one bright spot to all of this. If the Aliens stay holed up while Weyler's around, we'll only have to face one problem at a time."

"Possibly," the Colonel said. "But I feel that we must deal with the Aliens before we can deal with Weyler. A session of the Legislature has been scheduled for to-morrow to discuss the matter."

"I hope I have something to say to them." I scratched my chin, feeling the stubble. "Colonel, can you think of any alternative to war?"

"No, sir, I can't—but then my job is war. I do not permit myself to become involved in the decision-making process, as you know."

That was as close to a rebuke as I'd ever heard from

him. It also explained some things. Washington knew that he was mentally unbalanced, and he confined himself to activities where he would be harmless, or useful. He avoided areas where he didn't trust his judgment.

He thinks of himself as a weapon, I thought as we left my home. A tool. The only way he could cope with his past was by letting other people assume the responsibility for his actions. That put the responsibility for anything he did square on my shoulders.

We were three paces outside the door when Washington grabbed my arm. He reached for his pistol, then stopped as one of Weyler's warriors rose out of the shrubbery. The war-paint on his face hid his expression well, and he walked away in silence.

"They're too damned elusive for us," Washington said. "We can't confine them to their bivouac and we can't track each of them. That surely figures in Weyler's plans."

"It makes it damned easy for him to spy on us," I said. I wondered what this one had been looking for. Later it would occur to me that he had seen the obvious: the zapper had had no effect on me. That, too, would figure in Weyler's plans.

I met a lot of people as I walked to the government office building. A politician never complains about attention, but it didn't take too long for me to figure out what was happening, and I started judging people's reactions. I'd say half of them wanted to know if I'd turned into a chaser, while the other half took me as proof that the zapper wasn't as formidable as legend had it. I think Gwen was solidly in the second camp. She seemed happy to see me up and around, although we didn't get the chance to talk much.

The rain started around the time I entered my office. It built up rapidly, and it was coming down in sheets when the Alien walked into the room.

I looked it over carefully. Its silver suit was bone dry, which didn't impress me. It was wearing the same belt as the one who'd visited me yesterday, which told me nothing. The holster was empty, as the Speaker had ordered, although any of its tools might have been a disguised zapper. The idea didn't affect me one way or another. "What do you want?" I asked, hoping that it would understand my tone as unpleasant.

"Continuation, discussion of prior day."

Fine and dandy, I thought. It zaps me, and then it wants to talk as if nothing had happened. "Then you'd better tell me what you *want*," I demanded, as Gwen came into my office, dripping wet.

"Reiterate, information regarding social disintegration."

Gwen looked it over, satisfying herself that the beast was unarmed. "Aren't you afraid of the savages?" she taunted.

"Rain should immobilize one group in holding area. Speculate Woodman will not repeat action prior day." Dzhaz was shivering with fear. Maybe it thought *I* had attacked *it*. "Need outweighs risk."

"I know you're after more than information," I told it. "I want you to tell me what makes your expedition worthwhile. Otherwise, you may as well go home now."

"Reiterate, information regarding social disintegration. Such information has vital application."

"What 'application'?" Gwen said angrily. "So ships like the *Stinking Weed* can do a better job? Aren't you satisfied with what they did here?"

"Not understood. Request clarification."

"Dzhaz is playing dumb," I told Gwen, as if it wasn't present. "Socratic inquiry. It's pretending not to know that *Scented Vine*'s crew caused the Collapse."

At that, the Alien removed its translator plate, held it in front of its visor, then clipped it back on its belt. As expressionless as the helmet was, I had the impression that Dzhaz had just given the translator an incredulous look. "You can believe your ears," I said nastily, "if you have any. *Scented Vine*'s crew engineered the Collapse."

"Impossibility is self-evident," Dzhaz said. "Task too difficult for small crew, restricted timeframe. Study of social disintegration my specialty. Knowledge certain."

"Some expert," Gwen said bitterly. "You can't explain it, so you deny it happened."

"Denial, hypothesis blaming *Scented Vine*," Dzhaz said. "Crew involvement in events marginal, limited to terminal phase. Did not initiate disintegration."

"That's convenient for you." I leaned forward, over my desk. "You can explain why your species isn't responsible for what hit us. Honest scholarship at its best."

"Ritual statement of anger." The shaking had stopped. Dzhaz might have been scared of us, but no academic will take that sort of abuse lying down. "Challenge, prove guilt of *Scented Vine*."

"Oh, I'll prove it." Gwen sounded murderously calm. "Fact. Whenever *Scented Vine*'s crew said anything about humanity, they always belittled us. All of their questions implied that we were deliberately backward. When we asked them to explain things they said were 'obvious,' they suggested that the explanations were too hard for us to understand—even when they *weren't*."

"Request, explain why known falsehoods, subjective opinions of crew accepted as fact."

"These were people from an advanced civilization," Gwen said. "They'd seen who-knows-how-many worlds. They came here, looked around, and told us we couldn't make the grade. That was devastating."

"But it wasn't the only thing they did," I said. "The zapper. People got addicted to it. *Scented Vine*'s crew made a sport out of it."

"Understood," Dzhaz agreed. "Crew activities on record, ship's log and interviews. Agree, actions unworthy. Request, explain nature of addiction."

"You know how the zapper works," I said. "By direct stimulation of the brain's pleasure center. We tried similar, cruder things on lab animals, and they became addicted. All they wanted was the pleasure."

"Explanation inadequate. Difference, experimental animals not sapient beings."

"That's got nothing to do with it," Gwen said. "It's physiological. Once the brain is imprinted, all it wants is more pleasure."

"Partial agreement," Dzhaz said.

" 'Partial,' my tush!" Gwen said. "You never saw the chasers. Once people got zapped, that was *it*. And when word spread, other people sought out the zapper. Lots of people, all over the world. They just dropped out of society. That helped push us over the edge."

"Request, number of chasers, relative to total population?"

"Well . . ." What was the highest number I'd heard? A hundred thousand? "About one in fifty or sixty thousand."

"Request, this was significant fraction of population?" One of its hands made a small circle in the air with each sentence. Alien body language, I decided: a gesture of emphasis. "Request, chaser subgroup contained philosophers, scientists, artists, social leaders? Request, subgroup made large effort to describe effect of zapper to non-subgroup? Request, subgroup forced others to become chasers?"

"Okay, so most of them were bums," Gwen conceded. "And most of them didn't care enough to talk. But there was that minister, what's-his-name, and that Harvard professor. They got on the news a lot before they died. People listened to them."

"Self-evident, few listened," Dzhaz said. "Self-evident, speakers no longer sane. Request, explain why anyone listened, took statements seriously? Request, explain why chasers viewed as serious problem?"

"All right, I can't explain it." Gwen looked exasperated. "It's like asking me which straw broke the camel's back. The thing is that everyone saw it as a serious problem, and there was no way to stop it—"

"Request, describe attempts made to stop chaser subgroup's expansion."

"We didn't have the time to decide on anything," Gwen said. "Nothing like this had ever happened before. We didn't know what to do."

"Incorrect." Two of Dzhaz's hands pressed together. More body language, although I couldn't guess its meaning. "I speak as expert on field, able to make deductions concerning your past through study of other social disintegrations. Long before arrival of *Scented Vine*, you had problems with other addictions. Pattern identical to chaser issue. Limited size, most members non-important to social balance, attempts to curb ineffective, situation viewed with alarm. Addictive behavior seen only in individuals who feel society has failed their needs. This attitude, one of many signs of advanced social disintegration."

I stared out the window at the rain. I felt as bleak and cold as the dark sky. "You're saying that the chasers were a symptom."

"Correct," Dzhaz said. "Consider fact, you are not zapper-addicted. Additional fact, zapper effects non-physical. Addiction possible only in individuals who lack ability, or motive, to resist addiction. Single exposure ineffective on typical member of healthy society. Exposure not sought by such members, not truly enjoyed.

"Additional symptoms," it continued. "Before arrival of *Scented Vine*, great speculation made concerning potential dangers of contact, speculations unfounded but taken seriously, thus showing awareness of social instability. Long before arrival, high incidence of anti-social and asocial acts, crimes, matched by ineffective attempts to restrict. Superstitions, illogical social and political doctrines taken seriously. Warfare considered primary answer to nation-state disagreements—"

"Enough!" Gwen snapped. She looked rattled by Dzhaz's dry assertions. I felt the same way. Maybe the Alien had learned about Earth's problems from *Scented Vine*'s crew, but I didn't believe that even as I thought it. No, Dzhaz was describing typical events in disintegrating cultures. Ours was merely the latest in a string of intriguing, informative disasters.

You're a Polynesian, and white sailors and missionaries have left your tiny world in shambles. Your one consolation is that it wasn't your fault, that the outsiders were too much for you to resist. Then you came face to face with the fact that your society fell because it lacked the inner strength to survive—

Hell's bells, that comparison wasn't even fair. Most primitive cultures had fought to survive, and shown more resilience than we had.

Gwen's thoughts must have paralleled mine. "Maybe you have a point," she said grimly. "Okay, maybe what happened was our fault. But we might have solved our problems if it hadn't been for the war, and *they started it*. Why should they get away with that?"

"I can answer that," I said. "They didn't start it. It was human suspicion, with the Soviets thinking the Aliens had teamed up with us. Maybe folks in Washington thought the Aliens were working with the Reds, too."

Gwen gave me a look of betrayal. "There was more than that. They shot down all the missiles, which was the only favor they ever did us. Then they turned the war into a joke! A 'tribal squabble. Welcome chance to test repairs to anti-meteor system.' It was all a video game to them! And it brought the government down."

"Request, explain how," Dzhaz said.

"They didn't have enough time to accomplish anything," I said. The Alien's words had blasted me out of a mental rut, and things that should have been obvious all along were becoming clear now. I can't say that I felt any gratitude to Dzhaz for that. "Anyway, I think the governments are to blame. They failed, Gwen, they pushed the button. I doubt anyone would've let them have a second chance to blow us to hell, with or without the Aliens."

"We'll never find out," she said bitterly.

Dzhaz shifted around on his feet. "Request, continue talk at later time." After a moment of silence it left.

Gwen went to the window and watched it disappear into the rain. "They've done it again," she said, clutching the sill. "They're attacking our weaknesses. They won't be satisfied until we're all barbarians."

"I don't think that's what's happening," I said, feeling strangely bemused. "Or if they *are* trying that, Dzhaz just admitted it won't work."

She jerked around, startled. "When did it say that?"

"When it was talking about the zapper. What did it say? A single zap is ineffective against a member of a *healthy* society? Such people don't really enjoy getting zapped—right? It feels nice, but it's degrading, and you have better pleasures. Family. Work that means something. Accomplishment, hope, a future. When you have that you don't slip off into pipe dreams."

"What about the Colonel?" Gwen said. She still suspected an Alien trick, but she wanted to be convinced, to hear that there wouldn't be a second Collapse.

"The Colonel has his problems," I acknowledged. "But think about what he's like. A second Patton, the warrior incarnate. 'Duty, honor, country.' When he lost his first country, he set out to make a second one."

"The Republic didn't exist when he was zapped."

I nodded. "True, but his military unit did. He gave himself the responsibility of holding it together. He has a will that the zapper couldn't bend . . ."

Things clicked. Weyler had orchestrated the attack to get Washington zapped, assuming that it would break him. The spy at my house must have brought Weyler the impossible news that the zapper had failed with me and could not be trusted to work on the Colonel. If Weyler was going to remove Washington, it would have to be through other means.

And his warriors had a talent for sneaking around unseen—

I grabbed my coat and ran out the door. The path to the north slope and bivouac seemed all uphill in the rain, a waking nightmare. I was out of breath and my heart was pounding when I stumbled up to a sentry post. A soldier in a poncho kept me from falling over. I gasped out something about the Colonel and protecting him, and both sentries ran to his tent. I caught my breath and went after them.

The Colonel was in his tent, sitting up on his cot with the blanket over his legs. He was holding a revolver on a savage, although the look on Washington's face was deadly enough. "I cannot believe," he said in disgust, "that Weyler would try something so *obvious*."

I nodded absently at his soldierly esthetics. The savage glared at me. The rain had washed off his dirt and war-paint, revealing white skin and matted blond hair. It gave him an odd resemblance to a long-ago California surf bum. "Where's Weyler?" I demanded, as the sentries tied his hands behind him.

The savage—hell, the young man—spat at me. I noticed he had bad teeth. "Bring him with me," I told the sentries. I knew what I had to do now, risky as it was.

The rain had slacked off to a drizzle; the storm was passing. Weyler's camp had turned into mud, and the

savages squatted under their lean-tos. "Weyler!" I
shouted. "Get out here! Face me, you gutless wonder!
Crawl out here, back-stabber!"

He came out into the open. He had to, with me
calling him a coward in front of his advisors and warriors. He stood about ten feet from me. "What do you
want, Renaissance Man?" he asked in contempt.

"You sent your boy to murder the Colonel," I said, as
the sentries dragged the captive into the camp. "To kill
him while he slept."

"What if I did?" he asked. Some of his men smiled at
his cleverness. It was merely murder, an acceptable
gambit to them—just as we had been ready to go to
war to get what we want.

"You have no guts," I said. Using short, simple words
is hell for a politician, but I wanted his men to understand me. They spoke English, yes, but only in a crude,
limited way. I had to make certain that I left him no
escape. "You are lower than a snake's belly. You are the
dirt under the pile of crap. You send others to fight for
you."

He spat. "So I fight the way you fight. Guns, can-
nons, airplanes. Your people hide behind them and kill
at a coward's distance."

"We kill that way because you run from us," I taunted
him. "You can only face unarmed villagers, and you are
the biggest coward of all, hiding behind your warriors.
You would not even fight *me*."

Weyler looked me over, up and down, and smiled. I
was an old man, like him. I'd been zapped and I'd run a
half-mile, and unlike him, I wasn't in prime condition. I
was no hardy, hearty barbarian. "And you would not
fight me with spear and knife."

"I would," I said.

The Colonel stepped up to my side. "Mr. Secretary,
what in *hell* are you doing?"

"I don't have the time to explain." Across the muddy
grounds, one of his warriors had produced a spear and
knife. I sent one of the sentries to fetch it. "Think of it
as the soldier's dream, Colonel. The leaders are going
to slug it out."

"Single combat?"

"Just like David and Goliath." There'd been a time when armies sent out champions to do combat, allowing their gods to decide the outcome of battles through them. A good custom, I thought, peeling off my jacket. We couldn't have peace with Weyler, and we couldn't accomplish anything through full-scale war. This would give us a chance.

I looked at Weyler as he prepared for battle. He looked confident of victory, but he didn't know we were fighting according to my rules. To win, he had to kill me, but all I had to do was stay alive and wait for one opportunity.

Washington looked resigned, and far from optimistic. "Mr. Secretary, when fighting, keep your head down, to protect your throat. Face him sideways, to keep him from kicking you in the crotch. Keep your feet apart, so he won't knock you off balance easily."

"Okay, thanks." He'd taught me to fight years ago, when I'd joined him as a trooper, but it didn't hurt to hear that again. I removed my shoes and socks, and the sentry brought my weapons. The knife was poorly balanced, but I wasn't going to use it. The spear had a stone point, secured by sinew, and its shaft was good and solid. Fiber lacings served as grips. I tested them and decided they wouldn't slip or break.

"Weyler," I called. I had no right to make the Republic's foreign policy decisions, but I had to give Weyler a reason to fight without making him suspicious. "If you win, we will not attack your tribe, there will be no war. If I win, you will release, unharmed, all the captives taken on your last raid. Agreed?"

"Agreed," he said at once. Then he turned and faced Signal Hill, where the Alien force-field shimmered in the wet air. Several of the Aliens stood just inside the shield, watching us.

"Dark Gods!" Weyler shouted, raising spear and knife above his head. "*Ottar-idle, hai!* Give me victory!" Prayers said, he faced me and stepped forward, smiling.

I stepped forward. The long grass and mud squished under my toes. The mud was cold, but I'd never have kept my balance in my shoes. When I was within two or three paces of Weyler, I tossed the knife aside. I needed both hands for my spear.

He laughed as the knife splashed in the mud. "You won't win."

"Prove it." I circled slowly, waiting for him to make the first move. My feet grew numb in the cold mud, but as I moved around I tested the ground, noting which parts were slipperier than others, which might give decent footing. After a long moment I settled into a fairly solid patch of ground.

I heard grumblings from the barbarians. They wanted the warrior-king to prove himself in battle, and they disliked our dancing. Good. Every bit of pressure on my enemy helped.

He lunged at me with the spear. I parried it with mine, although the blow nearly knocked the spear from my hands. Gaunt as he looked, Weyler was stronger than me. Much stronger.

"Is that why you threw away your knife?" he asked. "To buy yourself more time?" He swung at me with the spear, twice, toying with me. He danced back, put his knife in his loincloth belt, lunged forward with his spear in both hands. He wasn't much faster than me, I saw. He was an old man, too.

I turned, and for a moment we were face to face, our spear shafts jammed together. "I'll never free any slaves," he whispered. "Even if you win."

"I know," I gasped. He kicked at my ankle and I tripped. I twisted away as he jabbed at me with the spear point. On my knees, I held the shaft above me as he brought his spear down on my head. The poles hit with a crack, jolting my shoulders. Weyler grabbed his spear with both hands and leaned forward, forcing me to support his weight.

"Still think you can kill me?" he asked.

"Don't want . . . kill you," I said.

You can't smile in a fight. Instead he grimaced. "You're soft, Civilized Man. Decadent. I'll free the world from your ilk."

"Really?" I grunted.

"You think me a fool." He could talk easily; he was in far better shape then me. "Your old world was a cancer.

Build it again, and you'll bring another Collapse. I'll spare the world that suffering when I destroy you."

I was sagging under his weight. Suddenly I pushed up with one arm and let the other arm drop. He dropped as I twisted aside, shoving my spear against his. Weyler landed atop his spear, face down in the mud—and I had the opportunity I'd wanted.

Kill him? No, not with his shamans' prophecies, all ready to turn his death into martyrdom. Spare his life and trust him to keep his word, overawed by my mercy and fighting prowess? Come, now. There was only one way to defeat him.

He started to get up, groping for his spear with one hand, wiping mud from his face with the other. He wasn't worried about me; he'd decided I was weak, and he knew I was unarmed, so he was in no hurry to get up. That's when I kicked him in the ass, in full view of his entourage.

The pain made him yell. I'd hit him in one of the most sensitive parts of the human anatomy, right at the base of the spine. I kicked again, harder, and I felt something crunch. He sprawled in the mud, then tried to stand. Weyler fell down again, immobilized by the pain, and I took his knife. It was a good, pre-Collapse blade, and I put it into my own belt. Symbolism is important among savages. Disarming Weyler sealed my victory.

Gwen was standing next to Washington, her face flushed with anger. "Do you know what you've *done?*" she demanded as I joined them.

"I think I broke my toe," I said. It was just starting to throb.

"You didn't win anything," Gwen said, looking across the grounds. Two of Weyler's warriors had helped him up and were wiping away the mud. "He's down now, but what about tomorrow? He'll be out for revenge."

"I know, but right now I'm in control." I faced Weyler and raised my voice. "Weyler! Tomorrow the Legislature will meet in the Forum. Before you leave, you and your men will go to the meeting." I waved a hand at Signal Hill and the Alien watchers. "*They* will be there also."

One of Weyler's old men nodded to me. In the face of their leader's humiliation, they could do nothing but listen and obey—until they got over this. If tomorrow's events worked out right, though, they would never recover.

I turned to Washington. "Colonel, would you send a messenger to the Aliens? Inform them that if they want any cooperation from us they will have a representative at tomorrow's sessions."

"What's the idea?" Gwen asked, as the colonel left to carry out my orders.

"Gwen, you know that everything Dzhaz said was true. We're going to have to learn to live with it. If we can't, then we're just setting ourselves up for another Collapse."

"Peachy," she said. "What are you going to do? Get up in the Forum and say that the human race is decadent? Why make the Aliens' job easier for them?"

"They aren't here to provoke another Collapse," I said. "If I'm right, we're not in any danger of a Collapse. I can prove everything . . . and when I do, Weyler won't be a problem any more."

"If you're right."

"We'll have to handle things carefully," I said. I planned to play games with beliefs, both ours and the outlanders. That would present more dangers than my duel with Weyler.

While the camp medic came over to examine my foot, I looked at our savages. One of them was ministering to Weyler's injuries, by chanting and waving a gourd rattle over him. The others were on their knees, bowing and praying to the Aliens, hoping for a miracle.

In my way I was doing the same thing, just as I'd done before the fight. My god was Reason, though, a much more demanding deity than any the savages worshiped. If it was going to deliver any miracles, I would have to work for them.

There was silence through the first part of my address. Shock, I suppose, at least among the other legislators. Weyler and his men seemed quietly pleased by my revisionist account of the Collapse. Perhaps it made up for yesterday's humiliation. They had chairs, but all of them were standing, no doubt because Weyler couldn't sit down. I was having trouble staying on my feet; willow-bark tea, our substitute for aspirin, wasn't doing much for the pain in my sprained toe.

Speaker Ryan had virtually handed control of the floor to me for the duration of my speech; only she and Gwen knew what I would say. Dzhaz had shown up, and he kept himself busy with his instruments while I talked about such things as decay, addiction, and the Collapse.

"So *Scented Vine* left and we started picking up the pieces," I said. "We never counted on a return visit from the Aliens, because *Scented Vine* was the equivalent of a tramp steamer, dropping anchor at a convenient port. We didn't think they'd tell anyone about their activities here. Even if they weren't responsible for the Collapse, they'd played a role in it, and some of their activities *were* criminal.

"Nevertheless, they talked. Word got around. A group of scholars heard about the incident. They interviewed *Scented Vine*'s crew, purchased copies of their records. They came here to study the Collapse. Isn't that right, Dzhaz?"

The silvery suit turned to face me. "Correct."

I looked around the Forum. "Fascinating, isn't it? *Scented Vine* kept nothing secret, but only a few academics took any interest in their crimes. No galactic government or space patrol became curious. In any event, these scholars came to Earth, detected our radio station, and homed in on it. That brings up another strange point. Why investigate us?"

"Because we're rebuilding!" a legislator shouted. That got a scattering of applause.

"Exactly," I said. "They're interested in us because we're working to restore civilization—or to build a new one. But we have nothing to do with the Collapse; the Republic didn't arise until *after* things fell apart. Yet the Aliens were clearly, undeniably desperate to study us—*us*, not the savages or the warlords. Why?"

No one answered. "It must be vitally important; they even agreed not to carry their zappers among us. Does

that mean they're willing to risk their lives to—what?
Study a mishap on an obscure planet? Get information
to write a footnote? What makes it worth their while?"

"Well, they're *alien*," someone suggested—an Expansionist legislator. I felt glad that a member of the
opposition had suggested that. Let *them* look obtuse.

"I thought the same thing, at first," I said. "Dzhaz,
one of the Aliens, visited my office the other day. We
discussed one of my constituent's problems—two of his
cats had been shot by a neighbor's boy. The questions
he asked proved that Dzhaz had trouble understanding
that we wanted dissent *and* order, that there's a difference between discipline and brutality, the need to assume responsibility—" Light began to dawn on some of
the faces in the amphitheater. "You see? What sort of
society produces someone like that?

"And what sort of society produces people like *Scented
Vine*'s crew? Or lets them run rampant? Without assuming responsibility for their acts?" I had to raise my
voice over a growing murmur. The savages looked angry; I was blaspheming against their gods. "They're not
'alien,' any more than the twentieth century was 'alien.'
They came here to learn about themselves." I faced
Dzhaz. "*Your civilization is collapsing, isn't it?*"

"Statement of fact," Dzhaz said. Odd, how the translator's flat voice could sound so reluctant. "As experts,
self, others able to recognize disintegration of own society. Organize selves into unit, ultimate objective, for-
mulate method to halt or reverse process. One of many
techniques, study social disintegration this planet. Last
known collapse three thousand local years prior to your
collapse; you present opportunity to collect information
from survivors, generate new insights, possible solutions."

"You expected to find total anarchy, but when you
got here you found the Republic," Gwen said. We'd
worked out a compromise the night before, after I
explained my perceptions to her. It was good politics to
let the head Expansionist handle some of the questions—
besides, she'd filled in a few of the gaps in my reasoning. "That changed your plans."

"Statement of fact," Dzhaz said. "Many known cases
of planet-wide social disintegration in galaxy. Approxi-

mately one half never recover. Of successful half, recovery normally begins only after hundreds or thousands of local years. Full recovery process requires similar time frame."

"We're the exception to the rule," Gwen stated with pride. "And you want us to tell you what makes us so special."

"Partial statement of fact. Improbable, natives understand factors behind own success. You lack training, experience in academic matter. Best chance of success, conceal true motive of investigation, learn answers through indirect approach."

I nodded. There'd been nothing sinister in that; far from it. "It's a basic law of any science," I said. "The process of observation changes whatever you observe. You couldn't risk losing what you might learn here."

"Statement of fact." That had become a litany, confirming my hunches. "We do not know many things. Extreme importance, things we may learn from you—"

There was a sudden upset among the barbarians. The sergeants-at-arms waded in and pulled them apart. Two of Weyler's advisors had taken him and shoved him to the floor. "How can anything be unknown to the Dark Gods?" one demanded.

"Fact, we are like humans." I don't think Dzhaz was addressing the savages. None of the Aliens had ever shown any interest in them. "All sentient species share many traits, fact which makes studies useful. Gamble, can uncover your secret, apply to galactic culture, prevent total disintegration. Alternative, social disintegration on galactic scale, all habited planets and artificial worlds to experience your conditions or worse."

The Alien turned slowly on its three feet, and I had the impression it was sizing up the audience in the amphitheater. "Probability of success low. Evident that your success product of mental, emotional attitude, in itself product of unique conditions. Unlikely to reproduce attitude in other minds. Ultimate failure indicated."

A galaxy-wide Collapse was beyond my grasp. My concerns were closer to home. The Republic was in no danger from the Aliens—or the barbarians surrounding us. If the looks Weyler's men gave their "king" meant anything, the day of the warlords was over, at least in our corner of the world.

Then Gwen walked up to Dzhaz, something that wasn't in our script. I started to leave the podium; I was afraid she was going to say something vengeful, something that would upset everything. "So you need us to keep your own society from collapsing."

"Correct. Possibility, still time, opportunity to prevent disaster."

I was halfway down the steps when she spoke again. "We'll do what we can to help you."

I had not wanted to see this, but you can't duck your responsibilities, even when the thing you're responsible for is justice. I'd engineered Weyler's fall, and I had to be there at the end.

It had been two weeks since the meeting in the Forum, but things were already changing outside the Republic. The story was slowly percolating through the outlands: the Aliens came to the Republic for help. Their empire was falling apart. They expected the Republic to save them. In the Neutral Zone, the raids had stopped.

The story of Weyler's fall was spreading, too, and our outposts reported cautious overtures from the neighboring warlords and chieftains. They wanted to make arrangements with us, before their own people turned on them as well. We were ignoring their appeals.

Weyler's "castle" was a crude stone blockhouse, surrounded by a dry moat and abatis. Our rehabilitation team had pitched camp outside it, and was laying plans to bring twenty thousand ex-barbarians and freed slaves into the Republic. Meanwhile, the people made themselves ready to join us.

Gwen had come out to watch the ordeal. She had been rather subdued since the last Legislature session. "Their ship left yesterday," she said, after we finished breakfast in the camp mess.

"Yeah, I saw the shuttle go overhead. Did they say when they would return?"

"It won't be for two or three years, maybe longer.

They can travel faster than light, but it's still a big galaxy."

"And we'll have a place in it."

"Along with the Aliens." Gwen looked bitter. "I didn't offer to help them because I forgive them."

"Gwen, you can't blame all of them because *Scented Vine—*"

"I blame them," she said. "Every time I looked at one of them, I saw my husband and children. We may have set ourselves up for the Collapse, but *Stinking Weed*'s crew played a role in events. They were killers, too. Dzhaz never admitted any of that."

"Did you expect him to? He's a product of his society." I shook my head. "I doubt we can really help them."

"I don't care about that, Tad." She toyed with her coffee mug, turning it around and around on the mess hall table. "I made that offer for us. They need *us* to survive. If anything can prove to us, and the rest of the world, that we're coming out of the Collapse, it's that."

Gwen had a point. I had one, too, which I couldn't mention to her. One of the driving forces behind the Republic had always been our hatred of the Aliens, the feeling that they were to blame for everything. We were losing that now; it had been comforting, but illusions never last, and hate can be one of the worst illusions. It had kept us from seeing the realities behind the Collapse, and that blindness might have put us on the road to a second such disaster.

Even though I was glad we were shedding our hate, I could see the danger in losing part of our motivation. The belief that the Aliens had caused the Collapse had made it possible for us to think that there was nothing wrong with the human race, that we could recover from what had been done to us. Now we would have to take pride in what we were going to do.

There was a metallic clattering outside the camp, a sound like a garbage can being hit by stones. It was time for Weyler's end.

Many of his ex-subjects lined the path from the castle gate. Some of them had walked for days to get here, and they looked eager. Gwen and I climbed to the top

The Crash of Empires

of a hillock, where we could see the gauntlet Weyler would have to run.

Two of his warriors dragged Weyler through the gate. He was naked, and tied into a crude yoke. They pushed him down the road, and he stumbled along while the people reached out for him, laughing and cheering.

"It's something I suggested to the rehab team," Gwen said, seeing the confusion on my face. "They need something to rid themselves of Weyler's influences . . . but it had to be something that would break the cycle of killing."

"So you turned him into a scapegoat." A final paganism, I thought. By touching Weyler, they symbolically placed all their guilt on him, and drove it out into the wilderness.

"Executing him would have been too much like a human sacrifice," Gwen said. "Then I remembered hearing about scapegoats in Sunday school. It seemed fitting . . . and after all he's done, Tad, I want to see him *suffer*. This way, he can spend the rest of his life remembering what he's lost."

"What happens when he gets to the border?" I asked.

She shrugged. "I suppose he'll take refuge with another warlord. Let him; he'll never be a king again, but he'll remind the other chieftains of what's in store for them—and show their subjects what to do."

Gwen's vindictiveness made me uneasy, but I knew it wasn't her motive for punishing Weyler. Her punishment rendered him harmless, and it was fitting. After using people for so long, Weyler was being used to help fix the damage he'd done. There was justice in that.

Weyler followed the road, driven by his people, and vanished as the path curved behind a hill. The rehab team was already down among them, beginning the work of leading them out of their long night.

Editor's Introduction To:

THE QUEST

Rudyard Kipling

Those who lose battles may yet win. Recall Lt. Colonel Oliver North . . .

THE QUEST

Rudyard Kipling

The Knight came home from the quest,
  Muddied and sore he came.
Battered of shield and crest,
  Bannerless, bruised, and lame.
Merrily borne, the bugle-horn
  Answered the warder's call:—
"Here is my lance to mend (Haro!),
  Here is my horse to be shot!
Ay, they were strong, and the fight was long;
  But I paid as good as I got!"

"Oh, dark and deep their van,
  That marked my battle-cry.
I could not miss my man,
  But I could not carry by:
Utterly whelmed was I,
  Flung under, horse and all."
Merrily borne, the bugle-horn
  Answered the warder's call!

"My wounds are noised abroad;
  But theirs my foemen cloaked.
Ye see my broken sword—
  But never the blades she broke;
Paying them stroke for stroke.
  Good handsel over all."
Merrily borne, the bugle-horn
  Answered the warder's call!

"My shame ye count and know.
  Ye say the quest is vain.
Ye have not seen my foe.
  Ye have not told his slain.
Surely he fights again, again;
  But when ye prove his line,
There shall come to your aid my broken blade
  In the last, lost fight of mine!
And here is my lance to mend (Haro!),
  And here is my horse to be shot!
Ay, they were strong, and the fight was long;
  But I paid as good as I got!
  Haro!
  I paid as good as I got!"